BUSHWHACKED

"You as good as I've heard?" Sly asked.

"Probabaly not. And you?" Spur replied.

"Better, and I'm modest."

"We do it mounted. Cavalry style. We ride toward each other and whoever wants to shoot first shoots. You have six rounds in your piece?"

"I do."

"Then let's get at it."

Before either man could move, two rifle shots cracked and Spur's horse bellowed in pain and shot out from under him. Spur bailed out to the left away from where his instincts told him the shots came from.

Also in the *Spur* series:

GIANT SPECIAL EDITION!

SPUR

TALL TIMBER TROLLOP

DIRK FLETCHER

LEISURE BOOKS NEW YORK CITY

A LEISURE BOOK

June 1989

Published by

Dorchester Publishing Co., Inc.
276 Fifth Avenue
New York, NY 10001

Printed in the United States of America.

1

Slim Gillette felt gut wrenching terror for the first time in his life. Some bastard out there was trying to kill him! Slim dropped the double bitted faller's axe next to a three foot thick Douglas fir and dove behind the big tree, then stared into the dense Oregon woods.

The shot had come less than a minute ago and thunked into the fir beside him. It wasn't some crazy deer hunter out shooting. Slim had been in a little cleared place around the big fir and was about to start chopping it down for the Thompson Lumber Company in Astoria. If he hadn't swung his axe into the heavy fir bark precisely when the gunman fired, Slim would be a dead lumberjack right now.

Slim lifted from his belly where he had dropped and edged around the big tree through the ferns and some scattering of foot high fir trees. He wasn't even sure where the shooter was, but he had to be in front somewhere.

Slim knew the woods, he was the top faller for Thompson, which was saying a lot since they had fifteen good fallers in the crew that cut down the big fir trees. He'd learned his trade and come up slow the hard way. Now he only cut when they got behind or he had two or three sticks in a row that needed to come down.

He felt a clammy sweat on his back. Could this have anything to do with that guy who talked to him after work a week ago? The guy wore a black suit with a black string tie and a pure white low crowned Stetson. He also had a six-gun tied low on his right hip. Nobody he knew in Astoria wore a six-gun.

"I'll see that you get a hundred dollars cash if you slow down the timber felled. Cut in half what you're supposed to do for the next month. You do that, and I'll give you five nice new twenty dollar bills."

Slim had grinned and said it couldn't be done, his men were too good. They would smell something rotten right away. The two men were talking behind the saloon and the young guy had pulled his six-gun so fast Slim barely saw him move. Then the black muzzle was at his throat.

"You slow down the fallers and earn the hundred, or you're a dead man, you understand?"

At the time Slim had grinned and said sure, sure, and gotten away from there.

The crack of a high powered rifle shattered the silent Oregon woods again and Slim rolled down the slight hill. He ran into a patch of alder, Oregon grape and vine maple. The heavy Oregon coast rainfall made the undergrowth on the mountains grow in magnificent profusion. It was close to a rain forest.

Slim straightened behind a foot thick alder and looked around it.

"Back here, asshole," a voice said behind Slim. He

2

turned slowly and there was the man he had talked to, still in the black suit holding an old Spencer rifle, the big .56 caliber model that fouled easily.

"Going somewhere, Slim? You didn't hold up your end of our bargain. You tell your boss about me?"

"Tell? No, why should I? You were drunk that night."

"Warn't drunk, asshole. Now you know." He walked forward, smiled in a condescending way and fired. He was less than six feet away when he pulled the trigger.

The big slug hit Slim in the chest, shattered three ribs and his heart, then slammed him backward against the alder which he slid off and fell on his face in the brush, crushing a cluster of wild flowers and a trillium. Slim Gillette never moved again.

The six men in his crew heard the shots. Four shots, they said later. They looked for Slim when he didn't come in for the midday food break. Two of his best friends found him a half hour later. One of them carried Slim out to the road, put him in a wagon and drove in to the sheriff.

Spur McCoy arrived in Astoria on the morning passenger boat from San Francisco. It paused briefly in the small town on the Oregon side of the wide Columbia river before it churned upstream on the mighty river to Portland.

Spur stood for a minute on the dock looking at the small town clinging to the shore. This was where John Jacob Astor had set up a fur trading fort in 1811 in an attempt to expand his fur trading monopoly. Astoria had become a fair sized little fishing town and a quick haven for ships off the Pacific Ocean.

McCoy settled his '73 Colt Peacemaker on his lower right thigh, picked up his carpetbag of necessaries, and walked toward the only building in town he saw with a "hotel" sign.

A half hour later he had settled in at the Astorian, found the name and office of the Clatsop County Sheriff and sat talking with the lawman in the first floor of the county courthouse.

Sheriff Zane Vinson watched him closely over half glasses perched on the end of his nose.

"So, you're one of them government men, Secret Service the telegram says, and you're here to see about the Ihander case."

"That's right, he was an employee of the Department of the Interior. 'Murder most foul,' as the British would say."

"The man was beaten to death in a saloon fight."

"My report said that three men did the job, and that all three are on the fringes of the law. All have been in jail, all are unemployed, yet all have money to spend."

"I tried, McCoy. I had three men checking into those guys for a month. I got no evidence other than a fight. Our District Attorney wanted a murder case bad, but not even his investigators could come up with enough evidence for a conviction. After the fight, two of the three carried Ihander to the doctor's office."

"But it was too late to save him. Nice touch."

"One guy's name was Poikela. He seemed to be the smartest of the three."

"What kind of a name is that? Poikela?"

"Finnish. We have a big settlement of Finnish fishermen here. They just about run every salmon

4

fishing boat around here.''

A deputy came into the room. ''Trouble, sheriff. Some timber faller got himself killed out in the Thompson woods.''

''How?''

''Shot. A rifle it looks like. They brought him in on a wagon.''

Sheriff Vinson stood and growled as he walked around his office. ''I get lots of help from the citizens. They couldn't leave the body there. Not a chance. Now how can I read any sign around it, get any clues? It's like trying to solve a mystery without knowing who the suspects are.''

Sheriff Vinson looked at Spur. ''You might as well take a look, too. Ihander was dealing with the Thompson Lumber Company when he was killed. This man was on the Thompson team as a timber faller. Thompson has the biggest logging/milling operation in the county. Must be tied in to them somehow.''

He waved and Spur followed him out to the alley where a wagon with foot high sides sat behind a team of mules. The body had a dirty blanket over it.

A woodsman with high boots, pants legs cut off just above the boots and red suspenders holding up his pants, pulled the blanket back. ''I found him, Sheriff Vinson. I'm John Pietula. Don't know much else about it.''

The man lay face up on the wagon. He wore cut off pants and high boots and red suspenders as well. There was little blood on his chest. The body was starting to stiffen as the sheriff rolled him over.

A chunk of flesh the size of a man's hand was pulped and blown away from his back. The jagged end of a broken, red-stained, white rib protruded from the chopped up flesh.

"Probably a rifle. You said you heard rifle shots, Pietula?"

"Yes sir, four of them. I was falling about three hundred yards away. Saws make a lot of noise but the rifle shot came clear."

"So you ran his way?"

"Yep. By the time I got there he was well down-slope from his tree on his belly, and dead like this."

"You see anybody?"

"One of the other fallers saw a hunter with a rifle stalking a deer about half an hour before."

"What was he wearing?" Spur asked.

"Funny about that. He had on a black suit and a string tie," Pietula said. "Did seem strange."

The sheriff looked at the man's chest again.

"His name?"

"Oh, Slim Gillette. He was my boss. Best damn faller I ever seen. He could figure where he wanted to drop a stick, pound a stake into the ground and drive that stake in with the tree when it fell. Damn, he was good!"

"Any trouble with his crew?"

"No, sir. We all got on."

"Anybody he had to fire lately?"

"No, sir. We been together now for over three years."

"Thanks, Pietula. I'll want you to write this all down for me and sign it. Go inside with this deputy and he'll get you started."

When the others left, Spur looked at the man's chest closer.

"Sheriff, notice anything else about the body?"

"Like what?"

"He wasn't just killed, he was executed. Look at those black burn marks around the bullet wound. Powder burns. With a rifle, the killer would have to be within five or six feet to leave powder burns. This was no accident."

"Damn! I don't like this. We had a nice quiet little town until a month ago when Ihander got himself killed. Josiah hates things getting out of hand. He's gonna be down on me like a hammer on a nail head. Gawdamn!"

Spur walked through the rear door to the jail and the sheriff's office as the wagon took the body to the undertaker.

"Have there been any other bad accidents around town lately, especially at the Johnson Lumber Company operations?" Spur asked.

The sheriff looked up and nodded. "Yeah, have been. Nothing that we could tie down as planned to hurt the company. Now we'll take another look. You best go see Lee Johnson over at the lumber company offices. He's a good young lad. Took over the business at 25 when his father dropped dead one day ten years ago. It's a family business, so they are a might close."

"I think I will just drop over there and get acquainted," Spur said.

He walked. Nothing was far from anything else in Astoria in 1875. The lumber company was situated on the east side of town along the spread of the mighty Columbia. A small inlet, backwaters of the river, was called Thompson Bay and had been cleared of snags and brush to form the mill pond where logs were held just prior to sawing.

Most of the firm's logs were rafted down the river along the gentle flow near the shoreline, and herded into the small bay to wait their turn at the big circular saws and the top man in the mill, the talented sawyer.

Spur walked into the small grounds and spotted the office in a building fifty yards from the whining, singing circular saws as they sliced through the virgin Oregon Douglas fir, with a few spruce, hemlock and cedar thrown in. Douglas fir was by far the most plentiful and produced the greatest revenue.

Spur stepped into the office building and for a moment was startled by the quietness. The thick door and walls kept out most of the constant noise of various saws, re-saws and cross cuts in the big sawmill itself.

The office was finished in wood, stained and varnished. A pair of soft chairs fronted a fireplace and to one side were three desks. The room was two stories high and extended thirty feet to a partition with three doors. It was well decorated in a lumber/logging/woodsy way.

A young woman rose from the closest desk and smiled. She looked a little past twenty, with long blonde hair that draped halfway down her back. She was taller than most women, maybe five-five, Spur decided.

"May I help you?" she said in a voice that was firm and sure of itself with a resonance that seemed to come from conviction. He walked closer and found her soft blue eyes watching him. She wore a one piece dress, tight at the waist and flaring everywhere else.

"Yes, you certainly may help. I'd like to talk to Lee Johnson, if he's not busy. It's about the Ihander affair and what happened today out in the woods."

Her face clouded and she blinked back tears.

"Such a tragedy! I've known Slim for years. His wife is going to be so crushed about this, and she's expecting their first child in less than a month."

She bit her lip, then wiped away the wetness and looked up.

"Pardon me, my manners. Please sit down. Could I bring you a cup of coffee? Lee is out right now talking to Slim Gillette's widow, but he should be back soon."

"My name is Spur McCoy."

"Oh. Excuse me again. I'm Karen Johnson, the office manager here. Yes, I'm one of the family. It's a family owned and run business and we're all terribly proud of it."

"From what I've seen you have reason to be," he said.

When he sat down, Spur saw a copy of a newspaper and picked it up. It was the *Astorian*, which came out once a week on Thursdays.

A picture on the front page showed a smiling man. Under the picture the article read: "Fred Ihander as he arrived in town after his trip up the coast. A timber expert for the U.S. Department of the Interior, Ihander was brutally killed in a fight in the Silver Goose bar two weeks ago. District Attorney Josiah Dangerfield stated that no suspects are in custody and that no charges have been filed as yet.

"Motive for the beating is still undetermined. The case is still open, however."

Spur hadn't finished reading about Ihander when the door closed and someone stopped in front of him.

"I'm Lee Johnson. Karen said you wanted to see me about Slim Gillette's murder."

Spur stood and took the man's big, rough hand.

Johnson was a working man owner, six feet even and about 185 pounds. He had blond hair with long side burns and a blond, full moustache. His face was tanned and he looked fit.

"Spur McCoy. Pleased to meet you, Mr. Johnson."

The smaller man wore a taste of a frown which quickly melted. "Welcome to Astoria, McCoy. Anyone who wants to talk to me about Slim's murder is more than welcome. Come right into my office!"

2

The blond man pulled his hat down to shield his face, then walked toward the house from the large open area at the rear. He knew this place like the back of his hand. He should, he grew up here. It was his father's old house, the Johnson family place. Quietly, he lifted the rear yard gate latch and eased open the panel. He looked inside.

No one was in the back yard. He slid past the gate, closed it and ran to the woodshed behind the house and around to the door leading into the kitchen. There might be nobody home. That was not likely, she would be there.

The man lifted up slowly at the kitchen window and looked through the double hung frame into the kitchen. A flood of memories came boiling back. It staggered him for a moment and he was surprised at the emotion. He beat it all down and shook his head and blinked so he could see clearly.

A woman sat at the kitchen table looking over a book that had belonged to his mother and held most of her old recipes. The man at the window snorted softly. Cilla's cooking had never been what he'd call wonderful, even with the big book.

He sucked in his breath in surprise. The woman was a beauty. Dark brown hair, still long, flowed around her shoulders hiding part of her face. Brown eyes he couldn't see but remembered so well. Her oval face lifted as she frowned slightly looking at the stove, then back to the book.

Had she been this strikingly beautiful five years ago? She couldn't have been. She had matured and her beauty glowed.

She still had the slightly prominent chin. He told her it housed all of her stubbornness, her bull-headedness. One of her hands went down and rubbed her breast and he smiled. There had been nothing coy about her when it came to pleasing a man. She was damned good at it and he always told her she acted like she enjoyed making love more then he did.

He had to have her! He was already excited, hard. He saw no one else in the kitchen, heard no one else in the house. He knew she had two kids now. They would be napping. He hoped.

He ducked under the window, went past the back door and slid into the small room at the back of the house. A few steps and he was at the door into the kitchen. Another look told him she was where she had been, her back toward him.

The man opened the door without a sound, moved on silent feet across the kitchen, nuzzled into her hair with his face and put his arms around her, settling his right hand over her right breast the way he always used to. She had jumped when he first touched her, but now she relaxed without looking around.

"Lee, why didn't you tell me you were coming home? Is there anything the matter?" She tried to look over her shoulder at him but he held her tightly. His hand pushed under the open neck of her dress and caught her bare breast. He rubbed it gently. She murmured with pleasure.

"You are worked up, aren't you, darling?" she said.

He responded with a soft moan of his own and kissed her ear.

"Lee?" she paused. "You are really feeling ready. Good! We have lots of time. The kids are both napping." She spun around, loosening his grip, and her smile exploded into anger.

"Martin Johnson! How *dare* you slip up on me that way!" she screamed. Cilla Johnson picked up a butcher knife she had been cutting up celery with and waved it at him.

"Martin Johnson, you get out of this house this instant!" She pointed the knife at his chest. "I know how to use this. You taught me how to skin out a deer and butcher it, remember? Right now I'd like to do the same to you, you *bastard*!"

She thrust the knife outward at him and Marty retreated. "You loved my hand on your bare tits," he said grinning. "You're the same as ever, half angel, half slut. Christ! but you are good in bed."

"Out! Out right now or I'll get the shotgun. It's loaded for rats just like you!" She ran to the broom closet and waved the knife at him as he started to follow her. He remembered the shotgun and Marty turned and ran for the kitchen door.

Cilla grabbed the 12-gauge Greener and hurried out the door behind him. Marty bellied up and over the

13

back six foot fence just as Cilla fired the shotgun. The birdshot peppered the fence nearly thirty yards away, and Martin Johnson, ex-husband of Priscilla, yelped in pretended pain as he ran away from her into the bare field of grass and bachelor buttons behind the house.

Cilla watched him hurry across the vacant field to the next street. She sighed grimly. Marty was back in town. That could only mean trouble. Damn, but he had hurt her five years ago. When she was sure he wasn't coming back, Cilla went into the house to the broom closet, automatically broke open the shotgun, took out the used shell and put in a new one from a half empty box. Then she returned the Greener to its usual spot.

She sat on a kitchen chair, shaking so hard she could barely stay on the chair. The bastard! How could he do that to her? She had no idea he was back in Oregon. The last she had heard about him was a year ago when he had been sentenced to serve a month in the county jail in San Francisco.

She would tell Lee as soon as he got home. At once she reversed herself. No, she wouldn't tell Lee, because he would get so angry he might go hunting his younger brother. Lee had enough trouble right now.

The wail of a small voice echoed through the big fourteen room, wooden, three story house on High Street. That was little Luke, awake, wet and hungry. She went into the nursery. They had set it up on the ground floor to make fewer trips up and down the stairs.

She loved the three story house but climbing the steps twenty times became a real chore toward the end of the day.

14

Outside the house and halfway across the open field, Marty walked along with a smile on his face. At least he'd touched her bare tits, that was something. Damn, to think he used to have all of her three times a day! Then the bird really got on his shoulder and he couldn't knock it off. Lee had bought his stock to bail him out from his gambling debt to Fu Chu and he sailed for San Francisco and a new start.

The lawyers said he had abandoned her. Grounds for divorce. Hell, he was coming back. He had a problem, that was all. So she divorced him. He only got one letter from some lawyer. By then it was too late to do anything but scream bloody hell at all of them.

Marty walked back to the street and on downtown. What Marty couldn't figure out was why Fu Chu had worked as cook for the Johnson family for so long. Sure he was a great cook, but he had so much else going for him. He had the big Chinese laundry that was raking in the money.

Then Willy Fu Chu always had his import business. Marty laughed. If the town knew how much money Fu Chu really had they would probably lynch him. Or maybe the Astoria vigilantes would string him up. Fu Chu, a lowly ex-family cook, could supply a sporting man almost anything he wanted.

The enchanted flower was his main source of revenue. The blood of the poppy and a growing demand for the refined product called opium were both tremendously profitable for Fu Chu. He had the franchise for the whole state of Oregon and much of Washington as well.

They said he had to cut back, but Marty wanted to find a pipe right now! Damn, but that stuff was wonderful. Once he smoked a little he didn't worry about anything, just drifted off in a pleasant fog where reality absolutely ceased to exist.

One time in San Francisco he floated on a lovely purple and gold cloud for two weeks without ever touching the ground.

But now there was one thing more important. One strong emotion that could make him put down the pipe . . . revenge.

That damn brother of his had stolen his 26% of the family company from him; he had sent him out of town in disgrace, and then he had moved in on his wife, made her get a divorce and then married her! The stinking son of a bitch!

The shithead did not deserve to live! He wouldn't for long. But first Lee Johnson had to be defeated in business, and then Marty would take back Cilla, his woman, and there would be disgrace for Lee Johnson before his agonizing, terrible death.

Maybe on the re-saw, where the finished sawed timbers were cut into eight, ten, or twelve foot lengths. Yeah, it had to be a saw!

Marty turned down the block, went into the alley close to the waterfront and entered an unmarked door. Down a long hallway he came to a well furnished reception room. Three doors led off it, all made of heavy oak with large brass doorknobs.

He knocked on one, then pushed it open a crack. "Yes, come in."

The windowless room was shadowed. One small lamp burned on a massive desk. A man sat in a deep leather chair behind the desk but his face was in total shadow.

16

"Ah, Mr. Johnson. I see you are still standing. Good."

"Don't worry, I have a new mistress. No longer is she the pipe. The pipe is now only a sometime lover. My new mistress is revenge, and I will do absolutely *anything* to reach my goal."

"Good. We're making progress. The pressure must mount on Mr. Lee Johnson and his Johnson Lumber Company. I have two weeks to make good on my bid. I rule out nothing except fire. *I do not want the mill destroyed!* Do you understand me, Martin?"

"Yes, sir. I understand. If I produce, I will be a twenty percent partner, as we agreed?"

"I don't renege on a deal, Johnson." He tossed a stack of bills on the desk in front of Martin. They had a piece of string tied around them. "Here is some more of your expense money. Be as economical as possible. We do not have unlimited funds. What you spend now will be recorded and come out of your share of the profits."

"I still don't like that, but it was the deal," Marty said checking the bills. He saw that they all were tens. There had to be seven or eight hundred dollars there!

"Turn up the pressure. I want every problem to look like an accident. You have to give Lee Johnson so many problems that when I make my offer to buy, at a low price, naturally, he will leap at it as a way out of all these problems and trouble."

"He's a tough nut . . . especially about the family business."

"I'm a hard case myself. I have ways of persuading people."

"Yeah, I hope so. I have some people to see before

it gets dark." Marty put the stack of bills in a large wallet and slid it into a light jacket pocket.

"I'll do my part, you just be sure that when the time comes you can hold up your end of the bargain."

The man in the shadows lurched forward, but restrained himself when he started to rise. "Get out of here, Martin, before I show you just how angry I can become."

Marty smiled and left the office, went out the front hallway that opened on the street. It was a nondescript door with no markings and no outside doorknob. The panel was always locked and could be opened only from the inside.

Marty grinned as he looked at his old home town. He had grown up here, slightly privileged because he was the son of the man who ran the large lumber mill operation. Even so, he had a lot of friends in town.

He headed for the Owl Hoot Saloon, not the best drinking establishment in town, but good enough. It had a private back room for high stakes poker games, and a large couch for more personal matters.

A man waited for him there. He had boots with sharpened hobnails in them, his pants legs were cut off with no cuff to catch on snags or branches. He wore red suspenders and a light blue shirt. A full red beard covered his face and matched the color of his hair.

His huge calloused hand gripped Marty's and when Ham Frazer pulled his hand away he found a ten dollar bill in it.

"Little bonus," Marty said. "You do good work. Got a big one coming up for you. Gonna take some doing, but I know you can handle it. Fact is, I have four jobs I want done, two tomorrow, two the next day. I don't want nobody killed, understand that? We get too many bodies, all sorts of lawmen gonna be dogging us."

Ham Frazier nodded. "Hail, don't cotton to killin' anyhow. Just what fun and games are you talking about this time?"

3

Spur McCoy looked across the rough hewn desk at the man who ran Johnson Lumber Company, Lee Johnson.

"Mr. Johnson, I'm here to investigate the death of Erkki Inhander, a government timber specialist. I was talking to the sheriff when your man was brought in. His death couldn't have been an accident. The rifle that shot him was so close to his body that it left powder burns."

"Damn! I hope that doesn't mean it's come down to a shooting war."

"You've had trouble before?"

"Trouble? It's become my middle name. I'm supposed to be a logger and lumber mill operator. Lately, half the time I've been running around looking at little 'problems' that are draining my patience and cash as well. A dozen axes vanishing from the faller's shack, a reel of cable that gets lost just when it's needed, breakdowns in the mill that look like they are man caused. I've had a rash of these sorts of expensive problems."

"I've heard this is a rugged business, Mr. Johnson, but nobody needs to have the added problem of somebody playing a tattoo on your head with a peavey."

"Peavey, so you do know something about logging. Most easterners have never heard of the word."

"My job here is to dig into the Ihander death, determine if it was an isolated, accidental death or a murder, find out who was responsible and bring that person or persons to justice."

"Could be you're hunting the same people who had my faller killed. Going to miss Slim. He was an expert at his job and got along well with the men. Damn!" Lee Johnson stood and combed his blond hair back with his fingers. He looked at Lee.

"That might be one way. You must be a U.S. Marshal or something similiar. If you help me find out who's behind all of my troubles, it might turn up Ihander's killer for you."

Spur smiled. "Rightly so, but seems a long way to go around the barn to get to the door."

"McCoy, I'm cutting timber off government owned land on a government timber contract. Shouldn't that entitle me to some help from you federal people?"

"Might, I can't rightly say. I could wire Washington and ask them. In the meantime, what can you tell me about Ihander?"

"He signed leases for timber rights on parcels that he surveyed out himself. Good man. Honest. Knew his job. Bid the lease rights fair and square. We got some, we lost some." Lee Johnson went to the other side of the room and brought back a tool with an axe length handle. The head was half axe and half wedge.

In his other hand he had a half-inch steel twisted cable.

"Look at the end of this cable. It's been chewed in half by about twenty swings of a four pound splitting axe like this one. Probably ruined the splitting axe. But it also let a water tower up in the woods fall over and held up work with our stream donkey engine up there for three days until we could haul up enough water in tanks."

He put away the cable and the heavy axe. "I know, I know, little things. But remember Ben Franklin. He said a little neglect or, in this case, mischief can breed disaster. For want of a nail the shoe was lost; for want of a shoe the horse was lost; for want of the horse the rider was lost; for want of the rider the battle and the war was lost."

"As soon as I tie down this Ihander situation. . . ."

"Mr. McCoy, I appreciate that, but by then I might be bankrupt. I'm convinced somebody here in town is trying to scuttle my business. They want me down and hard put. My guess then is that I'll get an extremely low offer to buy me out."

He waved at Spur's .45 on his right leg. "I see you go armed. Not many loggers and fishermen in Astoria do that. Yet there is a new man in town who has his gun tied low and tight the way you do. People who know say his name is Sly Waters."

Spur looked up quickly. "Sly Waters, late of Arizona Territory?"

"The same. With a sneer on his young face, and death hanging on his hip. So far he hasn't killed anyone—unless he did the job on Slim. Far as I can tell he's been in town only two or three days. I take it you know this young gunsharp."

"Know of his reputation. I've never met the man."

"But he is a fast gun, a gun for hire to the highest bidder, and he doesn't mind being a paid killer?"

"That's the rep on Sly."

Now it was Spur's turn to stand and walk to the window where he looked out over a steam belching lumber mill with a big burner at the far end where slab and sawdust and edges and other wooden waste was burned as it was produced. There was a constant roil of smoke rising from the three story high rust colored, cone shaped burner.

"If Sly Waters is in town and men are dying by gunshot, the chances are better than ninety percent that Sly pulled the trigger," Spur said at last.

"Which would mean this would be a government job as well, since Sly must be a wanted man and he's crossed a state and territorial line."

"Not necessarily. I just know of him. I don't have any wanted paper on the man."

"Let me give you another factor. My younger brother, Martin, is back in town. I just heard about it last night. He left here five years ago. I bought out his share in the company that Dad willed to Martin."

Lee frowned a moment. "You might as well know. Marty got involved with the opium pipe and gambling. It took almost all of his inheritance to settle up his gambling debts before the gambling people holding his I.O.U.'s towed him across the

Columbia River with a slow boat and a hundred pound weight for a life preserver. He wasn't happy when he left. He's probably not happy now that he's back. He also deserted his wife of four months. She divorced him and then I married her. So I guess you'd say he has a couple of reasons to hate me and the company."

"So you think he's the one behind all of these destructive accidents you've been having?"

"I'd bet on it. It's so obvious."

A knock sounded on the door and Karen hurried in.

"Word just came, Lee, there's been a raft breakup. It's about halfway between the Svenson flume and the mill."

"Damn, damn, damn! This one could cost us a whole lot of money. We'll never get those logs back!"

He grabbed his hat and a rifle, then looked at Spur. "You want to come along and see one of these expensive pranks first hand?"

Five minutes later the two men rode hard along the river road, the one that followed the level land beside the Columbia River and went all the way to Portland. Three miles out on the road they saw a large raft of Douglas fir logs cabled together and tied up to some large trees near the shore.

"Look at that!" Lee growled. "Maybe forty percent of the raft is gone, the whole front end and one side of it is missing. Somebody has a lot of explaining to do."

They rode on and Spur saw men running over the floating logs as if they were on dry land. They threw cables around logs, moved others into position with long pike poles and peaveys.

They rode down to the water and saw a small, powerful river boat nudging the raft of logs tightly against the shoreline.

Lee jumped off his horse, let the reins hang down ground tying the animal and ran forward to a big man with blazing red hair and a beard to match. He wore blue pants cut off just below his boot tops so they wouldn't snag anything. Red suspenders laced across a blue shirt. When he saw Lee coming he hurried toward him.

"Damnedest thing I ever saw, Mr. Johnson. Only way I can figure it is we hit a submerged rock, and it snapped one of the main cables. Water level is down in the river a little."

"How many are lost?" Lee asked.

"We had a count of 238 in this raft. I'd guess we lost near a hundred, ninety at least. Reckon it wouldn't pay to use a boat to try to round them up."

"You're right there, Frazer. They're halfway over the bar now. They'll wash up on the beaches all along the coast. Get the rest of that hole patched up and I want you on the raft the rest of the way into the pond. You lose one more log and I'll have your head in a bucket!"

"Yes sir, Mr. Johnson. I talked to the two riders. They say all was fine one minute, then the next, wham! Logs was bucking and pitching and spurting under and over them cables like they wasn't there. Leastwise we didn't lose either rider on the rafts."

"Get both men over here, I want to talk to them."

"Right away. Clem, he run two miles back up to the dock and told us what happened. He got the raft in here and tied her down fore and aft. Just missed by a whisker of losing the whole kaboodle.''

"Yes, send both men over here."

Spur looked at Lee. "Is he the foreman on this job?"

"Yes. He tallies, ties up the raft and sends it down to the mill with two rafters and the boat. Don't lose many logs. Damn things are worth at least twenty dollars each. If we lost a hundred that's two thousand dollars, not even counting the cost of cutting, bucking, yarding and rafting them. Damn!''

Clem and a man called Marshall came walking up. Both men were dripping wet, both looked as if they were about to drop from exhaustion.

A quick change came over Johnson. He sat down in the grass and asked the men to sit down with him.

"Either of you get hurt?" Lee asked gently.

They looked up with gratitude. First he was concerned about their welfare. They shook their heads.

"Lordy, Mr. Johnson I can't figure out what happened," Clem said. "I checked the left, the shore side, before we pushed off like always. Everything tight and snubbed down. Frazer, he checked the right side as usual, then he signalled, I waved at Harry in the boat and he nudged us away from the dock.''

"Any idea what happened, Marshall?" Lee asked the other man.

"If we hit a rock, Mr. Johnson, I never felt it. Course the water soaks up a shock between sticks. Can't say we didn't hit something, but figure I'd feel it. I feel ever time we scrape bottom in the shallows, ever time we nudge the dock or come in the slough. I still don't think we hit a blamed thing.''

"Then how did we lose near eight years of a

26

workingman's wages of cash money this afternoon in lost sticks?'' Clem said.

"Where were both of you on the raft when she broke?'' Lee asked.

Clem said he was up near the nose on the shore side. ''I usual ride there to watch for the shallows, and motion Harry to edge us out before we stick fast someplace. If the water level in the river drops a foot, it can make a big difference along here.''

"I was on the other side halfway back and I got dunked when she blew,'' Marshall said and stopped. ''I said blew, but I didn't mean dynamite. Weren't no blast. When those wires came off, logs went every which way. Lucky I didn't get squished between a couple. Big hole came right under me, dropped me in the river and I was swimming and coughing right smart. Got to a big knot on a log and heaved up on it. Ain't never gonna swear at a good sized knot again.''

"Dynamite?'' Lee asked looking at Clem.

He hesitated. ''Don't rightly know what it'd sound like under water. But guess the fuse would burn out.'' He shook his head. ''Nope, not dynamite. You ever river rafted and come to white water and a real log jam? When you find the key log and dig it free sounds like thunder when them logs break free. Kind of like that today out here, kind of like thunder.''

Lee nodded. ''I want both of you men to sit right there for half an hour. Then take those two horses over there and ride home. Leave them at the mill stable. Then you both go see Doc Ulman. Tell him I said to check you over. Then get home and rest up. See you tomorrow.''

The men nodded and stretched out on the grass, still so tired they could hardly talk.

"Frazer's side blew out," Spur said as they walked toward the log raft of two to four foot thick Douglas fir logs forty feet long. "He has to be a suspect."

"Frazer's been with me for twelve years, not a chance. I want to look at the cable, see if it broke, was cut or what happened."

Lee stepped on the first log, jumping nimbly, landing with bent knees and arms outspread. He looked back.

"You stay there. I want to look at the break. Then when you get brave enough, we'll get you on board so you can ride down to the mill. Whole lot easier than walking."

It took the men another half hour to bind up the gaping wound in the log raft, move some logs around, loop cables around the logs and tie them together so not even dynamite would break them apart. They used come-along on the cables, levers that tightened the already tight cables.

By the time the raft was pronounced ready by Frazer, Spur had ventured out on the raft, chose three logs the same size that had almost no water between them, and waved to Lee that he was ready to travel.

Lee ran around the raft as if he had caulks in his boots. The sharpened nails in the soles of the boots meant the men would not slip on even the wettest log that had lost its bark.

The cables were released from the shore trees, and the little boat nudged the raft into the water, angling it gently into the slow current along the shore line.

Spur had done some sailing. This was smooth, powerful, gentle. He could not imagine a raft like this breaking apart. It must have had help. Spur moved around a little but kept to the shore side.

28

Lee was all over the raft, watching the cables. When they floated serenely into Johnson Sough about 40 minutes later, Spur was not ready to get off. He wandered to the far side of the raft now and looked at the repair job. It meant nothing to him. He hoped that it did to Lee Johnson.

Lee walked with him up to the mill and then to the office. He held out his hand.

"Mr. McCoy, I hope you are around for a while. I like your no nonsense way of digging into a problem. After you settle the Inhander thing, I'd appreciate a hand on this big problem I have. It touches on government land. You should be involved.

"I can't say for sure, but when we find out who is trying to send Johnson Lumber into bankruptcy, we might very well find the killer of Erkki Ihander.

4

Spur thought over what Lee Johnson said about finding Ihander's killer. It seemed like a roundabout way of doing it. Still . . .

He walked back to the Astorian Hotel, put on a clean shirt and went down to try the hotel's restaurant. Often in smaller towns a hotel had the best eatery.

Spur soon hoped that wasn't the case in Astoria as he worked his way through a partly burned, partly raw steak. The cool beer helped him get through the meal.

It was now dark outside and a tour of the Astoria night life seemed in order. Plenty of gambling and drinking establishments. Four of the larger ones also served up an assortment of fancy women who looked more soiled than fancy. He stepped into the Silver Goose Saloon where Ihander was killed.

It wasn't much, mostly a saloon with a few tables for gambling. This was a serious drinker's establishment and several men stood at the long bar. Spur bought a beer and worked on it slowly as he studied the place.

His first impression was right. It was just a low class saloon one step up from a sawdust floor barrel bar.

On down the street, the Owl Hoot Saloon had girls to add to the mix and twice as many gambling tables. Spur sat in on a 25 cent limit game he had watched for a while. The players were not professionals, and nobody was going to lose the farm or get shooting mad.

He joined in with five dollars to lose. He lost two, came back to two ahead, then after an hour he was back to even. He finished his beer, and bowed out with hardly a murmur from the four men still frowning over the way Lady Luck was treating them.

Two doors down the street he came to the last watering hole: the Oregon Saloon, J. Randall, Prop. Inside it was a little classier than the others. It had a dozen lamps lighting the place; at the far wall sat a battered piano beside a six foot wide raised platform. Did that mean they had entertainment here?

Spur nursed a warm beer and watched a poker game that had over fifty dollars in one pot. Things were grim and serious around the table where two months of a working man's wages lay on the turn of a card.

A small bald man with red suspenders and a city shirt won the pot when he dealt himself an ace to go with a pair of aces he had showing in the five card stud hand. Nobody shot anybody else. Good, Spur thought, a civilized town for a change.

By eleven o'clock the saloon began to fill up. Not all of the men were drinking. There were no fancy women in this place. The men stood around watching the gambling and waiting.

Spur nudged the lumberjack beside him and the man who still wore his cut off pants over his logger boots looked at him.

"They really have entertainment here?" Spur asked.

"Yep. Best damn little songbird this side of St. Louis. She's good. Used to have a picture of her, but some jackass stole it."

At eleven sharp someone banged a dozen chords on the piano, then played a little fanfare, and a woman came through the door behind the bar and walked confidently to the stage. The men made a path for her and cheered wildly.

She held up her hands to silence them. Spur figured she was twenty-two or three, about five-four with sparkling red hair. She wore a dress that proved she didn't have a big bosom. That act in itself showed Spur that she was a lady with some class.

When the men quieted she smiled at them. "Hey, you guys, don't clap yet, make me earn it."

"We know how good you are!" somebody shouted. Everyone cheered and clapped again.

"Yeah and nobody charges us to listen!" another voice said.

Everyone laughed.

When it quieted again, she smiled. "So nice all of you could come tonight. My name is Nancy Reed, remember that name, you can say you knew me back when I played Astoria." The piano crashed with some more chords, then swung into a stirring rendition of "The Girl I Left Behind," which was a Civil War song, but still had a lot of meaning for many of the ex-soldiers.

McCoy was surprised by her voice, a full, rich and obviously well trained alto with a pleasing range. As he listened he realized that the lady could sing. She was pretty, could put a song across and showed on the first few lines that she was a good little actress as well. He joined in the applause when she finished the first song.

She did half a dozen more, then looked around the crowd for a moment and walked down through the tables and glanced at the men as she sang a saucy little tune about a girl looking for a beau. She passed Spur, then backed up and caught his arm and tugged him forward.

"No, no, really . . ."

She smiled at him, and one section of the song fit in perfectly.

". . . .But little boy I want you to come,
Little Boy, I know we can have some fun."

By then she had him up to the stage and held his hand as she stepped up on the low platform so she could look him in the eye.

She sang the last refrain of the song again and finished with a quick kiss on his cheek. The saloon was packed now and the applause shook the sturdy roof, but it didn't fall. She smiled at Spur.

When the audience quieted down she looked at McCoy.

"Thank you, thank you. It's always wonderful to have a fine audience who appreciates the finer artistic side of life. I want to thank the gentleman who helped me in that song. I hate to sing that without somebody to plead with directly.''

Spur grinned in spite of himself. She was bright and smart and could sing. How in the world did she wind up far, far out here in the wilds of Oregon?

Nancy finished with a romp through six more songs, then closed with a slightly naughty version of "Catch Me If You Can," and ran back to the bar before anyone could catch her. She waved at the cheering men and vanished through a door into the back of the saloon.

Spur sat a moment watching most of the crowd leaving the bar. The free show was over. Most of the working men were headed home for bed and a tough work day tomorrow. Ten minutes after her song ended, Nancy Reed came from behind the bar quietly and slid into the chair at the table where Spur sat working on a serious game of solitaire.

"Do you actually like solitaire?" she asked as he looked up.

He rose at once, tipping over his chair. Nancy grinned.

"Nobody has stood for me like that since I left Chicago." She held out a small, delicate hand. "My name is Nancy Reed. Thanks for helping me with the song.''

Spur took her hand and held it as he watched her jade green eyes.

"It was my pleasure, Miss Reed. My name is Spur McCoy. Can I buy you a drink, sarsaparilla, coffee, milk?''

She shook her head and motioned for him to sit down.

"No thanks, beer makes me get fat and I'm not supposed to." She watched him a minute. "Did I hear a trace of a Boston accent just now in your speech?"

"Might have, I spent four years at the Yard."

Nancy grinned. "I knew it. I served my time in Boston as well."

"Was that where you had voice training? You're good."

Nancy smiled and her face shone. "Thank you so much! Most people out here wouldn't know a great singer from a wailer. I'm somewhere in between. I will have that drink after all." She waved at the barkeep and he brought over a bottle of white wine and a small long stemmed glass.

"Private stock," she said. "Wine is less fattening than beer."

Spur lifted his brows. "I know an opera singer who said her voice wasn't full and mellow unless she maintained her full figure. She was chunky; no, she was just plain fat."

Nancy giggled. "That's just an excuse for someone who likes to eat. The voice box and the lungs and diaphragm don't care if you're fat or not. I've tried it both ways." She sipped the wine. "The Yard must refer to the Harvard University Yard. Did you graduate?"

"Yes . . . a few years back. Where did you study?"

"Actually, English Literature is my field. I have a college degree myself, a Bachelor of Arts from Mary Smithwyck College about 50 miles out of Boston."

"A Smithwyck girl?" Spur said astonished. "We used to have some socials with the Smithwyck girls.

35

Most of them were rich and snobbish.''

Nancy laughed and he smiled when he saw the pretty things it did to her face.

"Not all of us were snobbish and rich. Some of us were snobbish and just moderately well off. Now I make my own way and don't depend on anyone.''

"Oh, no!" Spur said in mock horror. "Not another suffragette!''

They both laughed. She smiled at him and stood. "I'm not all that anxious for the vote for women. It's a big responsibility. Now, it's late and I'd appreciate it if you would walk me back to the hotel. The street out there isn't always . . .''

"I'd be honored to walk you that way. Fact is, I'm staying at the Astorian. You too?''

"Best and only hotel in town,'' she said. The barkeep came and reached for her wine bottle. She shook her head. "Thanks, Chance, but I'll take it with me.''

It was less than two long blocks to the hotel, and they chattered about Boston and school days. She held his arm as they walked and now and then his elbow rubbed against her breast. She didn't seem to notice.

In the hotel she went toward the stairs. "I'm on the second floor,'' she said. "Room 211.''

When they reached her door, she unlocked it and then turned and looked at him. A beautiful smile spread over her face. "Spur McCoy, I'd appreciate it if you could come in for a minute, for a small glass of wine, maybe.''

He looked up and down the hall. No one was in sight. He nodded. She opened the door and they stepped inside. She closed the door behind him, then looked at him and gently slipped the bolt into place.

Finally, she turned and held out her arms. "McCoy, I've been waiting all night for you to kiss me. Can you handle the task, or is it too hard for you?"

He caught her shoulders and lifted her, his mouth coming down on hers gently. Her eyes closed and she sighed as she let her lips part to admit his probing tongue.

Nancy whimpered a moment, then sighed again and pressed against him with breasts and hips. Her arms laced around his back and she held him tightly. The kiss lasted a long time and when it ended she looked up.

"Oh, God, but that was marvelous. Don't . . . don't let go of me or my knees will buckle and I'll fall down. Do you think you can help me over to the bed."

He picked her up easily and lay her flat on her back. Nancy looked up at him and patted the bed beside her.

"Join me down here, Spur McCoy, and let's continue what we started. We can talk about Boston later, if we really want to do that."

Spur stretched out beside her, his arm went under her neck and then he rolled her toward him and kissed her again. His hand found her breast and he massaged it gently through the layers of fabric.

Her lips left his a moment. "Yes, Spur, touch my breasts, but inside on my bare titties."

She moved back a little and his hand snaked down the neck of her dress and under the chemise and wrapper until he found her small breast. He stroked and fondled it.

Nancy sighed, then moaned softly and her hand

reached down to cover the growing bulge behind his fly.

"Yes, yes, yes!" she said softly, then reached back to weld her lips to his as her tongue darted into his mouth. Spur felt the heat of her body radiating through their clothing. Her hips did a little dance against his and she worked on the buttons trying to get in his fly. He opened the buttons for her, then found her bare breast again.

Spur eased away and unbuttoned the fasteners down the front of her dress. They went to her waist, and he helped her sit up and lift the dress over her head. She slipped out of the chemise and then let him unwind the wrapper. Some women were now wearing them over their breasts. It was a length of pure white linen and held a woman's breasts tighter to her so they didn't bounce and jiggle so much when she walked.

Spur had always enjoyed the excited little jiggle of a full breast as a woman walked quickly down the street. It was one of the finer pleasures of life.

He bent and kissed her bare breasts as they came from the linen. He suckled on each a moment testing her reaction. She moaned and he kept her sitting up while he nibbled on her nipples, kissed around the small orbs, and then down her soft white stomach to a small belly and under the top edge of her drawers.

Nancy suddenly jumped up and pulled at his boots. She undressed him quickly until he was down to his short underwear. Nancy watched the sharp tenting of the cloth over his crotch and giggled again.

"HE must be huge," she said shyly. Then she pulled his underwear down and sat back on her heels on the bed, her eyes wide. "My God!" she said, "my God! So beautiful! Such a marvel. I never understand how it can happen. HE goes from a little worm into a spear!"

Slowly she bent and touched his shaft, then gripped it and came down and kissed its turgid, purple tip.

"Oh, God, I want HIM inside me this instant!" Furiously she pulled at her drawers, undoing buttons, pulling it down over her legs until it was free and she sat there naked and panting, her face flushed.

Spur touched the red bush around her crotch. "Be damned, you're a real redhead!" he said and they both laughed. Then she was on top of him, thrusting with her hips as she positioned herself over HIM.

"Now, McCoy, push HIM into me right this god-damn minute!"

Spur did, driving in so deep with gentle thrusts that he touched something far inside her. She pulled back her eyes wide in surprise.

"Nobody has ever been in that far before!" she said with wonder and surprise and then delirious joy. "Yes, Spur McCoy, you're the best. Now let's see if you know what to do with that huge stick of yours."

5

Spur and Nancy lay on the bed in each other's arms, talking quietly. They had been sipping at the bottle of wine and getting to know one another.

"So how come a proper Smithwyck girl like you went into show business and wound up way out here in Oregon?"

"I tried teaching, one year. The little school wanted to put on a play and the other teachers said the newest teacher had to do it, so we did a play with music, and I fell in love with the theatre again. I'd done some plays at Smithwyck."

"Some of us from Harvard were always invited, but we usually ducked out before the first act was over," Spur said.

"I started singing, and acting, and was with a small troupe touring Chicago and St. Louis. Then I got a chance to come west with a company doing Shakespeare. But we went broke in Portland and the sheriff took our costumes and trunks, and I came up here looking for a singing spot. So here I am. I have a contract for another two weeks."

Her hand snaked down between them to his crotch but he shook his head. "A man's got to rest a few minutes," he said.

"So tell me about yourself, Spur McCoy."

"Not much to tell. When I got out of Harvard I went back to New York City where my father has three stores. I worked in them and hated it for two years. Then the war started and I enlisted as a lieutenant of infantry and did my share of fighting.

"After two years in the war I was called to Washington D.C. as an aide to Senator Arthur B. Walton, a long time family friend.

"Then in 1865 the Secret Service was established by the Congress and I joined it. Later I was assigned to St. Louis where I dealt with problems across the western half of the United States. Actually, I got the job out West because I was the only one who could ride and shoot well enough to stay alive out here."

"What's the Secret Service?" Nancy asked.

"Can't tell you, it's a secret," Spur whispered and Nancy hit him in the shoulder.

"Okay, we were originally formed to protect the United States currency from counterfeiting. For a long time we were the only Federal law force authorized to cross state lines and go into territories. So we started taking on more and more crimes that had some bearing on the U.S. Government, its officials or agencies. Now we handle almost anything."

"Now I know. I won't tell a soul." She kissed Spur and nibbled on his lips, then bent and bit his nipples gently. "Are you rested up yet?"

He was.

Before morning the wine was gone from the bottle, and both Nancy and Spur lay exhausted on the bed. They got to sleep an hour before a rooster crowed half a block away. Neither of them heard anything until well into the morning.

High in the Svenson timber lease tract, ten miles upstream along the mighty Columbia River, John Kamara, the donkey stoker, came to work just as light broke in the east. It was only a little after five, but John already had sticks and chunks of split logs and branches from felled Douglas fir thrown into the firebox on the steam engine donkey.

The big machine furnished the power to run the pulleys that dragged the cut down logs from where they had dropped to the edge of the dry flume so they could be skidded down the big wooden trough to the Columbia hundreds of feet below.

John Kamara pitched the last of the wood into the firebox and sloshed a quart of coal oil over the wood. Then he twisted up some newspapers, lit them with a match and threw them into the box. He watched as the flames licked the petroleum-soaked wood, then flamed up and soon, he was sure, it would burn. He opened the draft, closed the door and stepped around to the front of the big engine.

He had just checked the oil and greased some of the gearing when a sudden explosion blasted the firebox of the donkey into a twisted mass of steel and shattered iron. Kamara was thrown backwards half a dozen feet and landed on his back. He jumped up and rushed around the wreckage to find the firebox shattered.

For a year, John had been blowing stumps out of

his twenty acres of land down on the river. He knew a blast such as this could be made only by explosives. Quickly, he checked the rest of the wood he had cut the day before and formed into a rick near the fire door.

He found some split pieces of the wood that had been nailed together. Hidden between the three sticks of wood, except from a very careful inspection, lay two sticks of dynamite. He could see a length of fuse extending half an inch from one end. Inside there must be a dynamite detonating cap.

John found one more such bomb and carried them with him as he hurried to where he had tied his horse. There would be no high lining today on top of the mountain. The fallers would get ahead. Perhaps some of the logs could be snaked up to the flume by oxen.

He rode down the trail quickly, the two bombs in his hands. He had to show this to Mr. Johnson himself. He knew he should have checked each piece of wood carefully, but this had never happened before in his ten years working with the big donkey steam engine.

"Damn them!" John Kamara growled to himself as he rode. "Gonna be old Billy Hell himself to pay for this one. Might be my last day's employment by the Johnson Lumber Company."

John stopped at the smaller, second skidder donkey, halfway down the mountain and told the man there what had happened. He and John inspected every piece of wood already in the cold firebox and stacked outside. None of it had been laced with dynamite. John rode on down and the other fireman got his steam tank up to the right pressure.

Well before John made it back to the mill, the

choke setters for the smaller donkey were busy rigging chains around the logs so they could be attached to a cable and pulled through the woods up two hundred yards to the flume.

Scotty Jones had just attached the cable hook from the high line to the forty-foot-long chunk of a three-foot-thick fir and stepped back. He gave a hand signal that was repeated by other choke setters along the way until the donkey operator saw it and tightened the drum on the engine and began drawing up the slack on the half-inch steel twisted cable.

The line came tight and Scotty could hear it "singing" as the steel tensed, then the big log groaned and skidded a half dozen feet toward the donkey.

There was no warning.

One moment the log moved slowly forward, and the next the half-inch cable snapped like a piece of dry spaghetti, the tension on it from the drum back at the donkey making it thresh and whip toward the steam engine like a lightning bolt. On one of its whipping motions it caught Scott Jones on his left leg.

Scotty bellowed in pain as the whipping steel acted with the force of a runaway train and sliced his leg in half between his knee and ankle.

Too late, the donkey operator heard the cable snap and he at once hit the whistle on the donkey that was a danger signal. Choke setters and cablemen dropped into the grass and weeds getting their bodies as low to the ground and as safe as possible. The flailing end of the stressed cable wrapped itself around a three-foot thick fir left as a seed tree and the danger was over.

Two choke setters ran to Scotty Jones. One man whipped off his belt and tightened it around the bloody stump of Scotty's left leg. Scotty was unconscious from the shock and pain.

Another man used his shirt, made it into a thick pad and held it as hard as he could over the bloody stump to slow the bleeding. Four more men rushed to the scene and helped. Two went for horses, three men carried the unconscious man out of the cut to the trail.

It would take them more than two hours to get him into town. Frank Long took off on his horse at a gallop to get to Doc Ulman and bring him out to the river road to meet them. Every minute counted now.

They sat Scotty in a saddle, with a rider behind him to hold him in place. One man walked alongside holding the compress on the stump wound and checking the tourniquet. They couldn't stop the bleeding, but they had slowed it to a few drips.

An hour and a half later they met Doc Ulman riding a galloping horse toward them. Doc spread a white bed sheet in the grass and they put Scotty on it. He ordered a fire built and using a red hot spatula type tool, cauterized the stump end of the wound. He checked releasing the tourniquet. Then settled down to watching and doing what he could.

A half hour later a buggy arrived and Scotty was placed in the seat and the horse led on a lead line back toward town.

The loggers stood around looking at each other. The foreman on that show shook his head. "We did what we could," he said. "It's up to the doctor now. We better get back up there and run some logs down that damn flume. They're shut down up on top. We got to get enough logs for Ham Frazer to make another raft run."

In the Johnson Lumber Company office, Lee stared at the two bombs planted in the firewood. He had used a hammer and gently taken the nailed pieces apart. There was the dynamite and the detonator. Lee carefully took the detonator out of the dynamite and took the fuse from the hollow end of the cap.

Spur had wandered in about a half hour before. Lee was still steaming.

"Somebody could have been killed!" Lee thundered. "If all eight sticks of dynamite had been in that firebox there would have been steel shredding trees over a quarter of a mile up there!"

"How long to replace the firebox?" Spur asked.

"Three days if we had one. Now we have to skid a whole new donkey in there. Take at least three days up that hill, no real trail up there. We might do better to take a donkey apart and haul it up a piece at a time. My head mechanic is still considering that."

"Somebody is stepping up the pressure on you," Spur said.

"Not somebody, it has to be that damned brother of mine."

A knock sounded on Lee's office door, then it opened and Karen looked in.

"One of the loggers is here. He says there's been another problem."

Frank Long stepped through the door. He had never been in the boss's office before. His left shirt sleeve was red with blood. His pants were spotted with blood.

"I'm sorry, Mr. Johnson, there's more trouble. Scotty Jones got hurt when a cable snapped on the

46

lower donkey high line. Cut his leg clean off like a cleaver.''

"Is he alive?" Lee said jolting to his feet.

Frank told them what they had done, that the doctor was on his way to meet the hurt man.

"I'm going out there. Come along, McCoy. See up close how serious this attack on the company is.''

They headed for the door.

Martin Johnson and his lawyer, Robert Erickson, came through the outside door.

"I want to see you right now," Martin said marching toward Lee.

The lawyer stepped forward. "Mr. Johnson, I'm representing Martin Johnson in this matter and we're notifying you that we will be filing a lawsuit against you for fraud and illegal conversion of property of my client, namely 26% of the total shares in this firm. We are willing to sit down and work out an equitable settlement of this case before it reaches the court.''

"Out of my way!" Lee shouted. "Marty, take your damn lawyer and get off my property. You have no rights here at all. You come around again and I'll have my men blow your head off!''

6

The two men rode hard down the river road along the silent, powerful flow of the Columbia River. About twenty minutes from the barn, they met the carriage heading for town. Doctor Ulman was still working over Scotty Jones.

"He gonna live, Doc?" Lee Johnson asked.

"I think so. Depends on how much blood he lost. These lads did well with that belt around his leg. He hasn't bled to death already, which is a good sign. He has a fighting chance now. Couldn't have done that tourniquet better myself. We'll get him back to town and in bed."

"When he comes to again, you tell him not to worry about his job. His pay goes on just the same, and he's got a job as long as I have a business. You tell him that, Doc, so he won't worry."

Lee got back on his horse and he and Spur rode on down the road—not quite so fast now—heading for the site of the accident.

When they got there, an hour later, nobody had

moved the cable that did the damage. They left their horses near the steaming donkey engine and hiked down to the site.

Lee picked up the end of the cable which had wrapped around the seed tree and now lay slack. He swore, the angry words spilling out of his mouth in a fountain of fury.

"Look at this damned cable!" Lee roared. "It's been cut halfway in two! Somebody with a hammer and chisel, I'd guess . . . a damn sharp chisel. Then they smeared it with grease and mud so nobody would notice. Not until it snapped."

He threw the cable down and called over a choke setter to get a new hook bolted onto the cable and get it back in action.

"That cable could just as well have killed two or three men. When those things snap it's like a blast of grapeshot across the woods. They said it was on Scotty's log, his choker set so he was closest. He's damn lucky to be alive."

Lee looked around and kicked at some bark on the ground. "Let's get back to town and have it out with that lawyer. If I start punching the bastard, you drag me off before I kill him."

By the time they rode past where the carriage had been for Scotty Jones, it was gone. They came back to the mill office and Lee fell into his big chair. The lawyer was not there.

Karen brought in fresh coffee and muffins for both of them. Her pretty face showed concern. "More trouble?"

"I'm afraid so, Karen." He told her about the deliberate cutting on the cable.

"Oh, I so wish this would all end," she said. Spur

watched her soft blue eyes brim with tears. She blinked them away. Her long blonde hair crowded around her face now and the straight bangs over her face bounced as she poured them fresh coffee. She looked up at Spur.

"Mr. McCoy. I'm sorry you're here right at this bad time for us. Usually we have a happy office."

"I know this is difficult for all of you," Spur said.

"I hope it's all over soon," Karen said and looked out the window a moment, refilled their cups and watched Spur. The touch of a smile around her mouth and the gaze from her blue eyes lingered on him. Then she nodded as if deciding something and left the two men alone in the room.

"Lee, I've decided to look into your problem," Spur said. "If this is all tied in together, it's a lot more than a simple murder of a government timber cruiser."

Lee stared at a list on his desk. He smiled when he heard what Spur was saying. "Good, good. That will help us get to the bottom of this and get it settled. I've kept a list of the 'accidents' that have happened in the past month. Simply too damn many of them to be normal."

He stood and held out his hand. "Welcome to Oregon and to Astoria. I hope we can clear up this mess in a hurry."

Spur remembered the slightly shorter version of Lee he had met a few hours earlier in this office.

"Your brother, Martin. I thought you said he was probably broke again. If so, how could he be behind all of these problems? They sound to me like somebody has been spreading a lot of cash around to cause all these 'accidents' for you."

"That's been bothering me, too. But knowing Marty, he might have hit a lucky streak at the tables, or got somebody else to finance it. If I had to sell this business at half of what it was worth, Marty could offer a prospective partner a highly lucrative deal."

"True." Spur worked on his coffee. "First I'm going to try to talk to the three men involved in the Ihander death. I wasn't satisfied with what the District Attorney told me. I might get some kind of a pointing from them."

"Far as I know, they still make the Silver Goose their headquarters when they aren't working. Right now they don't have a job."

Spur looked up.

"It's a little town, everyone knows the other guy's business."

Spur finished his coffee, thanked Karen for it on the way out, and was surprised by the big beautiful smile she gave him.

Spur made two stops at the saloon before he found the three men there. They were making a mug of beer last around a poker table in the far corner of the bar. The apron pointed them out to Spur and must have signalled the men at the same time. All three were standing when he walked over to them.

"Afternoon, gents. My name is Spur McCoy and I want to talk to you for a minute. Would you get mad if I set each of you up to a fresh beer?"

Lou Poikela laughed. "Hell, no! Beers don't come for us as often as we'd like. My name is Poikela, and this is Harvey and Bolt."

Spur told them what he wanted to talk about after they were into their new beers. Bolt stood up and almost left, but Poikela waved him back in his chair.

"Bolt, damnit, we got nothing to worry about. This gent is just talking. The law isn't charging us with a thing. It was just a fight. Relax."

After talking with them for almost an hour, Spur was satisfied. The three men had got into a brawl with Ihander after they had angry words. Ihander had been half-blind drunk and started the wild insults and threw the first punch. Ihander was not a diplomat and called Poikela every lumberjack swear word he could think of.

"So help me, McCoy, it was just a fight. We didn't want to hurt the man. Hell, we didn't even know his name or what work he did. Why would we want to kill him? Beat him up a little, but not kill him."

Spur set them up to another beer. He paid the barkeep on his way out. Beer was ten cents a mug, he could afforrd to blow another thirty cents. He'd figure out some way to put it on his expense report.

It was near closing time at the mill when Spur came out of the saloon. Too late to go over the list of accidents and problems the mill and woods had been having lately. He'd dig into that tomorrow.

Food sounded good right now. He remembered he'd missed any noonday intake. A big supper somewhere, not at the hotel. He spotted Delmonico's, named after the famous New York restaurant. He hoped the food was half as good.

Three men dressed in black melted into the deep shadows in the alley in back of the Silver Goose Saloon. They waited patiently, there was no rush, they had all night.

A half hour after they arrived to take up their vigil, a man stumbled once coming out of the saloon door, looked around and walked quickly to the outhouse on the far back corner of the big lot and went in. He came out and went back into the saloon.

Almost at once another man came out. A morning dove called softly and the three men in black ran at the man, knocked him down, bound his hands behind him and wrapped a gag around his open mouth. Then they hustled him down the alley to a wagon and lifted him on board. They tied his feet and ran back to their positions.

Ten minutes later another man came out and they captured him the same way. It was nearly twenty minutes before the next man they wanted came out.

"It's Poikela," one of the men whispered. The man coming up behind him slugged him on the side of the head with a six-gun and Poikela went down in a heap. They carried the big man down to the wagon, dropped him over the sideboard, then tied his hands and feet securely and gagged him. The men threw a tarp over the human, live cargo and they drove slowly toward the docks two blocks away.

The wagon and its two mules pulled up on the pier beside a three-masted sailing ship. Many wooden sailing ships still plied the trade winds. Manpower was often a problem. The tallest of the three men went on board and talked with the First Mate who came and stared at the men in the wagon in the light of a pair of lanterns.

"I'll take all three," the First Mate said.

"We can offer you only two," the taller man said. His face was in shadow.

"Will they be missed? Are they family men?" the first mate asked. "I got in a hell of a lot of trouble in Portland on the last trip that way."

"Won't be missed. None are married. They have done considerable drinking in the past."

"Bring them on board."

"That's your job, First Mate," the taller man said. He held out his hand. The First Mate reached in his pocket and took out a shiny gold double eagle.

"Ten for each, as usual," he said. Then he called to the ship and four men hurried down the gangplank, hoisted the two tied men between them and carried them onto the ship.

The First Mate turned to thank the tall man and his two shadowy friends, but they were already in the wagon as it rolled on past the rest of the docks and toward the road that led to Upper Town.

Three more men rode up to the wagon on horseback and led the wagon on its climb along the road past Upper Town and on to the highest point overlooking Astoria. A gnarled oak tree stood there that had been buffeted by on-shore ocean winds until most of its branches now grew on the inland side. It looked like half a tree from one angle.

The heavy wagon stopped at the tree and one of the men displayed a rope, a half-inch hemp with a hangman's knot on the end. They carried Poikela from the wagon and slapped his face until he came back to consciousness. His hands had been tied behind his back.

The largest of the men now pulled a black hood over his head that had eye and mouth holes cut in it. The rest of the men did the same. The tallest of the men stood before the prisoner and spoke for the first time to the man.

"Lou Poikela, we, the Vigilante Committee of

Astoria, hereby charge you with the murder of one Erkki Ihander, a member of this community of long standing, and well liked. How do you plead to the charge of murder?''

One of the men pulled the gag off Poikela's mouth and he coughed and sputtered.

"Bastards! Fucking bastards! I've heard about you shit heads. Don't matter how I plead, you've already convicted me. It was just a fight. He started it. He happened to get his neck broke and he died. Tough shit. It was more his fault than mine. You thinking about some kind of justice, you should charge Ihander with killing himself.''

One of the hooded men slugged Poikela in the stomach and smashed half the wind out of him. He couldn't talk for five minutes.

When he screamed at them again, the tall hooded figure stood in front of him. "Since you, Lou Poikela, have offered no defense, and since the evidence against you is overwhelming, this body hereby finds you guilty of the murder of Erkki Ihander. The sentence of this body is that you shall be hanged by your neck until dead, dead, dead. The sentence will be carried out at once.''

Two men lifted Poikela on board a horse without a saddle. They held him there as two other men rode horses on each side of him and they moved under a six-inch thick limb growing on the big oak.

One threw the end of the rope over the limb. The man on the other side of Poikela fitted the noose over his head, tightened it around his neck, and carefully aligned the thirteen rounds of the thick hangman's knot alongside of his right ear and pointing straight up.

"Take up the slack," the noose man said. One of the men on the ground wrapped the rope around the oak tree's trunk near a big knot and tightened it until there was no more slack in the rope, then he tied it off securely.

"Lou Poikela, do you have any last words," the taller leader asked.

"It was a fight, I told you. Bastards! You won't believe me, will you? The D.A. didn't even charge me. How can you do this?"

"We help out the law to preserve order when our courts can't do the job," one of the men said.

Poikela twisted around. "I know that voice! I know who the fuck you are! You got no right doing this!"

The leader gave a signal. Men on each side of the big horse yelled and slapped his hind quarters and the startled animal jolted forward.

Lou Poikela slid off the back of the horse and fell to the bottom of the rope. It had been tied off well. He hit the end of the rope and in that instant the hangman's knot performed its work perfectly. The bulk of the knot jerked straight upward with the force of his body going down. The thickness rammed Lou Poikela's head sideways, breaking his neck with a sickening, audible crack.

The leader nodded.

One of the men gasped. "Oh, God!" he whispered.

Lou Poikela's feet twitched for two minutes as the lingering nerves got messages from a dead brain as it shut itself off. Then he hung there twisting slowly in the midnight breeze. His eyes were open, his tongue hung an inch out of his mouth. His broken neck slanted his head at a 45 degree angle.

"May the Lord have mercy on his black soul," the leader said, then he jumped up on the wagon and stood as it turned and the driver took it slowly down the hill through Upper Town and into the west part which many people were calling Lower Town. The six men with the black hoods pulled them off, folded them and tucked them away.

They met for just a moment, then all six went their separate ways. Each man in his heart knew that the cause of justice had been served, even though it had been accomplished outside of the rule of law.

7

The dinner at Delmonico's was not New York quality, but it was three times better than that at the hotel, and Spur was pleased with his big steak with four vegetables, a salad, two kinds of bread and a pot of honey on his table for one. His coffee cup was never empty.

During the meal he didn't think about the dead man, Ihander, the problem of finding out why he might have been killed, or the attack on the Johnson Lumber Company. He put it all aside and enjoyed his meal.

After his dinner, he walked the streets of Astoria for an hour but nothing new developed in his mind about his problems. So he took the next creative step. He went into the biggest gambling hall and invested ten dollars in a poker game. He lost seven dollars before he pulled out, had a beer and then went over to the Oregon Saloon to listen to Nancy do her eleven o'clock show.

Nancy didn't spot him in the audience until she

came down to hunt for someone to sing to. This time she sat on the edge of his small poker table and sang directly to him the haunting strains of a sad song about a lost love. The saloon went wild when she was done. She winked at Spur.

"Stay after the show," she whispered, then hurried back to the small platform to finish her singing numbers.

Five minutes after her final song, the saloon was back to its more normal customer level. Nancy came out of the back room, talked to a few people and worked over to Spur's table. Her red hair was piled high on top of her head tonight and her eyes were flashing green fire.

She sat down and Spur saw that she could hardly hold some good news in.

"Tell me about it before you pop your buttons," Spur said.

"I can hardly breathe! The boss, the *owner*, just told me he wants me to stay for six months! He's going to give me a raise to twelve-fifty a week, *and he's paying* for my hotel room. Isn't that just fantastic!"

"It certainly is. Congratulations. You'll be heading for New York and the big show houses back there pretty soon."

"Don't tease. This is a big step for me. I was only making five dollars a week with the touring company. They did pay for the hotels and transportation. So this is a big raise."

"I'm pleased for you, Nancy. You deserve it. You sing like a nightingale."

"So we're going to celebrate in your room tonight. I'm bringing the wine, we need some cheese or cookies or crackers or something."

At the hotel, they pried the desk clerk off his station to go to the kitchen and rustle up some cheese and crackers. He got a dollar tip for his trouble, and smiled.

"Why my room tonight?" Spur asked.

Nancy shrugged. She wore a plain white blouse and a flowered skirt that swept the floor. "I just thought it would be fun. See what you travel with, find a man's smell. Mostly curious. Anyway it's your turn."

Once the door was closed to his room and the bolt thrown, Nancy ran to Spur and kissed him hard.

"Ooooooooh! I'm so excited, Spur McCoy. This is the biggest success I've ever had and it means a great deal to me."

"It should, I agree."

He scooped her up and held her in his arms. He kissed her and then dropped her on the bed. She squealed in delight and Spur was glad the bed boards didn't pop out and let the mattress and springs fall on the floor.

She scurried off the bed and opened the wine bottle. She poured two glasses. Tonight she had brought two wine glasses from the saloon or from her room, he wasn't sure which. She lifted one in her hand.

"A toast to my new job, and my contract, and the first big step on my career. I'll work here six months and then get a job in Portland at twenty a week, and then start working back toward Chicago where I'll get a manager or a booking agent and *really start* making some money!"

"I'll drink to that," Spur said and lifted his glass.

"Now, to the next important point. How in the

world could a common man like William Shakespeare, with a minimal education and no access to the noble houses of England or Europe, write the plays and sonnets and poems usually ascribed to this low-born Englishman?''

She turned, a scowl on her pretty face. "You're joking. Not that old argument that somebody else wrote the Shakespeare plays and used Will to hide behind?''

"Of course, it's almost a certainty that Sir Francis Bacon wrote all of the Shakespeare plays. He was a brilliant man, extremely well educated, moved in the royal and monied circles of his day. He had the wit, the intelligence, the touch to write the so-called 'Shakespeare' plays. Old Will, a common worker with a common and sparse education and part time actor, had none of that background.''

"Ridiculous! All hogwash. Of course William Shakespeare is the true author. A man doesn't have to kill someone to write a story or a play about a murder. He simply must have a keen imagination and an insight into how people act and react, and to be a remarkably good observer of the condition of man.''

"I can see that we're going to have a rather long discussion of this problem.'' Take *Hamlet* for instance. How could a common working man such as Will Shakespeare know about the political intrigue, the maneuvering, the royal clashes, the misconceptions, the double crossing, all of that which went on in a royal court? It's totally impossible. Just as it would be for you and me to know about the political infighting and problems and hatreds that go on every day in our government in Washington D.C.''

Nancy plopped on the bed and crossed her arms

across her breasts as if protecting them. "Sir, I spent four years learning the best about English Literature, including one William Shakespeare, Ben Johnson and Sir Francis Bacon. He was a fop for the queen, a quarrelsome old man who had delusions of glory. What's more I'm not about to get undressed for anyone who thinks that a lout like Bacon or Johnson or any of those other hack writers could even cross the T's of a William Shakespeare comedy or tragedy."

"Fine with me," Spur said.

"Fine."

Nancy did look around the room. "This is not to say that I am not going to get some sleep, and I am not about to sleep in my clothes, so you may have that side of the bed, and this side is mine, and if you so much as straggle a finger across the centerline, I'll chop it off!"

"More wine?" Spur asked. She nodded. He poured her glass full, then gave her more cheese and crackers. He replenished his own supply, then renewed the attack.

"What about *The Taming of the Shrew*? What did Will know about Italy or Verona or Padua or Pisa? He never traveled more than fifty miles from Stratford on Avon."

"You must be joking. Either that or everything you said is out of spiteful lying. William Shakespeare was a magnificent talent. What playwrights of today are going to be known in five hundred years?"

Spur settled back. He had been known to argue this Old Will Shakespeare problem for months at a time with other students. Now he had only the night, but it would be enough.

Sometime around three in the morning the wine was gone and the cheese as well. At last they declared a truce, kissed to make it binding and then fell asleep, each believing secretly that they had won the battle.

About six that morning Spur roused, opened his eyes and saw Nancy pulling on her skirt.

"You're awake."

"Almost."

"Where you going?"

"Back to my room." She paused. "You don't really believe all that trash about Bacon?"

He watched her slip her blouse on over her bare breasts and grinned. "Love to see a pretty girl putting on her clothes."

"Do you believe that?"

"What, a pretty girl's bare bosom?"

"No, silly. About Bacon?"

"Usually I can argue on either side."

"What? That's terrible. Remind me never to speak to you again!" She grabbed her underclothes and hurried to the door, then looked for her reticule and found her key.

"Goodbye, Mr. Bacon," she said and slipped out the door.

Spur had another nap.

When he walked across the street and down to Delmonico's, everyone was talking about the hanging.

"Yeah, must have been the Vigilante Committee again. They hung some poor bastard last year, too."

Spur took a detour to the sheriff's office. Sheriff Vinson looked up and scowled at him.

"Yeah, yeah, I know. My boys cut him down early this morning, but not before half the town saw him."

"Who got lynched?" Spur asked.

63

"Your friend, Lou Poikela, the guy who killed Ihander in that fight."

Spur took a turn frowning. "Poikela? Damn! It was the local vigilantes?"

"Yep. They kick up once in a while. Nobody has a clue who they might be. So, I guess you'll be moving on now that the Ihander thing is settled."

"Not a chance. Who says it's settled? I'm not convinced it wasn't an accident. Anyway, my standing orders instruct me to aid local authorities any time vigilante activity crops up."

"I'll be working on it. This time we have an eyewitness. A guy who saw three men on a wagon and three mounted men drive up the hill just before midnight."

"Any identification on any of them?"

"Too dark, but this is more than we've had before."

Spur left and had breakfast. Everybody was talking about it at Delmonico's and all over town. The speculation was highest about who the six men were. Were they actually from right there in Astoria, men they all knew? Or did they come in from Portland, or maybe Vancouver?

Spur listened to the talk as he ate. The general opinion was that Poikela was no great loss to the community. Even if he was a good Finn, he had not been productive.

Somebody wondered where the other two were who were always with Poikela and had been in the fight with him. Were they hanged, too? An out of work fisherman said Poikela had been with his two friends at the Silver Goose Saloon last night. Evidently nobody had seen them this morning.

When Spur finished his breakfast, he went back to talk to the sheriff.

"Sure I checked on them, first thing. They didn't stay at the boarding house last night, Mrs. Fuiten doesn't know where they are. She told me when I found them, to collect the money they owe her for being a week behind in their rent."

"So where are they? Maybe they could give us a clue who Poikela was meeting last night?"

"Doubt it. After I knew they were missing I went down to the docks. One wooden-hulled three-mast ship sailed with the morning tide about five A.M. It was the *China Star*, outbound with a light load and heading for Hong Kong."

"I don't understand?"

"From time to time we have some shanghaiing around here. The sailing ships still need a lot of bodies to make them run. Let's say you were stuck with three men, one you wanted to hang, but the other two didn't actually kill anybody. A good lesson would be good for them. How about selling them to a ship's captain for an all-expense-paid cruise to China?"

Spur chuckled. "A little sea air might be good for the boys. I talked with all three yesterday. I got the feeling that there was no hidden motive in the death. From what I heard it was a fight that turned ugly and in the end Ihander got himself killed. From what the three said, Ihander started the bad-mouthing and brought the whole thing on himself."

"Same feeling I got when I talked to the three," Sheriff Vinson said. "Which is probably why the District Attorney didn't file charges against them. So, McCoy, what are you going to do next?"

65

8

Orville Ames sat in his small office shack at the edge of the large curing yard of rough-sawn lumber and made a tally on the sheet. The wagon of lumber was heading for the *Portland Queen*, a leaky old bucket that plied between Portland and Astoria and sometimes San Francisco with lumber.

The joke was that the *Queen* would never sink as long as she was filled full of dry Douglas fir. This was the last wagon load for the old ship. Orville pushed down on his chair and stood. It was time to report in to the mill office.

He used to hate going over there, but now it was the best part of his day. Little cute-tits was there, that Karen Johnson. Every time he went he used to wonder how good she would be between the sheets. But she wasn't the kind for an afternoon fling, especially with a married man. Her knees were glued together and it would take a marriage certificate to pry them apart.

Still it was fun to wonder. Orville combed his hair

and his full brown beard, then washed his face in the bowl and rubbed some of the gunk off his teeth. His shirt was clean, which was more than most of the mill hands could say.

Hell, he was as good as she was any day. He took his tally records for the past two days and the totals on the lumber loaded that would go on the manifest and walked the three blocks up the hill to the mill site. It was more a slope than a hill, but it gave the lumber carts a good roll down to the curing yard.

Orville knew there were troubles at the mill and in the woods, but so far none of it had touched his operation.

He pushed into the office and walked toward Karen's desk. She wasn't there. He waited a minute and she came out of one of the big offices. He smiled at her. She had that damn tight blue blouse on again today and the soft blue skirt. He wondered if she wore a wrapper under her blouse.

Then he saw the excited little jiggle of her breasts under the blouse and knew there was nothing more than a thin chemise of some kind. His wife tried to wear a binder and he burned the damned thing up.

Karen looked up, saw Orville and nodded.

"Sorry to keep you waiting, Mr. Ames. We have another one full?"

"Yes, ma'am. Here's the tally sheets with the sizes and number of pieces the way we always record it. Took two days to load her because of the dock men."

"Yes, I understand. They do get difficult sometimes. But that's out of our control," Karen said.

"Miss Karen, you certainly do look all spruced up and pretty today. It's a real joy to come over and see you."

She glanced up, serious at first, then she smiled. "Why Mr. Ames, you are the old flatterer, aren't you? You be good now or I'll tell your wife on you."

She went back to the paper work, wrote out the manifest with all the proper figures on it and gave it back to him.

"Just give this to the ship's purser or first mate and they're all set to go," she said.

"Yes, Karen, I certainly will."

He watched her a moment as she reached partway behind her for a record book. The motion brought the blue cloth of her blouse tightly stretched over her breasts and Orville's eyes went wide for a moment. Before she saw him staring at her straining blouse, he turned and walked out of the office.

He moved slower than usual on the way back to his shack and on to the dock. He had worshipped this young, fine-titted woman for two years, and he decided it was past time to do something about it. He wasn't sure just what, but it had to be something.

As he walked, he imagined how it would be with her. He would walk into the mill office, and everyone else was gone. Karen had turned down the lamps low and motioned for him to come to the second office where one of the owners had a small couch. Karen would sit on the couch and tell him how she had wanted him.

She asked if she could run her fingers through his beard. She told him that really got her all sexy feeling. As she ran her fingers through his beard, he massaged her breasts. She moaned and told him that was wonderful.

A moment later he would have her blouse off and be kissing those glorious orbs and sucking them into his mouth. Then neither of them could wait any longer. They would tear their clothes off and couple on the couch until they satisfied each other three times without ever coming apart.

They would dress and she would make him promise to be there two nights from then at the same time and they would discover some more interesting games to play on the couch.

Orville shook his head as he walked on toward his shack in the curing yard. What a dream, a daydream! But now he was tired of dreaming. It had to be real. He had to have that little cunt one way or another!

The rest of the day he tried to decide what to do. At least he could go and see what the big house looked like. He had never been up there on the hill.

That night he slipped out of his place and walked up the hill to Upper Town and through the grassy field behind the Johnson's big house. Most of the lights were on. He watched the various windows, staying well back in the darkness. Then he saw the blinds come down on a second story window.

As the person pulled down the shade he saw the flash of Karen's face and her mass of blonde hair. Yes!

He edged closer and discoverd that there was a considerable tear in the blind on the right hand window. The tear gave him a view into a portion of the room he guessed was her bedroom. Twice he saw her cross the opening, then she sat down at a small bench in front of a mirror and brushed her hair. When she turned around he saw that she wore only her chemise over her breasts.

She finished combing her hair, then stretched and lifted the chemise over her head. For a moment she looked in the mirror at herself. Her breasts were large, with big pink areolas and deep red nipples that stood tall. She brushed some powder on her breasts and smoothed it around.

Orville moaned. He had dropped to his knees, then lay in the grass on his stomach. He pounded his hips against the ground as he watched her rubbing the powder on her breasts. His hard-on jolted forward with each stroke and after a dozen more he erupted and shot his load into his summer drawers. He didn't even mind the wet mess. What a feeling! He'd almost nailed down Karen Thompson. He'd seen her bare tits!

He bet he was closer to fucking her than anyone else in town. As he watched she slipped a white nightgown over her delicious body and walked out of sight. Then the light went out and he sighed. He sat there for ten minutes remembering that marvelous set of breasts, then he felt himself getting hard again as he remembered. He turned at last and walked toward home.

He should marry her and they would have six kids, he'd own part of the Johnson fortune and they'd build a big new home up here on the hill.

There was one problem . . . his wife, Ida. She wouldn't like that arrangement. Ida was a tough woman. She'd borne him two children but also led him around by the nose. He admitted it. She would definitely be his main problem.

The idea came to him quite simply. The only thing to do was to get free of Ida by killing her.

Orville thought about it for a moment. All early love for his wife had vanished five years ago when she turned into a bitter, hard-driving complainer. He never made enough money. He never bought her enough pretty things. He never took her anywhere. He didn't like her relatives. On and on and on. He was sick of her voice, of her looks. That's why he blew out the light every time he humped her.

Yes, he would kill Ida. Now all he had to do was figure out how to do it without getting caught. Simply killing her wasn't enough, it had to look like an accident, like he was in no way responsible. It was a problem, but he would work on it until he had the ideal, perfect solution.

The man's name was Tom Monroe and he regularly ate his breakfast with the four other boarders at Mrs. Kincaid's boarding house a half block off Main Street just down from the bank corner. Tom Monroe melted into the background at the boarding house.

Mrs. Kincaid put him down as a perfect boarder. He never stayed out late at night, never drank or cooked in his room, and he paid his bill promptly. He had been in town for only a week, but she was pleased the way he had fit in. At breakfast and at supper, he was the perfect gentleman.

He nodded his thanks now for the pancake, bacon, toast and coffee breakfast, rose and stacked his dishes, then walked out the front door and down the street to Main. She didn't know where he went every day or what he did. But that was none of her business. Still, a body wondered.

Tom Monroe walked to the alley behind Main, went down four buildings, and turned in at a door with no name on it. Inside was a narrow hallway beside the outer wall that extended for forty feet, then opened into a small lobby-type room with two soft chairs, a table and a lamp. There were no windows and three doors opened off the lobby.

Monroe used a key, unlocked the middle door and went into his office. The room was twelve feet square and had the feeling of a temporary situation. No pictures hung on the walls. The only furniture was one small desk and two chairs. No plants, flowers, no stacks of books or papers and no windows.

One pad of paper lay on the top of the desk. Monroe took off his jacket, hung it on a peg on the wall and sat down at the desk. Two items were written on the paper:

Banker . . . 9:30

Sly . . .

Monroe was short and fat, about six inches over five-feet tall, and almost bald. Fringes of brown hair had been neatly trimmed low on his neck. His brown beady eyes set too close together and only accented his slender nose and thin and almost feminine lips.

Monroe was not a man to boast a granite chin or even a strong chin. In fact, his faded away to almost nothing on the way to his prominent Adam's apple.

He made some notes on the paper, then checked around the floor to make sure nothing had been slipped under his door during the night. Monroe slammed his open palm down on the desk and slipped back into his coat.

First a walk around town to use up some time, then he'd go see the damn banker. It had to be done, he had to keep up the front that he was in the process of scouting out a major retail store for Astoria. He would sell dry goods and ladies and children's clothes. It would be nearly a general store but without groceries.

That was what he wanted the locals to think. Monroe wasn't even sure he needed such a smoke screen, but he had started it on the spur of the moment when it seemed needed and now he had to follow through.

He stopped at the far end of the business district at the Korner Kitchen and had a cup of coffee and a cinnamon roll. Ten minutes later he knocked on the door of the bank a half hour before it opened and the president himself came and unlocked the door.

"Yes, Mr. Monroe, right this way. I was hoping we could have a little talk. I think I might have found you a good location for your store."

They talked for twenty minutes, then went for a walk and looked at the corner lot that Monroe got enthusiastic over.

"See what kind of a price you can get for me on it," Monroe said. He checked his watch. "Now, I'm sorry to run off, but I do have an appointment in about five minutes. Thanks for your help in finding this spot."

Monroe shook hands with the banker and walked quickly down the street. When he was sure the banker wasn't watching him, he went down the side street, into the alley and then to his door.

In the small reception room, Marty Johnson sat waiting. He jumped up when Monroe came in. Monroe harumphed, and opened his door with a key.

Inside, the small man built up a frown. "I thought we agreed that you wouldn't come here," he said.

"We did, but this is an emergency. One of those dirty tricks almost cost a logger his life yesterday."

"We're playing for high stakes here, Johnson. If we lose a man or two along the way, that is to be expected. No army wins battles without taking some losses."

"Yes, but now the damn vigilantes are cropping up again. Did you hear what they did to Poikela?"

"Strung him up. So?"

"So if they start looking into the accidents the lumber company is having, who are they going to come after? Probably me, because I'm the one out front stirring things up."

"And getting paid well for your trouble. Look. You bought in on this deal and there's no welshing now. I have less than two weeks to get this all wrapped up and guarantee that I can produce. If I can't give them a certifiable mill operation under my control by then, they'll move on to another bidder. We're talking about a profit here of a quarter-of-a-million dollars. Do you know how much money that is, Johnson?"

"Yeah, a lot."

"A lot? It's the average yearly wages of one thousand men, that's how much it is. A working man makes about $250 a year. Now, down to business. Your work yesterday was fine. We need more and more, at least one serious accident each day to keep up the pressure."

He watched Martin closely. "What was the company worth when you sold out five years ago?"

"About a hundred and fifty thousand dollars for the whole thing. Now it's at least twice that big, twice as many workers."

"Three hundred thousand?"

"My guess. The mill provides half the payroll for the town."

"More than I estimated. Well, we'll work with

that. Get out of here and figure out some more accidents for the Johnson Lumber Company. The better you work, the quicker you'll be a rich man.''

Martin headed for the door. ''You don't think the vigilantes are a problem for us?''

''Not at all. If they become a problem, we'll simply eliminate them. They understand power and violence.''

Marty watched Monroe for a minute realizing he did not know the man at all and understood him even less. Just as Marty reached for the door, someone knocked. Marty opened it and stepped aside as Sly Waters swaggered into the room, quickly checked to see who was there, then eased his hand away from the butt of his six-gun.

Marty nodded and walked out. As he closed the door he heard Monroe getting up from his chair.

''Sly,'' Monroe said warmly, ''glad you dropped by. I've got another little piece of work for you.''

9

Sly Waters looked at Monroe and snorted. "Hell, you call this work? This is a damn vacation." Waters was 24, cocky, four inches shy of six feet, wore his black hair short and had a pencil thin moustache and modest side burns.

He slouched down in the chair and put one cowboy boot up on the edge of the desk. Monroe frowned at the boot and Waters shrugged. "Don't worry about the furniture, you rented it. What you got for me?"

"Nothing, actually. I was just trying to impress young Johnson so he would renew his efforts. All you have to do is stay out of sight and not go on any drunken binges. If you get into a gunfight on your own, I can't use you anymore. Right now, I'm holding you in reserve until I need you. Understand? Remember that. We just don't have fast guns running around Astoria shooting up the place. I'm saying this isn't Tombstone."

"For damned sure. Lot hotter over there."

"You have enough money?"

76

"Always use some more, but yeah, I'm fine."

"That's about it then, Sly. Just wanted to talk about a few things. I might have another situation coming up that will need to be resolved."

"Yeah, you let me know." Sly stood. "This whole setup is weird, you know. I'm used to going in and doing a job and leaving. This is strange."

Monroe stood. "This is the way it is. Get a girl to take to your room."

"Got me one. Gets expensive."

Monroe handed him a twenty dollar bill. "This should help. Now, I have some people to see."

Sly waved and went out the door.

Monroe put his feet up on the desk and thought through the project again. He did have a two week deadline. He had to show them that he had a sawmill that could turn out the needed product on time and in the right quantity. He should go into Portland tomorrow and stall them, tell them it was almost in his hand. He had a choice of going up on the passenger boat or taking the stage. Neither one was his favorite. A train would be better.

Yes, a train! He grinned and opened up a folder and began going through his estimates again. He had to come up with the right-sized offer for the mill, woods and timber leases. He would get the right figure, then cut it by at least 50% for his first offer. It left bargaining room.

But what if Johnson was tough enough to simply absorb the accidents, fight back and refuse to sell at any price?

Monroe laughed and shook his head. Lee Johnson had a wife and two kids. Amazing how a man can change his mind when he's not sure where his family is. Damn interesting what that does to most men. A business doesn't look all that important any more. Of course that would be a last choice option. It wouldn't go that far, he was sure.

Spur McCoy arrived at the Johnson Lumber Company a little after nine that morning. Karen looked up as he came through the door.

"Good morning. How about some coffee?" She smiled.

"Yes, Karen, I would appreciate that."

"Do you like huckleberries? I made some red huckleberry muffins this morning."

"Can I have three or four?" Spur said. "Yes, I like them better than cinnamon rolls."

Karen wore a bright blue one piece dress that tucked in at the waist and surged outward over her breasts delightfully. The fabric covered her all the way to her chin in the usual fashion. Her long blonde hair looked brushed to a sheen and blue eyes watched him as she put the plate with three muffins and a dish of butter down in front of him.

"Pull up a chair and use the front of my desk as a table," Karen said. "Then we can talk. I'm curious how you got into this kind of work."

Spur broke one of the big muffins in half, took a bite of it and grinned. "I got into this work so I could sample muffins. Now that is a great muffin!"

"You're teasing me," Karen said. "The hucks grow on the hills around here. Takes a while to pick them. They're the first cousins of the more famous blue ones."

"Speaking of blue, I like that dress."

"Thank you. Most people don't even notice. You're all spiffed up yourself with town pants and brown shirt and vest. Is that buckskin?"

"True. Now, tell me why you're here in Astoria instead of down in Portland finding yourself a rich, handsome husband."

"Oh, I've been there. Too many people. I used to go down twice a week on the passenger boat to take dancing lessons. Ballet. I liked it but it's just too far away, over a hundred miles. I had to stay over and come back the next day."

"So that was the end of ballet."

"Yes. Now I'm interested in the company. I'm part owner so that helps, and it's my job, too."

Spur buttered the other half of the muffin and munched on it. "If you ever give up this job you can always open a bakery. This is the best red huckleberry muffin I've ever tasted."

She grinned. "Probably because it's the *only* one, right?"

"Caught me. Is Lee coming in this morning?"

"He's working on that new donkey engine for the one that got blown up. At least we haven't had any bad news today, yet." She looked up at him, her face serious, but still pretty. "I earnestly hope, Spur, that you stay a while and help us get to the bottom of all this trouble. Lee says somebody wants to force us to sell out cheap."

"That's what it looks like, Karen. I'm going to be here a while for that and to dig into the vigilante problem as well."

"Let me give you some more coffee," Karen said. She reached out to hold his hand on the cup and when their hands touched she pulled back for a moment, then looked up at him and smiled. Spur had felt it too, a spark, a flare of emotion. This was a girl he wanted to know better.

He tasted the coffee.

"I grew up in a big city. I bet you had more fun growing up here in Astoria."

"Yes, it was fine. We could fish in the river or the ocean, we could build sand castles, and soak in the sun in the summer when the wind wasn't blowing too hard. Then there were hikes in the woods, and games on the sand. I'd say I enjoyed growing up here."

Karen watched him from serious blue eyes. She was beautiful. Her hair swirled around her shoulders, some falling in front.

"Spur McCoy, what was it like growing up in the big city? Which one?"

"New York City. My father had enough money so we lived well. I remember the parks and nurses and then playgrounds. Summers we went to Long Island. My father and mother still live in their town house in Manhattan."

The outside door came banging open and Lee stalked in. Spur saw the anger in his face and in his manner before he spoke.

"Goddamnit! Won't this ever stop! I just came from the main saw. Somebody drove spikes into a log and tore up the big blade. Chunks of the saw flew every way until they got it turned off. Somebody could have been killed. Going to cost us a half day to get a new blade on and check all of the logs for spikes."

"Oh, no!" Karen wailed.

"Any way to tell who might have done it?"

"Not a chance, unless somebody confesses."

"Your problems are getting worse. I know you probably aren't looking for advice, but from an outside viewpoint, I might have a good idea."

"Damnit! I'd like just five minutes with the guy who pounded in those spikes and his hammer. I'd have a bigger hammer and pound that bastard right into the ground."

"Lee, did you hear Spur? He said he might have an idea."

"I heard, I'm still too mad to listen. Give me about ten minutes to cool off." He charged into his office and slammed the door.

"Do you know who that lawyer was who came in with Marty yesterday?"

"Sure, Victor Trumbull. Not exactly a favorite of the company."

"I gathered that. I think it's time to get him and Lee together and see what's going on."

"I agree. So many times problems can be talked out face to face." She watched him a moment. "Want another muffin?"

"Three are enough. I'll spoil my dinner."

They talked about growing up for a few minutes, then Lee's door opened and he leaned against it.

"Okay outsider with a clear, uncluttered, non-emotional mind, what's your big idea?" Lee asked.

Just before eleven o'clock, Spur, Lee, Trumball and Marty met around a large desk in an office that once had been Marty's. Lee started the talks.

"Yesterday, I think it was yesterday, Mr. Trumbull made a challenge to this company and some demands. Now I think it's fair that I get to talk first.

"I'm sure both of you know that for the past

81

month this firm has been having a series of attacks by outsiders made to look like accidents, but which are really vicious, deadly invasions of our company in an attempt to force us into wanting to sell out. I've all but proved that Martin Johnson is responsible for these attacks, as well as for the man who was killed and the other man who lost a leg yesterday.

"Mr. Trumball, as Marty's lawyer you should know that I'll be filing criminal charges of assault, murder, mayhem, and a series of other dangerous and illegal acts against the personnel and corporate structure of this company."

For a moment there was silence. Marty started to say something but Trumbull's hand on his arm stopped him.

"That was a good speech, Mr. Johnson. You should have been a lawyer. Except for one small point. To file charges and to win in court, you need evidence. You can't have any, because my client is not involved in your mismanagement, poor maintenance and your rash of accidents. Now, let's move on to a legal problem.

"Tomorrow or the next day we are filing in the circuit court charges that five years ago you illegally froze out your brother from this company, at an outrageously low price for his stock. Now we intend to prove that the true worth of the company at that time was at least twice what you purported it to be—"

"Hold it!" Lee thundered. "This is hogwash. I have legal documents of three independent appraisers of the company at that time. All parties agreed to the appraisal, including Marty's lawyer and the circuit court judge."

Trumball looked at Marty. "You didn't tell me this."

"You never asked. You said since it was worth more now than it was then that we could declare that. . . ."

Trumbull shook his head. "He's right, you don't have a case. You can't get another dime out of Johnson Lumber. But if you are named in a criminal procedure you're going to need a damn good lawyer."

"Evidence, remember," Martin said. "Lee doesn't have any evidence. It's just a bluff."

"I'll put an axe handle alongside your head for evidence!" Lee thundered.

The brothers stood and glared at each other.

"If you weren't such a pig headed prude!" Marty shouted.

"If you weren't such a worthless, drugged out gambler!" Lee snarled back.

"Get him out of here," Spur told Trumbull.

The lawyer grabbed Marty's arm and led him out through the front door. Spur stood in a place where he could stop Lee if he stormed after his brother.

Lee took a big breath and dropped into the chair. "Damn, but he makes me mad! Always has. He was the favored one. Dad spent five times as much time with him as with me. Pretty soon he got to expect it. He was spoiled rotten. When he had to get by on his own he floundered and got in a hell of a mess. Drugs, gambling. That's when I tried to bail him out before the gambling guys chopped him up for crab pot bait.

"He still resents it, I guess. If he's trying to put the company out of business, he'll try even harder now."

"So I had a rotten idea, sorry," Spur said.

"Forget it." Lee sat there a minute. "You want to help find out who's behind this?"

"Yes."

"Go see a little man by the name of Percival X. Northcliff. He's a saddlemaker. Half the cowboys from Pendleton and eastern Oregon come over here to get him to make their saddles. He also is one of the smartest guys in town and knows more about more people here than anyone, including the sheriff."

"Percival?"

"Right. Most of us call him P.X. Can't miss him, he's just the other side of the bank."

Spur watched the lumber man. "You going to be all right?"

"I'm fine."

Spur walked out, waved at Karen and worked his way over to Main Street. Just past the bank he saw the leather shop and pushed open the door.

A midget stood on a four-foot step stool putting the finishing touches on a fancy Denver saddle with a sturdy horn and a double cinch rig that would hold the 40 pound saddle in place in the heaviest roping work. The small man turned and smiled.

"The new guy in town, Spur McCoy. Welcome to the land of leather. If it's made out of leather, I can do it." He grinned and held out his hand.

"Yeah, that's me, Pecival X. Northcliff. No, I'm not English, and yes, I used to be with the circus until I ran away, took a wife and learned how to make saddles from the best saddlemaker who ever picked up an awl. How about a spot of coffee. I'm out of cinnamon rolls."

10

Spur liked P.X. Northcliff at once. There was nothing about him to dislike. He stepped to the floor, went across the room to a low bench built for him and took a pot of coffee heating on a one burner wood stove that was almost as tall as he was.

"Black?" P.X. asked.

Spur nodded.

"Easiest way to fix it on the trail. From your sun-tanned face I'd say you spend a lot of time outdoors."

He held out his small hand. "I'm P.X. to my friends. I hear you're with the Secret Service, federal government group from Washington D.C. I played D.C. once."

Spur took the coffee. It was black and hot and strong. "Just the way I like it." Spur took a deep breath. "Leather. That's the best smell in the world. I might drop in two or three times a day to get a few lungs full of that."

"Leather is God's gift to man. The Indians must have used it first. Well, not before Europeans, but here in this world. A lot of those early Americans are very bright when it comes to the land and the animals." P.X. sat on the bench beside the coffee pot.

"From what you've said so far, Spur McCoy, I'd say you're an educated man. Isn't hard to tell. Who was Archimedes?"

Spur laughed. "I didn't know there was going to be a test. The old Arc was a Greek who lived two or three hundred B.C. and specialized in mathematics and inventions. Reaching way back, I'd say his best known gadget was the Archimedes screw, a bent spiral tube used to raise water for irrigation."

"Ha! Absolutely right. I'd forgotten about the screw. Now that Arc was a smart man, but he's been dead and gone almost two thousand years."

Spur sipped the coffee. "You sure like your coffee hot."

"Keeps me awake. You ever stick a leather stitching needle through your finger?"

"Not lately. Mind if I check out the saddle?"

"Be my guest. But I get to watch."

P.X. bounded off the bench and up the steps and watched closely as Spur lifted parts and checked out the long, heavy Denver saddle.

"These Denvers are great, but I've always found they tend to put sores on a good horse's back. I saw a saddle down in California last year I liked. It was shorter, ten pounds lighter, had a slightly higher and slimmer horn and usually a single cinch arrangement. Back of the saddle came up straighter. The one I saw had tooled leather and brass stirrups."

"That is getting fancy. Almost as fancy as the mess you walked into here when that timber cruiser got himself killed."

Spur pushed it gently. "I talked to Poikela before he died. Seemed to me it was only a fight, from what I could tell. Poikela said Ihander was a loudmouth who started the whole thing."

"Probably. But even alive Poikela wasn't what you'd call a good witness." The small man sat in the saddle and began sewing on one of the straps that came around the horn.

"Everybody knows that the lumber company is having a lot of hard luck, accidents and all." P.X. looked at Spur sharply, but caught no giveaway expression. "Most people figure they aren't accidents at all. I do know there's some big money behind this operation somewhere."

"That doesn't sound like Marty Johnson."

"The prodigal son? Not a chance. Grabbed his inheritance and paid off his gambling debts and took off for California and wild women and song. Sure, he's back, but the trouble began before he came back, two weeks ago. Yes, the accidents and incidents have increased since he's been here. But he never has had any money."

"Maybe he's a lower echelon man, a flunky."

"Could be."

"What about the vigilantes? Are they tied into this mixture, or was it only concidence that the conscience of the town rose up and lynched Lou Poikela?"

"I've got some theories on those gentlemen. Not exactly popular ones. Fact is, they should be hanging themselves, but that's hard to bring up for a vote in most vigilante committees." P.X. chuckled and Spur grinned at the small man's dark humor.

"So, government man, your killer is dead, justice has triumphed. Will you be moving on to another assignment?"

"Nope. Not satisfied with the vigilante form of justice. The big question is, was it real justice? If it was a brawl and nothing more that got Poikela killed, then I'm duty bound to dig out the vigilantes. Looks as though I'll be around for a while."

The small man pushed the awl through the leather and quickly forced a needle with beeswaxed string through the two pieces of leather and pulled it tight. He looked up.

"Not many men wear guns in Astoria. But one does besides you. Be watchful of him. Only saw him once, but he's not a good person."

"True. You mean Sly Waters. He's a back shooting skunk, wanted in several states and territories. But I didn't come here to match up six-guns with him.

"Just so he doesn't get a shot at you first."

Spur stood. "I like the looks of that saddle. I'd bet you have all the business you can handle."

"Most of the time."

"You ever have cinnamon rolls in the mornings?"

"Every day."

"Save me one in the morning."

Spur settled his wide brimmed black hat with the row of Mexican silver coins around the headband on his head and walked back out onto the Astoria street. Automatically, he checked to be sure his .45 six-gun was snug in the holster.

Behind him, P.X. Northcliff smiled. He nodded

ever so slightly, then went back to working with the awl and needle on the nearly finished Denver-style saddle.

The notch in the tall, two-foot thick Douglas fir tree had been cut the night before. The big tree stood halfway down the dry flume which funneled the big logs from the mountain to the Columbia River backwater below on the Johnson Lumber Company leased tract of saw-log land.

Even part of the undercut had been made with a six-foot, just-sharpened, cross cut saw. Now as the sun rose over the mountains, all that was needed were a dozen more strokes with the big saw to sever the last fibers holding the tree skyward.

The man's muscles bunched as he picked up the saw. He would leave it there once the tree was down, jump on his horse tied nearby, and race out of the area before anyone could see him. Neat, clean and he was earing a fast ten dollars, half a month's pay for some.

The lumberjack slid the steel into the flat saw cut. He noticed the Johnson Lumber Company brand burned into the wooden handle. That made him grin. Doing the job with his own saw!

He stroked the steel through the cut and watched with satisfaction as the drag teeth cleaned out the cut spewing sawdust at his feet with every back stroke. A few more. He watched the top of the tree. It was wavering.

The man made six more fast strokes with the saw and heard a crack. He jumped back and sprinted ten yards away from the tree so the butt couldn't bounce back and hit him. He'd seen it happen too many times.

The final fibers holding the tree upright snapped and it fell in the direction of the under cut, slashing past smaller trees and then the heavy trunk smashed into the flume, shattering the heavy two-by-twelves, splintering them into rubble, and crashing all the way to the earth right through the heavy planks on the bottom of the trough.

When the sound of the falling tree quieted, he looked at his handiwork. The flume was mashed up so bad it couldn't be used until a damn lot of repairs were made. Yeah, his job was over.

The man ran for his horse, walked her due west along the side of the ridge and gradually angled down hill toward the River Road. Johnson had no fallers in this area. It was a hundred-to-one that anyone would see him. Nobody did.

It was almost four in the afternoon before Lee Johnson got to the site of the smashed flume. Obviously, this one was no accident, rather a deliberate destructive attack on the company. More than a dozen logs had shot down the flume from high above and smashed into the break before someone saw the trouble and raced up the hill to stop the logs being sent down.

Lee stared at the disaster. Big logs lay everywhere like a stack of jackstraws. The foreman had started repairs at once. First he had to buck up the logs into smaller pieces so horses and mules could drag them out of the way.

Then the smashed flume would have to be sawed

away and a new section built. They were still in the process of sawing the forty-foot logs in pieces. That would take at least the rest of the day. One three-foot-thick log stood almost straight up where it had smashed through the shattered floor of the flume and dug itself six feet into the soft Oregon forest floor.

A cable was being attached to the top end of the big log with the hope that it could be toppled to one side so it would not have to be cut up.

Lee stared at the mess. His foreman was doing a good job. He went over to the end of the killer tree, the one that had been deliberately felled across the flume. The axe used was gone but the saw was where an animal had waited for some time. The tracks through the soft forest floor were easy to follow, but to what end? He would lose them on the heavily traveled River Road.

Lee kicked at the saw, stared at the Johnson Lumber Company logo, then picked it up and carried it over to the men working on the big sticks.

The foreman talked with Lee for a few minutes, and gave him a list of lumber he would need to rebuild.

"I'll load it in the morning and have it start up here by wagon. First load of the heavier stuff will be here before noon."

The foreman nodded and went back to take his turn at a saw to cut up a four-foot-thick giant of a log.

Lee didn't even want to estimate how much this would cost the company. Deliberate destruction like this was what hurt the most. It slowed production of saw logs, and that sooner or later would stop the mill if it went on long enough.

He rode slowly back toward the River Road. At least no one got hurt this time. The doctor said that Scotty Jones would be fine. He weathered the loss of blood and was getting stronger. Scotty was determined to come back as a choke setter and work up to faller, the highest paid job in the woods.

Lee figured Scotty would be safer working in the mill, but he'd wait and give him a chance to work where he wanted to.

Lee snorted. "Hell yes, if I still own this company." He rode back to the River Road as dusk settled in. It was fully dark when he got to the office. The lights were on. Inside he found Spur McCoy and Karen talking over coffee.

"We waited for you," Karen said. "I invited Spur home for dinner and to meet your family."

Lee nodded, not feeling like entertaining company. But then he figured that Karen would do the entertaining. Right then he was so mad he didn't care. Damnit!

He told them what had happened out on the flume.

"Smashed one section all to hell. Take a week to get it fixed and back in production. We can cut and skid lower down on the hill, but we were saving that for bad weather work."

"How is the cold deck?" Karen asked.

"Good enough. We won't run out of logs, but it just puts another crimp in our operation. How many of these deliberately destructive moves can we absorb? About the only thing I don't expect is somebody to burn down the mill. Whoever is doing all of this wants the mill up and running, I'm convinced of that. So far it's just been nicking us around the edges."

"Let's go have dinner and think about something else for a while," Karen said.

"Karen, I don't think this is a good time for Lee to be socializing," Spur said. "Why don't I take you out to dinner at Delmonico's instead, and we both can get out of Lee's hair for a while?"

She grinned, then looked at her big brother. He simply nodded and went over and slumped down in a chair beside her desk.

"Yeah, I've got some thinking to do."

Dinner at Delmonico's was pleasant. Karen was attentive and they talked about early Astoria. For a moment Spur had a feeling that he was courting this pretty girl. They ate the seafood plate of clams and oysters and crab and slabs of fresh salmon.

"If I keep eating this way, I won't be able to get into my clothes," Spur said.

After the meal they drove her buggy back up the hill to Upper Town. On the dark porch Karen waited to be kissed. When Spur made no move, she reached up and kissed his lips gently.

"Nice," Spur said. Then he kissed her with more authority, pulling her hard against his chest until he felt her press her breasts against him. It brought a little sigh from Karen. Then he let her go and stepped back.

"It's been a nice evening," Spur said. "I especially like the way it's ending."

She grinned. "I enjoyed it too, Spur McCoy. You could come in for a while and meet Cilla and the kids."

"Another time. Then I'll get to kiss you good night again."

Karen lifted on her tiptoes and kissed him softly on

the lips, then spun around and went inside the big door with only a teasing smile over her shoulder.

"Now there is a woman," Spur said, and began his walk back down the hill and his hotel room.

11

Orville Ames growled just enough to make his wife feel comfortable because he had to take her fishing, and then pushed off from the dock in the rowboat he borrowed from his buddy Phil. It was a good eight-foot rowboat that Orville could handle well on the edge of the channel of the mighty Columbia River. Orville had been a fisherman for a while and grew up rowing boats.

Orville and Ida were heading out to try for some salmon. The run had started. More than thirty small boats worked the near side of the Columbia as the big fish turned out of the Pacific Ocean in a drive to find the headwaters where they themselves had been born. They would charge back up the very river and branch stream and tiny creek where they were spawned four or five years before.

Instinct told them to fight upstream to spawn in the exact same area. It was nature's way to perpetuate the species.

"Damn well better be good fishing tonight," Orville barked, "or one woman named Ida gonna be in a hell of a fix."

Ida was a large woman, almost five-ten, raw boned and not at all pretty, but with wide hips for easy child-birth. Orville often said she was as easy to breed as a milk cow.

He made sure she knew he was unhappy, then rowed out to where they could drop in their lines with three hooks on them all baited with a cross cut piece of a small fish they called a sardine.

They hit the first edges of the current and drifted downstream so the big salmon, silver sides and Chinooks, would find the bait as they swam upstream against the current.

Ida hooked up a fish almost at once and Orville rowed out of the current so she could reel in and land him. Orville didn't have a net, just a fishhook he made himself from an old piece of steel, but it worked and he flipped the ten or twelve pound salmon over the rail of the rowboat and bashed it on the head to kill it before it flopped out of the shallow craft.

They went into the current again but neither of them hooked a fish. After they drifted half a mile downstream toward the bar, Orville rowed out of the edges of the current into the calmer water. Out there he wouldn't have to fight the current as he rowed back toward Astoria's pier again where they would pick up the current for another try.

They made three drifts that way, and on the second Orville caught a fifteen pounder, and Ida got another ten pound Chinook.

"One more drift!" Ida begged.

"Damn right, woman, if'n you want to do the

rowing.'' That always shut her up because she was the world's worst rower. Orville headed for the pier with 35 pounds of salmon and started an almost daily fishing trip out on the river. He wanted it to be firmly established that he and Ida went fishing regularly.

He hadn't decided for sure yet how he would kill Ida, but the more he figured it, the more it seemed a natural to let the Columbia River help him in the task.

Late that same night, six men met in the back room at the general store for their weekly poker game. The doors were all locked, there was no chance anyone would break in on them. Cards lay on the table but no one was playing the hands that had been dealt.

The man who held the deck was taller then the rest. He had black hair cut short in the business fashion and wore a suit and tie. His name was Josiah Dangerfield and he was District Attorney for Clatsop County in the State of Oregon.

''Gentlemen, I hope you're all as pleased as I am with our recent work. We eliminated a dangerous man from our community and we sent two more packing where they won't harm us for a long time.'' He stopped and looked around at three merchants, a barber and the man who ran the biggest fishing cannery in the harbor.

''Do we have any new business to talk about?'' Dangerfield asked.

One of the men spoke up sharply. ''Damn right, the gunsharp in town. He probably is the one who killed Slim Gillette, the faller for Johnson who got shot.''

''The man's name you're talking about is Sly Waters, a real gunner from Arizona who wears a tied down gun,'' one of the men said.

"Yeah, that's the one. Don't see much of him, but he's still around. The girls know he's here. I move we run the little bastard right out of town.''

"You gonna go up against him with your six-gun?'' another voice asked.

"Hell, no, I'll use my deer rifle.''

"No!'' Dangerfield's voice was cold and final. "We will not sink to bushwhacking or mob violence. To keep any good will of the citizens, our vigilante committee must act in a responsible and logical manner. I'll do some thinking on Mr. Waters and see what I can come up with. The Sheriff might even have a wanted poster on him. If that's the case, then it's open season on him just like a buck deer.''

"What about Darwin Hart? We've talked about him before. He needs some kind of a lesson. Leaves his wife and four kids alone half the time. He's a boozer, a bar bum. I'd vote to run him out of town, but then his wife and younguns would hurt.''

"Shame him,'' another man said. "Shame him in front of the whole town. We've done it a time or two before on other men and it worked wonders.''

"Tar and feathers?'' someone asked.

"Dangerous. A man can get burned to death with hot tar.''

"Wish we had some village stocks where we could tie him up for a while the way the pilgrims did.''

"How about a sturdy logging chain, a padlock, and fasten him naked to the hotel overhang post?''

"Gentlemen, I think we've arrived at a favorable solution to one of our problems,'' Dangerfield said. "All in favor of such a lesson for one Mr. Hart, say Aye.''

It was unanimous. Two of the men went out the back door of the store for the chain, a half-inch link sturdy logging choker chain that would hold ten thousand pounds. They said they would bring two heavy padlocks as well.

The store man went into his office and came back with a thick bladed pen and a piece of cardboard.

"We need a sign," he said and proceeded to print it out:

DARWIN HART IS A DRUNKARD! the sign read.

Two more men left to find Hart and bring him to the back of the store. The promise of a bottle of rot gut whiskey would be enough inducement to lead Hart anywhere.

By eleven-thirty they had everything they needed. The chain was looped around Hart's waist and cinched up so it would not slip over his hips, and then padlocked securely in place. Then they let Hart drink as they took his shirt and pants off as well as his filthy underwear and his high topped shoes.

The six men kept Hart there until nearly two A.M. Then they made sure the street was empty and walked him over to the hotel. They quickly used the other padlock to chain Hart firmly to the eight-by-eight-inch post that held up the overhang of the hotel that extended out eight-feet over the boardwalk.

Hart grinned, emptied the bottle and sat down on the boardwalk and promptly went to sleep.

About 3 A.M. a deputy sheriff found Hart and studied the padlocks.

"Damn, but somebody's having some fun with old Hart." The deputy saw that he couldn't solve the problem, so he checked the doorknobs on all the stores in town, as usual, and wrote a note on his report back at the jail about finding Hart.

Rob Wilson, making his early morning run with fresh milk, saw Hart and got off his milk wagon to check. He decided at once that he couldn't help the man who was still snoring in his drunken manner. Rob continued with his route, telling anyone he saw that there was a free freak sideshow on down at the hotel.

When Sheriff Vinson arrived at his office slightly before seven A.M. the deputy reported on Hart's problem and the head lawman in Clatsop County ambled up to the hotel for a look.

"Be damned," Sheriff Vinson said. "Looks like Darwin will be tied up for some time."

Already there was a crowd of twenty people around, including five or six women. Somebody threw a towel over Hart's private parts, but he clawed it away in his sleep and used it as a pillow.

The sheriff woke Hart up by sloshing a bucket of water over him. The water came from a horse trough. Hart sputtered and sat up trying to wipe the water off his face.

"What'n hell?" he asked. He squinted as he peered at the twenty-five faces staring at him. By that time most of the faces were laughing at him. Two of the women screeched in delight at his nakedness.

Hart scowled and spit, then looked down at his crotch. "M'God, I'm naked!" he yelped.

Sheriff Vinson walked up. "Morning, Darwin. How you get in this pickle?"

"Damn if I know. I . . . I might have been drinking?"

The crowd roared with laughter. Five or six more

women hurried up. Hart pulled the towel over his crotch. Somebody ran up and snatched it away from him. The crowd clapped and howled and the cackling laughs of the women were easy to hear.

"This man has real shortcomings!" a woman shouted. The crowd cheered.

Sheriff Vinson knew Darwin well. He'd spent more than a day a week sleeping off a drunk in the county jail.

"Darwin, how we going to get that chain off you?"

"Damned if I know, Sheriff."

"You wouldn't have the key in your pocket?"

"Not likely. No pockets."

Quade, Astoria's locksmith, came up and studied the padlocks a minute. He shook his head. "Multiple tumblers with variable notches. I can't pick it open, Sheriff. Got the key?"

The Sheriff sent for the blacksmith, Mark Hardison. "Tell him to bring a hammer and chisel and an anvil to work on," the Sheriff directed.

It took Blacksmith Hardison twenty powerful hammer blows against the chisel on the anvil to cut the half-inch chain link. That freed Hart from the hotel support post.

There wasn't room to do the same thing on the chain around Hart's belly.

"I'll get a hacksaw, the big smithy said. The hardware store man brought one out and ten minutes later the last of the chain was off Hart. He grabbed the towel back and pulled it around him as he ran down the block toward his house.

Sheriff Vinson watched him go. "That should cure Darwin of his drinking . . . for about a week is my guess. What do you think, Dangerfield?"

The District Attorney had walked up during the hacksawing. He shook his head. "Had my way I'd lock him up for good. But then the county poor house would have to feed his family. Maybe this mortification will cure him."

"Don't count on it," Sheriff Vinson said. "Josiah, a few things I need to talk to you about. You have time this morning about ten?"

"I'll make time, Sheriff. That's my job. About ten in my office?"

Sheriff Vinson nodded and went back toward the jail.

Spur McCoy had first seen the small circus when he left the hotel and the blacksmith was whaling away on his chisel. Now as the small crowd broke up, McCoy spotted Marty Johnson in the edge of the crowd and he worked over toward him.

He caught Marty's elbow with his left hand and shoved his finger in Marty's side simulating a gun.

"Marty, don't panic, nobody is going get hurt. You know I always carry a gun, right? So just relax and let's walk over there into that first alley. You and I need to have a small talk."

"Just a talk?"

"Sure, what else? I'm not absolutely positive that you're the head man directing all of these destructive problems against Johnson Lumber. It's a good chance, but I'm a man who has to work with definite proof."

They walked halfway down the alley and stopped. Spur pushed Marty against the wall.

"That wasn't a gun. . . ."

Never draw it unless I'm ready to kill somebody. You're a lucky man . . . so far. Your big problem right now are these damn vigilantes. You saw what they did to a lush like Darwin Hart. You know about them hanging Poikela. What are they going to do to you when I tell them that you're the man behind all of these costly problems, and the murder of Slim Gillette.''

Marty's face blanched, his eyes went wide and his chin quivered. He stared at Spur for a minute and then shook his head.

"Naw, you wouldn't do that. You can't, you don't know who the vigilantes are.''

"Don't need to. I just start talking around town how you're the man responsible for all of these accidents. The right people will hear. Some of them must be merchants. If they think you're going to close down the mill, and stop all those wages, it'll make a big difference to their sales totals.

"They'll be losing money and you'll be to blame. How long do you think you'll last with the vigilantes and their rope and their oak tree up there on the hill just waiting for you?''

"No! No, it can't happen. The mill won't close. It can't. Besides, I'm not doing a thing to hurt it. Bad management, bad maintenance.''

"That's what caused that tree to be cut down across the flume yesterday out on the Svenson timber tract?''

"Well, no, but. . . .''

"I'm sure you'll be able to reason with the vigilantes. Everyone says they are logical, methodical. They never hang anyone unless they really deserve it.''

Spur eased away from Marty. "Just thought I should tell you, Marty. Don't let anything I've told you hurt your chance to have a happy day." Spur grinned, and walked out of the alley and into the hardware store. He stopped near the front windows and watched the street.

Only a minute later Marty left the alley and walked quickly down the street. Spur eased out of the store and followed him. Marty didn't look back. He went down the block, turned left at First Street and walked to the alley. Then he stepped into it and Spur ran to the edge of the building and looked down the way Marty had vanished.

He was just in time to see Marty open the second door from the far end and go into a building. Spur ran through the alley and eased the same door open. He saw the long hall and the stark reception room on the other end.

A blind entrance to something. He'd come back later and investigate. Not a chance he could do it now.

Marty hurried down the hallway and knocked on the middle door in the reception room. He pushed it open and went inside. Tom Monroe looked up, his surprise turning into a grim-lipped tolerance.

"What's the trouble now, Marty?"

"You know about this new guy in town, the guy with the black hat and the tied down six-gun?"

"Yeah, his name is McCoy, he's pretty thick with the Johnsons."

"You think they brought him in as a fast gun to balance out Sly Waters?"

"Nope. They aren't that smart. What's the problem?"

"He just forced me into an alley and threatened me. Said he was going to tell the vigilantes that I'm

104

responsible for all of the accidents and slow down and the deaths and injuries at the mill and in the Johnson logging show."

"So? You arranged most of them."

"Yeah, but I don't want him blabbing it to the vigilantes!"

Monroe put down the wooden pencil he'd been writing with on a pad and rubbed his face with his hand. "Marty, you are a miserable little son of a bitch, you know that? He's bluffing you, trying to scare you. He must be working for the Johnsons. He's trying to chase you off."

"But the vigilantes! They strung up old Poikela, and run off them other two. Jesus . . . they might try to hang me!"

Marty slumped in the chair beside Monroe's desk.

"Get a hold on yourself, Johnson!" Monroe snapped. "You're in this deep with me, and you've got to learn to take a little bit of the danger and responsibility for your twenty percent." He stood and walked around the room.

"All right. I see your point. I guess it's time to show our hand a little more. We'll start with wiping out this McCoy character. I've got too much riding on this operation now. Not a damn thing can go wrong."

He lit a big cigar and puffed on it as he walked. "Hell, only way to deal with a threat is to kill the threat." Monroe went to his desk and sat down and wrote out a short note. He took five twenty-dollar bills from his wallet and put them in an envelope with the note and sealed it.

Marty had been watching closely.

"Take this envelope to Sly Waters. He's at the

Miller boarding house. You know where it is?"

"Hey, I grew up in this town. I'll get over there right away. You gonna have Sly gun down this McCoy?"

"Not that way. But if the two of them have a fair fight, a shootout, nobody gets blamed and we get rid of a bad influence with the Johnsons. Go find Sly."

Marty took the offered envelope and hurried out the front way into the street through an unmarked door beside another door that went to the upstairs of the same building.

He walked two blocks and then down to the Miller house. He'd known it since the time he could remember. Mr. Miller got killed in a woods accident, and Marty's grandfather had set up Mrs. Miller in a boarding house.

He found Sly in his room cleaning his matched pair of six-guns.

"Yeah? Who the hell are you?"

"Marty Johnson. I was the one who got you the job here. Mr. Monroe has some work for you."

Sly took the offered envelope, tore it open and checked the money first. He folded the bills and pushed them in his front pants pocket, then read the note.

"Yeah . . . yeah. I've heard of this McCoy. He's some kind of a government lawman. Don't know just what kind, but he's been in and out of Arizona. Be my pleasure to get him out of your hair. Not much pay, but what the hell, I'd face this guy down for nothing."

He finished cleaning the revolver and checked its firing system. It worked perfectly.

"Now is as good a time as any. You know where McCoy is?"

Sly Waters prowled the Astoria streets most of the morning, and it wasn't until he had given up hunting for McCoy and went to Delmonico's for some coffee that he spotted the lawman eating his dinner with a lady.

Waters walked up and from ten feet away challenged Spur. "McCoy, I understand you've been calling me a back shooter. You want to stand and go for your gun like a man right here, or should we go outside and save the china?"

Spur McCoy watched for a moment. He had seen him once, but not for long. McCoy was surprised how small the gunman was, but he knew any finger could pull a trigger. All that mattered was how fast and how straight the gunhand could fire.

Spur eased away from the table, kept his hands well above his waist and stood. His glance told Nancy Reed to stay where she was seated across from him and not to move.

"Outside would be much better. No reason I should spoil all of these good people's dinner with your blood."

"Actually it would be your blood, McCoy. But outside is fine with me."

The two men walked toward the front door, neither giving the other a chance for a surprise shot. By the time they got to the boardwalk a crowd was already starting to form. Word had shot around town faster than a .45 round.

"Main Street all right with you, Waters, or don't you want that many people to see you die?"

"Not worried about dying. More interested in what the good Sheriff of Clatsop County thinks he has to do with this."

Spur turned and saw the sheriff and two deputies running up the street. All three carried shotguns. They pushed people out of the way and stopped twenty feet from the two gunmen.

"No gunplay in town," Sheriff Vinson said. "Now, I know you two aren't local, but this is still my county. Ain't been too happy having either of you here. But once things get this far, I figure it's better to have at it and get it over with.

"But not right here. I'm giving you fair warning. You two try to shoot it out here in town, I'll charge you both with breaking all the laws I can find that fit. Murder for one, and the one who lives gets hung for murder in my town. So you both lose."

Spur relaxed. "Not going up against three shotguns, Sheriff Vinson. You got a suggestion?"

"Sure have. I'll bring you both horses and send you out opposite ends of town. You circle around somewhere up on the River Road and have your little kid's game up there. I want no part of it. If I don't see it, I can't rightly charge anybody with a crime."

The sheriff looked at both of them. "Those arrangements all right with both of you?"

"Fine," Spur said.

"Yeah, let's get started," Waters said.

Ten minutes later the sheriff had brought up two saddled horses from the livery and pointed the two men in opposite directions.

"I don't want to know anything more about this," the sheriff said. "Far as I'm concerned I'm booting

108

both of you out of town. Just how you come back is up to you.''

"The River Road in ten minutes,'' Waters said.

They both rode away.

Spur checked his Colt. He had twenty rounds in his cartridge belt. He was headed away from the river. He turned at the next street and angled at the River Road. He saw Waters a quarter of a mile away going in the same direction.

Waters would get to the road first, but then he would turn and come toward Spur who was farther upstream. He would wait. Spur rode faster then, got to the road and sat his horse, checking his six-gun. It slid in and out easily, no hangups.

Spur watched the gunman coming at a walk on the roan. He'd heard wild stories about how fast Sly was. How much was true and how much was myth?

Spur considered something else, the question that always surfaced when he had time to think about a gunfight like this one. Was he ready to die? It was always a potential. A lead slug goes exactly where it's aimed. It makes no distinction between right and wrong, between good and bad. One could just as easily kill him this warm Oregon day as could kill Sly Waters.

Waters came steadily ahead. Now he wasn't rushing up to the confrontation. He stopped his horse thirty yards from McCoy.

"You as good as I've heard?'' Sly asked.

"Probably not. And you?''

"Better, and I'm modest.''

"We do it mounted. This way. Cavalry style. We ride toward each other and whoever wants to shoot first shoots. You have six rounds in your piece?"

"I do."

"Then let's get at it."

Before either man could move, two rifle shots cracked and Spur's horse bellowed in pain and shot out from under him. Spur bailed out to the left away from where his instincts told him the shots came from.

Even as he dove for the ground, Spur was calculating the odds. Had Sly been fired at? Was he still mounted? Where were the gunmen? Two at least. Who were they? Vigilantes on a move to erase both the gunmen in town?

Spur hit the ground, tucked the six-gun next to his chest and rolled. He came up in some high Oregon ferns, their tall tender fronds unfolding in a thick cover of light green. He rolled again into the ferns, then crawled and dove behind a long-since fallen fir log beside the river road. The two feet of wood gave him protection as rifle fire nipped at the ferns and thunked into the half rotten log.

Was Sly fired at? He still didn't know. He crawled down the log and lifted up for a look. Sly was still on his horse. He rode into the brush. Evidently no one had fired at him. Why? Then it wouldn't be the vigilantes. They must know that Spur was a lawman. They would have no argument with him.

The rifles snarled again and Spur crawled deeper into the brush. Now he knew where the riflemen were. He had to get across the road. He squirmed behind a big fir and stood, then darted to the next tree upstream. He heard no more firing. By the time he was twenty yards up the roadway, he had worked closer to it. Now he saw no one. Sly must still be in the brush on this side of the road.

The riflemen were on the other side. He crouched at the side of the trail behind a tree, took a deep breath and in one surge dashed across the open space and slammed into the brush and small trees and rolled twice.

Three shots jolted into the brush around him but all well over his head. He worked his way behind some trees and stood. Now he began a silent trip downstream toward the two riflemen.

Ahead he heard movement, a broken branch, a soft curse. He moved faster. Then the sound of someone crashing brush, running through it hard with no thought of being quiet. Spur picked his spots and rushed faster. He came to a thinning section where little brush grew. On the far side of the opening two men started to mount horses. Spur held his six-gun steady, gave it a little elevation for the 40 yard shot and fired four times. One of the men screamed and sagged as he stepped into the saddle. Then he threw up his hands and fell off the saddle as the horse spurted away.

The second man mounted and rode into the brush evidently unhurt.

Spur worked around the opening in the thick brush, making no noise, but not ready to move into the clear. Sly Waters was still out there somewhere.

It took Spur ten minutes to slip up on the wounded gunman. When he saw him plainly he figured the man was dead. He hadn't moved since he crashed off the horse. The man had fallen on his head and shoulders and his head lay at a strange angle. Broken neck. His chest was a mass of blood where he evidently had bled before he died.

Some distance away, Spur heard a horse call, then there were hoofbeats on the ground as a rider moved away from the area quickly.

Spur gave it another five minutes, watching the dead man and the whole area. Nothing moved.

Then to the left he heard something. A horse edged into the open area munching on the thick grass. Spur moved then, walking up slowly to the horse through the brush, taking its reins and leading it back near the body. He rolled the man on his side and saw that he had to be dead. A rifle lay beside the corpse. Spur pushed the weapon back in the saddle boot, then lifted the body over the back of the horse just behind the saddle and tied his hands and feet together under the horse's belly.

Spur stepped into the saddle and rode back toward town. He had a dead bushwhacker on his hands and expected Sly Waters at any moment to come charging out of the brush at him with his six-gun blazing.

12

Spur kept the jittery horse to the open ground as much as he could as he rode back toward Astoria. There were still two gunmen out there who could be waiting for him, but so far they hadn't shown. He watched every direction as he rode, the rifle across the saddle and ready.

His six-gun had been reloaded with six rounds and he played the game of stay alert and stay alive. By the time he entered the first buildings at the edge of Astoria, he began to relax a little.

He wasn't fully at ease until he slid into a chair in the sheriff's office.

"I've got a dead body outside. Nope, it isn't Waters. Don't know who he is. He decided to join in the little contest from the brush with his rifle. You mind taking a look at the guy?"

Sheriff Vinson nodded as he identified the body and asked a deputy to take the corpse over to the undertaker.

"His name is Sloan, Kurt Sloan. He was a logger,

113

when he could find work. Wasn't too steady, drank some. Usually hung out at the Oregon Saloon. Has a wife and three kids.''

"Sorry, he didn't tell me that when he tried to kill me from ambush. One of the rounds hit my horse and she reared and took off.''

"Probably come back to the livery when she gets hungry. Where's Sly?''

"When the shooting started he rode into the brush. There were two bushwhackers. The other one got away. No idea who he was.''

"You had a pistol and you took on two rifles and won?'' The sheriff asked.

"Sometimes a body gets lucky.''

"Or is just plain damn good.'' He sighed as they walked back inside. "I'll have you write out a statement about what happened and sign it. You being a law officer and all, I got to take your word on it.''

"Thanks for the support.''

"The other bushwhacker wounded?''

"Don't think so.''

"Watch your back.''

"I certainly do aim to do that, Sheriff Vinson. Thanks.''

When Marty rode into the edge of Astoria, he dismounted and whacked the bay on the flank sending her down Main Street toward the business section. He had "borrowed" the horse on the spur of the moment and didn't want to get arrested for horse stealing.

He stood for a moment breathing deeply. He would not pass out. That was stupid. Ever since he was a little kid he had fainted when things started going badly. He was not a damned little kid any more.

Christ, Kurt was dead! Marty was sure the man he had hired to go with him on the shoot was dead. One minute they had been joking and laughing and sending hot lead into the brush, and the next they tried to mount up and . . . God, the bullet ripped Kurt's chest apart and then he fell.

Marty hurried to the first bar on Main and took two shots of whiskey as fast as he could down them. It helped a little. Not enough. Not by a hell of a lot!

Marty walked out of the bar and down the street to the Astoria Chinese Laundry. He went in, nodded at the clerks, pushed through to the back room, and then climbed the steps to the second floor where he knocked on a door and waited. He hadn't been here for a long time. Five years! So long, but it seemed like day before yesterday.

The door opened and Willy Fu Chu stared at Marty. The small Chinese man wore his Old World clothes. His hair was braided down his back and he looked nothing like he used to many years ago when he had been the family cook at the Johnson home. Marty felt that he had almost grown up with Willy Fu Chu.

"Gotta come in," Marty said.

"You have a great need? You think Willy can help you?"

"Oh, God! Don't use that tone of voice. I'm here because I can't stay away. You know what's going on. Now I think the damned vigilantes might be looking for me. You got to let me use a pipe. Just for tonight. I promise just for tonight. For old times sake."

Willy smiled. "For old times sake, and twenty dollars. The price has gone up, small Johnson."

"Twenty? It used to be a dollar."

"It also used to be twenty-five cents a day. But that was many years ago."

"And you still have a monopoly on the import, right? You always were a sneaky little slant eye. Come on, I need it. I wouldn't be here if there was something else I could do."

Willy smiled, bowed and led Martin into a private smoking room where a large bowl of an opium pipe had many tubes leading from it. No one else was in the room.

"You know I haven't touched one of these for months, many months. But right now, with the damn vigilantes and people shooting at me . . . it just got to be too much."

Willy smiled. Marty decided the little Chinaman was always smiling.

"Then my friend, you have earned a turn at peace and joy, at a relaxation that is magnificence and beauty. Smoke. Smoke and enjoy."

Just a few puffs, Martin vowed. He wasn't going to get himself blown into a week long binge. Just a few puffs.

Willy sat down with him on the soft mats and they took turns with the pipe. Soon Martin smiled and giggled and then he lay down and wouldn't give the pipe back to Willy.

The Chinaman watched Marty with curiosity that was tightly controlled. He knew the pipe would do its work. At last the right time arrived and he took the pipe away from Martin who sat up reaching for it.

"Martin, you were telling me about your current work, about doing bad things to your brother."

Marty laughed. "Yes, yes, we hit him again and again until he gets tired of it and agrees to sell out. Simple, very simple. Now give me the pipe."

"Soon, Martin, soon. You were telling me about the men you work with."

"Yes. Not good men, but they got the job done. Tom Monroe is his name. He says it's coming soon and he has to have the mill so he can produce the ties for it. He has a contract to produce four million of them. Four million. Make just a few cents on each one and I'll be a rich man!

"Rich man. Always wanted to be a rich man. But I didn't kill Slim. Didn't know nothing about that. Tom probably did that, had somebody do it. Hated that." Tears welled up and rolled down Marty's face. He sobbed for a moment.

Willy gave him the pipe and he sucked on it greedily, then held it with both hands and curled up on the mat. It would be too hard to get the pipe again, Willy knew. He watched Martin. He would let him use the pipe for two hours, and sleep it off. By morning he would be in the alley with no more than a bad headache, and wanting the pipe again.

Willy smiled. He knew now what he had tried to find out. Now he had to figure some way to take advantage of the information. He knew little about this Tom Monroe, but now perhaps it was enough. Ties could only mean one thing, a railroad. It must be coming down the coast.

If they wanted ties here, the line might start here or more probably in Portland. If the ties were here they could build from Portland this way and haul the ties up the Columbia. The rails could be brought in by boat either here or in Portland.

Willy took all but one of the pipes from the big opium bowl and walked from the room, a dozen ideas churning in his mind.

Spur sat in the chair beside Karen's desk. He had tried to explain it to her, but she kept shaking her head.

"I don't see how any angry or insulting words will make a man risk his life. It's so . . . so illogical."

"It's a part of the code of the West, a part of death before dishonor, a part of being a man." Spur stood and walked around her desk. "Then too, it's practical. From what Waters said, he was bound and determined to have a shootout with me. If I didn't agree then he would be free to gun me down from the first dark alley I passed.

"That meant I'd have to watch my back everywhere, every waking and sleeping minute of the day. I'd be a jumble of nothing but shaking nerves in two days. In these cases it's easier to face the man and get it over with like the Sheriff said. Only it didn't work out. Somebody tried to do the job for Sly and I'm not sure if Sly knew they were there."

Karen nodded for the first time. "That makes more sense to me. I just wish you never got into this kind of a situation."

"It didn't start here. Sly and I had heard of each other before. What is interesting is that Sly has been in town since before I came. He must have known I was here. Why did he wait until today to call me out?"

Karen stood now and paced with him. She had on a

fancy split skirt and ruffled blouse of blue polka dots. Spur thought for a moment how pretty she was, but he pushed that idea out of his mind.

"The only thing I can think of is that Sly was suddenly turned loose and told to get rid of me. Which means I must be stepping on somebody's toes, or they are afraid that I'm getting too close to the truth."

Karen stopped in front of Spur, standing much closer than she needed to. "Why don't you come out to our house and stay. You'd have better protection there. I could keep better tabs on you that way."

Spur grinned. "Thanks, Karen. But I can still take care of myself. Protection is what I wanted to talk to Lee about. Do you have any night guards on the mill?"

"Just one man who watches for fires. He's not really a guard, just roves around."

"See if Lee is busy. We need to talk."

A few minutes later, Spur had outlined his idea to Lee.

"You mean put on a real guard force, six or eight men with rifles and pistols and guard the mill during the nighttime hours?"

"I don't see how you have any choice. I'd get men on tonight who have been laid off or are new hires. At least six men on two shifts, seven to twelve and twelve to five. It could pay in the long run."

Lee stared at the idea on paper for a few minutes more, then nodded.

"I'll go out into the yard and get a few men I really trust. Then hire five or six more downtown."

"Might be a good idea to consider hiring ex-soldiers. They at least would know what to do with a

119

rifle.''

When Lee left to hire the guards, Karen called Spur over.

''I wonder if tonight would be a good time to come out and see the house?''

''It would but I have an important bit of research I need to do tonight. I'm not sure how long it will take. Actually, I'm going to break into an office and see who works there.''

Karen's eyes went wide. ''You are, really?''

''Really. I saw Marty go into an office downtown that has a blind entrance. I figure Marty isn't smart enough to put this whole conspiracy together. He must be working with or for somebody. Now I want to see who Marty went to visit. It might give us a big boost to know what is going on.''

''I agree, that's important.'' Her face darkened for a moment with a frown. Then her clear blue eyes brightened and her hair came to a stop on her shoulders. ''Then why don't we have supper down at Delmonico's and I'll take myself home afterwards.'' She laughed at the surprise in his eyes. ''I'm a grown-up person, Spur McCoy. I see nothing wrong inviting a handsome man out to dinner. I'll even pay if you want me to.''

Spur chuckled. ''I'm not surprised at anything a beautiful girl does or says these days. The times are changing. Miss Johnson, I'd be proud to have supper with you at Delmonico's tonight. Since it's nearly five o'clock, why don't we close up and ride down there in that fancy little buggy of yours. I'll even let you drive.''

13

Karen and Spur had a fine supper at Delmonico's. He paid over her mild protests, then he handed her into her small, smart buggy.

She bent down and kissed his cheek. "I guess that's the best I'm going to do tonight," she said smiling.

Spur stepped into the buggy beside her. It was nearly dusk and few people were on the street. He touched her chin and turned it toward him, then kissed her hard on the mouth. Her lips started to open, then closed and she leaned against him.

When the kiss ended she clung to him, her face against his shoulder. "Spur McCoy, I know I shouldn't, but I'm becoming tremendously fond of you. Not supposed to say that, but I just nearly melt when you kiss me like that."

"Good," he said softly, lifting her face where he could see it. "That's what is supposed to happen." He touched his lips to hers so softly they barely connected. He came away at once. "Now you hurry on home and don't pick up any riders."

Karen eyes were still dreamy. She looked at him and blinked, then bobbed her head. "Yes, Spur. I certainly will. Can you come calling later on?"

"I don't think so. Better not count on it. I'll see you tomorrow."

"Oh, but that's such a long time!"

"I promise to come see you."

"Yes, all right."

She reached out and touched his arm, then his hand. She didn't want to let go. Spur stepped out of the rig and waved and slowly she moved the buggy down the street. Spur smiled. Karen Johnson had never made love with a man. He must be tremendously careful with her.

A few minutes later, Spur found a spot he liked in the alley where he could watch the unmarked door that led to the private offices. He was beside a trash barrel and behind some cardboard boxes and completely out of sight.

For an hour nothing happened. Then two men came out. Spur couldn't remember seeing them before. A few minutes later another man left. These people worked late. He sat there for a half hour more, and when there was no more action, he stood, stretched and walked to the unmarked door. It was not locked.

Inside he found the hall lamps had been turned out. Good. He struck a match and felt his way down the hallway. Since he didn't know which office Martin went in, he tried the one on the left first.

It was not locked. He opened it, found a lamp and lit it. The office was lined with books, legal books. On the desk was a name plate. L. Preston, Lawyer.

Martin could have consulted another lawyer but not likely.

Spur carried the lantern to the middle door and tried it. Locked. He put down the lamp and using a pair of small stiff wires, picked the lock and swung the door open.

Inside by the lamplight, he found a mostly bare office. It held only a desk and two chairs and a small table. Temporary? Spur pulled the doors open. There were few papers. Nothing with a printed letterhead like a real company.

He found a pad of scratch paper with a lot of lines and dots and numbers on it. One number stood out. Four times the person had written 4,000,000 in figures. Why? What did it mean? Four million what?

He found the words, "Portland, Astoria, Seaside and then San Francisco." It made no sense. He checked the other drawers and found an envelope addressed to Tom Monroe, General Delivery, Astoria, Oregon.

The man in this office must be Tom Monroe. Spur burned the name into his memory. He battled with his conscience a moment, then opened the unsealed envelope. There was no letter inside.

Nothing else in the office revealed anything about Monroe or why he was in town. Spur put everything back as it had been and went out, locking the door with the snap lever behind him.

The third door was also open, and it plainly was not occupied.

Spur left the complex by the front door. He saw that it, too, was unmarked and opened on Main Street. It was slightly after ten o'clock.

He wanted to talk to the midget again, P.X. North-cliff, but his small shop was dark. Spur checked into three saloons but did not find Sly Waters. After all of the dangers Spur had faced, he would just hate getting killed now by being shot in the back.

When he didn't find Sly, Spur wound up at the Oregon Saloon in time for Nancy's number. She didn't see him tonight until her songs were almost over and she winked and then belted out a furious *On The Banks of the Walbash,* and *When My Johnny Comes Home*, to roaring, table slapping approval. Then she was done. She was good. He hoped that she did well wherever she went.

Nancy slipped onto a chair beside him at the table where he was working on a beer.

"Beautiful lady, your talents are far, far too great for this grungy frontier saloon. Let me take you away from all of this and put you on the stage in New York."

"You got it, Buster!" she cracked and they both laughed.

He reached over and kissed her cheek. "You were good tonight, as usual."

"I'd like to be even better for an audience of one."

"A small audience is always good."

"My room," she said leaning close. "Let's go, I'm getting all warm and damp feeling."

"I stocked up on essentials the other day. Cheese, crackers, two bottles of wine and a small bottle of sipping whiskey for emergencies like snake bite."

"You spoil me."

"Bound to happen to a beautiful, sensitive woman like you." He leaned forward and whispered, "Who also likes to play bedroom games."

Nancy giggled. "Right now, we're leaving!"

They walked quickly to her room in the Astorian Hotel and she closed the door and threw the bolt.

She put her arms around his neck and pushed up against him with her hips and leaned back. "When I sing a love song, I always think of you," Nancy said. "In a minute I'm all panting and damp down below. It makes the song just that much better."

He carried her to the bed and put her down gently, then sat beside her. "Sing a love song, just to me. Softly and like you mean it."

"Not here," she said. "No piano."

"Especially here. With your voice you don't need a piano. Besides, as you sing, I'll start undressing you and begin making love to you."

Nancy shivered. "That's the most romantic thing I've ever heard of. Yes, I want to do it." She began singing a favorite that had spread across the country. It was, *I'm Waiting for You in the Moonlight*.

Spur smiled as she began the first haunting strains. He kissed her throat, then her chest, then both small round breasts through the fabric. Gently he unbuttoned the fasteners down the front of her dress and spread it aside. He lifted her chemise and stroked her mounds, then bit the nipples gently and kissed her breasts until she stirred and brought one of his hands down to her crotch.

She still sat on the bed. He urged her to stand and slipped the dress and chemise over her head, then nuzzled her globes until she sighed and missed a verse.

She undressed him as she sang softly. The tune wasn't important now, just the words.

"I'll save my love for you, I'll keep watching every day, I'll be loyal to you and true, I'll be faithful and never stray."

Soon they both were free of their clothes and Spur lay on the bed. He drew her slender form over his. His lips closed over her mouth shutting off the song.

She rubbed her crotch against his surging penis, and leaned up so she could see him better. "Spur McCoy, let's get married."

"Why?"

"Because, we're a good match, and if you say you'll at least think about it, I'll have an easier time making love to you without thinking that I'm a fallen woman."

"You're a beautiful lady."

"But I let you ram me without even talking about making it legal."

"You like it that way. No attachments, no strings."

"McCoy! Listen to me! If you don't listen to me I'll feel no better than a whore in a saloon!"

Spur held her tenderly, kissed her lips and settled back to listen.

"I was a good girl at home and all the way through school. I had plenty of chances. Even the football hero tried to get my clothes off one night. I slugged him in the eye, blackened it. He said he got it in the game. Nobody got my skirt off during college.

"Then . . . then after I went with the touring troupe, the manager called me into his room one night in Chicago. He told me there were two singers for one part. If I wanted it, I could have it, but he needed a favor. So . . . so I gave him my maidenhead for the job."

"I'm sorry, Nancy. The first time should be better

than that. Lots of love and understanding and hope. . . ."

"Shut up, McCoy. I've had my little cry, I've done my good thoughts for purity and virginity. Now please, take me hard and fast and at least four times!"

Spur lifted her body. She helped and he lowered her down, impaling her vagina with his mighty shaft. She climaxed at once, shrilling in ecstasy, then grinding and riding him and bringing on his first climax before he wanted to.

"You're a devil," he said. "A succubus, except you attack me when I'm awake."

"The devil you say. You have ten minutes to recover, then I'm going to attack you again . . . totally without mercy. And if you so much as mention the greatest literary genius of all time past, present and future, I'm going to bite your nose off."

They didn't argue about Shakespeare and got to sleep at little after 2 A.M.

The next morning, Spur walked into the saddle shop and stopped and inhaled deeply. "Damn good for the sinuses," he said.

P.X. was cutting leather on a table he had made to fit his size. He had a pattern for the underside of the saddle that would cover up the hardwood frame. The cowhide was well over a quarter-of-an-inch thick.

P.X. looked up and nodded. "You're late, cowboy. The cinnamon rolls are all gone."

"You said you'd save one," Spur growled.

"In the morning, I saved it. The time is now ten minutes past ten in the nearly noon time." P.X.

laughed. "Have a good sleep, or did you get any sleep at all?"

Spur looked up and chuckled. "Does everyone in town know every move of every other person?"

"Nope, but I mostly do. You couldn't have picked a nicer little lady. I used to listen to her every night until my wife started whopping me with a broom. She's what I call a full size lady, so she could trash me around if she wanted to. Lucky I married the nicest lady in California."

"She's a big person?"

P.X. laughed. "You giants always seem to be embarrassed by size. My size is not hereditary, mostly a problem with my pituitary gland. Yes, my wife and I fit together well and all the plumbing works. We have two sons, and the oldest one is nearly five feet ten now."

"Some of us are just plain dumb, P.X. That's why we come to talk to smart folks."

P.X. grinned. "Amends made. Look under that cloth there on the low bench."

Spur found the biggest, gooeyest cinnamon roll he had ever seen.

"I told Beth to make a big one for a good friend. Coffee?" P.X. jumped down and brought over a steaming mug of coffee. "Now, what questions are on your mind, big person?"

"The hidden offices. Who uses them?"

"The Lowden secret. Everybody knows about them. One is used by a lawyer who works mostly by mail for a Portland firm. The other one right now has a man renting it by the name of Tom Monroe. Nobody knows much about him. Stays at Mrs. Kincaid's boarding house."

128

"So what does this Monroe do?"

"Nobody knows for sure. He says he's here to open a big retail store on Main. He talks to bankers and lawyers and property owners, but he hasn't bought anything yet. I'd say it's a false front for what he's really doing.

"He's about five-seven and fat. Maybe forty-five to forty-seven. Mostly bald and usually wears a hat. Man has close-set beady little brown eyes and almost no chin. I never trust that combination. But he must have a normal pituitary gland and that always irritates me."

Spur munched on his cinnamon roll. The melted brown sugar and walnuts on top kept him busy licking his fingers and wiping his mouth. The coffee and roll made coming in a double pleasure.

P.X. grunted and went back to cutting the heavy leather for the saddle.

"As for you, Secret Service Agent, Spur McCoy, are you satisfied yet with the death of the government timber cruiser?"

"No, or I'd be gone. What about Sheriff Vinson, can I trust him?"

"About as far as to the moon and the stars. I'd trust him with my oversexed seventeen year old daughter—if I had one. True blue, four square and solid. Not a worry there."

"How about Lee Johnson?"

"Near perfect. Keeps Astoria afloat. Runs a fine business that's growing every year. Fine gentleman."

"Brother Marty?"

"Now there is a problem. Marty, the spoiled, wild brat. His father spoiled him into mush, then died. Marty just hasn't grown up. Got involved with smoking opium when he was in his teens. Then went into gambling. Took off with what was left of his inheritance. Now he's the prodigal son returned. Absolutely no moral principles, no belly, but lots of gall.''

Spur finished the cinnamon roll. "Give my compliments to the cook. Best damn cinnamon roll I've had in a year and four months.''

"Good, I'm about ready for a cold beer.''

"Cold? You don't have an ice house in Astoria.''

"Course not, but I have a cool sink.''

"A what?''

"A cold bucket. I put a bucket of water outside every night. The water picks up the cold from the cool air and early in the morning I bring the bucket in with the four bottles of beer in it, and wrap it in blankets. Cold moves downward, and if there's no spot for it to get out, it keeps the beer cold until middle of the afternoon.''

Spur took the cool bottle of beer from P.X. and grinned. "Damn, I might stop by this food and drink place again. Best service in town!''

"Fire!'' Somebody yelled outside.

A bell clanged somewhere in the distance.

P.X. scowled. "That's the fire bell out at the mill. Must be a fire out there. Only heard that bell ring once before.''

Spur drained the beer and ran for the door.

"Thanks for the brew, I might be able to help.'' He charged through the door and ran with a dozen other men toward a spiral of smoke he saw coming from the Johnson Lumber Company mill.

14

The cone shaped burner where the saw end cuts, trash wood, bark and sawdust were burned, sat at the side of the Johnson mill near the close end of the stacks of drying, just-sawed lumber. There were ricks of two-by-fours and four-foot-square stacks of two-by-eights and one-by-ones and all manner of neat vertical stacks of ship lap. It all was piled up ten feet tall.

The fire seemingly had worked out of the burner cone and attacked the first stack of two-by-fours. It fell into another stack of drying cut lumber, and that made the burning sticks tumble into another one. Until something stopped them, the stacks would play like dominoes until the whole block long yard would be burning furiously.

A force of twenty fire fighters from the mill were battling the fire by the time Spur and other men from town arrived after their six block run. They manned a bucket brigade from the mill pond a hundred feet away.

Six men ran up with a new hand cranked pump.

One hose ran into the mill pond, and another out of a small tank. The faster the men cranked, the harder the water squirted out of the nozzle. It provided a steady if unspectacular stream of water into the stack of lumber burning three down from where it had started.

For a time the raw lumber blazed up from the still fresh pitch of the Douglas fir and roared like a giant bonfire. Men pushed over stacks of lumber so the fire would not reach them.

They battled for an hour before they saw progress. Almost a dozen stacks of lumber had been ruined, but they had the farthest part stopped. No more new stacks could catch fire.

Slowly the buckets of water and the stream from the half-inch nozzle began to make headway against the flames. The first stack was put out and the burning lumber between both ends were battled to a halt. Then the process of making sure all of the fire was out began.

Hundreds of buckets of water hit the charcoal blackened wood, and hundreds more came up from hand to hand. After more than another hour the weary fire fighters sprawled on the grass. The fire was out, the danger was over.

Lee Johnson dropped beside them and stared in anger at the blackened lumber. This was a loss he could count up accurately. He could figure precisely what each stick on those three stacks could have been sold for.

It wasn't worth the trouble. He had fought them and won again. It was possible that tens of thousands of dollars worth of cut lumber could have been burned, but an alert guard spotted the fire shortly after it must have started.

Lee pointed to the area where the fire could have come under the side of the burner and caught the stack on fire.

"Not a chance in the world that it could have happened," Lee said. "That side metal is firm and solid. No hole, no spot where a spark could have popped out and lit the grass that burned the wood.

"This fire was set," Lee told the men around him. "I want all of you to be especially watchful these next few days, checking on people who shouldn't be around the mill or the logs or the lumber. If you find anything out of the ordinary, call your boss or me, or one of the roving guards we're going to have on duty night and day."

There was still a lot of the day left and the men trudged back to work at the mill which had shut down for the emergency.

An hour after the mill began working again, Marty walked through the open field in back of the Johnson house and knocked on the rear door.

When Cilla came and opened the door so she could see who it was, she simply stared at the man who had been her husband. She shook her head. "You shouldn't be here, Marty."

He made no move to go inside the house. "I know. I just got to thinking how it used to be. We were so good together. Remember those great times we used to have?"

"That's all over. You deserted me, we're divorced and I'm married to Lee."

"Oh, yeah. Do I know that!" He shook his head

sadly. "Damn but it was good, just you and me in that little house. I think those were my happiest times."

"You better go, Marty. I don't want either of us to get in trouble."

"Trouble? We're just talking. I'll never forget the first time we made love. You said it was your very first time. You were so fantastic. I didn't have to show you a thing. You did it all by . . . just by instinct."

"Marty, you're embarrassing me."

"I don't see why. It was beautiful. You always did have a great body, still do. Damn but you're pretty."

"Marty. That's all over."

"I know. I'm just remembering. Just talking." He laughed. "I remember that first week after I got home from work you'd be there in some wild lacy things, then you'd pull off the top and run around with your tits swinging and swaying around getting me so damn hot I could hardly stand it."

"I was young, Marty. Please."

"Oh, but you were good. You're still the best I ever had. And I had lots of girls. You just know how to get it moving, what to do for a man. Christ, you're beautiful!"

"Marty."

He opened the screen door and she moved back.

"You shouldn't be inside the house, Marty."

"I know." He reached out and touching her only with his lips, kissed her mouth. It came open at once. His arms went around her and she moaned.

"Oh, God, Marty. You shouldn't."

"I still love you, sweetheart." His hands pushed

down the top of her dress and closed around her bare breast.

"Such great tits! You always had the best tits I've ever seen. And that slender little pumping ass! Christ, but you are a lot of woman."

"Marty . . ."

He ripped the front of her dress open, popping two buttons, then his mouth covered one big breast and he nibbled at her nipple.

"Oh, God, Marty, you can't do that."

"I know. But you're so sexy, so good at taking care of me. Remember when you used to ride me! Jeeze but you are good at that."

Marty reached down with one hand, lifted her skirt and pushed his hand up her bare thigh. She had on little beside the skirt. His fingers hit her crotch and he felt it wet already. Gently his fingers massaged the wet spot through the thin underwear.

"Damn but you are hot, Cilla. What a wonderful love machine." He pushed his finger into her clit taking the soft fabric with it, stroking the clit a half dozen times, knowing what it did to her.

"Oh . . . damn! . . . Marty . . . oh . . . shit!" She kissed him, her mouth open and waiting. Then locked together, she pulled him down on the kitchen floor and spread her legs.

"Marty! You've got to poke me right now. Right now! I can't wait another second! Rip my panties. Rip them apart. Get right in me, Marty. Now! God, Marty, do me now the way you used to! I really need you to do it!"

Marty grinned, tore her soft cotton underwear at her crotch and pulled his sturdy tool from his fly. He grinned as he knelt between her thighs. Her knees lifted, her slot glistened, wet, ready and she panted.

"Now, Marty, now!"

He lowered and aimed and hit her juicy slit. He plunged into her all the way on the first solid stroke. Her hips rose to take all of him and then they slammed together, each stroke a jolt of desire.

Cilla bellowed out in a loud raucous screech as she climaxed, her whole body shaking and jolting and pumping furiously. Then she panted and after two more solid strokes, she climaxed again.

She had reached her peak of rapture six times before Marty could hold it no longer and blasted his hot juices into her, then came out at once, and rolled away.

She rolled with him, caught him and fell across his body, one breast dangling near his mouth. She pushed it up to his face and he sucked it in and chewed.

"Once more before you go, Marty. Please, like we used to, you know, on all fours!"

"I can't, not for a while."

"I'll help. I used to, remember?"

Then she was at his crotch, petting him, stroking him, licking, and as he started to show some life again she sucked him into her mouth and cried out in delight when he hardened and popped out.

She laughed and kissed him and got up on all fours with her round ass facing him.

"Do it, darling Marty!" she said. "Once more for old time's sake."

He laughed and crawled up behind her there on the kitchen floor and lifted and aimed at her still slippery hole and slid into her from behind.

"I love it doggy fashion!" Cilla squealed. She promptly climaxed, and then again.

Marty leaned forward and lay on her back reaching round and grasping both of her breasts and squeezed. Cilla purred and rocked back and forth.

Marty wasn't sure. Two in a row had been a long time ago, but he tried. He got off his knees and to his feet, squatting and holding her waist now and powering into her with serious thrusts that brought a small moan from her each time.

He pounded against her a dozen times, then again, and Cilla squealed into another fast climax before Marty slammed her so hard she lost her balance and fell flat on the floor on her stomach.

The change in position was all Marty needed and he surged into the most powerful climax he could remember, snorting and bellowing and humping until he was exhausted. This time when he fell on her he lay as if dead.

Ten minutes later he struggled to move off her and they both sat on the floor grinning.

Then with her libido satiated, reason returned to Cilla and she slapped her forehead.

"My God! You've got to get out of here! What if Lee comes home early or somebody stops by. I'd be ruined, my marriage ended. Out, out!"

Marty pushed himself back inside his pants, buttoned his fly and looked at Cilla sitting on the kitchen floor, satiated. He knew she wouldn't tell Lee. He was safe there. Marty took a deep breath, stopped his own racing heart and hurried to the door. He took one more look at her, skirt around her waist, her crotch open, ready again, her breasts both exposed.

She was still the hottest woman he had ever taken to bed. He had been a fool to leave her. He snorted. This afternoon he had come here with only one purpose, to get her so sexed up she would be the one who seduced him. Yeah, it had worked. It would never happen again. She would make sure of that. Now she knew his magic still worked.

"Any time you need a good sexy session, send me a note," Marty said. She looked for something to throw at him, but laughed.

"Not likely. You slipped up on me."

"I'm not making any bets," Marty said and turned and walked out of the kitchen, through the open field behind the house and down to the woods that led to the road to Union Town. No matter what else happened today it had been a fantastic afternoon.

He had awakened that morning in the alley in back of Fu Chu's laundry, and knew what had happened. The pipe had pulled him past one small crisis. He might not need it again.

Cilla had provided him with the lift he needed for today. Now he had to figure out how to get things moving against brother Lee again.

15

That same evening, just after darkness closed in around the Port of Astoria and the mouth of the Columbia River, Willy Fu Chu moved away from the small dock at the end of the harbor and cut deep into the current to cross to the Washington side. About half a mile into the river a freighter sat waiting for the morning light so it could sail up the river to Portland.

Fu Chu knew where it would be anchored. His small steam powered boat cut through the current of the mighty Columbia and soon he had the freighter in sight. She sat on the Washington side just out of the current but still in the deep channel. She was a three master with the name *Marlin Maru* on the side. He came alongside and waited for recognition. Soon a rope ladder spilled down the side of the big wooden ship and Fu Chu went up the rope like a sailor.

Ten minutes later he came back over the rail and into the puffing steam boat. A moment more and two large bales three feet square lowered over the side of the tall ship on ropes. The bundles settled on the rear deck of the rocking steamboat and Fu Chu and his two men untied the ropes and their craft steamed away into the darkness.

The trip back to the dock in Astoria took another twenty minutes. Two large Chinese men met them at the dock. They put the heavy burlap wrapped bundles on a wheeled dolly, and rolled them away.

Fu Chu led them to one of his buildings on the dock, a small, two storied structure less than forty feet wide that had been used at one time as an office for an importer. The venture ended in bankruptcy.

Fu Chu bought the building for a hundred dollars as an investment. He knew he would be needing it. Now he unlocked the side door, went in with the goods and closed and locked the outer door behind them.

The Chinese men were immense, standing six-feet six-inches tall, and weighing an even 300 pounds each. They were not fat, rather solid and sturdy and intimidating. Neither one spoke a word of English even though they had been in the United States for more than five years working for Fu Chu. They took the outer wrapping off the two packages. Inside the burlap and another wrapping of tough paper, they found a dozen smaller packages in waterproof seals.

Fu Chu took one of the foot square bundles and cut through the wrapping and peeled it back, exposing a solid lump of blackish-looking gum like substance. The bricks of raw opium weighed more than five pounds each.

Fu Chu nodded and the bricks were stacked on the table. He consulted a list and repackaged the bricks, one or two to a smaller cardboard box he sealed, gluing the top secure. The boxes had been used for other merchandise and had names of products on them.

Each box was marked with a number corresponding to a number on a list of addresses. Twelve boxes were prepared, the rest of the bricks were neatly stacked in a large iron box with a heavy hasp and three padlocks on it. The iron box was then covered with a heavy wooden table and the table stacked with a variety of old china, fine glassware, and small vases and statues.

One of the huge men drove a wagon around to the side door and now the twelve boxes were loaded in the wagon. One of the Chinese men moved to the front of the rig, climbed up on the small seat and drove the mule away heading for the River Road.

It was over a hundred miles to Portland, but taking the opium there this way would be no problem with the customs people. Opium was not an illegal drug in the state of Oregon or Washington, but the import duty on it was extreme.

By stopping the shipment here, Fu Chu saved many hundreds of dollars on each bundle. Then he transported it to his establishment in Portland, and to other customers in that area.

Fu Chu nodded as the wagon and its cargo vanished into the Oregon darkness. Another successful purchase. His fortune was growing. Soon he would be able to leave Astoria and place trusted people in charge here. Then he could go back to Portland and build a grand house in the tradition of Old China.

He could bring his family around him and enjoy his grandchildren in his old age. He sighed. "Soon," he said, then bowed to the remaining Chinese giant and walked with quick steps back to the laundry where he also had his living quarters.

Willy thought that he had done well here since he had been a lowly cook in the Johnson household. He had learned much there, including the white man's weakness for smoking the opium pipe. Slowly he built his contacts and began importing the "joy everlasting." Five years ago he had quit the Johnsons and spent more time with the laundry he had opened fifteen years earlier.

He had been extremely careful. While opium smoking was not illegal, all church people railed against it, and many conservative anglos were totally opposed to it. He had heard of some opium dens and dealers who were driven out of towns. So Fu Chu maintained his position as lowly laundry owner, who gave money to worthy charities, and helped the poor. Few people in town knew of his small opium palace in the upper rooms over the laundry. Few ever would unless they were sworn to secrecy.

In the morning, the mists hung over the Columbia before the sun came up to burn them away. On the Svenson landing, the Johnson Lumber Company rafting crew was already hard at work.

Six men ran over the floating logs as if they were on dry land, their caulk boots gripping fast as they heaved and pulled and jostled the big sticks into order, closely packing them together and then chaining them tightly so there would be no breakup like there had been before.

By seven-thirty that morning, the raft was finished. Ham Frazer ran the sides of the raft checking cables and tie downs. When he finished he sent his number two man around in the other direction to do the same job.

He came back and nodded his agreement. The number two man and a pair of helpers stepped on board the big raft and Ham waved at the small steam powered tow and push boat which promptly pulled on a cable that led the raft forward out of the backwater and into the near Oregon edge of the current which would float the logs gently, and economically, down to the mill six miles away at Astoria.

Ham and the two men beside him watched the raft move away, then at once they began putting a new raft together from the logs in the water. They gathered some in with a row boat, pushing them easily. As they slid into place cables wrapped them. By eight-thirty they had fifty logs formed into a small, slender raft with a pointed nose.

They tied it and bound it with cables so none could escape. Then Ham waved his arms and soon a medium sized tug boat came around a bend in the backwater from upstream.

Ham ran out to the point of the raft where the tug nosed up. The man gave Ham a paper sack which Ham stuffed inside his shirt, then they hooked a heavy tow cable onto the hook that had been cabled to the point of the raft and the tug backed off tightening the line.

Then the three men leaped off the raft to the dock and to shore as they watched the tug pull the raft slowly upstream toward Portland.

Ham watched it go, a big grin on his face. He dug into the sack and took out fifty dollars, giving half the greenbacks to each of his two friends on the show.

"Hell of an easy way to make two months pay,"

one of the men said.

Ham snorted. "Lots of ways to make money, if a man just has his wits about him." He patted the sack still in his shirt. He had sold a thousand dollars worth of saw logs for five hundred. He had cleared four hundred dollars for three hours work. Over a year's pay! He laughed.

"Hell, now we got to get building another raft before them three buddies of ours come riding back up here on company horses and think we been just as lazy as all hell!"

The men patted their purses and ran to the water as they began forming up another raft. Two big logs came slamming down the dry flume and spraying water a hundred feet in the air when they hit the back-water of the river.

Once a month Ham could get away with a deal like today. He couldn't do it too often or the tally sheets wouldn't match. But he could rig those too, shorting the logs marked as coming down the shoot.

Yeah, Ham thought. He had a real money making machine here!

All that morning Spur had been walking around the Johnson Lumber Company mill and the big drying yard, watching the workers, looking for problems. He had on work pants and shirt and a pair of heavy gloves and pulled lumber off the green chain for a while.

That was work. The sawed lumber came along on a steam operated chain that moved them from the re-saw which cut them into ten- or twelve- or eight-foot lengths. For a while only four-by-fours would come, then it would be two-by-fours, and then maybe one-by-sixes.

Each stick had to be put on the right pile so each size was stacked neatly together for grade and size. After an hour Spur begged off and let the regular man go back on the job.

He wandered round the place where the fire had been. He had found no coal oil cans or other obvious arson clues. But he was certain the fire had been set. It was the type that could be costly to the owners, but not hurt the mill itself or its output capacity.

The fire had started at least forty feet from the big burner. It was always possible that a spark had dropped from the top of the tall cone, but not likely.

Spur looked down a row of the eight-foot-high stacks of drying lumber. They were in a pattern to allow enough room between them for quick drying. A man moved past the row Spur was looking down. He came back and tried loosening the upright that was one of two that held the side of the stacked lumber on the platform.

Spur edged back out of sight of the man but so he could still watch him around the edge of the stack. The worker used a hammer, prying the side stake upward out of the metal holder. He tugged it free and stepped back, then pushed on the side of the stack until half of it clattered down to the ground from the pile.

Spur raced down the row and caught the man before he had moved a dozen feet.

"Well now, what do we have here?" Spur asked.

"It fell down, I swear," the man said. He was unshaven for the past few days, wore an old hat and had a front tooth missing. "Fell down. I just walked by and it fell down."

"Right, we better go see Lee Johnson about this."

"I ain't going nowhere!"

"You don't say."

Before the man could move, Spur's big fist slammed into the side of the jaw knocking him sideways into the spilled lumber. More of it fell down.

The man staggered away from the wood and shook his head. Spur caught him by the arm and marched him up to the office. Lee came to the porch and worked on a cigar while Spur told him what he'd seen.

"You've never been in trouble around here before, Zanely. But right now once is too often. You're fired. You get back down there and restack that lumber, then come and pick up your pay figured for this week."

The mill hand tried to protest, but Lee held up his hands.

"I've had too much trouble around here. Anybody causing trouble is through. Now get to work." Lee pointed at Spur to watch the man.

"Come on, Zanley," Spur said. "You've got some work to do."

The lumber worker swore for the first five minutes as he pulled the top half of the stack down so he could get the rest straight and start the stack again. Lee helped him get the side poles into the hangers, and then stood back as the man kept swearing as he restacked the two-by-fours.

"Be glad it wasn't a stack of one-by-ones," Spur said. "Then you'd have twice as many to put up."

146

It took Zanley almost two hours to restack the wood. Then Spur took him back and Karen had his cash envelope ready for him.

"I'm sorry this happened Mr. Zanley," Karen said.

He only nodded, took the envelope and looked inside, then hurried out the door. Spur waved at Karen and watched the man. When the fired man was far enough away, Spur went through the office door and trailed him.

The man never checked his back trail. Spur moved closer as Zanley stopped in the first bar he came to. The place had two windows and Spur watched through one as his target bought two beers and sat at a table by himself drinking both. Then he headed for the street door and walked away with rapid strides.

A block down, Zanley turned to his right and halfway down that block he went into a boarding house. It was the same one where P.X. said Marty stayed.

Spur worked around the side of the house and peered into the side window. It was the parlor and Zanley stood in front of Marty Johnson talking fast. They had some kind of an argument and a moment later Marty stood up and slapped the mill worker hard, then dug in his pocket and came out with two bills and pushed them into Zanley's hand.

The mill worker headed for the door and slammed it when he went out. Spur ran around to the front of the house and caught Zanley just as he started back downtown.

Spur grabbed him by one arm and marched him down to the side of the first business building. He pasted the now quivering lumberman against the brick wall and glared at him.

"You have about twenty seconds to tell me exactly why you went to see Marty Johnson, Zanley. If you don't tell me I'm going to mop up the street with your bloody body. You understand me?"

He nodded.

"Then talk!"

"The little bastard! He . . . he promised me twenty dollars if I could tip over half a dozen stacks of lumber and make it look like an accident. I said sure, why not. I could use the money. Three weeks pay!"

"But I caught you."

"Yeah, and I had to restack it and I told Marty and he got mad. Told me to forget all about it, our deal was off, and he gave me two lousy dollars."

"We're going back to the mill office, Zanley. You're going to write down everything you just told me and then sign it. You know what I'm saying?"

"Yes. What else can I do? Marty made me try. We used to play on the baseball team when we were in school together."

16

Twice a day for the past three days, Orville Ames and his wife, Ida, had been fishing. They had caught 14 salmon, smoked three of them, given eight away to neighbors and were experimenting with canning them in glass jars from a new firm called Ball.

Ida told everyone how much she enjoyed the fishing and bragged that Orville was probably the best fisherman in town.

Today they left for the river the minute Orville got off work and walked home.

"Salmon are still running out there," Orville said. "Let's go out and get some more before they all swim upstream."

They used the same eight-foot boat. Orville was a good boatman, and rowed out to the edge of the current and let it carry the little craft along. Their baits were weighted so they trolled along behind them about fifteen feet below the surface, all ready for the first school of salmon swimming upstream.

Orville saw only a half dozen boats in the mouth of

the river on the Oregon side. None of them ventured into the main current, it moved the bait too quickly through the water.

Orville watched and fished. It didn't matter, whichever one of them hooked up first would start it. This was the day. He felt nothing unusual, just a little eagerness to get on with it now that his mind was made up.

"Got one!" Ida called.

She set the hook and let the big fish run a moment under the water, then lifted the tip of her pole so the bend of the rod would take some of the fight out of the salmon. She began reeling the fish in. Ida was a good one with a fishing pole.

"Let me help you." Orville called. "Don't let him get away!"

A boat drifted by twenty feet away with the fisherman concentrating on his bait and line. A hundred yards inland another boatman rowed strongly back upstream through the quiet water for another drift.

Yes, now!

Orville stood up in the short boat. "I'll get my fish gaff ready," Orville said. The boat rocked as he stood. He almost lost his balance, lunged one way and then steadied the boat.

"Careful, idiot, I almost lost him," Ida bellowed.

Orville grinned.

"I'm the boatman in the family, woman," he said and moved toward her in the stern. He stepped on the side of the small seat she was on. The boat tipped dangerously. Then Orville pretended to lose his balance. He jumped with all of his weight on the far edge of the small rowboat to catch himself.

His 160 pounds tilted the boat until the edge

touched the water and a little trickled inside. Then the angle was too much and Ida lost her grip. She screamed, and then fell against Orville on the right side of the little craft. The combined weight of the two adults flipped the rowboat over in a half second.

Orville screamed as he fell into the Columbia. His first thought was how cold it was, and then as he sank below the water he felt an excitement, a satisfaction. He stayed under as long as he could. He had gulped in a big breath before he went down. Now he came up and thrashed his arms and screamed for help.

The boat that had been slightly ahead of them had turned and the man rowed back strongly against the sluggish current.

Orville was a strong swimmer. "Where's Ida?" Orville screamed into the afternoon light.

He splashed some more. The upside down boat was a dozen yards away. He swam to it and went underwater but Ida had not come up under the boat. She was not hanging on the sides.

He dove again and swam around until his breath gave out. The Columbia was not a crystal clear river, silt and dirty water clouded it so he could see only four or five feet.

He came to the surface sputtering. Two boats were now there. One man tried to right the rowboat.

"Ida can't swim!" Orville screamed. "Where's Ida? Has anyone seen my wife?"

"Haven't seen anyone but you," one of the boaters called.

"Look downstream!" Orville screeched through a face full of water. "She must have drifted that way. She can't swim!"

"Come over here and hang on," one of the boaters

said. "We don't want to lose you, too."

Orville let them talk him to the side of the boat. He rested for a while. He was winded. He hadn't swam this much for years. Then he pushed off and dove underwater again, searching, searching. He had to make it look good. There could be no doubt.

He dove six more times, and by then they were coming to where the mouth of the Columbia narrowed to cross the bar. The boatmen tied his upside down boat to theirs with a rope and pulled him into their craft, and then two men rowed him back to the Astoria dock.

The sheriff was at the dock waiting. He talked with the two men in the boat and three more fishermen who had come to help. Then he came to talk to Orville who huddled under a blanket. The sun was down by that time. A brisk wind had sprung up. Orville shivered in the chill.

"Orville, I'm afraid none of the other boats found anything of Ida. Can't be sure, but you said she couldn't swim, and nobody has seen a thing of her since she went under. I'm sorry."

Orville cried. He broke down and cried with a sense of loss. Partly it was for Ida. She'd been a good wife, she was just in the way right now. Then he cried with joy because he had done it. He had gotten rid of Ida when he wanted to, and nobody could prove a damn thing!

He let the sheriff drive him home in his rig. His fishing gear was gone, but that didn't matter. By the time he got home, his sister had come and collected both the children and taken them to her house for a few days. She had left him a note. News travels fast in a small town.

152

Orville thanked the sheriff, went inside and lit a lamp, then he found a towel and rubbed himself dry and put on clean clothes. He lay down on the bed so exhausted he didn't think he would be able to sleep.

That night Orville Ames slept like a baby and woke up in the morning feeling better than he had in ten years. He almost went to work, but realized he couldn't do that. He was a grieving widower. There were funeral arrangements to be made.

That same morning, Spur stopped by to talk with P. X. Northcliff in his saddlery. Most of the talk was about Ida Ames. Northcliff couldn't imagine why a grown woman wouldn't learn to swim, especially when she had lived all her life around the water there in Astoria.

Spur moved on to the mill office and accepted a cup of coffee from Karen. Before they could talk, Lee waved Spur into his office.

"Three more small incidents yesterday and today," Lee said. "Nothing earth shaking, but irritating. I just wonder when these idiots are going to stop. I finally got the donkey back in place on the Svenson show, and now the flume is still out of action."

"I'm not being much help," Spur said. "Sure, I'm finding out a few things about the people in town, but nothing definite yet. You know my favorite in the whole place is P.X. He's an amazing man. And the way he works with leather. He's an artist."

Spur sipped his coffee. "What do you know about this new man in town by the name of Tom Monroe?"

"Not much." Lee shook his head. "Keeps to himself mostly. I hear he's trying to open up a big new retail store. Couple of other store owners aren't happy about it. Far as I know it's all still in the planning stages.''

"Any reason that Marty would talk to him?''

"Marty? I wouldn't see why.''

"He's been to see the man at least twice in the last couple of days. Not a sure thing, but I don't think Marty is smart enough to put together a conspiracy like this. Somebody is spending a lot of money. You said Marty didn't have any.

"Oh, you were gone last night when I brought Victor Zanely back here. I had him write out a complete confession. Marty paid Zanely to tip over the lumber. I followed Zanely after you paid him off yesterday. He hit one bar and then went to Marty's boarding house and they talked.''

"The little bastard!'' Lee shook his head. "Hell, I don't know what to think any more. It's enough work and worry just trying to run an operation this size, without having somebody trying to ruin me all the time.''

He tossed an envelope to Spur who sat across the desk. "This came in the morning mail. It's from a Portland attorney and contains a certified offer to buy out our whole operation here for a hundred and fifty thousand dollars.''

"Not bad, but you think it's worth more than that?''

"I had an offer from a big outfit down in Coos Bay for the mill and my cut lumber and my timber leases. They said they would pay me two hundred thousand cash, and another hundred thousand spread over the next ten years.''

"So this offer is about half of what you're worth?''

"Somewhere near.''

154

"So maybe you should talk to the District Attorney about all of this."

"Hell, McCoy, I've been over it with Dangerfield three or four times. Last talk with him was when Slim was shot in the woods. Just no way that we have enough proof even to file charges."

"So, it's up to us." Spur laughed. "How did I get so wrapped up in this problem? I'm supposed to be finding out who killed Ihander, and be working on blasting loose those vigilantes."

"You are. Somehow it's tied together. I don't know how, but in a town this size everything is attached somehow to everything else. Besides, I need you here right now, McCoy."

A knock sounded on the partly open door and Karen looked in.

"Pardon the interruption, but one of the fallers is out here and he says he has to see you, Lee."

"One of the fallers?" Lee asked.

"He says he's been elected spokesman and he wants to talk about wages."

"Oh, damn!" Lee dropped a pencil on his desk and stood. "Have him come in. Sit tight, McCoy."

The man came in right from the woods. He still wore his boots and his jeans were cut off at mid calf so they wouldn't snag on the brush. He wore a blue shirt and red suspenders two inches wide.

"Olmstead," Lee said. "You talking for the fallers now?"

"Seems like. When Slim got shot, the guys sort of put me up for talker."

Olmstead was about 25, thin and short with bunched muscles in his arms and shoulders produced from long hours swinging the saw and axe. He had a round baby face and a day's growth of beard and a red hat in his calloused hands.

"I thought Williams was the new foreman up there?" Lee said.

"Yes sir, he is. But he said he didn't talk money. Said he couldn't ask for more money. So the guys sent me."

"Higher wages?" Lee asked.

"Yes, sir. Been a year since our last raise and we keep cutting better, faster. Figure we got the most dangerous job in the woods. Highest skills and all. We want a 15% increase in our pay."

"That much, Olmstead?" Lee thought about it. "Now, Paul, we've known each other for what, eight years? I brought you up through the ranks and gave you a shot at falling, right?"

"My wife and I both appreciate it, Mr. Johnson. I'm also one of the best fallers you got. But all of the guys say they really need a raise and we're only asking for 15%. We're not talking strike or anything like that. We figure you're an honest man who will sit down and talk it over."

Lee walked to the window and looked out a minute. "Damnit, Paul, that's what makes it so hard to run this company. I know you guys, almost everyone on the payroll I grew up with, and I know your folks and your wives and kids. Be a lot easier if I didn't know any of you."

"You wouldn't have such a good company that way, Mr. Johnson. Us guys bust our asses for you out there in the woods. Just wanted to tell you what I told you, and the guys say we'll give you a week to work it over. Now, I better get back 'cause I got to work extra time to earn my wages for today. We always give a full day's work for a full day's pay."

Paul Olmstead, master timber faller, grinned and walked out the office door.

Spur watched the woodsman leave Lee Johnson's office and finished his coffee.

"About time I officially met your duly elected District Attorney, I would think," McCoy finally said.

"Right," Lee confirmed. "He was voted in as sheriff for one four year term, then read for the law and now is our district attorney. He just won his second term in a walkover. Good man, you'll like him."

"Courthouse near the sheriff?"

"Upstairs."

Spur went out to Karen's desk. She tried to feed him more coffee and a blueberry muffin, but he begged off.

"You don't like my cooking." She pretended to pout.

"Love your cooking, and your muffins, and other things."

Karen grinned. "Then how about a picnic supper along the river? I'll help Cilla fix it and we can take the kids and have fun."

"Ants and sandwiches and everything?"

"Everything," Karen said, smiling. "Well, almost everything."

"What time?"

"Meet you here at four-thirty."

"I'll be here," Spur said.

District Attorney Josiah Dangerfield was two

inches over six feet tall, solidly built with black hair and a square jaw. Spur liked him at once.

"Heard a lot about you, McCoy. But the Sheriff says you're one of the good guys, so welcome to town."

The district attorney's office was solid and sure of itself. One wall was paneled with red cedar varnished to a gloss. On it were two elk heads and a moose, its big glass eyes glaring at everyone. The desk was oak, the top cluttered with a dozen books, papers, files and stubbed out cigars.

On the wall was a large, hand drawn calendar with boxes four-inches square for meetings, trial dates and appointments. Most of the squares had at least three entries. One week was outlined in red with the only words across the spaces: Circuit Court Here.

The man wore a conservative black suit and a real necktie. On a hat rack/coat stand by the door, hung a slicker rain hat, a rain coat and a summer jacket. The D.A. was prepared.

They talked for five minutes about the town, the weather and the great salmon fishing this year.

Then Spur got down to cases. "Mr. Dangerfield, isn't there something you can do to help ease the pressure on the Johnson Lumber Company? They're having crimes committed against them every day. A death, a leg cut off, a fire. Isn't there something that can be done?"

Dangerfield toyed with a small replica of a train engine on his desk. It had a three foot long track with wheels that moved and he rolled it back and forth.

"McCoy, you're a lawman. You know what I need, a suspect and some evidence. You bring me both of them and I'll arrest half the town."

"You don't have anything?"

"A little physical evidence, some suspicions, but absolutely no suspects. Who can you point me at?"

"Nobody. All I have is malicious mischief, not even enough for a misdemeanor. But I have some strong leanings."

Dangerfield pushed the train back the other way. "Got to ride on a train back east once. Been fascinated with them ever since. If I was rich I'd build a rail line up here from San Francisco, into Portland, bridge the Columbia and go on up to Seattle." He rolled the little engine again. "But as you can see, I'm not rich."

"Pity."

The district attorney looked up and chuckled. "I like to see some sense of humor in a lawman, McCoy. But there's still not a damn thing I can do."

"You have any investigators?"

"Two, and I keep them busy on civil cases. More than 90 percent of my work is civil here. This is not a crime riddled community."

"Except for the past month. Crimes all over the place. You might keep your eye on Marty Johnson. Yesterday I caught a man he paid to do mischief around the lumber yard. The man was paid to push over stacks of lumber."

"Not exactly a vicious criminal act."

"That's what I mean. I don't have much. But these small destructive actions are wearing down the Johnsons. This town would suffer if the firm went broke."

D.A. Dangerfield sat up straighter. "Indeed it would. More than half of the jobs in town are with the Johnson Lumber Company. It would be a disaster to Astoria if that firm ceased to function. I'll see what I can do.''

"I can give you a dozen more examples: the raft breakup, the dynamite in the donkey engine, the flume being crushed, the fire at the mill."

"I understand. One thing we have that I can work with is a criminal conspiracy, that's evident. Yes, I'll do some work on that. Now, I do have an appointment."

"Fine, glad to meet you, and I'll dig up what evidence I can for you. Oh, anything more on the people who lynched that man on the hill?"

"No, not a thing. Strike in the night. Hard to get any witnesses, any evidence."

Spur nodded, thanked the lawman and walked out of the office. He stopped in the jail. Sheriff Vinson was working on a cup of coffee and a pair of baking powder biscuits with a pot full of honey on the side.

"Anything new, McCoy? I figured a federal agent like you would have this whole thing wrapped up and tied with a string by now."

"No such luck, Sheriff. Anything on the murder, Slim Gillette's killing?"

"Not a whisper. Nobody's spending money fast, nobody is talking. Must have been one man."

"Like Sly Waters."

"Like him, maybe not him."

"Seen him around since our set-to?"

"Nope. Heard he's here, but far as I can see he ain't broken no laws. I can't touch him."

"No wanted paper on him?"

"I don't keep that southern California and Arizona paper. Too damned much of it. I'll have somebody go through the stack again. That'd be too easy."

"True. I'll keep digging."

"Yeah, do that, McCoy, and watch your back. Hate to hang Sly Waters if I had to do it for gunning you down."

"Sheriff, you have a point. That would certainly spoil the rest of my day if you had to do that."

Spur wandered the town, checked the saloons, but came up with no sighting on Waters. He patrolled the mill and and the drying stacks, but found every one of the men on the alert now for any mischief. In effect, every worker in the place was also a lookout and a guard.

He noticed three of the mill workers wearing gun-belts and six-guns. One man nodded. "Damn right I got my gun. Ain't gonna let some damn hoorah burn down the mill and put me out of a job."

Spur walked to the mill office and slipped into the chair beside Karen's desk a little after four. Karen saw him and a smile broke over her face.

"You're here, good. I was afraid you might forget. I drove up to see Cilla this noon and she's making the picnic supper. We're having fried chicken and ham sandwiches and everything!"

Karen glowed like a just lit candle. She wore a print dress that swept the floor and came to her throat with a series of bows that continued across the bodice. The fabric stretched tightly across her bosom and Spur noticed it with a grin.

"You're looking pretty enough to kiss today, Karen," he said.

She blushed but didn't look away. "That's a nice

thing to say, Spur McCoy. I enjoy it. My work's all done. Let's go grab Lee and drag him away so he can forget all about the mill and the problems for a while."

Lee at last gave up, closed the account books and rode up the hill to the Johnson house. They picked up Cilla and the two kids who were only one year old and two years old, and the big picnic basket and rode down the hill and along the coast road to the Klaskanine Bay and up to the river.

It took a half hour to get there, but it was a small stream compared to the Columbia and gave a whole different feeling. They found a grassy spot that ran right down to the small river and Spur and Lee had a rock throwing contest before the women called them to eat.

Two blankets spread out on the grass and the picnic turned into a Roman feast, with not only fried chicken and ham sandwiches, but potato salad, pickles, three hot vegetables, two kinds of pie, apple sauce, and two varieties of grapes. There were also dishes of cherries and raspberries and blackberries.

For a while the conversation stopped as they all ate. Spur took his third chicken leg and frowned.

"Funny kind of chicken, Cilla. It had three legs!"

Karen sat beside Spur and when most of the meal was over began feeding him grapes.

Cilla whispered to Karen, who nodded. A minute later she picked up the ball they had brought.

"Spur, let's play catch," she said. "I used to be able to catch and throw."

They moved off a ways to an open meadow and played with the ball, then Karen caught Spur's hand. "Could we take a little walk?"

"Sure."

Karen laughed. "You saw Cilla whisper to me. She said she gets all worked up on a picnic and she wanted us to go away for at least a half hour." Karen rolled her eyes. "I can't imagine what she wants to do there in the grass."

Spur pulled Karen to him and kissed her gently. "I can imagine, and I bet you can too, so let's leave them alone for a while."

"Not unless you kiss me again."

He did.

They walked upstream and soon found a grassy place and sat down. There wasn't another person within half a mile of them. Spur kissed Karen again and she sighed and leaned against him.

"This is so nice. Why does it ever have to end?"

"Because you live in Astoria, and I'm a traveling man. I'll be gone as soon as the trouble here is over."

"You could stay."

"I'm not much of a logger. I hate the green chain. I don't even stack lumber too good."

"You wouldn't have to. I own fifteen percent of the company. You'd be in management, like me." Karen kissed him long and hard and somehow she leaned against him and they fell over backward, with Spur laying on top of her.

The kiss ended and Karen sighed. "Oh, yes, that is so nice. I like you right where you are."

He bent and kissed her again.

"You know that nice girls don't kiss this much. I guess that makes me not very nice."

"Any nicer and you'd sprout wings and fly with the angels."

Karen shivered. "What do we do next, Spur?"

Spur kissed her with more fire, and she moaned softly.

"That feels so good. I feel so good all over, kind of warm and hot and I know I'm breathing too fast." She caught his head with both her hands.

"Spur, I'm . . . I'm not very experienced in this sort of thing."

"Not experienced . . . like you never have before?"

She nodded. "But . . ." Her voice was so soft he could hardly hear it. "But, Spur, now I want to."

Spur let her reach up and kiss him. She shivered and then broke off the kiss and smiled. "I . . . I could open the top of my dress."

Spur sat up and lifted her beside him.

"Young lady, are you trying to get me killed? That's your brother back there, remember? If I were to go ahead . . . make love to you like you're suggesting . . . Lee would hunt me down with a pistol and kill me dead. I certainly don't want that, do you?"

"Oh, no!" She kissed his cheek and hugged him. "I want you alive and with me, forever. Is it nice for a girl to ask a man to marry her?"

"Yes, it's nice."

"Spur McCoy, will you marry me?"

"No."

"Then will you ravish me and make love to me and make me feel like a woman?"

"No."

Karen frowned. "You are a stubborn man." She took his hand and put it on her breasts. "At least you can touch me up here a little. That can't hurt me.

Please touch me and rub me, Spur. I'll be ever so angry if you don't.''

Spur kissed her lips and felt the blazing hotness there, the hunger. He left his hand over her breast and rubbed it gently. Karen sighed and leaned against him.

"Oh, yes. I can remember this." She reached up and kissed his lips urgently. Then she undid four buttons and pushed his hand inside her dress.

Spur worked through the chemise and something else and then his hand settled around her big breast.

Spur fondled her and kissed her and whispered. "You know this is the fastest way to get a man worked up, to let him touch your bare breasts.''

"I hoped it might help."

He moved her hand over his fly where his erection was full and hard and pulsing.

"Oh, glory!" Karen said.

Spur fondled her breast a moment more, then moved to the other one and tweaked the nipple as Karen sighed softly. She spread her legs and began lifting her skirt.

Spur came away from her hidden flesh, buttoned the fasteners and stood quickly.

"It's time we get up and continue our walk or I'm going to be a dead man.''

Karen put her arms around him. "Spur, I need to know. Do you want me even a little bit now?''

"Lord, woman, yes!"

"Then I'm pretty enough and . . . built well enough so you wanted to make love?''

He kissed her, hard, demanding. It was all he could do not to push her to the ground and take her maidenhead right then. He at last pulled away.

"Yes, yes, yes. And the next man you lead on this way might not be worried about your brother and will go ahead and rape you whether you want him to or not. So you be good. Never do this again unless you're ready to go all the way."

Spur stopped and looked at her.

Karen giggled.

"Yes, I know. I just haven't done it yet."

Karen hummed a little tune as they walked back toward the picnic. As they came up, Lee was putting on his shirt and Cilla was arranging her skirt. Spur decided their action was over. He held Karen's hand as they stopped at the blankets. She was almost glowing. He had never seen this lady happier, or more at ease.

17

Orville Ames had carried through as a good husband should. He let his sister make the funeral arrangements, then he went that afternoon to the church and on to the small cemetery up on the hill and buried his wife Ida. It was an empty coffin, but he told them even though she was never found, he wanted a coffin and a burial. They put a message in a sealed jar inside the coffin explaining the circumstances.

If her body was found washed up on some beach in the next few days, they would pull up the coffin and rebury her inside.

Orville hugged his sister who said she would keep the children for a week or two to let him get adjusted. He went home and ate salmon steak for his dinner, then turned out the lights and slipped out of the house and went up the hill.

Damn he was feeling good!

Orville lay in the grass just beyond the Johnson house lights and watched Karen's window. She went to bed early, and he saw her doing a little dance as she undressed. Tonight the blind was not down quite as far and the rip was still there and he saw her slip out of her chemise.

Glorious! Such tits. Beautiful!

Orville dropped into the grass. His penis came into his hand and he pounded off as he watched her powder her breasts lightly. Christ they were beauties, must be thirty-eight, maybe forty-inchers! Biggest damn bare tits he'd ever seen. He'd give a week's pay to play in them for about half an hour. Then pull them together and have a tit sandwich! Oh, yeah, he was a tit man all the way.

He watched her slip into her nightgown and go out of sight of the window.

Orville lay there for an hour thinking about her. He got hard again and climaxed by pumping furiously before he ran back down the hill. He knew he'd have to wait a while before he approached Karen. Damn, those tits were worth waiting for. But he was single now. True, a widower, but SINGLE! So he could talk to her and court her and marry her pretty little ass and have his future secure as a member of the Johnson goddamned family!

He figured a week would be enough to wait before he contacted Karen. If he could stand it for a week. If anybody fixed the tear in Karen's blind he'd kill them!

That same night, the vigilantes gathered on the outskirts of town and knocked on the door of a run-down house where a family of Chinese lived. They worked for Fu Chu and had come into town only last week.

Hard pounding on the door just after midnight

brought the old father to the door. He stared at the six men, frowned and said something in sing-song Chinese.

"Get anybody who speaks English," Josiah Dangerfield bellowed. "Anybody here understand English?"

A young girl came forward. She wore a thin night-dress, her small breasts showing plainly.

"Yes, I speak some English."

"You have an hour to pack everything you own. We're running you out of town. We don't want you in Astoria. Understand?"

"What have we done?" the girl asked.

"Done?" Dangerfield roared. "Your parents did it years ago when they conceived you. You're Chinese, and we don't want no more Chinks in town. We got enough. So you're the ones that we run out."

He reached down and rubbed the girl's breast. She slapped him, then darted back inside.

"Burn it down!" Dangerfield roared.

The others pulled him back and another man told the family they had an hour, then they would be escorted ten miles up the River Road toward Portland.

"If'n any of you come back, you'll get your hands chopped off, you savvy?"

The young girl who spoke English nodded and the family began packing the meager belongings that they had only started to take out of boxes.

"You got a wagon?" the black-hooded vigilante asked.

"No wagon," the girl answered. "Two mules."

"Load up the mules, that's all you take except what you can carry."

It was nearly two A.M. when the procession headed down the River Road. There were eight in the family, three generations. Only the fifteen-year-old girl spoke any English. The vigilantes herded them forward. Two men led the mules and the rest of them walked slowly behind.

About six miles out, just past the Svenson logging show, Dangerfield stopped the caravan and talked to the Chinese girl.

He called her up, grabbed her by one arm, and with his other hand fondled her young breasts.

"Just trying to help them grow," he said and laughed. "Missy Tiny Tits, you see that your family keeps going all the way to Portland. You understand?"

She nodded, frowning at his hand on her breasts.

"You come back and we find you, we'll chop off your hands. Now you get your slant-wise little self out of here. We got too damn many Chinks in Astoria already."

She pulled away from him, said something to the family and they all continued up the road. Once she looked back. There was anger and a sense of shame in her look. Then she picked up the smallest child and carried her as they all walked into the darkness.

"Good riddance," Dangerfield said.

"And you got a free titty feel," one of the men said. They all laughed.

"What about Fu Chu?" One of the men asked. "His laundry is fine as long as he doesn't bring in any more Chinks. But we all know he's got his opium den open again. We closed it up two years ago, but he's working it again."

"Hell, nothing illegal with opium," Dangerfield said.

"But it's wrong, it makes addicts out of our men. I know one guy who stayed in that old den for three weeks. He almost died of starvation. Never was worth a lick after that."

"Well, hell," another man said, "we know we got to do something about Fu Chu. We don't want to burn out his laundry. Ain't he got some other buildings around?"

"Sure has. Owns half of town, almost. I'll check the county records and see what he does own."

"Now let's talk about that damn Medicine man. He still in town?"

Dangerfield said he was. "He needs moving along about next. We do it tonight?"

"Might as well. He won't give us no trouble. Otherwise he's on foot with no medicine and no mule and no rig."

They rode back to town and near the bank where the Medicine man always parked. The six men took off their hoods and tucked them inside their shirts. The Medicine man had been there three days selling worthless female potions and high energy elixirs. Both of them were mixtures of alcohol, coloring, and some flavors used in cooking. Potent, sweet, and useless.

Dangerfield knocked on the back door of the wagon. It was the regular type with fancy painting all over it, wooden sides, and a door on the back that locked up tight. Inside were the Medicine man's living accommodations, laboratory, as he called it, and his supply of elixir and female potions.

When he came to the door, Dr. Dunsmuir was still half asleep. He saw the six mounted men and laughed, then promptly stopped and swallowed hard. Dr. Dunsmuir was about fifty, had seen almost everything and knew a vigilante posse when one came to call.

"Gentlemen?" he began.

"Get dressed and hitch up and get out of town," one of the vigilantes said. "You have ten minutes to get moving."

"Now, gentlemen. Didn't I tell the city council that ten percent of all my revenue would be dedicated to building a new room on your school house? Didn't I promise to send my customers to church every Sunday? I don't understand what's wrong."

"Now you have only nine minutes. You're pushing your welcome here, Dr. Faker. Get moving."

"No recourse? A donation to you gentlemen's fine cause. . . ."

Someone threw a knife that stuck into the side of the door not a foot from the Medicine man's head.

"Or perhaps not. I'll be gone. Let me get my pants on. This is embarrassing."

"Not half as embarrassing as swinging from our favorite oak tree up on the hill. You now have seven minutes to get moving."

The Medicine wagon made it. Two of the riders watched from well back. They had ridden behind the wagon to the edge of town. They waited in three spots until they were sure the wagon was out of town. Then two men were assigned to roust it on its way.

As soon as Dr. Dunsmuir left the city limits, one of the vigilante riders put on his hood, raced up beside the plow horse pulling the wagon and grabbed his

172

halter. The rider pulled the big horse into a labored run as they clattered out the coast road and down toward the small village of Seaside about 20 miles away.

When the horse was running, the two men fired a half dozen shots over his head and through the top of the Medicine wagon to hurry it on its way.

Spur McCoy was up early the next morning, had a quick breakfast at Delmonico's and settled himself against a tree a half block down from Marty Johnson's boarding house. By eight that morning Marty still hadn't come out. Three men had left for work in the mill with their lunch boxes. One had come out and ridden away toward Portland. Marty had not shown.

It was nearly ten before Marty sauntered out picking his teeth as if he'd just had a late breakfast, which he probably had. Marty walked the street, went in and out of two bars as if hunting someone, then he shrugged and went into Fu Chu's laundry.

He must be picking up something, Spur decided. Spur settled into a chair propped up against the General Store and waited. Spur figured it couldn't take more than five minutes.

An hour later Marty hadn't come out. Spur did a slow walk up and down the sidewalk, but always keeping an eye on the laundry's front door. Marty could have seen the tail and gone out the back of the laundry. If he did he was gone and Spur would never find him. He had to stick to the idea that Marty was still inside.

Spur went back to the chair and sat another hour. It was about one o'clock when Marty came out of the building. He had no laundry. He walked as if he were half drunk. McCoy walked up to him and was about to talk to him, when Marty grinned and waved at Spur and then grabbed him to keep from falling down.

Marty was completely gone on opium, but he was awake and could still talk.

"Hey, Marty, have a good smoke? Where you get the pipe, anyway?"

"Where?" Marty looked at him wide eyed for just a moment. Then he giggled. "Fu Chu and his laundry. Upstairs . . . Good pipe. You want some?"

"Not now, you can't walk so good. Besides, what about the mill? What's next for the mill?"

"Dunno. Got to work out something. Maybe another log raft. Hell, I don't know." He looked at Spur. "Who'n hell are you?"

"Just a friend, Marty, a good friend."

"Yeah, right. Good to have good friends. Good for good old you." Marty giggled again, then his eyes rolled up until only the whites showed and Marty passed out in Spur's arms.

McCoy pulled him to the back of the boardwalk and sat him down against the side of the newspaper office. Marty was still out. He could be stoned for hours. He reeked of smoke. Spur sniffed again. Damn, that was opium smoke all right. Spur knew the smell, he'd been through an opium den or two before. Marty had just zonked himself out on a pipe. He wouldn't be of any value to anyone for a long time.

Spur stood, left Marty there sleeping it off, and went across the street to a small cafe that specialized in seafood. He had a big fresh crab salad and a toasted cheese sandwich. It took almost an hour for

Spur to eat, and Marty never so much as moved a finger.

Trying to look busy and alert when you've got absolutely nothing to do but watch a sleeping, zonked out drugged man was hard work. Spur had been up and down the street for a block each way three times. He had been in every store where he could watch Marty out the window.

Now he was half a block down on Main when Marty stumbled to his feet, shook his head and walked as sober as a fencepost down the boardwalk toward the livery. Spur followed. Marty hired a horse and rode out the River Road.

Spur was a quarter of a mile behind him, half in and out of the brush along the road. Marty never checked his back trail. Where was the little bastard going, Spur wondered. Then he remembered the logs down at the Johnson Slough.

"Not again!" Spur said and picked up the pace.

Spur ran the last quarter of a mile to the rafting dock through the light brush and timber along the landward side of the river. He moved across the road and into some light growth thirty yards from the dock where he saw the six raft men hard at work.

One came off the raft and looked around a minute, then walked across the road and into the woods. Spur frowned, then realized that Marty's horse and Marty himself were not in sight. In the woods? He stood and walked across the road as if he belonged there, and heard no shouted challenge.

Then he moved as silently as an Apache through the Oregon woods, never breaking a stick, not letting a live branch swish back. He stole from fir to fir, covering himself. Ahead he heard a horse nicker.

Another twenty feet and he spotted Marty who had just shaken hands with the other man.

Now Spur was close enough so that he could tell the rafter was Ham Frazer. The two men stood talking. Spur took a chance and crept closer until he could understand the words. After two more moves he listened critically.

"So you can take care of it on the next raft," Marty said. "This one is tied together well, but on the next one, you get it started while those other three men are herding this one down to the mill. I'd like almost all of this one to go downstream, right into the Pacific. If it does, you get double what I'm going to give you."

"Sounds good to me. I'll probably get fired if it breaks up completely. Lee ain't that stupid. How about half of this one going and then doing it again?"

"No, we've got to speed up things, make them tougher. This will help. Any other problems?"

Ham shook his head.

"I better get back to town. You take care of your other two men."

Marty reached in his pocket and took out a roll of what looked like paper money. He counted off a stack of bills and gave them to Ham.

"Don't let me down on this one, Ham. We'll have a spot for you after this is all over, so don't go far."

Marty ran to his horse, stepped into the saddle and rode through the woods back toward Astoria before he hit the road again.

Spur caught Ham just before he got to the road. He had stayed where he was while he counted the money. He grinned and pushed it in an inside pocket.

Spur stepped out from behind a tall fir and aimed

his .45 at the logger. He clicked back the hammer and Ham looked up at the sound.

"Going somewhere, Ham?"

"What the hell?"

"About the size of it. This is a stickup. Empty out your pockets."

"Not a chance. You're that damn detective or something. You've got no right on this property."

Spur shot Ham in the right thigh, made certain the bullet nipped no more than an inch of flesh and muscle, but it put the logger on the forest floor swearing.

"You shot me! You bastard!"

"It's only a nick. The next one will break your leg, and the one after that will smash your knee cap so you'll never work the woods again, let alone ride the river rafts. Now empty out your pockets. I want that cash that Marty just gave you."

"Marty? I don't know a Marty."

"For that I should shoot you again. The cash. NOW! How much is he paying you to break up the raft tomorrow?"

"Oh, hell!" Ham reached into his pocket and took out the wad of bills. He handed them to Spur who counted them.

"Two hundred. Not bad for a day's work. Let's go talk to the other men."

Spur asked who the next senior man was. A kid who looked about nineteen raised his hand.

"Take over here, Ham won't be working for the firm much longer. Do whatever you usually do, and make damn sure that no logs get away and that no rafts break up or it's your ass. You hear?"

The kid nodded.

"Frazer, get your horse, we're going for a ride."

Spur tied Frazer's hands behind him and then led his horse the six miles back to Astoria. They went the short cut through the mill to the office, and when Spur marched Ham into the office, Lee took one look at his tied hands, the bullet wound in his leg, and the wad of bills Spur held and slammed his fist into Ham's jaw. Ham slumped to the floor.

"Seems that Ham here has been taking money from Marty to let the log rafts bust up on the river. He probably has been selling logs upstream as well. You better check your log tallies on how many went down the flume and how many arrived at the mill."

Spur tossed the money to Lee.

"Two hundred dollars he got for breaking up about five thousand dollars worth of logs. Ham works cheap. Seems like Lee will want to have a long talk with you, Ham. Why don't the two of you go into his office."

When Lee's office door slammed shut, Spur was alone in the big room with Karen.

She hurried over. "I've never seen Lee so angry. Ham has always been one of his favorites. Now this." She shook her head and the long blonde hair swung. "I just don't understand some of this."

"It's called life. Not all sweetness, not all sour. A little of each."

She reached up and kissed his lips and clung to him for a moment. "I hope that was some of the sweetness."

Spur grinned, caught her, pulled her close and kissed her again.

"Oh, my, yes," Karen said as he let her go.

"That could get to be a habit," Spur said.

"I earnestly hope so," Karen said. "Are we having dinner tonight at Delmonico's?"

"I hope so, but you never can tell. If I'm free, I'll be here at five. If not, sorry, next time."

"I understand. Thanks for catching Ham. Lee has been worried about the rafting."

"See you later," Spur said and walked out heading to see P.X. Northcliff. He wanted to ask the small-sized saddlemaker a few important questions.

The story about Ham being ridden into the mill with his hands tied behind him must have flashed through town like a hurricane. Spur felt the surge of interest as he walked down the street. Bad news travels fast.

Spur had just passed the sturdy two story brick bank building and headed past the alley when a shot exploded across the street. He felt the bullet slice through his upper left arm and he dove toward the horse trough. He heard a second shot and then a third round hit the solid wooden trough. Spur raised his hat over the top of the tank on the barrel of his gun and a slug tore through it.

In a flash of a second, Spur saw the blue powder smoke from the four rounds that had been fired on the far side of the alley where a shining pistol barrel poked around. He put two rounds into the wood at the edge of the building and then another lower. He sprang from the trough and came up running for the store across the street.

Two women had dropped to the boardwalk near the alley. Half a dozen men and kids scurried out of the line of fire. Spur raced to the building, looked around it in time to see someone dressed mostly in black turn around the building at the end of the alley

179

and run down the next street.

He could be in any of a dozen stores down there before Spur could get to the end of the alley. It was an impossible chase. Spur gave it up at once and checked in with Dr. Ulman, who cleaned out the wound on his upper arm, put some ointment on it and bandaged it up tight.

"Should heal easy. No big problem. Damn, boys playing with guns again," Dr. Ulman said.

"Playing is not the right word, Doc. Right now I'm supposed to be a corpse. Somebody paid to have me killed. Only he missed and now his ass is in trouble from two of us. Has to be Sly Waters. Probably the only man in town that good with a six-gun."

Doc finished the bandage. "Probably the only man, but don't bet your life on it, McCoy. I'd say you better watch your backside with considerable care."

Spur finally got to P.X. Northcliff's shop. He had reloaded his six-gun and slid it back in leather. When Spur let the screen door slam at the leather shop, P.X. chuckled. "I agree, it's no fun to be shot at, but don't take it out on my brand new screen door."

"Sorry," Spur said. "You out of coffee?"

"Never, pot on the back of the stove. Help yourself."

P.X. paused as he put bee's wax on a piece of strong cord he was using to stitch a piece of saddle together.

"You know, we used to have a quiet little town before you come here, McCoy. Now we got gun play in the street. A man hanged. Another man shot dead and one with a cut off leg. You really stir up a town."

"None of it my doing. Things were stirred before I

got here. I'm the one trying to settle things down."

"You think it was Sly Waters?"

"You know anybody else in town good enough with an iron who could do the job?"

"Not likely. Least he missed."

"This time."

"You think he'll try again?"

"Does the sun come up in the east?"

"Yeah, yeah. So, how you doing on the vigilantes?"

"Lousy. How *you* doing? Any idea who they are?"

"Ideas? Everybody got ideas. But the gentlemen are starting to make mistakes. They ran a family of Chinese out of town. Now who in Astoria doesn't like Chinese? Maybe some of the merchants who are looking over their shoulders? They are getting sloppy, leaving loose ends. Sooner or later all of this will trip them up and they'll be boosted by their own petard."

"Let's hope so. Any idea where Sly Waters lives? Some boarding house? He isn't at the hotel."

"Haven't heard. He stays to himself a lot."

"Waiting for an assignment."

"True. How's the coffee?"

"Better than yesterday."

"I must be slipping," P.X. said and grinned.

Spur bought a box of .45 rounds at the general store, stashed them in his jeans pocket and headed back for the mill office.

At least he had supper to look forward to. Karen could be a minor inconvenience, but nothing he couldn't handle.

18

Spur was in Lee's office at the mill when they heard a scream out front. He pulled his Colt and eased Lee's office door open an inch.

Two men with guns stood over Karen who had been ready to start working on payroll envelopes. Most of the men were paid by cash in small 2 x 5 envelopes that were then sealed and the men's name and amount written on them.

Karen had the work records, and a steel box taken from the company safe on her desk. The payroll money was always brought down by the bank on Friday afternoon so the men could pick up their pay on Saturday afternoon. The payroll for two weeks for the lumber and mill workers was over $1,500. The cash was all in the steel box on her desk.

Karen stood with her hands over her head and two masked men reached for the cash box.

Spur shot the closest one in the chest and he went down and never moved. The second one fired at Spur, then darted for the front door.

"Get on the floor, Karen," Spur bellowed. She dropped just as two men at the front door fired half a dozen times into the office, at the far window and at Lee's office door.

When the firing ended, Spur saw both men run in front of the office and jump on horses.

Spur surged out of Lee's room, checked on Karen who was unharmed, then he raced for the front door. He fired twice at the retreating bandits, but they were too far away. The third man's horse stood at the hitching rail. Spur ran for it, jumped into the saddle, and saw with satisfaction that there was a carbine in the leather boot on the saddle.

The men didn't go through town. Instead they angled around the mill and went directly east up the slope to the ridge of hills that ranged along the Columbia River. The woods there were thick from the rain, and it would be hard to find the bandits if they tried to hide.

Spur urged the unfamiliar mount forward up the slope. He took out the rifle and when he saw the two men ahead go through an opening on the slope above, he sent two quick shots at them. Both missed but the pair ducked back into the forest cover as they worked east.

It was easy tracking the pair. Riding through the Oregon rain forest is like leaving a pair of boot tracks in a foot of snow. Broken ferns, trampled small bushes and bent over young fir trees no more than two feet high drew a line simple for Spur to follow.

He stopped and listened. Ahead he heard the two horses crashing brush. He moved forward then, past a small opening on the side of the hill.

Then he was on the top of the ridge and the trail

kept moving east along the highest point in that area. It was a true ridge, perhaps carved hundreds of millions of years ago by the struggling Columbia River. Now the slope had forested and moderated and spawned a forest that would hold the soil in place for hundreds of years if it were renewed by seedlings.

Spur plowed ahead into a small opening. On the far side, less than fifty yards away, he saw his quarries with their rifles up and both pointed directly at him at this hard-to-miss range!

Spur McCoy didn't consciously decide what to do. His survival instincts took over and he dove off the horse on the left side, pushing with his left foot, slamming his body through the air toward a two-foot-thick fir tree.

He heard the rifles blast almost together, then again and again. He hit the dirt hard and rolled, came up behind the fir tree and eased upward, his right hand now holding the Colt .45 which he must have drawn while he was in the air.

The riflemen paused, then both surged forward in a charge, coming across the open space at a gallop. Spur saw the nostrils of the two mounts flaring, their eyes wild from the unaccustomed gunfire, their manes flowing in the wind and both men hunkered down on the saddles to make small targets. Spur watched from the very side of the tree. His hat was gone. Some feathery leafed vine maple grew just in front of the fir and half shielded him.

Spur cocked the .45 and waited. His horse had ambled off a few strides and had her head down munching grass. It left an open alley for the riders. Their charge carried them up to the trees.

The two had not been cavalrymen. They still had

184

their rifles out which are hard to use for close-in fighting, too slow to move and aim and point.

Spur lifted his Colt and tracked the rider closest to him. When he was less than ten feet away, Spur fired. The round caught the man in the chest. By then McCoy had triggered the weapon again and the second round hit the same man in the side of the head and blew him out of the saddle.

With the sound of the first round from Spur, the second rider had shied to the left away from the danger and now plunged into the brush. Spur had a slight angle on the man and fired twice, but neither round found flesh.

Spur leaped for his own horse, grabbed the reins and stepped into the saddle. He rode ahead again, tracking the man. He had glanced at the first one on the ground, but he did not know the face, or what was left of it. The round had come out the robber's eye and changed his appearance for all of eternity.

Half of Spur's attention was riveted on the noise from ahead on the trail. When the sounds stopped he halted his mount and listened. A meadowlark gave its call somewhere to the left. Two squirrels chattered at each other. A raucous crow angrily disputed its territory with a smaller bird.

Spur heard the sound of crashing brush again. The rider was moving, but angling downhill on the river side. Spur turned toward where he figured the direction of the sound would place the rider and charged quickly on the down slope. Spur lifted the rifle, an old Henry repeater that should have twelve rounds in the magazine. He checked. There was also one in the chamber. He found a tree and stopped behind it and listened. The crashing continued.

It still came downhill and this time toward him. Spur lifted the rifle and watched the brush for the first movement.

A moment later the muzzle of a horse nosed past a mountain laurel and then the rest of the horse came out. Spur saw the man on the horse's back at almost the same time he saw Spur. The man was Sly Waters.

Spur had no shot at the man who dove off the horse but he changed sights and shot the horse through the head, putting it down and kicking its way to death.

Put a man on foot and he was halfway dead.

Spur sent four more rounds into the woods around the spot where Sly had dropped, then waited, moving behind the tree so that no lucky pistol shot would hit him.

For five minutes he waited, then he rode around the spot watching it. Sly was in there somewhere. He had not walked out. Spur guessed that Waters was not a good enough woodsman to get out without making some noise. He was waiting. Like an Arizona Apache. You never see them until they kill you.

Spur pulled his Colt and pushed another round in the empty cylinder. Now he had a gun in each hand. He rode slowly forward. Behind a large fir tree, Spur slid off the horse and whacked it on the flank. It charged ahead into the brush directly over the place where Waters had dropped.

Ten feet away to the left, Waters jumped up and fired four times at the horse before he realized Spur wasn't on board.

Spur used the rifle and put a round through Water's left leg dropping him into the brush.

"Bastard!" Sly shouted. "You tricked me."

"One trick deserves another. I don't suppose you're going to give yourself up, just to save that leg from being amputated."

"Don't reckon." A rifle shot slammed past the tree so close Spur could feel its hot breath.

"Nice try." Spur went to his belly, moved forward toward where he had last seen Sly. He worked six feet, then stopped and listened.

Sly lifted up and ran downhill. Spur chased him. The runner has the advantage. He knows where he's going. He doesn't have to stop every dozen feet to be sure the movement continues. Anything less for the pursuit man could mean an ambush and quick death.

Spur worked it by the book and got down the long slope to where he could see the River Road next to the Columbia. Now Spur figured Sly Waters' plan. He would try to get a ride with the first person passing by.

Spur lifted the rifle and shook his head. It wouldn't work.

Ten minutes later, Spur found where Sly had walked into the River Road and crossed it. He would be in the brush on the far side waiting.

Spur picked out a slight rise where he could see a hundred yards both ways on the road and waited. Ten minutes later a lone horseman came down the road from Astoria. He rode a bay at a walk, and Spur watched him carefully.

Nothing happened until he was well past Spur heading for Portland. Then Sly jumped out of the brush and grabbed the reins of the horse. Spur put a round from the rifle into the dirt at Sly's feet and he jolted back.

"Rider, get the hell out of there, the man's a

criminal," Spur shouted.

Sly lifted his six-gun to blast the rider from the saddle, but the man skittered the horse to the left. Spur's second rifle shot slammed into Sly's six-gun, jolting it from his hand, bending the cylinder and freezing it in place until a gunsmith could fix it.

Sly dove into the brush and crawled out of sight.

"That's not going to work, Sly. What's your next move?"

"To kill you, McCoy."

"Come get me."

"A fair fight, in the road."

"You don't even have a weapon. Want me to use a knife on you?"

"You too much of a yellow-belly to do that."

"I'm taking you in one way or another. You shot down Slim Gillette, the timber faller."

"Sure, I was just doing my job. You a damn marshall or something? I never did know."

"Close enough. Come out and I'll see that you get a fair trial."

Spur waited a moment but there was no response. He ran across the road, paused and listened. Off to the left Spur could hear a man running. Sly was trying for the river.

Spur ran hard for the water. It was less than fifty yards away, and half of that was swampy and wet from where high water came and left its sticky slime and rotted wood. Spur crouched behind a bush and stared through it east, upriver, but saw nothing move.

After five minutes Spur lifted up and ran up the bank, keeping to the solid footing, skirting any brush and trees where Sly could be hiding.

The jangle of harness came from the road. Spur ran

back to the River Road and watched a farm rig going toward Astoria. Sly plainly was not on or in the wagon, so Spur only waved and let the man go on his way.

Spur walked up the River Road and watched through the light brush toward the river. Sly was there somewhere. The man had admitted that he shot down the faller. Now Spur had a reason to bring him in.

Spur saw a figure dart from one tree to a clump of brush. He sent a lead rifle slug zinging through the brush but heard only a laugh from Sly.

"Missed me again. You're getting short on rounds. I hope you're counting."

Spur realized he wasn't counting his rounds expended. Any shooter worth his Colts always knew exactly how many shots he had left in any weapon he used.

Spur walked rapidly now directly toward the brush where he last saw Sly. No sense in dragging this out. It would be dark in another two hours. He saw movement behind the brush and Spur increased his speed to a run and stormed through the brush only to find his quarry gone.

More brush showed closer to the river, and Spur realized that was the only direction Sly could have taken unseen. He ran again, and came past a clump of thick brush too fast. Sly swung a heavy branch with all his strength. It caught Spur on the left shoulder, making him drop the rifle.

But he lifted the .45 and fired. The round hit Sly in the left arm, but already he had swung the branch again. Spur tried to duck. He fired but he was off balance. The heavy branch crashed into his gun hand jolting the weapon away as Sly Waters charged into Spur and they both crashed to the ground.

They rolled over twice and Sly pounded Spur in the face with his fist twice before Spur got a hand free and smashed Sly on the side of the head. They broke apart and both jumped up. Sly grabbed a knife from his belt and Spur brought up a larger one from his boot.

Sly snorted, turned and ran. Spur started after him, then found his Colt and tested it. Still worked. He picked it up and began to run after the other man.

Spur looked ahead trying to find Sly. He was gone. There was no place he could go. The road was too far away. Only the bogs and the river on this side.

The river! Spur stared at the shoreline now. He saw several logs twenty feet long that had been lost or broken free from the rafts. There were five or six of them along the edge of the water, some of them still afloat.

For a moment he thought he saw one move, then he was sure of it. He ran toward the river and saw an arm over the inside of the log. Now he could see the edge of Sly Waters' head on the other side of the log. He pushed it and then splashed with his feet as he kicked the log back into the slow moving waters of the big river.

It was over a half mile wide here, surging with a strong current down the channel in the center, and decreasing in speed until the backwaters didn't move at all.

Now Sly had kicked his log into the edge of the slow moving current. He was out of pistol range and drifting slowly downstream.

Spur turned and began walking along the bank, easily keeping up with the speed of the current.

"Damn you!" Sly shouted. The sound came plainly across the water.

Sly moved to the end of the twenty-foot log and angled it into the faster current.

"You get out there too far you'll never get back to shore," Spur shouted.

Sly only waved at him.

McCoy worried now about some boat picking up Sly. But as he looked up and down the Columbia, Spur saw no boats of any size heading in either direction.

Spur looked up and Waters was well ahead of him now. McCoy used some of his Indian training and began to trot forward. He stayed on the solid ground and quickly made up the time on the floating log and its passenger.

Then Spur saw the log hit yet a stronger current and a rapids from some water motion or underwater obstacle. The long log bounced in the water, one end vanishing for a moment. Sly screamed and went underwater. When he came up he swam furiously to catch hold of the log again and made it.

Now Spur had to run to keep up with the pace of the current as it swept Sly downstream. The stronger current had also pushed Sly farther into the river until he was nearly in the middle of the current and the water roiled and rolled.

Spur could see the log bouncing again. A scream and a wail came from Sly as the log caught the current and shot forward out of his reach and he splashed into the Columbia, suddenly alone and on his own, a quarter of a mile from shore, and with the strong current to fight.

Spur ran faster to catch up, then paused and

watched the water. He saw the splashing. Then Sly went underwater. A moment later he surfaced and splashed again. Sly screamed for help. He turned over and tried to float on his back, but kept sinking.

With one more scream, Sly Waters struck out for the far shore with a strong crawl stroke. It lasted only eight strokes. Then Sly wailed in lonely defeat and slipped under the water.

Spur ran down a hundred yards and searched the river waters again, but found nothing. The books on Sly Waters could be closed at last.

Spur wondered if he could find the third horse. It had not been shot. He noticed now that his arm was still bleeding from some tear or scrape. He cut off the tail of his shirt and wrapped it around the wound, then got to the road and began walking toward Astoria. It was getting dark.

There would be no more traffic to offer him a ride. Spur wondered how far he was from the small town. Too damn far, he knew. He walked. It was full dark now, with the stars out and a chill in the air. The wind died down and that helped. Spur rested twice and at last came to where he could see the lights of Astoria. He took the shortcut past the mill to the office and saw a light on.

19

Karen sat on the little porch waiting for him.

She grinned when she saw him. "I knew you'd be back," she said. Then she saw the bloody bandage on his arm and she frowned.

"Don't worry, it's just a scratch," Spur said and dropped on the porch beside her. He was so tired and sore that he wasn't sure if he would ever move again.

Spur sat on the steps and without realizing it, sagged in fatigue against Karen.

She put her arms around him. "Right now, Spur McCoy, I want to hug you and kiss your hurts and make them all well. Is that a bad sign?"

"Probably. I could use a shot of whiskey."

"You wait just a minute. I'll bring round my rig and drive you up to the house and get you cleaned up and your wounds all bandaged and then a good big dinner inside of you, and you'll feel a lot better. Any objections?"

"Would it matter?"

"Absolutely not! Should I get three big gorillas and

have them carry you to the buggy?" Karen laughed and kissed his cheek. "Now don't move."

She hurried away and brought her one horse buggy around so close to the steps he had to pull in his feet. She tied the reins and climbed out, her movements revealing one shapely leg almost to her knee.

"Oh, sorry," she said. Then she shook her head. "No, not really. You've felt a lot more of me than that." She shrugged and helped him stand and step into the rig.

"Hey, I'm not crippled."

"What happened to those robbers?" she asked as the horse pulled the buggy along the street toward Upper Town.

He told her quickly and leaned back against the seat. "So none of them will bother us anymore."

"You'll have to tell the sheriff."

"Tomorrow. That one robber in the office die?"

"Yes." Karen looked away. "I . . . I'd never seen a person die that way, especially not right in front of me. After you shot him he just fell down, looked at me with wide eyes, then gave a little sigh and I guess that's when he died."

"People who use guns have to be ready to die," Spur said.

"Are you?"

"Yes, have been for quite a while now. Sometimes I'm surprised that I'm still alive." Spur felt her stiffen where he sat close beside her, but she kept looking straight ahead.

At the house, Lee met them and helped Spur into the living room.

"I'll tell you what happened later, Lee," Karen said in a takeover kind of voice. "Get Spur into that

194

guest room on the first floor. He needs some nursing and cleaning up. I'll see if there's any hot water.''

Lee grinned. ''When Karen takes over like this, I kind of step out of the way.''

Spur nodded. ''I got the other two guys who tried to rob you. No more worry there.''

''Figured. We had another small problem at the mill. I fired the man who caused it and told the men if there was any more tricks like that one, the men would be fired without any hesitation. I don't think any of the men will take any more money from Marty for dirty tricks on us.''

''Good. Lee, about Karen.''

''Take a blind man not to see that she's interested in you. She's a grown woman. What she does is up to her. Hell, wouldn't matter much what I said anyway.'' He looked at Spur sharply. ''I know you're a fiddlefoot, be gone in a week or two. I want to be certain that you don't break her heart.''

Karen came in then with a bucket of water, a big pan, two towels, wash cloths and brown soap.

She put them down and came to Spur where he sat on the edge of the big bed and began to unbutton his shirt. He helped her.

''Lee, where did that doctoring box of things go? Can you find it for me? We've got a nasty gash in Spur's arm that need some fixing.''

''I'll find it.'' Lee walked to the door, watched Karen for a minute and hurried out when she glared at him.

''You don't have to do this, Karen, I'm not that bad off.''

''Then let me pretend. I'm enjoying taking care of you.''

She pulled his shirt off.

"Lost your hat, I'd bet."

"Yes."

"It already had a bullet hole in it anyway. I'll get you a new one."

She reached for his belt. Spur caught her hands.

"Half a bath will be enough, thanks."

Karen grinned. "Nurses do that all the time."

"You're not a nurse, no basic training."

"But I am a fast learner."

Spur let her wash his arms and torso and his face and then he dried himself. Lee came back with a shoe box filled with all sorts of small bottles, tape, scissors and rolls of cloth for bandages.

Karen cleaned the wound on his arm again. It was only a three-inch scratch no more than a quarter-of-an-inch deep in the center. He'd ignored many wounds worse than that. She insisted so he let her put some salve on it and then bind it up tightly. She changed the bandage on the bullet wound and looked at it.

"It must be healing, I don't see any redness. You heal quickly."

"One of the requirements for the job."

She flashed him a slight frown. "Don't talk that way. I won't let anybody else hurt you."

"Good, I'll call you for my next fist fight. I hate those the worse. Don't get killed or cut up, just hurt all over the next day."

"How do you like your steak, medium rare?"

"Fine, am I having steak?"

"Yes, biggest one I could find, and a plate full of fresh fried potatoes and onions and cheese with just a touch of garlic, lots of fresh peas and a lettuce and tomato salad. I'm not sure that you've been eating right."

"And then you'll tuck me in for the night?"

"I'll try." She smiled. "In a situation like this, a girl has to figure out how much she can push."

"Don't count on tucking me in. Now how about a shirt?"

She grinned. "Not that grubby old thing. Besides, I kind of like you all bare topped that way."

Spur shrugged. "Fine with me, only you have to go bare topped, too."

"Oh," she started to blush, then controlled it. "Lee and Cilla might not understand."

Spur chuckled. "Cilla would."

Karen laughed, too. "You're right about Cilla. But you're not supposed to know. You rest up a bit. I'll go get your supper."

Spur tried to stay awake, then when his eyes dropped closed the second time, he gave up and slept.

A kiss on the lips woke him. He started to reach up then remembered where he was.

"Nice way to wake up," Spur said.

"For me, too. If you'll sit up, I'll get one of those little tray things to put your supper on."

A half hour later, Spur finished the meal, found his shirt and shrugged into it and stood in the bedroom looking down at Karen. Her blue eyes were like a piece of a summer sky. The wheat straw blonde hair swirled around her face and shoulders. When she smiled he knew he had never seen a prettier woman.

"Thanks for the doctoring and the nurse work. Thank your cook for the food, it was just what I needed."

"I never did get you that whiskey."

197

"Food works better, if there's time."

"What are you going to do now? It's almost nine o'clock."

"Time working men were in bed and asleep."

"You're not a working man."

"Was today. Damn hard work."

He pulled his gunbelt off the bedpost and buckled it on, then took the rawhide thong through an eye in the tip of the holster and tied it tightly around his lower thigh.

"What's that for?" Karen asked.

"Keeps the holster from moving when I pull out the six-gun."

"Why can't it move a little?"

"When it moves the gun doesn't. That hundredth of a second could be enough to get a man killed."

"Oh."

"May I go out and talk to Lee, now?"

"One more treatment." She came up to him and pushed her full breasts against him and lifted her mouth and put her arms around him.

Spur kissed her lips. She hugged him so hard he thought her breasts would crush. Damn, but he liked it. His arms came around her and she didn't let the kiss end. Just held it and nibbled at his lips and her tongue brushed his lips.

His hands rubbed her back and then she eased away from him. He dropped his hands and she stepped back.

"What would the little old gossip ladies say if they knew I kissed you like that in a bedroom!"

"They would have a fine day of gossiping," Spur said.

She caught one hand and brought it toward her

breasts but he shook his head and pulled away.

"No," he said softly. "You're not ready, and if you were, I'm not ready."

He turned and walked out to the hall. He found Lee in the front room going over a list of all of the dirty tricks that had been played and what he figure it cost the company.

"Right around ten thousand dollars," Lee said. "Didn't have to but I gave Slim Gillette's widow three thousand dollars and paid off the three hundred and fifty she still owed on the house. She's going to take in boarders. She said she can make it all right. She's building on two more bedrooms to rent out."

Lee stood and walked around the lamp. "You're looking almost alive now. Rested up a little?"

"I'm fine. That supper was great. Now I better get down and talk to the Sheriff before somebody else does."

"Lots of times. He makes the first door check about ten. You should be able to catch him on his rounds."

Spur thanked Lee and got down to Main Street a few minutes later. He found Sheriff Vinson coming away from the General Store. The lawman stood for a moment and stared at Spur.

"Heard you took off after them last two robbers. What happened?"

Spur told him and the Sheriff shook his head. "He was a damn fool to try to ride the river on a log. Even if it is deep there's some rough spots. He didn't know that. Not a chance in a thousand that he's alive."

They walked along as the Sheriff checked to be sure the merchants' doors were locked.

"Think you can find that other body tomorrow?"

"Figure as how."

"I'll need to know who he is at least. We better go down to the office so you can write out a statement for me. Three dead in one day is a first for the county in a mighty long time. Better have a good record of it in case anybody asks questions."

"The gunman at the mill office. Was he a local?"

"Yep. Used to run a fishing boat, but he was never a good fisherman. Finally lost his boat 'cause he couldn't pay back the bank. He was nearly two years behind on the payments before the bank had to take it over.

"Bank sold it for what the guy owed and now the boat is turning a profit every month. The guy was just a loser." Sheriff Vinson rubbed his face. "You said Sly admitted that he shot Slim the faller, but he didn't say who paid him to do it."

"Right, we didn't get around to who hired him."

"A shame. At least we've got the murder cleaned up and off the books."

"You must keep a neat office, Sheriff. Could we get this done with so I can catch some sleep."

It took almost an hour for Spur to write out the story of the death of the three men. He left blanks for the second gunman's name and would fill it in the next day. At last both of them were satisfied and Spur made it back to his room. He was still stiff and sore, but mostly dog tired.

He fell into bed after taking off his boots and his pants. The dirty shirt he threw in a corner and lay on top of the covers in the warm room in his short underwear drawers. McCoy slept as soon as he hit the pillow.

Sometime later he heard a knock on the door. At

first it was in a dream, but as he groggily came awake he realized it was on the door. He stumbled over to it and unlocked the latch and took away the chair.

Nancy Johnson came in with a bottle of wine. She looked at him and grinned.

"You were going to start without me!" she said in mock anger.

Then she closed the door, bolted it and put the chair back in place. She kissed Spur firmly on his mouth and opened hers invitingly.

Spur walked her to the bed, then lay down and was sleeping soundly even before Nancy took off her clothes and lay down beside him.

She kissed the back of his neck, then his cheek. At last she lay on her side and kissed his lips almost in the pillow. He kissed her back in his sleep, and rolled over.

"Oh, damn," Nancy said. Spur lay on his back and Nancy grinned as she reached for his crotch. She knew one way she could wake him up.

But even after five minutes of playing with his limp genitals, Nancy couldn't wake up Spur McCoy. She couldn't even bring him to an erection.

She sighed and lay down beside him. If he was that exhausted it wouldn't do any good to wake him up anyway, she decided. By morning he would be rested and she would demand her own satisfaction!

20

Spur was surprised when he woke up the next morning and found Nancy beside him. She slept nude and presented a tempting picture stretched out beside him. She lay on her back with one arm across his chest. Her red hair sprayed on the pillow, and the red triangle of soft fur at her crotch matched the color exactly. He eased her arm away from him, and slipped out of bed.

Today he had work to do and he needed an early start. It was a little after six-thirty when he left the hotel and stopped at an early morning cafe. He had coffee and a roll, took a fast walk through Lower Town.

Most of the businesses were built over the water on long pilings and the water fell and raised with the tides twice a day. He went upsteam along Concomly Street to the water, then on Sequemoqua across to Scow Bay.

Uppertown lay across the bay five or six blocks and was connected to the rest of Astoria by a foot path around the beach. He turned back and walked along the waterfront and wondered at the canneries that were springing up to can the yearly run of salmon.

When he got back to the saddle shop, he sat on the small porch and waited until the small man opened the front door.

P.X. snorted. "What's the matter, lawman, couldn't you sleep? Or did she kick you out of bed early?"

"Both," Spur said grinning. Inside he poured himself a cup of coffee and broke one of the still hot cinnamon rolls off the block of eight.

"You expecting a convention here this morning?" Spur asked.

P.X. was already at work stitching on a saddle. He shook his head. "Not at all. I knew a couple of freeloaders would be around. I can't say no to a hungry man."

Spur chuckled and sat on the regular sized chair and watched the midget working.

A normal sized woman came into the room from the back. She stopped when she saw Spur.

"Oh, I didn't know a customer was here," she said softly. She was the picture, the personification, of gentleness. Spur had never seen such a softly beautiful woman. She was about five-two, with brown hair cut shorter than the current style and thrown back with no concern, yet it fell in a pleasing shape.

She was slender with no breasts showing through the simple, loose calico dress. Her face was what captivated him. Tender blue eyes that mirrored her love and concern for P.X. Her hands, thin, sensitive, talented, communicated a language all their own as she brought P.X. a small bottle.

"Your medicine," she said, the voice a caress of gently falling rose petals.

P.X. had been watching her with love shining from his eyes. He motioned her closer and reached up and kissed her cheek. It made her smile and Spur wanted a camera to preserve that perfect, dedicated, unselfish expression.

"You're much too good for me, Sandra." P.X. looked up and motioned to Spur. "This gentleman works for the United States Government as an anti-crime man and one who catches outlaws. His name is Spur McCoy. Mr. McCoy, this is my beautiful wife, Sandra."

She looked at him for just a moment, smiled, nodded ever so slightly.

"It's a pleasure to meet you, Mr. McCoy. We'll have you to supper one of these evenings. Now, if you'll excuse me." She said something softly to P.X. and moved like a dancer back through the curtain into the rear of the shop.

P.X. chuckled. "Mr. McCoy, your mouth is open." P.X. went on with his work. "Yours is about the usual reaction for a first meeting with Sandra. Isn't that Sandra of mine something? Best wife in the whole world. The most fantastic person I've ever met. Yes, yes, I know, a thousand times too good for me, but for once I got lucky.

"Most things I must work tremendously hard for, but this time I was fortunate. Sandra actually courted me. Marriage was her idea, at first anyway." He watched Spur a moment more.

"McCoy, either eat that cinnamon roll or I will. Your small introduction to Sandra is over. Now, back to business. I hear that Sly Waters is no longer among us.''

"Uh . . . yes. What a fantastic lady," McCoy said at last. "You are indeed a lucky man, P.X."

"Sly Waters?"

"He went for a swim on a log. The Columbia water gods grew angry at him and unseated him. Evidently Sly wasn't much of a swimmer. The turbulence and the current swept him under. Last time I saw him he was headed for the bar, underwater.''

"Waters wound up in a watery grave. Poetic justice. Sometimes things work out better than we expect.''

Spur told him quickly about the robbery attempt and what happened.

"Astoria will not miss those three. When do you ride with the Sheriff?''

"Probably anytime I get over there."

"I've been doing some thinking," P.X. said. "Who would want the mill so bad that they would go to all of this trouble to steal it from Johnson? There's an outfit in Portland who gets wild eyes every six months or so about building a railroad down the coast. They are at it again and supposedly taking bids on all sorts of services and goods.

"I saw a story that six firms had bid to supply the railroad ties needed for the job. One quote I heard was that they would need four million ties with an average cost of somewhere around 12 cents each. That's almost a half a million dollars.''

Spur was nodding before P.X. got through. "Somebody wants the mill so he can make a bid on the ties. Sounds reasonable. If he can get the mill at a steal, the thief wins both ways.''

"True. Now all we have to do is figure out who here in Astoria the front man might be."

"Marty has been talking to somebody in those closed offices. The one guy is a lawyer. The second office is vacant. What do you know about this so-called retailer store builder?"

"Tom Monroe is the name. He's as slippery as he was when he first came to town. He could be up to almost anything. But why else would Marty be going to see him? He looks like the best prospect for the Astoria connection with the mill buyers. I'll do some probing and see what I can find out."

Spur finished the cinnamon roll and sipped at the coffee.

"All of that and she cooks too?"

"Damn right!" P.X. said smiling.

Spur put down the coffee cup. "I better go see the sheriff and take a ride. Don't look like Sandra is going to come back out here."

"Not likely," P.X. said. "Have a pleasant ride."

They took along a spare horse to bring back the body. Spur followed much the same route as he had used the day before, got lost twice but at last came to the spot where the robbers had turned to fight.

Sheriff Vinson looked at the man's face. "Yep, Jeb Turner. Been around town for a year or so, works on and off at the cannery and on the boats. Worst part is he's got a wife and four kids. They got kin in Portland. Jeb hasn't been working lately. One of my deputies been wondering. He seemed to have enough money."

They pulled him out of the weeds and hoisted him on the horse. Rigor mortis had stiffened the body in a slumped over position. They wound up tying Turner on the horse in the same slumped over posture. They took him back to town through back streets to the undertaker.

Wallace Jones was fat, red cheeked and always happy. He looked at Jeb and shook his head. "Used to play a little poker with Jeb. Thought he'd do better than this. Sheriff, you know I'm gonna have to break him up some to get him in a casket."

"I won't tell the widow about it, Wallace, if you don't."

An hour later Spur had the name filled in the report he'd made out the night before, and penned a small addition.

"What have you found out about Tom Monroe, Sheriff?"

"Nothing more than what I already knew. You want me to send a letter to Portland asking the sheriff there if he knows anything about him?"

"Might be handy, Sheriff."

The rest of the day, Spur walked the mill area, checked out a raft of logs that came in and walked around the burner. Everything seemed in good shape. With luck they would get through a whole day without some kind of expensive accident.

After dark, Orville Ames lay in the tall grass just beyond the lights of the Johnson family house. He took little naps until he saw the light come on in Karen's bedroom. Tonight she forgot to pull the blind and Orville lay there his eyes bright as Karen undressed.

When she got down to her chemise she combed her long blonde hair, and Orville waited impatiently.

Then she slid the chemise off and stood in front of her mirror. She turned and he saw her glorious breasts swinging slightly.

He was hard at once. His hand moved to his crotch. Then she moved again and he saw her bare little bottom as she walked away from his view toward her bed.

For an hour, Orville lay there fantasizing what it would be like the first time with her. She would beg him for it. Get down on her knees and take him in her mouth and then pull him over on top of her in that same bedroom and it would be so good. He would use her eight times the very first night. It would be a record for him!

It was after midnight before he slipped back down the hill to his house in Lower Town on Fourth Street. Someday soon! Some day damn soon, he would have that woman for real.

When morning came, Orville went back to work. He figured almost a week had passed and it was time. He took over his regular job and the man doing it went back to his usual duties driving a lumber wagon.

Well before noon, Orville took his report to Karen. He had put on a clean shirt that morning and fresh pants, shaved carefully and even combed his dark hair.

Orville stepped into the office and saw someone else talking with Karen and waited. He stared at her. The white blouse was strained to hold in her breasts. He knew exactly how large they were from last night. He wiped his mouth as a bit of wetness dripped down. He glanced around. He had to be careful.

He looked away for a while, then back at her. The man in the chair next to her desk was gone. Orville walked up and stood a moment until she looked up. He used his best smile.

"Miss Karen, I have the report for the manifest ready."

"Oh, Orville. I didn't expect you back at work so soon. I'm terribly sorry about Ida." Her face was worried, concerned. He didn't like to see her that way.

"Thank you. I understand. But we must go on. The preacher told me that. So I'm working."

She brightened. "That's wonderful, Orville. I admire that in a man." She reached for the sheets of papers.

"Miss Karen, you're looking so pretty this morning, like a white buttercup."

"Thank you, Orville, the report?"

He handed it to her and his hand brushed her fingers.

"You're so pretty it just gives me goose bumps."

"Now, Orville. You're still in mourning."

"Yes, Miss, I know."

She did the paper work and gave him back the forms he needed for the ship captain.

"Here you are, all ready to go." Karen felt a little disturbed the way Orville stared at her. It was like he was trying to see right through her blouse.

"Thank you, Miss Karen. Oh." He stopped and moved closer. "Miss Karen, I surely would like your permission to come courting. Like the preacher said, life must go on."

"But . . . but, Orville. Ida was lost less than a week ago! No, I won't hear of any such thing. You shouldn't even be *thinking* about courting for at least six months."

"But. . . ."

"Absolutely no, Orville Ames. And I'll thank you not to mention the idea again. If you please." She stood up and Orville thought her blouse was going to split. When it didn't he nodded, scowled and turned so he could walk out of the mill office door.

Karen watched him go, her own face a cloudy frown. She walked straight into Lee's office. The door was open and he wrote something on a paper.

"Lee, I don't know what to think. That . . . that was Orville Ames and he just asked me if he could come courting. Have you ever heard of such a—"

Karen felt someone behind her and saw Spur standing by a bookcase. Evidently he and Lee had been talking.

"Oh . . . sorry. I didn't know you were having a conference. I can come back."

Spur moved toward the door. "Family business . . . I'm the one who will take a walk."

"No, Spur, we need to work this out."

Karen shrugged. "Well, I guess I don't mind Spur hearing. I was just so surprised and now I'm getting angry. His wife is hardy cold yet and here he's staring at me and . . . and . . . well, he was no gentleman. No self respecting woman would even consider letting him come courting for at least six months. At least.

"Besides, I never have liked Orville Ames. There's something about him that I can't stand. And he's old. I mean he's well over thirty-two or three." She looked at Spur. "Not that thirty-two is old for some people, but Orville . . . not in a million years!"

"You always smile at him when he brings in the reports," Lee said.

"Of course. I smile at everyone. It's good business,

210

and most of the people I work with I like. Actually, I'd be twice as happy if he never came into the office again.''

Lee fired up a cigar and took a puff. ''I heard somewhere somebody saying that he wondered if Orville tried as hard as he could have to find Ida.''

Spur looked up. ''I heard something different. Somebody in a saloon said the way Orville stood up in the boat he had to know that was a guaranteed way to tip over an eight-footer.''

Karen watched both men her, eyes wide.

''You mean. . . . Are you two suggesting that Orville might have *wanted* his wife to drown? No, no I can't think that. You're suggesting that Orville deliberately tipped over the boat and then deliberately did not try. . . . No. That just can't be true.''

She hesitated. ''Lee, would you do something for me? Could you tell Orville to have somebody else bring the tally sheets up to me. Tell him his place is on the tally board. He should delegate running the forms to someone else. I'd really rather not have him coming up to the office anymore.''

''That bad?'' Lee asked.

Karen nodded. ''I don't know . . . he just makes me feel like I want to go wash my hands.''

''I'll drop by and tell him today, don't worry about Orville anymore.''

She went out and Spur eyed the mill owner. ''Some others are worried about Orville's story?''

''Quite a few. I know the man who was the closest one to Orville out there fishing. He said he saw the whole thing. He said Orville couldn't have dumped the boat any easier. And Orville almost grew up in row boats and bigger boats. He was an old hand on the river.''

"Now him making a play for Karen . . .'' Spur said.

"Kind of makes you think twice about it, doesn't it. I'll have a talk with the sheriff. Can't hurt.''

"I'm going to try to follow your brother today. See what he's up to. This might be the day he steps over the line and I nail him for some worthwhile charge.''

21

Spur was on his way to Marty's boarding house about ten that morning when he saw the man entering a saloon on Water Street. It was one of many drinking and gambling establishments in Astoria built over the water. More than one shanghaiing had taken place here when a trap door was opened in the back of the saloon and a drunk rolled down stairs to a small dock under the building. There a First Mate of a sailing ship waited eager to buy another hand for ten dollars and row him straight out to the ship.

Spur made sure Marty stayed inside the saloon and that he was drinking. If the pattern held he might be there all day. Three saloons later, just into the afternoon, a barkeep hired two men to walk Marty to his boarding house and drop him on his bed to sleep off his drunk.

Spur patrolled the mill and the lumber stacks but no new mischief came about. He had supper, won two dollars in a slow and poorly played poker game, and by eleven was in his hotel room and ready to call it a wasted day when Nancy knocked on the door.

"You can't be too tired two nights in a row," she said with a sly grin.

"Redheads as pretty as you, who can sing like a nightingale, are always welcome in my room, and in my bed," McCoy said. It wasn't going to be a wasted day after all. Not if the night proved as fine as he figured it would.

He was right.

Just after one o'clock that same night, six figures slipped down Concomly Street to the wharfs. They made sure they had the right building, a twenty-foot-wide dockside warehouse about sixty feet long that sat by itself and the sign over the door said, "Far Eastern Import Company."

Four of the men went to the four corners of the building and sloshed a can of kerosene on the raw wood weathered by the wind and rain, then scratched matches and set the building on fire. They faded away into the darkness and waited. The building was burning on all four sides when the fire siren sounded.

Someone at the volunteer fire station cranked the old siren that wailed as long as it was cranked. As the six men knew who had started the fire, Astoria had almost no fire fighting equipment.

A tall pumper on six foot steel wheels with two inch hoses and powered by four men turning cranks was the only means of throwing water other than by buckets. Tonight there weren't enough men to work the pumper. Most of the volunteers still slept.

The warehouse of the import company burned to the ground in half an hour. The outer section fell into the water where it had been built out on the wooden

214

pilings. Soon the building was simply no longer there.

Fu Chu stood in the street and watched the last of the timbers fall from the roof and the walls cave in. His fists were on his hips and his eyes narrowed in controlled anger.

The six men wearing dark clothes had left the scene of the fire when they were sure it could not be put out. They shook hands, then walked three blocks upstream to the east and stood across the street from another building.

This structure sat on the corner of Cushing and Seventh Streets. At one time it had been a general store, then a boarding house and lately it belonged to Fu Chu who used it for some of his warehousing and for those who wished to experience the opium pipe in more privacy than the loft of the laundry building provided.

Josiah Dangerfield carried a can of kerosene as did three of the other men. This building had ground floor windows on both sides. One on each side was broken as quietly as possible. No lights showed in the structure. The cans of kerosene were poured in through the windows and wadded newspaper lighted and dropped on the petroleum.

Again the six men moved well away from the blaze. This one was reported quicker and for a time it seemed the building might be saved. Enough men worked the tanker, but it was not near enough to the water for easy water pickup.

Fifty people who crowded around the first blaze were on their way home when they saw this one and hurried over. A bucket brigade beat back the flames on the front corner for a while, but the heat was too intense and it soon won the right to burn the building as it saw fit.

Fu Chu was on the water line and screamed at the workers to move quicker. But old-timers on bucket brigades knew the faster the buckets moved, the less water they had in them when they came to the throwers.

The men who pitched the water on the flames were changed after every tenth bucketful in the intense heat. But it was a futile try.

Fu Chu stood watching his second building go up in flames and he swore in Mandarin until he ran out of words.

"They will pay! They will pay!" he said.

He had been at the fires early enough to smell the coal oil. He knew the fires had been deliberately set. On both properties he found the mark he hunted. It was a piece of wood that had been branded with a hot iron.

In the wood were the burned letters: VCA. He knew what the meant, the Vigilante Committee of Astoria. They would pay!

The six men dressed all in black retreated to a large house on Jefferson Street. They met in a small room where no lights showed outside.

Dangerfield poured a drink for each man, then lifted his glass of whiskey. "To the VCA!" he said. "Long may we serve justice and the American Way. Long may we rout out the lawless, the riff raff, the scoundrels who would enslave us all!"

"Here here!" the other five chorused and all drank.

"Damn Chink gonna think twice before he pushes that Devil Weed on any more of our people," a man said. "Opium might not be illegal, but it damn well

216

should be. Had a clerk who took to it. First week he came to work just two days. The next week I had a long talk with him and he came to work only one day. That was the last I ever saw of him."

"We cut half of Fu Chu's opium business right out from under him," a new voice agreed. "But I'm still in favor of taking care of the laundry and running the little bastard out of town."

"All in due time," Dangerfield said, trying to calm the waters a little. The little man is on our list. We have plenty of time. He might just take the hint and move out by himself."

"Don't count on it," another voice said.

They finished their straight whiskeys, had another all the way around and then called it a night well spent and slipped out the dark door to go to their homes.

Three blocks away, Fu Chu was not yet ready to end his night's activity. He had hurried back to his laundry, rousted two of his sons out of bed and brought them and the goods he needed to a large store on Chenamlis and Main.

They started in the alley behind the store, soaking three gallons of coal oil along the outside and through one window. The same treatment was given both sides of the store. It took up almost all of the city block facing Chenamlis. It was the largest store in town, the Putnam General Store Emporium.

It was nearly three in the morning before Fu Chu was ready. Then he ran from one side to the other and to the back. He set each part burning and then moved back three blocks so no one could accuse him of being there.

The fire siren rang out again, but this time only two of the volunteers answered the call. They had not gone to the two other ones. The large store burned quickly, then cans of paint began to explode from the heat, spraying more volatile fuel around the already furiously burning interior.

After an hour the roof fell in and then the front wall. Fu Chu went home and ordered four men to guard the laundry building. Each man had a double-barreled Greener sawed off shotgun and 25 shells. The men were told to shoot anyone who tried to set the laundry building on fire.

George Putnam had been roused at three-thirty A.M. He struggled out of bed and saw the bright light of the fire four blocks from his house.

"Not the store!" he bellowed. But he knew it had to be his treasured store or he would not have been called. Tears streamed down his face as he rushed down to the fire. He screamed and wailed from across the street. Volunteers used buckets of water to wet down the surrounding buildings so they wouldn't burn. So far it had worked.

"How did it start?" Putnam asked everyone he talked to. Most of the people shook their heads.

One man insisted that he knew. "We got a damned fire starter in town. Could burn down the whole sorry place. Three fires tonight alone! What's it going to be like by sunup? We could have a dozen more fires!"

George Putnam held his head. Fire bug indeed! When they set the fires on Fu Chu he had no idea that the same thing might happen to him. Slowly he slumped against a wall across the street.

Fu Chu knew!

Fu Chu was a wise old Chinese bird. He had been around Astoria for twenty years. He knew almost everything. He must know that the vigilantes burned him out . . . and that George Putnam was one of the band.

Now Fu Chu had to die. There was no other way around it. First they would burn out his laundry and his opium den. Then the leader of the Chinese himself would be hanged on the oak tree. Hanged by the neck until he was dead, dead, dead! That would teach the little bastard.

George Putnam sat on the step of a store and let the tears come. For thirty years he had built up the Emporium from a hole in the wall little store to the biggest retail establishment this side of Portland. Now all he had were ashes and charcoal and a debt that could never be paid off.

For a moment Putnam wished desperately that he had never helped organize the vigilantes. Then he steeled himself. No, by God! He'd see it through. He'd ruin the little bastard the way he had been ruined. By fire, by God! By fire!

Spur McCoy had seen the second fire. Now he and Nancy looked out the window at the biggest blaze of them all.

"Big," Spur said. "A lot of fire out there."

Nancy had come awake when the sirens went off the last time. Now she pulled McCoy back to the bed.

"Fires make me all wild and crazy inside," she said. "I bet you have a hose that could put out my fire."

"That hose has been used four times already."

"Not man enough to put out my fire?"

"Anytime, anywhere," Spur said.

"How about on my little stage down at the Oregon Saloon right after I finish my last song tomorrow night? Both of us bare-ass naked and humping like wild?"

"I'm willing, but the management probably wouldn't pay my thousand dollar a performance fee. I can't perform without getting paid."

"You still wouldn't do it," Nancy said, her hand stroking him gently.

"Neither would you, I wouldn't let you. I won't share that much of your body with all those horny old men."

"Good, they get bad enough as it is. Tonight one got his hand all the way down the neck of my dress and around one of my boobies."

"You slap him?"

"Sure, and he loved it."

Nancy rolled over on top of Spur. "You're ready again, sweetheart, and I'm past ready and you got to play fireman and douse my fire."

She raised herself over him, positioned him and slid down on his tool.

"Come on, horsy, let me show you how I can give you a good ride."

It was fantastic.

22

Spur sipped his coffee as he watched P.X. work on a set of saddlebags.

"What's the talk around town about the fires?" Spur asked.

"That we've got a fire starter. In a mostly wooden built town like Astoria, that's bad news. As you saw last night, no way to stop a fire once it gets a good start."

P.X. pulled the bee's wax string tight in the stitch through the two thicknesses of leather and watched McCoy. "Last night was some of the action around here that you didn't get to take part in."

"Plenty for everyone last night. Who set them?"

"One thing you can be sure of: Fu Chu didn't burn his own two buildings. Another is that the same guy or group that burned one of them, torched the second. Lot of people in town ain't all that happy having Fu Chu around peddling his opium pipe. I know, I know, it's legal, but by all civilized standards it shouldn't be."

"Now that you've given me your sermon, Reverend, who torched Fu Chu's places?"

"Why not the vigilantes? They've run more than one minority man and his family out of town. We had a black family for about three days a year back. They put a tent on a wooden frame. One night the whole thing burned up. Family was lucky to get out alive. They left the next day."

"So, vigilantes. Why'd the big store, the Emporium, get the torch? Fu Chu doesn't own it."

"Retaliation," P.X. said and grinned.

Spur scowled at him. "Don't make me think so hard this early in the morning. You're telling me the vigilantes could have burned out Fu Chu. To retaliate against them he'd have to know who some of the vigilantes were. . . ."

"You're getting the idea."

"Pushing that same logic, Fu Chu must think or know that George Putnam is one of the Astoria vigilantes."

"Bravo for Spur McCoy! Fu Chu has been around town a long time, thirty years or more. He knows where a lot of bodies are buried."

"So he could know who the other vigilantes are?"

"Could, you'll have to ask him that yourself."

Spur sipped at the hot coffee. It had a touch of cinnamon in it that made it just right this morning. Yesterday and now today he felt as if he were running through deep mud. He was struggling and pushing and trying but not moving very far or fast. He could not prove who killed Ihander, even though the killer was probably dead. It could have been an accident. He was making little progress helping the Johnsons on the mill takeover threat. Maybe he had a first lead on the vigilantes, he wasn't sure about that.

Spur lifted his coffee cup in a salute to P.X.

"Time I'm moving. Remember, a stitch in time. . . ."

P.X. threw a piece of leather at him and Spur ducked out the door chuckling. At once his mood changed. What the hell was he going to do now?

Tom Monroe sat in his interior office brooding. Everything was moving too slow. There had been only silence in response to the first letter offering to buy the mill and the company. Silence was the worst problem in a situation like this.

Monroe heaved his bulk out of the chair and paced around the room. He took out a folder and stared at it. The engraving was good, the certificates ready to issue. "The Portland and San Francisco Railroad!" He would be a millionaire! If only he could bust into this first big one.

Monroe did not think of himself as a failure. Just because he had left his family in Chicago and came West, that was not a factor. They had been holding him down. In Seattle he had done well for a while. Then some petty dispute about the physical presence of a gold mine to back up the gold stock certificates he was selling. Difference of opinion.

Portland had been great. He had money in the bank. He had a small import/export business and made lots of money for a while. The one failing he would admit to was the ease with which he spent money. His or other people's. He went through his funds and then lost a small fortune at that damn gambling table.

So he was in Astoria with a new name, a great

223

connection, and opportunity nudging him to get busy.

He took out the bid request letter and read it over again:

"Bidder will furnish to the Portland and San Francisco Railroad Company four million railroad ties of standard specifications made of any Pacific Coast conifer except cedar. First increment of 5,000 ties to be delivered on site in Portland for the start of the construction, and thence may be milled and supplied anywhere down the line to Astoria and hence down the coast to San Francisco.

"Buyer shall pay for the ties as delivered in lots of two thousand, the sum of fourteen cents each. Bidder to deliver to the job site or any rail siding of the P&SFRR, which ever is closer.

"All bids must be in by June 11, 1875.

"Bidder must post a thousand dollar bond, and show evidence that he is the owner of a sawmill capable of producing the required ties, and has available logging rights and timber leases on tracts with sufficient standing timber to fill the contract."

Monroe folded the much creased sheets of paper and put them in his inside pocket. He sat down and spread his hands across his bulging belly. He had gained twenty pounds since he arrived here. That boarding house food was good. The widow wasn't all that bad herself.

The first day he took the room she came in and asked him if everything was all right. Then she told him how she liked a man with a little meat on his bones. He grinned and kissed her cheek. She moved his face and kissed his mouth.

Ten minutes later she was humping him on the bed.

Monroe snorted. An easy woman didn't get his job done here. What more could they do to the Johnsons beside burning them out? Then he wouldn't have a mill to certify to the railroad company. Damn! He had to light a fire under Marty. The little bastard was probably drunk again.

Monroe slapped the desk and stood. He had to find Marty.

It took him two hours of plying the saloons to find the younger Johnson. Monroe hadn't realized that Astoria was such a wide open town. It had been the main stop for coast-wise sailing ships between San Francisco and Seattle for several years now. The anything goes saloons, gambling halls and the easy availability of ladies of the evening made Astoria a favorite stop.

Sailors said they could find anything they wanted in Astoria, any time of the day or night. Drunken sailors staggering down the street with whores trying to hold them up was a common sight around the waterfront saloon area on Concomly and Chenamlis.

He found Marty at a back table in the Owl Hoot Saloon. He had a whore pushed against the wall and her blouse open as he played with her breasts.

Monroe pulled Marty away from her and the woman swore at him better than most sailors could manage.

"You owe me two dollars, you bastard!" she spat.

Monroe gave her a greenback out of his pocket and pushed her back in the chair. Without a word he piloted a weaving Marty out the back door where he slapped him across the face six times.

Marty whimpered and shook his head trying to sober up before he got killed.

"Don't, damnit! Stop that!"

"I paid you for action, not slobbering over whores. We've got to figure out some more hell for your brother, since he hasn't responded to what we've done so far."

"A fire," Marty said. "Lots of fires in town."

"We can't burn down the mill, stupid, we need it."

"Not the mill, the family house. That'd shake him right down to his highfalutin toe joints."

Monroe grinned. "Yeah, sonny boy, you might have a point there. I'm going back to my office. But I don't want to be seen walking with you. You get over there in five minutes and we'll work out some more tricks on your brother. You be sure and come, and no more boozing today, understand?"

"Yeah, yeah. I'm not even drunk."

Monroe left him with more ideas of devilment churning in his head. He got into his office, took a quick shot of whiskey from a flask in his desk and was ready when Marty walked in five minutes later.

"First we do the house," Monroe said. "Get that done tonight for sure. Tomorrow I want you to concentrate on the lumber yard. Must be ten thousand dollars worth of lumber out there drying. Get some coal oil and light about a dozen of them stacks so they'll fall over. Do that tonight right after the house gets torched."

Marty nodded. "Yeah, I got just the man to do both jobs. Then I pay just one. Exactly the man."

"Good. Now stay sober until we get this finished. Go back to your place and take a cold bath and have some coffee. Then get that man set up for tonight. Now get out of here. It's almost noon already. You don't have much time."

* * *

Cilla had listened to the family talk about the mill and the problem with all of the damage and destruction. She wanted to do something to help, but didn't have any idea what she could do. She thought about it all morning and just after the kids' noon meal she had an idea.

She wrote out a note, sealed it in an envelope and had the neighbor boy deliver it. She told him exactly where to take it, and then started getting ready.

She kept the kids up longer, for an hour past their nap time, then put them down so they would sleep almost to supper. Then she put on one of her fanciest dresses, combed her dark hair until it shone and then opened two more of the top buttons on the dress until she could see the swell of her breasts.

He was a tit man, always had been. She put on perfume, then dabbed a generous amount between her breasts and on her bare thighs under the dress.

Then she waited.

It wasn't until nearly two that she heard the back door open. She ran into the kitchen her heart pounding, a smile on her face. She knew it would work.

Marty stood there watching her.

"You mean it, sweet tit?" Marty asked.

Cilla put her hands under her breasts and lifted them higher and higher until they popped out of her dress.

"Oh, yeah, big cock, I mean it. What took you so long? I got to have more of you. You're so damn *good* in bed."

Marty rubbed his growing erection and walked toward her. Cilla met him halfway. Marty went down

227

on her breasts, nibbling them, sucking them into his mouth, moving from one to the other.

Cilla threw her head back and moaned.

"So good, darling Marty. So wonderful! Why did I ever divorce you?"

He picked her up and carried her to the sofa in the living room and ripped off her dress. There was nothing under it. Furiously he spread her legs and went on top of her. He tore open his fly and pulled out his penis and drove into her without a moment's hesitation.

Cilla shrilled a soft scream of pleasure. Her hips bucked and pushed his crotch high in the air before she was satisfied he was in as far as he could go.

The first time was not making love, it was raw sex, fast and hard, sweat pouring off both of them, and then relaxing on the softness of couch and the cushioning female pillow.

"Lee says you've been doing bad things to the company, but darling, I don't care. I just want you! Love me forever! I'd even help you if I could. I don't care about the mill or the company. You were my first love, my only love."

They made love again, slower, with more feeling. They moved to the braided rug on the floor and he put her legs on his shoulders lifting her high in the air as he pounded away.

Afterwards, as they rested on the floor, he looked over at her.

"You really want to help me?"

She took his hand and pushed it into her crotch gripping it with her thighs.

"I'll help you do anything, anywhere, anytime."

Marty grinned. He still had the old charm. Once

into her pussy she'd do *anything* for him.

He played with her breasts. "There might be something you could do. You know where those papers are I signed when I sold my part of the company to Lee?"

"No, but I can find them. You want me to burn them up?"

"Yeah, little cunt, you get the idea. No, first bring them to me and we'll burn them up together."

"Easy. What else can I do? What are you going to do?"

"Couple of things. That drying lumber in the big yard. It's going to be one big bonfire tonight, late. And then some more spikes in the logs until they'll have to inspect every one and not get them all.

"The next log raft is going to have dynamite on it. Oh, I've got a lot of things planned."

She looked at the clock. "Damn, the kids are due to get up any second, and Lee is coming home early. You've got to go. Damn but I am sorry!" She rubbed her crotch up at him and stopped with it just over his face. He reached up and gave it a kiss, then she rolled over.

He dressed.

"I'll find those papers tonight. I think they're at the office. Come by tomorrow." Cilla picked up the pieces of her dress, then kissed him hard on the lips and watched him slip out the back door and into the heavy timber behind the house.

Cilla dressed in her usual at home clothes, and got the kids up and played with them.

She had no pangs of shame from her afternoon frolic with Marty. She had learned three attacks he was going to make on the company. She would tell Lee, and he would stop them. She dressed the kids, took the buggy and drove as fast as she could down to the mill and had a mill hand ask Lee to come out and see her.

He came at once.

"Lee, I found out three things Marty is going to do to the company. Don't ask me how I found out, just listen. All right?"

Lee knew at once how she found out. She was still flushed, and her eyes were bright the way they always were after making love. He calmed his anger. It was her way of helping. He listened carefully, then thanked Cilla, kissed her firmly on the mouth and sent her home.

In the next hour, Lee took immediate action to prevent all three of the events from happening.

23

Orville Ames got to the Johnson house early that evening. It was barely past eight o'clock, and he knew Karen never went to bed until nearly ten, but he lay in the weeds dreaming about her anyway. They would be married in the fall.

A small wedding and then a honeymoon in Portland and come back to a big new house next to the family place here. There was plenty of land for two or three more houses.

Their honeymoon night—the very first time he would get his hands on her tender virginal body—would be in the hotel here before they went to Portland. She would be shy but interested, hesitant but excited, and then she would tell him to turn around while she undressed.

Orville caught the glimpse of movement out of the corner of his eye. He must not be found here! He turned slowly and stared at the spot in the woods just below him. It wasn't full dark yet. A man lay in the brush evidently waiting.

If the stranger tried to spy on Karen as she undressed, Orville knew he would kill the man. She was his!

The man did not move. He seemed to have something in a box with him. Orville couldn't make out what it was. Right then he wished he was an Indian, then he could sneak up on the bastard and push a knife in his belly.

Neither man moved for a half hour, then a moonless night settled down over Astoria and Orville watched the man more intently. He was up to no good.

Slowly the man crawled forward. He carried two gallon tins now, cans of something. Orville knew what it was then, coal oil, kerosene! That was what fire starters used. The bastard was going to try to burn down the Johnson home!

No! That couldn't happen. Karen might be hurt. Orville moved up silently behind the man, staying back out of the man's sight, yet close enough to move on him quickly.

Orville waited until the man had sloshed one of the cans of kerosene on the lower wall of the house.

Then Orville lifted up and charged. He hit the fire starter just as he turned to empty the other can of kerosene. The can spilled one way and Orville rammed the man against the side of the house and they both tumbled to the ground.

Orville let out a nerve jangling scream as he jolted into the man. They struggled on the ground and then one of Orville's big fists came free and he slammed the man twice in the jaw.

The fire starter sagged on the ground, then drove his fist into Orville's crotch hitting his testicles and bringing a cry of pain from Orville.

The fire starter lifted up, struck a pair of matches and ran for the side of the house.

A revolver shot blasted close by from the soft darkness. The fire starter pitched forward, the matches smoking out.

"Get a lamp out here," Lee Johnson called. He walked up to the two men on the ground. First he looked at the shot man and saw that the bullet had caught him high on the shoulder, probably shattering a bone.

"You move one finger and I'll shoot you in the head," Lee growled at the fire starter. He backed up and looked down at the second man.

"Orville! I don't know what you're doing here, but I saw you clobbering that guy with the matches. How did all of this happen?"

Later in the kitchen, Orville explained it the best he could.

"I was out for a walk. Since Ida died I don't know what to do with myself. I saw this guy sneaking around way down the road. He had two cans I figured were kerosene. With all the fires lately, I figured I'd follow him. He came up here and waited in the woods until it got dark.

"Then he slipped up and poured out that one can of kerosene on the side of the house.

"Didn't wait no more, I just jumped him hoping he couldn't get the fire going."

"I saw him punch you in the old gonads," Lee said. "You gonna be all right?"

Orville laughed and said he was. "Glancing blow," he said. "But still hurts like fire."

Lee watched the man for several seconds.

"Orville, don't know how I can thank you. Without your quick thinking, this house would be on fire right now and burning all the way to the foundations."

He turned and walked to the window, then came back. "You come up to the office tomorrow, I'll have a voucher for you that the bank will trade you for two hundred dollars. And I'll see about getting you a better paying job at the mill if you want to move. Fair enough?"

"Lordy, Mr. Johnson, you don't have to do all that. Just did what I knew was right."

"That's the kind of man I want working for me, Orville. Come on and help me get this polecat down to the sheriff's office. I'll hitch up a rig and tie his hands. Bastard won't say a word, not even give his name.

"Wonder why he was going to burn the house," Orville said.

"Plain enough, somebody paid him to. More of the same trouble we're having at the mill."

Lee dropped Orville off at his house first. He held out his hand. "Thanks again, Orville. You come just after midday tomorrow and I'll have that draft ready. You think about a better job, too."

Lee took the fire starter on to the sheriff's office and filed a complaint against the man. Now he would have to put a guard around the house as well. He was angry that this whole thing had come to this.

The next morning, Spur McCoy signed on to work a regular shift on the green chain. He figured the work level view of things might help.

His foreman knew who he was, but the other men didn't. He explained it as he would to any new man.

"The steam engine runs the belts that run the chains that make those rollers move. They pick up the slabs of sawed lumber that come off the re-saw and the cutoff saw. Now what we have are two-by-fours, and four-by-fours, and one-by-sixes and even some one-by-ones. All shapes and sorts.

"Your job is on station twelve. All you pick out are the two-by-fours. You grab them that come down the chain and pull them off and stack them on this little dolly cart so they can be wheeled out to the drying yard."

"Sounds simple," Spur said.

"Even looks simple, but wait until you hit hour three. Remember you have to stack the two-by-fours close together, get twelve of them across on the first row and then stack them as high as you can reach. Give it a try."

After an hour Spur thought he was going to die. His arms felt like they were going to drop off. At noon he was sure he would die. By three that afternoon he hurt so bad he was afraid that he *wasn't* going to die.

He called the foreman and begged off the rest of the day. As Spur sat beside the green chain, he saw someone walking through the mill. What was he doing? Then the man was hiding. Spur lifted up and followed the man. He was in mill working clothes, blue jeans and an old print shirt.

The man slipped around to the long chain that lifted the logs from the pond up toward the big circular saw. Then the man vanished. It took Spur fifteen minutes to figure out where he went. The whining scream of the saw biting through the two-foot- and three-foot-thick logs overpowered every other sound.

Men used hand signals to communicate. Spur looked closer at the chain that hoisted the logs and then he saw him. The man had a heavy hammer and was pounding on a huge spike. Every time the saw screamed, the man hit the big spike with his sledge.

Spur worked around behind him. The big chain hoisted the log another six feet up the ramp toward the carrier that would move it against the saw.

Then the chains stopped and the man whaled away at the spike until it was sunk into the log.

Spur darted around a pile of cutoff ends of boards and grabbed him. He swung the hammer at Spur who ducked and slammed his right fist into the man's jaw.

He went down and didn't move. When Spur dragged him out into the open, he saw the man was Marty Johnson.

The log next on the carrier was inspected carefully by the men. They found no spikes. On the log where Marty had been pounding, they found three.

The old sawyer, the top man in the cutting process who earned more than any man in the operation, sent a squirt of tobacco juice into Marty's face where he lay on the sawdust.

"Damn, that would have ripped my main saw apart. Pieces could have sprayed around and could have killed three or four good men. This the jackass who done it?"

"He did and I'm taking him right to jail," Spur said.

"Should just string him up," the sawyer said. "Hang the son of a bitch!"

"There'll be none of that," Spur said sharply. "The law will take care of him. He couldn't have ruined more than one log, but it wouldn't hurt to check the others on the chain."

Spur kicked Marty in the side. "On your feet, Marty. You've got a date with the sheriff, and then a nice long rest in jail."

It took Spur an hour to get the report written out and Marty lodged in jail. When word got around town a lawyer came in and in five minutes Marty was out on the street after he paid bail of fifty dollars.

Spur gave up and headed back to his room and a change of clothes from his green chain work. He was so tired he could hardly move. Now he believed the men who said the green chain was the toughest physical work in a sawmill.

In the lobby, Spur saw someone coming toward him. He looked up and found Karen standing in front of him.

"Looks like you've been working. How was the green chain?"

"Murder, I'm dead. Just not buried yet."

"I'll revive you by taking you out to dinner, courtesy of the Johnson Lumber Company for spotting Marty and his spikes in the log. Lee says you saved the company at least five hundred dollars."

"I can't eat that much," Spur said. He took a deep breath. His body wanted to lay down and stay that way for ten hours. "Let me go up and wash and put on some clean clothes. Can you wait for half an hour?"

The dinner was good, but Spur hardly remembered what he ate. He was so tired the food didn't even taste good. Karen tried to talk bright and interestingly, but Spur still found himself drifting off.

Then Nancy Reed walked up and looked at Spur

and began tapping her foot.

"So, who is this?" Nancy asked. She was dressed for the show in a tight black dress that showed off her every curve. She had a touch of rouge on her cheeks and light red lipstick on her lips. Nancy stared at Karen who now seemed drab by comparison.

Spur stood. "Nancy Reed, I'd like you to meet Karen Johnson, one of the managers of the Johnson Lumber Company."

The women stared at each other. Karen nodded her head ever so slightly.

"Good," Nancy said. "It must be business. I've signed that contract for six more months here. Stop by and catch my act." She winked at Spur and swept on past toward a table across the room.

"She's a singer at one of the saloons," Spur said. "Really quite a good voice."

"I can imagine," Karen said.

Spur was having trouble staying awake again. Before dessert came he gave up and said he had to get back to his hotel.

Spur put Karen in her buggy and stumbled twice getting to the hotel. He was sure people thought he was drunk, but he didn't care. As soon as he got to his room he pulled his shirt off and washed his face in cold water. He had just dried it when he heard a knock on his door.

If that was Nancy he was going to disappoint her. He got the bolt open and swung back the door. Karen Johnson walked in with a bottle of wine and smiled at him.

"Tonight's the night," she said. She closed the door, threw the bolt and put the wine on the dresser. Then she smiled at Spur and began unbuttoning the fasteners down the front of her dress.

Spur couldn't believe it. He didn't get her stopped until she had them open almost to her waist.

"Karen, no," he said. He caught her hands. She brought them upward toward her breasts and he pushed them down.

"Why not? I want you to. You did it with that Nancy person. Why not with me?"

"Because it wouldn't be right. You're beautiful and sexy and young and desirable. But it isn't right. It's not fair to you."

"You can't believe that. I want you to make love to me."

"It's not right. Your first time should be with a man who loves you and you love him and you're married to him."

"You made love with that singer."

"She wasn't a virgin. You are."

"What . . . how . . . never mind. I still want to." She reached up and kissed Spur, hard and firm and with her lips closed.

He came away and held her close. "Sweet Karen, you have time. Don't push it. Besides, Lee would probably kill me." He kissed her and Karen almost melted.

Slowly Spur buttoned up the fasteners all the way to her throat being careful not to brush her firm breasts.

"Now, you're going to go downstairs and get in your buggy and go back up the hill to your house and go to bed and dream about getting married."

Karen pouted. She tried to kiss him, but he held her.

"I'm mad at you, Spur McCoy. I never want to see

you again." She pranced to the door, then ran back and hugged him. "I don't mean that. I want to see you tomorrow. Do you hate me?"

"Of course not."

"Then kiss me good night."

He kissed her and led her to the door. It was a nice kiss and Karen grinned.

"At least that I can handle. Thanks!" She went out his door and down the hall. Spur got the door closed and all the way to the bed before he fell on it and slept at once.

Sometime during the night he woke up and took off his boots, then he slept again. His dreams were about the green chain.

24

That same night the vigilantes met in the small closed room. George Putnam had been drinking and he couldn't wait for them all to get there. He nearly exploded when the last man, Dangerfield, came in the door.

"About goddamned time you got here, Josiah. We got to do something 'bout that damned Chink. Somehow he found out I'm with the group and he took out all of his hatred on me.

"I'm ruined. Absolutely ruined, and I've got bills to pay and no cash. My store, my merchandise, all wiped out. I figure I had over fifteen thousand dollars worth of goods in that store and it's gone!

"I want fifteen thousand worth of skin off that little yellow bastard!"

Dangerfield knew Putnam would be in a rage. Putnam had called the meeting. Josiah looked at the six men and let out a long breath.

"All right, all right. It seems the consensus that we do something. Let's sit down and figure out what will be the best response, how we can do it, and do it with the least danger to ourselves."

"Obvious what to do," Abe Quincy said. "George lost his entire store. Fu Chu has one more business. We got to burn his laundry to the ground and run the little bastard out of town bare assed and begging for his life."

Abe looked around at the others. He had a store too, Astoria Boot and Shoe, and he didn't want to get burned out. Abe also sat on the County Board of Commissioners, the county legistative body.

Several heads around the table nodded.

"That's a start," Putnam said. "We burn him out for damn sure, then I think we should chop him up in little pieces and dump his worthless yellow carcass in the channel to feed the salmon."

"I brought five gallons of kerosene with me," one of the other men said. "I reckon it's high time that we should use it, and I mean tonight."

Dangerfield sensed the mood of the group. He'd be outvoted even if he made a dramatic appeal. "Let's see, the brick bank building is on one side of Fu Chu's Laundry. On the other side is that little ladies' wear shop."

"Yeah, but the Chink owns the building," someone said.

"That's the last building on that block," Dangerfield went on. "So we burn both of them and donate a few dollars to the woman who runs the hat shop."

"I don't like it," a voice said from the end of the table. "We're doing too much. It's getting personal. We started this group to make sure our county had evenhanded, pure and simple justice. Now we're learning some of the hazards of absolute power."

"What the hell you mean?" Quincy asked.

"Absolute power, such as we have and have been wielding, leads almost always to absolute corruption of that power. We're not talking justice here, this is pure and simple revenge."

Dangerfield felt a vote on his side and he powered in. "That's a good point to remember. Another one I'm thinking about is that Fu Chu knew for damned sure that George was one of us. If he knew one of us, did he know the rest? If he knew, how many others in town have figured it out as well? The folks around here might be fishermen and cannery workers and loggers, but that doesn't make them stupid. I'd urge that we show some caution right now."

"Vote," Putnam said. Any member could call for a vote at any time. Majority ruled. If they split three-three the measure was defeated.

"Vote that we burn out Fu Chu and run him and all of the Chinese family out of town. That we do it tonight."

The vote passed four to two.

"Will he have guards out?" Dangerfield asked. "I would."

"Not Fu Chu," Putnam said. "He'll think that we won't touch the laundry. If we were going to hit it we would have done it last night. He won't have no damn guards."

"Everyone have his hand gun?" Dangerfield asked. All were supposed to bring a short gun of some kind for personal protection. They all nodded.

Putnam took over. It was his show. He got four gallon cans and filled each from the five gallon tin.

"We'll come up in two groups, three in front and three behind. Start the fires at both spots in exactly

243

fifteen minutes from now. Let's set our timepieces so they're all on the same time."

It was ten minutes past one in the morning when the two groups of men converged on Fu Chu's laundry on Squemoqua Street, one block up from the water. Dangerfield moved up with the two men in the rear of the building. He saw one of the giant Chinese standing solidly against the back door. He had a sword in one hand and a shotgun in the other.

"No guards, huh?" Dangerfield said.

"Shoot the Chink," one of the men said.

"That's crazy," Dangerfield said. "We shoot him and then try to get the fire going? The whole idea is to do the job silently and slip away."

Just then a shotgun blasted from the front of the building. The guard on the rear lifted his head and stared into the darkness. He raised the shotgun and Dangerfield could see where the twin barrels had been cut off a foot from the breech of the deadly scatter-gun.

Another shot roared from the front of the building. Dangerfield shook his head. "Not a chance I'm going to take on that monster with his sawed off shotgun and sword. This round goes to Fu Chu as far as I'm concerned." He turned and slipped unnoticed out of the dark alley.

The other two men with him scowled for a moment, looked at the shotgun and pulled back with Dangerfield.

Out front, George Putnam had already fired one shot from a .25 caliber six shot revolver. He missed the huge Chinese who neatly reloaded his shotgun and waited.

He had fired the first time down the middle of the

street when he saw the three men coming toward him with the cans. They had rushed behind a farm wagon that stood at the edge of the boardwalk across the street.

"We gonna let some damned Chink stop us?" Putnam said, his voice almost a hiss. He leaned around the wagon box and fired twice more at the big man and saw one of the rounds hit his thigh. The Chinese jolted for a second, then fired directly at the wagon box.

"Damn him!" Putnam howled. "Buckshot hit my leg." He looked at Quincy who huddled beside him. "Like in the big war. We surround the bastard, we come at him from both sides. He can't shoot two ways at once. You game, Quincy?"

"Right! Let's shoot the son of a bitch down and then set fire to that building and get the hell out of here."

The men went to opposite ends of the wagon box, waved and charged around at the Chinaman. He fired low hitting Putnam in the legs with the birdshot, not wounding him severely, but turning him back to the wagon, limping on one leg and half dragging the other.

By then the Chinese shooter at the front door of the laundry had taken another slug, this one in his massive shoulder. He shrugged it off, picked up a pail of burning kerosene and ran toward the second man attacking him and threw the whole bucket of flaming kerosene at him.

The burning liquid splashed over Abraham Quincy. The gush of flames caught him by surprise. He had been in the act of aiming for a death shot at the giant's head when the fire splashed into him. He fell

245

and rolled, then stood and ran behind the wagon. The rolling had quieted the flames, but as soon as he ran the wind surged the flames turning Quincy into a human torch.

His hair flamed up suddenly and burned away as he staggered around the wagon. Putnam screamed in anguish and fell on Quincy, smothering some of the flames, then rolling him in the dirt of the street until the last of the fire died.

Putnam looked up straight into the sawed off twin barrels of a Greener shotgun. The big Chinese still held it. Putnam saw death in those black holes.

Then someone rounded the wagon from the near end, said something sharply in Chinese, and the big guard steadied his finger on the trigger.

The smaller man was Fu Chu who held a Colt Peacemaker .45 with the hammer cocked and aimed directly at Putnam.

"Putnam, get out of here," Fu Chu said. "Run now or die, take your choice."

Putnam stood slowly. "This man is burned . . ."

"I'll take care of him. Are you ready to die?"

Putnam turned, thought of the pistol still in his shirt, but instead of trying for it, ran into the darkness, through a sifting of men from two nearby saloons who had been attracted by the shooting.

Fu Chu looked at the man on the ground, spoke softly in Mandarin, and the big guard gave Fu Chu his weapon and picked the burned man up gently and carried him into the front door of the laundry.

Just after the laundry door closed a sheriff's deputy ran up with his gun out.

Somebody on the sidewalk laughed.

"Little late, boy," one of the gawkers said. "The fun's all over. Couple of Chinks having a shooting match in the street. Don't look like nobody got hurt none too bad."

For an hour Fu Chu and a Chinese woman worked over the burned man. He was still alive. His hair was burned off and his scalp blistered. Half of his clothes had been burned away and both his legs were blistered by the flaming petroleum.

They put salve on his wounds and sprayed a fine mist of water over him. He was still unconscious. The misting of water seemed to ease his pain.

By morning Abe Quincy could sit up. By noon he could walk. Fu Chu watched him closely. No one had spoken to the man. Fu Chu supervised the making of two signs that were tied together with heavy cord. Both signs said the same thing:

"I AM A VIGILANTE."

When the signs were done, Fu Chu showed them to Quincy who snorted. "Who you talking about?" he asked through burned lips.

Fu Chu took him to the front of the laundry. He had not given him any new clothes, or wrapped his burns. Quincy could walk with only a slight limp.

Fu Chu watched Quincy for a moment.

"Quincy, we have never had trouble before, but now you try to burn down my laundry. You succeeded in burning my other two buildings. You are one of the six members of the Astoria Vigilante Committee. Now we will tell all of Astoria about you and your crimes."

He placed the signs as a sandwich board over Quincy. They came waist high.

"Mr. Quincy. I'll have a revolver that will be pointing at you all the time. You do anything but what you're told and I'll shoot you with infinite pleasure. Do you understand?"

Quincy nodded.

Fu Chu put a light rope around Quincy's neck and led him out the door. Twenty feet down Squemoqua Street he picked up a crowd of amazed and surprised Astoria residents. Most walked along at the side and behind Quincy making comments.

Fu Chu let them talk. He walked down the street three blocks to Denton Street and the courthouse. On the other end of the block stood the jail. Fu Chu led Quincy into the sheriff's office in the court house, took the rope of him and smiled at the deputy sheriff.

"I wish to charge this man with attempted murder, assault and battery, attempted arson, and completed arson on my two buildings here in town. I also wish to list as a participant in all of these crimes, George Putnam."

The deputy sheriff hurried into the back and brought out Sheriff Vinson who listened to the charges.

"First we'll take him over to Doc Ulman and get him patched up, then he'll come back to jail." The sheriff motioned one of the deputies to do the task.

"Vigilantes, huh? I've been wanting a line on these guys for three years now. Sit down Mr. Chu and we'll be glad to write up the charges. You have witnesses who can back up these allegations?"

"Yes sir, three witnesses to each fire, and the mark the vigilantes leave at each of their illegal acts."

Sheriff Vinson grinned at Fu Chu. "Haven't

always agreed with you, Mr. Fu Chu. But on this one you and I are going to get along just fine."

He turned and motioned another deputy over. "Go to his home and bring back George Putnam. Tell him he's being charged with arson, and attempted murder."

25

Orville Ames reported to the mill office just after the noon whistle. He had on a pair of Sunday pants, a clean shirt, and had shaved and splashed some bay rum on his face just before he left the house.

He was coming for a two hundred dollar check! That was more than eight months of wages. Damn, but he had done good!

Orville opened the big door and walked in. He saw the two doors to the private offices and then Karen at her desk. He hoped one day to own one of those private offices.

Orville walked over to Karen's desk. She looked up and smiled.

"Orville, I didn't get to thank you for what you did last night. It certainly was a fine act of heroism. I hope our thanks are going to be enough. All of us appreciate your saving our house from being burned down."

She stood as he walked to the desk. Now he stepped around the desk and stood closer to her.

"Just did what I thought was right, Miss Karen."

Orville knew no one else was in the office. She was so close to him. He could smell her perfume. For a moment she watched him, and her smile was still in place.

He saw her bosom rise and fall as she breathed and he remembered her breasts all bare and at once he was stiff and ready.

Orville grabbed her. He couldn't stop himself. She was so close and smelled so wonderful. He caught her and pulled her to his chest and tried to kiss her, but she turned away. He kissed her cheek and around toward her mouth.

She was screeching at him, but he didn't pay any attention. One of his hands caught at her breast and he pulled away the cloth, surprised when it tore so easily. His hand covered her bare breast and she clawed her fingers down his cheek.

Her fingernail caught in his eyelid and tore it down as she screamed again and again. The pain from the torn flesh startled Orville and he let go of her and touched his wounded eye.

Karen jumped away from him, ran to the other desk and opened a drawer pulling out a six-gun. She had to hold it with both hands. When Orville laughed at her and walked forward, she closed her eyes and pulled the trigger.

Her hard pull on the trigger jerked the muzzle to one side and the gun went off with a booming roar in the closed building. The round missed Orville.

A mill hand heard the shot and rushed inside, saw the situation in an instant and knocked down Orville with two hard punches in the face. The mill man sat on Orville as Karen put down the gun and pulled up her dress to cover her breast.

"He . . . he tried . . . he tried . . ." Karen couldn't say anything more.

Lee ran into the office from outside, stared at Orville and then at Karen who now sat sobbing in her chair. He took Karen into his room and calmed her down and talked with her. When he knew for sure what happened, he went out to the main part of the office and told the mill hand to let Orville stand up.

As soon as Orville got to his feet, Lee knocked him down with a furious barrage of six hard blows to his head and belly.

Lee panted from his sudden fury.

"Drag this animal out of here and run him off the property. Pass the word, Orville Ames will never set foot on this company property again or he gets brained with a peavey. Get him out of here!"

Karen insisted that she was all right. "I'll pin up my dress and then put a light sweater over it. No one will ever know. I tell you that I'm all right."

"Karen, I'm sorry that I wasn't there when he came. Orville really did have a thing for you, Karen. Am I going to have a whole series of men going wild over you?"

"No, of course not. Be serious. I guess I led him on too much, I treated him like a human being."

"With him that's all it took." Lee watched her. "Little sister, you can go home if you want to."

"I know, I'm management, too. I just don't have quite as much stock as you do. I have work I need to do."

Sheriff Vinson came around an hour later looking for Orville.

"Is it about the fracas here?" Lee asked.

"Nope. What fracas? I want to talk to him about his wife's death. Sam Tyler was out fishing that day and says he saw the whole thing. He swears that Orville tipped that boat over on purpose. Tyler said Orville is such a good boatman he would know that standing where he did would upset that little eight-footer.

"He says the more he thinks about it the more he's sure that Orville dumped the boat on purpose. Want to talk it out with Orville. What happened here?"

Lee told the sheriff, and also about Orville asking to come courting Karen a week after Ida died. Then he told about Orville being up at the house last night and then his attack on Karen today.

"Could it be what it sounds like, Sheriff?"

"Sounds like it more and more. I've heard of a man killing his wife so he'd be free to court another woman. I'm more interested in talking with Orville now than ever."

Spur spent most of the day resting up from his long day on the green chain the day before. From now on whenever he thought of torture he'd recommend the green chain. It was a killer. He made the rounds of the bars, spotted nothing, talked to P.X. a while, then had an early supper and played some small-change poker before Nancy came on to sing.

She was good, and she changed parts of her program every night. Half of the songs were new. He wasn't sure when she would run out of new songs. The men in the bar certainly enjoyed it, and the cash drawer kept sliding open and taking in money.

Spur walked her back to the Astorian Hotel and she insisted that he stay in her room.

"I need you," Nancy said, putting her arms around him. "I know I'm not a virgin like some girls you've been taking out to dinner, but I'm a hell of a lot easier to get into bed."

She kissed him and pulled him down to sit beside her on the bed. "Hey, big guy, I can be a virgin if you want me to. I'll mew and whimper and cry a little and fight you as you try to violate my sacred titties and my unapproachable cunt hole. You want me to play the virgin?"

"I'd rather talk about Ben Johnson. Take his play, *The Alchemist,* now there was a beautiful play."

"I don't remember it. Who was Johnson, some small-time English fop who thought he could write?"

"As you know, Johnson was a contemporary of Shakespeare, wrote some of the most elegant poetry of his generation, but also was a colorful outlaw and a convicted murderer."

"A murderer? You're kidding?"

He grinned. "You didn't know that last part, and you're an English Literature expert?"

"A girl can't know everything."

"But you do know all about Shakespeare?"

"Yes, everything ever written about him, and by him and all of the spurious fops and dandies who tried to claim that they wrote what the one true master of the English language has accomplished."

Spur grinned. "I'm getting too bored to argue. Shut up and take your dress off."

Nancy grinned. "Now that's the kind of talk I like."

Spur lay on the bed watching her. She made it a

strip tease. Her blouse came open and she kissed him, pushing her tongue deep into his mouth. Then she slid down his body and rubbed his crotch until she felt the first sign of hardness.

"Oh, yes, come on big boy, grow!" She slid out of her blouse and lifted her chemise for a second, then dropped it and lay on top of Spur, pushing her covered breasts down to his face.

"Want a little nibble of a goodie?" she asked. "Just a small bite?" Nancy lifted the chemise to show him her breasts, then pushed one into his open mouth.

"Yes, yes, yes. That's the kind of torture I need. Bite me hard, suckle on me like a newborn babe."

She pulled the chemise over her head and sat astride him, opening his fly, working out his now turgid member, letting him rise into the air, hard and long and purple tipped.

Gently she kissed his lance, then licked off the head and jumped off the bed and stepped out of her skirt and two petticoats.

She now wore only a thin silk pair of short panties that were skin tight revealing her body outline.

"I bought these in New Orleans. They came straight from the naughty ladies of France. The whores over there all wear them. What do you think?"

He grabbed her and pulled her on the bed and rolled her over until he sat on her thighs.

"Like them a lot better than this angle," he said.

Then he bent and kissed her eyes closed and pecked at her nose, toyed with her lips, then moved down to her breasts flattened now against her ribs. He played with them, watching her nipples rise and harden.

With that accomplished he moved farther down, trailing a hot line of kisses across her ribs and down her flat little tummy to the very tops of her blue silk panties.

"Kiss them off me," she said, her voice getting husky with anticipation.

He pushed them down an inch and kissed down until he came to the soft red muff over her crotch. He parted the hairs and dove lower until he found the pink slit and licked at it.

Nancy screeched in delight, then climaxed in a rolling thunder of vibrations that shook her again and again until she was panting from the excitement of it.

She caught his head, pulled his face into her crotch moaning and yelping, her hips doing a brisk tattoo against him as his tongue searched for her heartland.

"Oh, glory!" she said, her hips quiet for a moment. "Oh, glory, how you do get me going."

She kicked off the Paris panties and stood on her knees on the bed beside him.

"Ever try it standing on your knees this way?" she asked.

"Not possible," he said.

A gleam in her eye made Spur know she was going to prove to him that it was possible, if at all possible. They tried for an insertion a half dozen times, then collapsed on the bed in a fit of giggles.

"You win," she said, "it ain't possible."

Spur stood, carried her to the wall and stood her against it facing him. "Put your arms around my neck and hold on," he said. She grinned and did as she was told.

"Now lift up and put your legs around my waist and lock your ankles in back."

After the second try she did. He moved them apart for a moment at their midsections, then adjusted her and drove into her slippery, ready vagina, and Nancy moaned in wonder and marvel.

"That's a first for me," she said.

Then she was too busy to talk. Spur began pounding into her, keeping her back firmly against the wall, driving in hard and full, exciting himself so quickly that he couldn't stop and play. He wheezed and growled and moaned, then panted as he slammed hard into her six times, spurting his seed deeply into her furrow with never a thought if it might take root and grow.

When she felt him finish and he leaned against her, she grinned over his shoulder.

"What the hell are we supposed to do now?"

Spur dropped her. She held on to his neck, swung her feet down and he slid out of her. They both dropped on the bed laughing and squealing.

"That way it can be done," Spur said. "Now I get a ten minute intermission."

"Between emissions," she said.

She lay on her back and looked up at him. "You don't know how good it is to talk to somebody who has a vocabulary of more than two hundred words. Sometimes I feel like I'm in a third grade classroom out here and can't get out."

"Have you met P.X. Northcliff?"

"The cute little midget? No, but I've heard about him."

"He's probably smarter than both of us put together."

"Both? You're talking to the person who was third in a class of eighty. You're talking to a woman who has a B.A. degree from a prestigious university. You're talking to a woman who just loves the way you put out my fires.''

They convulsed with laughter and rolled on the bed, bouncing on the springs, daring the cross boards to drop out.

"This would be perfect if you had anything to eat in this room," Spur said.

Nancy started to spread her legs, then grinned and jumped off the bed. She opened the dresser drawer and pulled him over to look. It was stocked with three kinds of cheese, three kinds of crackers, a half dozen ripe apples and six bottles of non-alcoholic sarsaparilla.

"Yes, sarsaparilla. I don't want you to get so drunk you can't perform. Tonight we eat and make love and eat some more. If we get any sleep at all before dawn, it certainly won't be any fault of mine."

"Amen, sister!" McCoy said.

26

The next morning, Spur was out early to talk to P.X. about Orville and to speculate about who the other four vigilantes were. He had walked a block down Concomly Street when he smelled smoke. He looked around to see what building was burning this time, but saw none. Then to the east he spotted a plume of white smoke showing over the top of the fir-covered hill along the river.

A rider came pounding down the street into Lower Town. His horse was lathered.

"Forest fire!" he screamed. "Forest fire." He was like a town crier.

Somebody near Spur stopped him. "Where, man?"

"Up the river two miles, on the Johnson tract. Get shovels and axes. Every able-bodied man supposed to get up to the fire line right now."

Men came out of stores and stared.

"Come on, don't stand there. We need men on the fire line. Axes and shovels. Move, now!"

Sheriff Vinson came along the street. "Have wagons moving up to the fire meet in front of the courthouse in ten minutes. Close up your stores, and let's go. Every able-bodied man on the fire lines! If we don't stop this one where it is, it will come this way and burn down every building in Astoria. Let's go!"

Spur walked toward the courthouse with a group of other men. There was no decision about going or not going. Fire call—it was a duty of every man to fight a forest fire. Especially in Astoria with the timber coming down to the streets on three sides. Most of the men had no tools. The hardware store man came to his front porch with an armload of shovels, then a dozen double-bitted axes.

Spur took one of the shovels and at the courthouse got in one of three wagons lined up waiting. Other men rode away on horses. A few of the younger men gave up on the wagons and began trotting upstream.

None of the men hesitated. It was the thing to do. Save the town. Spur sensed that it was like a war, a holy war almost, and a man simply had to respond. Timber and stumpage came right down to the city street ends in many cases. A roaring fire through the pitch-heavy Douglas fir would spread across the city in a few terrible minutes. The devil fire had to be stopped now.

McCoy had never fought a forest fire. He had heard about them. With a good wind and dry conditions a forest fire could be the most terrible of natural disasters.

They could see more smoke as the wagon moved up the River Road. Soon ashes began to fall on them. A cloud of dark smoke covered the morning sun blotting it out entirely, turning the morning into dusk.

Wind whipped the cloud away and brought with it more smoky air and a whisper of heat.

"How'n hell you fight a forest fire?" one man asked.

"Mostly with hope," another man said. "Hope the wind turns it back on itself, or hope it starts to rain. Today not much chance of either one."

When they got as far as they could go on the wagon, they were directed up the hill toward plumes of smoke.

"All you men with tools, come this way. The rest wait here." The man wore a red hat and was a fire boss. He had taken charge and everyone followed his orders. Spur was getting tired by the time they had climbed up a quarter of a mile to the fire.

Some places it looked like an inferno. Hundred-foot-tall trees standing untouched one moment, then a gushing tower of flame the loggers called "crowning" whipping in from another tree. In a moment the whole pitch filled fir needles and small branches exploded into flames and the very fire itself caused an updraft that surged the fire hotter and blew it to the next tree.

This crowning fire was impossible to fight, it was fifty, sixty feet off the ground.

The fire boss moved twenty men to a spot where small fires burned through the foot thick mulch on the forest floor. It ate at the humus and dry leaves and needles.

One man showed them what to do. Trench around the slow-moving ground flames. They used the shovels and grub hoes to dig down a foot through the mulch, throw it away from the fire and dig a two foot wide dirt trail around the creeping flames.

"Stop this part here and it won't have a chance to get to the heavy Irish Gorse and flame up again into the tops," the fire boss said. Then he ran on to instruct another twenty men.

Spur dug. After five minutes he had blisters on his hands but he tried not to notice them. He should have gloves. Too late. He dug on.

After an hour they saw some small success. This arm of the fire had been stopped. Men came in with axes and cut down brush overhanging the fire trail. Their trail met that of another crew and they cheered.

Spur realized he had been on the fire line less than two hours. He was soaked with sweat, had smears of black charcoal over his face and clothes, and his hair was filled with ashes.

"Down this way!" someone shouted. "We got a breakout."

Forty men charged along the side of the slope a quarter of a mile to where they saw new flames. High above, some of the flames were crowning and on the forest floor an inferno burned white hot, feeding on three-foot-thick fir logs and their sap, the volatile pitch that was like solid turpentine.

The fire boss looked at it, evaluating the fire, trying to figure out where they could work.

He took them a hundred feet in front of the slow-moving flames.

"Right here," he shouted. "Line up six feet apart. We're going to back fire here. I'll go along and set fire to the mulch and leaves and brush. Your job is to beat it back from coming toward you. Easy when it's just starting.''

He lit some fires. ''We want this to burn back and meet the fire coming this way, then it will burn itself out. It's a back fire.''

Then they all were too busy to talk. Spur dug a start of a fire trail before the burner got to him. He nodded at Spur, lit the mulch and brush in front of Spur's trail and moved on. Spur pounded some taller brush with his shovel to beat it down on the fire side of the line. Then the fire ate gradually back toward the rest of the raging fire a hundred feet away.

''This better work,'' someone said. ''I'm running out of energy.''

Spur moved down the line working on another section of fire trail, slashing down some brush that fell over the line.

''Down here, it's breaking out!'' somebody screamed.

Twenty men charged the area. They beat the flames with shovels, threw dirt on them, and fought down the six-foot-wide breakout of flames that had jumped the trail. They had to stop it here or it would make the whole back fire a useless exercise.

The fire boss came back shouting encouragement. ''Watch out!'' he bellowed suddenly. ''That snag is falling!''

A seventy-five-foot-tall snag, long dead and standing by will power alone, was caught in the flames up the hill and burned enough to be toppled by the wind. It came crashing down directly at the men on the backfire.

They had warning and scattered in time. The

burning snag crossed their fire line, extending twenty feet into the unburned forest.

"Get on it!" The fire boss yelled. "Trail around it and throw dirt on anything burning."

The men forgot their blisters and leaped to the emergency. In a half hour they had the new fire line built around the smoking snag.

The fire boss for that sector came back. "I need ten big men with shovels." He picked out the men including Spur and they jogged deeper into the woods, through a small canyon that hadn't burned and higher on the hill.

They soon came to a spot fire, one started when a burning branch was carried high in the air by a furious firestorm updraft and then blown ahead of the main fire to start a new blaze. These spots were the hardest part of a fire to fight. They could send the flames in a whole new direction and make worthless thousands of man-hours in trailing a fire.

The fire was less than twenty yards across, but was gaining. Already twenty men were fighting it, chopping down brush, throwing dirt, starting to trail it.

The men were all woods workers. Spur knew at once by their "tin" pants, heavy shirts and red hats. The pants were made of heavy course cloth and then soaked in water repellent until they were so stiff they would stand by themselves and hardly bend at the knee.

"Trail down here!" the fire boss shouted, and Spur and the other fresh men began to work. They got one side of it beaten down before it could get out of hand. Then the loggers cut down three small trees, felling them back into the fire, and in another two hours they had the spot put out.

Back at the main fire, Spur saw that the back fire had done its job on that section.

Another fire boss led them around a half mile to the other spur of the fire. Then suddenly, and with no warning, the wind changed. Fire burst toward them, surged along a small ridge cutting off their retreat that way.

The fire boss wiped his arm over his ash-spotted face. "Down the hill," he bellowed. "We'll have to outrun the damned thing."

They ran. A quarter of a mile down the hill they came to a marshy spot and went around it.

Suddenly the weather changed. A thick, wet fog billowed up the river canyon and swept up and over the hills. The fire fighters gave a cheer.

It was nearly four o'clock.

Spur lay on the soft forest floor beside a towering Douglas fir tree and sucked air into his lungs.

The fire boss came by and dropped beside them.

"Take a break," he said and grinned. "That fog is doing the job. The crowning is done, the hot spots are burning out. The wind blew the fire back on itself and all we have to do is trail this side and the other side and we'll have it beaten."

"Damned fog saved our asses," one man ventured.

"Never gonna swear at the fog again," another voice said.

A half hour later the men went back to the fire trail. Now the urgency was gone. They worked slower, digging out a trail the fire could not creep across in the night. There would be a patrol walking the trail all night and all day tomorrow.

About five-thirty the men gathered near the River Road and attacked a wagon load of sandwiches and coffee. Somebody said there were five hundred sandwiches on the wagon, but nobody counted.

Spur ate four of them and two apples and three cups of coffee. The fire boss ate with them, then told the men they were free to go back to town. There would be a new crew from the mill to work the fire lines that night.

There was no wagon to ride. The men walked back, talking about the fire. Reliving the falling snag. Marveling that the fog had come in.

"Without that fog the other side of the fire could have burned thirty miles to the coast," one man said. "That would have put two hundred loggers and mill workers out of work and begging on the streets."

"Hey, we did a good job," another voice said.

Most of them, including one Secret Service agent, were too tired to talk. One foot ahead of the other one. Spur looked at his hands. He had blisters on blisters. His hands wouldn't heal up for two weeks.

If he thought he was tired after the green chain work, he hadn't felt anything yet. The emotional response to the fire had been amazing. Nobody said, why me? Nobody asked to be paid. It was a community emergency and everyone ran to do his part.

Word came from group to group as they walked the two miles back to Astoria. One of the fire bosses had found where the fire started. There was a whole box of wooden matches at the spot, and the fragile remains of a dozen of the wooden matches that had been lit and left to burn.

Somebody had deliberately started the fire.

Spur growled. It was on land with timber leases to Johnson Lumber Company. The lease price was set and would be paid whether the timber was taken off or it was burned to the ground.

Another shot at the company. Now Spur was plain mad. He had been about ready to move on. Close out the Ihander case as an accidental death after a fight. He could pass on the vigilante situation. The Sheriff had it somewhat in hand with two of the men charged with attempted murder.

But now he was mad! He was going to find out for damn sure who was doing it and exactly why, and he was going to see that they were punished.

Back at the hotel he ordered a tub of hot water and took a long, burning hot bath, soaked for a half hour until the water cooled and then crawled into bed. Already he was getting stiff. He had some ointment that he put on his blisters. He hoped he didn't have to do any fast draws for a while.

Spur wondered how the Johnsons were. He had seen Lee twice during the day. He was on the fire line the way everyone else was, doing his part.

He grinned at the way Karen had tried to get him to make love to her last night. Had that only been 24 hours ago? She had been honest and straightforward and not embarrassed. But it was just not the right time. Not yet. Maybe later. He took no special pleasure in deflowering virgins.

Actually a virgin was usually not that enthusiastic and that good in bed. As with most artistic endeavors, making love took a lot of practice.

He thought of Karen, and then of Nancy. Now there was his kind of woman. He was sure that she liked making love as much as he did. He was going to ask her about that the next time.   .

For a moment he drifted to sleep and a huge, burning snag fell directly for him. He cried out and tried to move but he was frozen in place.

He sat up, his eyes wide, his ears still ringing with his own startled cry. He looked around at the room and the forest fire around the snag faded.

Damn dream, he decided, and lay back down. He wasn't going to get out of bed until at least noon tomorrow, he thought as he drifted off to sleep.

27

About six A.M. someone knocked on Spur's door.
He shouted for them to go away. The knock came
again, then again. Groggily, Sput got up and went to
the door. He peeked out, saw Nancy in a robe and
opened the door.

"You're a grouch this morning," she said. Then
her nose quivered. "Oh, you fought the fire yesterday
and you're beat and tired and singed."

Spur just looked at her frowning, half awake.

"Good, we can sleep until noon," she said.

Nancy led him back to the bed and he dropped on
it. She let her robe fall to the floor and then got in and
lay naked beside him under the light sheet.

"Good morning and good night," Spur said. He
kissed her, petted her breasts for a moment, then
dropped off to sleep before she could attack him.

"You are exhausted," Nancy said.

She snuggled down beside him, put her hand down
on his genitals and went back to sleep herself. That

was a luxury she could indulge in since she worked nights. She got to sleep in mornings.

They woke up about eleven o'clock. Spur moaned as he moved.

"You want me to get dressed and bring us some breakfast?" Nancy asked.

"It would be more interesting if you didn't get dressed and brought us some breakfast."

She hit him in the shoulder.

He shook his head. "Not hungry, don't even feel sexy, and looking at your luscious little body all naked and ready, that is a marvel. I'm not sleepy either but I don't want to move an inch in any direction."

"You're crazy is what you are. You just lay there and I'll ravish your body."

"You can try, but I won't ravish. I couldn't get it up for the Queen of Sheeba or even that cute little fourteen year old sexy Juliet."

"You are mad, mad, mad." She shrugged. "So tell me about the fire."

"It was like a war. Our side was the men, the other side was the fire. We fought all day and nobody won. Then the wind shifted and the fog rolled in and the weather won the war for us after all."

"Helped you win. Somebody said there were 300 men up there on the fire lines. I could have walked naked down Concomly Street and nobody would have touched me. I didn't see a man on the street all day yesterday, except for the deputy sheriffs with shotguns patrolling the streets."

"The fire was awesome. I've never seen anything like it. It was so damn powerful. It went where it wanted to and burned anything that got in the way.

Everything from the tender little green ferns just coming up to the giant fir trees.''

"Like a war?"

"Like war."

"You were in the war? Tell me about the war. Nobody will ever tell me what it was like. The anger, the blood, the death. Tell me."

"You don't want to know."

"I do. How else can I understand it? Please tell me." She kissed his cheek. "Pretty please?"

"It takes me back. I'm not sure I want to go. The Wilderness was bad enough. But most of that was in thick woods and brush. At the Crossroads we were in the open and chopped to pieces. I was with General Winfield Scott Hancock on the turnpike out of Fredericksburg.

"We were supposed to cover the retreat. But soon our corps was squeezed together by the Rebels. We were pressed so close that we had one division backed up against another division only a few hundred yards apart.

"The Rebel cannon were firing from five hundred yards, so close they couldn't miss. And they were using canister shot, nails, ball, wire, chunks of railroad ties, anything that could stuff down the muzzles of their guns.

"I saw two horses and their officers suffer a direct hit. The animals were blown into shreds and both officers had their legs blown away. They died in agony five minutes later from loss of blood.

"Everywhere men and horses were going down. Just at the start of the firing, a Lieutenant Stevens rolled into the open space between our defensive lines with his 5th Maine Artillery Battery. They fired at the

Rebel gunners at once.

"Half of the Rebels must have turned their guns on the new target. They sent over exploding shells on the battery and then hit them with canister shredding men and animals. They also fired solid shot to hit just short and riocohet off the hard ground and slam into the battery men at waist height.

"Horses went down screaming. Half the caissons blew up. The limber chests were blown apart. Stevens told half of his gunners to fire at Rebel infantry and half at the Rebel artillery. Within minutes Stevens and every officer in the battery was dead or grievously wounded.

"My infantry company was dug in at the side but we could do nothing for the battery but send some fire at the artillery that was cutting them to pieces.

"I saw one man hobble out of the battery with one leg, the other shot off above his knee. He clubbed along using a rifle as a crutch, but got only a dozen yards from his gun when canister shot caught him and his body disintegrated. There wasn't enough left of him to identify as a human being."

Spur looked down at her. Tears had welled in Nancy's eyes and rolled silently down her cheeks.

"You don't want to hear any more of war. That was what some of it was like, the worst of it. You don't want to hear." He kissed her cheek and put his arms around her and let her finish her cry.

Later she had wiped her eyes and blown her nose and looked up at him. "Weren't there any good times at all? There must have been some women."

"The good times were when it wasn't quite so bad, like simply camping out in a tent when it rained for six days in a row and everything was wet. Or marching through the mud in Virginia for two days hardly able to get one foot out of the muck. The good part was that nobody was shooting you, wounding you, killing your friends.''

"No girls?''

"A few here and there. A man has needs. But nothing as sweet and with the appetites that you have. How come you like sexing so much?''

"I don't know. I never tried to figure it out. I've liked boys since I was thirteen and got this itch and the fourteen-year-old boy who lived in back of us scratched it for me.

"What a summer that was. I'd slip away and swing in our back yard and he'd come watch me from some bushes in his back yard. Nobody could see him from either house, except me swinging. He'd pull down his pants and get his whanger all hard and then show it to me.

"The first time I ran into the house. The next time he showed his prick to me, I stayed there and watched. The third day I went into the bushes with him and we explored each other all over. I liked his hands on me. He got all worked up and climaxed. I'd never seen that happen before. I was fascinated and made him do it three times.

"After a week of messing aorund we figured out where his prick should go. After that we played in the back yard almost every day all summer until he moved away in August. The day before his family moved he rammed me six times. I was sore for a week.''

"You've loved it all ever since,'' Spur said.

"I have. Tell me about the first girl you ever poked it in.''

"First I have some business with P.X. He knows more about everybody in this town than anyone else. I'll meet you for supper at Delmonico's. All right?"

He stood, then bent and kissed both her breasts. She sat up pouting. "If you have to go."

Spur dressed, kissed her nose and went to the door. She still lay on the bed nude.

"You sing in that costume tonight and you'll bring down the house. The tips should be terrific."

She stuck her tongue out at him.

Spur went out and closed the door.

Five minutes later P.X. poured Spur a cup of coffee and laughed.

"Of course I have some ideas who the other five vigilantes are, but I don't want to get burned out."

"They might not be so active now that two of them are in jail."

"Were in jail. They made bond and are out. They might slow down, then again they may strike out of desperation. Who do you think the other four are?"

"No idea at all. I thought there would be some merchants, but I'd guess not more than two, maybe three. We already have two of the merchants."

"What about Lee Johnson?"

"Not a chance. No."

"The sheriff, Mr. Vinson?"

"Be a good inside spot for them to have a man, but I don't think so. One of the deputies could be a possibility, just thinking from an organizational point of view."

"Fishing boat people, or from the big canneries?" P.X. asked.

"Maybe, what do you think?"

"Not likely they would be working hand in glove with these two we know about. The fishermen stick to themselves. They aren't invited to the best parties that the merchants throw."

"So I'm back to nowhere."

"You don't seem worried about Ihander's killing any more. Why is that?"

"I've decided that his death was the result of his picking a fight with three men. Not too bright. The death was not premeditated or the part of any plot. A lucky punch or a bad fall, however you read it. Poikela used bad judgment and carried the fight too far. He killed Ihander but it was an accident."

"So you can close up shop and get back to Washington."

"I work out of St. Louis, but I'm almost never there. but, no. I'm not ready to leave. Johnson is cutting timber on government land. So I have a stake in his fight for his mill. Then too, I should clean up the vigilante mess."

The wooden screen door swung open and closed softly. Spur turned and saw the district attorney, Josiah Dangerfield, coming in the leather shop.

"Well, our district attorney," P.X. said. "When are you getting that new horse so I can make you a silver trimmed saddle?"

"Soon as the county raises my pay. I can't even afford one of your silver buckles." He sat in the second full sized chair in the shop.

"P.X., I know you've got your ear to the ground. What in hell have you been hearing now that two of the vigilantes evidently have been caught red-handed?''

"Hearing almost nothing. The hottest topic around town is wanting to know who the bastard was who started the fire.''

"We're working on that. But a box of kitchen matches is hard to trace. I've got two or three in my house, I'm sure you do too.''

"No other evidence?'' Spur asked. "No horse tracks, boot prints, anything?''

"Fact is, we did find some horse tracks coming into the spot and leaving. Both went to the River Road, but trying to track anything on there with all the traffic is impossible. We think the rider came off the river, set the fire and then rode back toward town. Not sure, mind you.''

"I think our spike driver is a good suspect,'' Spur said.

"I do too, Mr. McCoy. But until one of us gets some evidence that will stand up in Circuit Court, I can't even tell him to stay in town.''

"You could arrest Martin and make him think you have more evidence than you do,'' P.X. said. "Wouldn't that scare him a little bit.''

Spur chuckled. "You really think lawmen do that sort of thing, Percival?''

"Damn right they do,'' P.X. said. "We all know it. Just depends how it's done, who is being scared.''

Dangerfield pulled a piece of paper from his pocket. "Sheriff asked me to check on a man in Portland. He said McCoy asked him to look at the man. Tom Monroe is not a known name in Portland. They do have another name that matches the description of Tom Monroe.

"Then he called himself Archibald Dommington. Claimed to be a mining engineer from Colorado, and he was working a fake gold mining stock swindle. He got out just before they closed in and if he is still here the sheriff in Multnomah County would dearly like to know about it."

"That figures. About Monroe's style. So, being an officer of the court and a law enforcement man, I'd guess you shot a letter back to Portland police at once."

Dangerfield shook his head. "Afraid not. If he is tied in with anything crooked going on in Astoria, I want to nail his fat little ass to the wall right here and prosecute him to the fullest extent of the law. I've heard that you two think he might be tied in some way with the trouble that the Johnsons are having.

"If I can tie him to starting that fire yesterday, I'll have him right where I want him."

"Makes sense," Spur said. "You know that Marty Johnson is a frequent visitor to Monroe's little office."

"We are aware of that."

"Good. You seem to be on top of this thing. Any hope for any arrests soon?"

"Evidence, Mr. McCoy. I shouldn't have to tell you that. We have enough on Marty to get him maybe three months in county jail plus restitution. For lack of more evidence, that's it."

"Josiah, how is the vigilante prosecution coming along?" P.X. asked.

"That could be a problem. We have only two witnesses to the actual shootings, and they both are interested parties. Could be a tough one to prosecute."

"Both the witnesses Chinese?"

"Matter of fact, yes."

"Any progress on identifying the other four members of the vigilantes?" P.X. asked.

"Unfortunately, no. I've questioned both separately. Both men have posted an appearance bond and are out of jail."

Spur finished his coffee. "Well, I have some work to do. I better dig up some evidence that will stand up in court."

Dangerfield nodded.

P.X. grinned and waved Spur out the door.

28

It was just before two that afternoon when Spur walked into the Johnson Lumber Company mill office. He didn't see Karen at her usual desk. One of the mill hands looked up and recognized him. He nodded.

"Mr. Johnson is busy right now with the sheriff," the hand said.

Lee's door wasn't closed.

"Well, what the hell else are you doing?" Lee's angry voice demanded.

Spur wandered over near the door and looked in. Lee paced the office. He saw Spur. "McCoy, get in here, we've got a problem."

Spur walked in.

"I'll take care of it," Sheriff Vinson said.

"You've had over an hour and got nowhere." He looked at Spur. "McCoy, somebody kidnapped Karen. Probably it's Orville. Sheriff is getting nowhere."

"When was she last seen?" Spur asked. His gut turned over and he felt a pain that surprised him.

"She drove home at noon to get some things and never came back."

"Thanks," Spur said. "You have a horse I can borrow?"

Lee pointed to one at the hitching rail outside. "It's got a rifle in the boot and twenty rounds in the saddlebag. I was getting ready to go hunting."

"I'll be back," Spur said. He ran out of the office, mounted the mare and turned her up the hill toward the big Johnson home. When he rode up a few minutes later, Cilla sat on the front steps crying.

"Mr. McCoy, I never heard a thing. Karen had a bite to eat with me, and took some things back to the office she forgot this morning. Then a few minutes after she left I looked out and her little black buggy was still parked behind the house. I went out and she wasn't there.

"That's when I remembered seeing two saddle horses near her buggy. But they were gone then."

Spur had her show him exactly where she had seen the horses. They had been tied at the back of the buggy and would be partly obscured from the house.

Spur bent and checked the ground. Two sets of prints, all right, and some horse droppings. They had stood there a while. He found heavy boot prints, and then saw the lighter, smaller outline in the dust of small shoes.

"Tell Lee they're on two horses and I have a trail. I'll be back when I get here."

Spur led his horse as he followed the tracks the first few rods on foot. They headed up hill into the timber. Once under the cover of the big trees, the trail was easier to follow. Small ferns poking up out of the forest floor had been smashed and broken. The horses walked side by side, as if someone were leading the horse but keeping to him.

Karen's hands might be tied to the saddle horn. Soon the horses made one track. The kidnapper had moved ahead to find the trail and led the other horse on a line.

Spur followed the simple trail up to the top of the low hill, across a saddle to another ridge and along the side of the slope. They were moving along the same direction the River Road went, but much higher into the mountains.

Twice the trail cut across well worn tracks that showed wagon ruts extending deeper into the hills of the coast range of mountains. Spur went up each track aways, found no fresh hoof prints and picked up the trail again on the other side.

At first he couldn't figure it out. There was no attempt made to conceal the trail, no back tracking, no circling, just a move straight ahead. Didn't the kidnapper think anyone would find the trail and follow it?''

Spur decided here in the woods country tracking and trails and signs were not that important. The man might not even know that he could be tracked through the woods this way.

If he had moved down to the River Road, then it might have been impossible to trail him.

An hour later, Spur looked at the sun. Plenty of daylight left. He checked the trail. They still worked along the side of the range of hills. The man was not searching, he had his target in mind and was going to it. They had been well south of the forest fire, but

Spur had smelled the charcoal tinge to the air as they passed.

Not that it was far behind them. They swept downhill for a quarter of a mile and came to what looked like a small logging road that had been used years before. Spur made sure before he turned in. The trail followed into the road and along a small creek that wound up the little valley.

Spur got off and tied his horse, then took the rifle and his six-gun and started up the trail on foot. He checked the rifle, put a round in the chamber, and put the box of shells in his back pocket.

The trail of the two mounts was plain. They were walking, nothing seemed unusual. One came behind the other.

The track lasted for almost a half a mile winding upward slowly along the small stream. Twice they crossed it for easier riding.

Spur sniffed the air. Smoke. He had been out of Astoria long enough for his nose to clean itself. The acrid smell of the fir wood smoke came sharply to him now. He paused on the trail and watched the small turn ahead.

McCoy slid into the heavier brush and advanced slowly to the bend in the trail.

Two hundred yards ahead he saw an old cabin. It had been there a long time. A new stovepipe extended from the chimney. One of the walls sagged inward but still held. Heavy moss had grown on the shakes that formed the roof. It was a frame building but at least 40 or 50 years old, Spur decided.

He worked through the edge of the hill in the thick timber as he moved around the cabin. Two horses stood tied to a hitching rail at the side. The hitching rail was new; freshly peeled poles had been used and probably nailed together on the ends where the uprights had been driven into the ground.

Smoke came freely from the chimney now. At the side of the front door, Spur saw a stack of split wood. The split wood showed bright and new, not yellowed from sitting in the sun.

Someone had planned this kidnapping. It could be Orville. The man seemed to figure out his moves ahead. Orville had killed once already; he had nothing to lose by doing it again.

Spur moved around the cabin to inspect all four sides, then returned to the back. There was no window there. The brush grew to within fifteen feet of the back of the cabin. A rough pole ladder leaned against the back of the shack. It could have been used to put up the new stove pipe so the chimney wouldn't smoke inside.

Spur considered the ladder and the smoke coming from the pipe. He used his knife and cut four inch-thick fir boughs off a tree and carried them with him. He moved cautiously, saw no one and went up the ladder without a sound. On the roof he stepped with care. The old shakes were rotted and crumbling in places. He hoped sheeting had been used over the rafters.

The roof held. He moved a slow step at a time so he would make no noise as he walked the ridgeline to the stovepipe.

Once there Spur put his six-gun in leather and folded the ends of the fir boughs back a foot and pushed the folded end into the stovepipe. He got three of them in before the smoke stopped seeping through. Then he drew his six-gun and crouched beside the chimney.

Quickly he heard swearing from the cabin below. A door slammed and a moment later Orville ran out of the cabin and looked at the roof. He ducked in the same motion as soon as he saw Spur. The shot blasted from Spur's weapon, but too late as Orville ran back inside the cabin.

Spur rushed to the edge of the roof and jumped the six feet to the ground, rolled and charged the front door. He stood just at the side of the door and heard a shot as a slug rammed through the air head high.

"Come on out, Orville. You're caught. It's all over. The sheriff is here with six men. You're surrounded."

Spur hoped the bluff would work. He risked a look inside the cabin. Orville stood across the room. He had a lamp burning and smoke was filtering out of the stove pipe and forming a strata at the ceiling.

Orville held his left arm around Karen's throat. She was buff naked, her face frozen in a glare of hatred.

"Put your weapon down where I can see it, lawman, and I might just let you live. You move a step and this little doxy gets a slug right through her head. You hear me, lawman?"

"I hear you, Orville. Course, you kill her, you lose your protection. Then no way but I got to kill you. You know I can do it. Only person you ever killed was your wife."

"That was accidental."

"Not a chance, Orville. That's why the sheriff is looking for you. You killed Ida so you could court Karen. Isn't that so?"

"No. Ida died in the river. Boat tipped over."

Spur was silent, watching, waiting his chance.

"Stop trying to confuse me. Throw down your gun or Karen is dead."

"It's a bluff, Orville. That six-gun isn't even loaded. Besides, it's on safety."

"Safety? Is not. I pushed off the safety."

Confusion shook Orville for a moment. He didn't know much about guns. He looked down at the weapon, lifted it away from Karen and looked closer.

Karen bit his arm. Blood spurted and he jerked his arm away from her. Karen darted toward the door, blocking any shot Spur had on the kidnapper.

Karen hurried out and trembled against the side of the wall.

Spur moved toward the doorway again so he could see inside.

Glass shattered as Spur looked in. All he saw was Orville's back as he jumped through the window and was gone.

Spur raced around the cabin but Orville had vanished into the thick brush. Spur ran to the closest point and stopped and listened.

He heard brush crashing ahead of him. He ran in twenty feet and listened again. More brush noises, but this time moving back toward the clearing. Spur moved to the edge of the clearing and waited a few minutes. He saw Orville part some brush and look out.

Orville took one step into the open and paused looking around.

"Hold it right there or you're a dead man," Spur thundered.

Orville turned and fired. Spur shot a fraction of a second sooner. Orville's round buried itself in the dirt. Spur's round hit Orville in the right shoulder, spinning his weapon away. He turned and raced back into the woods.

Spur ran after him. This time Orville kept running. Sometimes Spur saw him through the thinning timber. Sometimes he was only a sound ahead.

Gradually he slowed. Spur had to stop to listen to be sure he was still on the right track. At last they came to a broad meadow and Orville got halfway across before he fell to his knees and began crawling.

Spur put a round over his head, but he evidently didn't hear the shot.

Spur jogged until he caught the man, then stood directly in front of him.

"It's all over, Orville. Time to go back to Astoria."

He charged. Spur kicked him in the side of the head and he went down screaming in rage.

This time Orville stood up before he ran at Spur. The Secret Service Agent sidestepped and slammed the side of his .45 revolver against the side of Orville's head as he rushed past.

Orville rolled in the meadow and lay there. Spur approached him with caution. He lay on his stomach, a welt of blood showing on the side of his face.

Spur pushed his toe against the downed man's side.

Suddenly, Orville burst up from the ground swinging a heavy stick he had been lying on. The wood whacked Spur on the shoulder and glanced off hitting the side of his head. It jolted Spur so he fell to his knees. Orville lifted the heavy stick again, victory in his eyes as he started to swing it at Spur's head.

Spur's .45 fired twice.

The heavy stick fell to the ground. Orville grabbed his belly, surprise on his face as he dropped to his knees, then forward on his side.

Spur shook his head to clear the last of the fluttering black curtains from it. He blinked, still on his knees, his Colt still aimed at Orville.

"My God, you shot me!" Orville said. "Bastard, you shot me!"

Spur shook his head once more and the world came back clear and plain. He moved up beside Orville and rolled him on his back. His eyes were open and angry.

"Didn't have to kill me."

"You were about to kill me, Orville. Rules say when that happens, you're fair game."

"Christ, but it hurts. Why does it hurt so damn much?"

"What about Ida? Do you think she hurt at all before she died?"

"Yeah, Ida. Bitch of a woman. Always nagging. Now that Karen, she is something!" Orville shivered, then gasped and cried out as the burning pain bored through his belly.

"Oh, Christ!" He weathered it. "Karen. Yeah. She kept me going. You know I used to sneak up there by her house and watch her get ready for bed. Undressed and . . . and all. She sure does have great tits. Doesn't she? You seen them."

He shook again and brayed at the sharpness of the pain in his gut. Spur had seen gut-shot men live about an hour. Orville had two .45 slugs through his belly. He wouldn't last another ten minutes.

"Then you did tip over the boat so you could court Karen?"

"Hell, yes! Wouldn't you? Look at Ida, then at the sweetheart that Karen is. I just had to have her, had to get my hands on her tits, had to get my dick inside her. Know what I mean. I had to get her."

287

"So you were there watching for Karen at her bedroom window when you grabbed that fire starter?"

"Yeah. Shit, I got him cold. Would have had it made at the company if I hadn't pawed at Karen's tits that way. I really messed up there."

"And now? Why did you kidnap her?"

"Hell, only way I could have her. Had to have her just once. Wouldn't have hurt her, you know that. I would've poked her about three times and then I was going to Portland. Get a new start. Oh, damn!" He lifted off the ground, almost sat up, then dropped back.

He wiped tears from his eyes. "How much longer you figure that I got?"

"An hour or more."

"Not so. Maybe ten minutes. Damn, but that hurts!"

"Anything else you want to talk about?"

"Tell Karen I'm sorry. I loved her. Really I did. Just wasn't my time."

"You have anything to do with the accidents, the damage around the mill or the rafts?"

"Hell, no. Marty did all of that. Or hired it done. He asked me I want to do anything. I beat the piss out of him. Hell, Johnson Lumber been good to me. Damn good!"

Five minutes later he died.

Spur slung the man over his shoulder and carried him the half a mile back to the cabin. He found Karen where he had left her beside the outside door. She hadn't put on her clothes.

He took her inside and helped her into her clothes. She stared straight ahead, eyes not blinking, not saying a word.

He tied Orville across the saddle of one horse, fastening his hands and ankles together under the horse's belly. Then lifted Karen into the saddle.

"Karen, can you ride? Will you be all right."

Her eyes moved for a moment and she looked at him, then away. He led her horse with the second one tied onto her saddle behind. When he came down the trail to his horse, Spur mounted and rode beside Karen all the way along the River Road to the outskirts of town. Spur left the horse with the body on tied in a clump of brush and took Karen home.

Cilla met him at the door.

"Thank God she's safe!" Cilla said.

"She's scared or in shock or something. Be gentle with her."

Spur rode back to pick up the horse with the dead body and brought it back to town, then tied up outside the courthouse. Spur frowned. Now he had another damn form to fill out.

29

Lee found Spur in the Oregon Saloon. He'd had a few beers by that time and had just lost five dollars at poker. Spur folded and left the game. Lee bought beers and they sat at a table at the side of the room.

"You always sit with your back to the wall," Lee asked with a grin.

"Yep. A good way to stay alive. I've had a man or two try to gun me down in the past. Every time I put some outlaw in jail or in boot hill, there's another man or his kin who'll want to even the score with me."

"I'll be glad to side you any time," Lee said. He held out his hand. "I can't thank you enough for what you did for Karen. I don't know the whole story. Karen isn't talking yet. Just sits by the fire like she's cold. Wants coffee all the time."

Spur told him what he found when he got to the cabin. "I can't be sure that Orville hadn't already violated her, but I don't think so. I told Karen he didn't. I told Cilla he didn't. But to you I've got to say that I can't be sure. Orville didn't say one way or the other."

"We'll assume that nothing happened. You brought her back to us, we're all thankful for that."

"Orville admitted that he killed Ida, so the sheriff can clear up that case."

"Good. We had him figured right on that. Karen doesn't have to know why he killed his wife."

"I'll try to make the point that it had nothing to do with her."

"Good, that's worried me some. On the fire, we didn't come out so bad. It might have cost the company a bucketful of money. Lost trees. But I've got a theory that just because a fir tree is burned clean of branches and killed, that doesn't mean the tree is hurt as a saw log.

"I've sawed down dead snags that were rock solid in a three foot log. Why wouldn't a just killed healthy tree stay good for a year or two? In two or three days we're going to fall a dozen of those old growth fir that were burned clean of branches. We'll skid them down to the river with oxen and make up a special raft and float them down and saw them. I got a feeling that lumber will look exactly like the rest of it we cut."

"So the loss will be the younger trees coming up, but they belong to the land owner, not you the leasee."

"Right."

They finished their beers and Spur signalled the barkeep to bring them two more. He waved Spur to the bar. Spur went over and got them, paid for them and brought them back.

"You ever hear Nancy sing?" Spur asked.

Lee said he hadn't.

"Like an angel. Stay for her show tonight. I could use the company. If I talk I won't drink so much."

Lee nodded. "I've never killed a man up close. Did some long range in the war, but it isn't the same, I'd bet."

"You'd win," Spur said. "Even when you know you have to kill him or you're going to get your head bashed in, it isn't any easier."

"Kill or be killed," Lee said. "Works at the moment. Don't help the memory any."

Later on, Nancy sang, Lee was impressed, and left for home before she came out after her show.

That night Spur and Nancy sat in his room staring at each other. "You're different tonight," Nancy said. "You want to talk about it?"

"No. I just want to go to bed and put my arm around your shoulder and your head on my chest and go to sleep. You know that: '. . . sleep that knits up the raveled sleeve of care . . .' "

"*Macbeth*. . . ."

"No, *Hamlet* . . . whichever."

"Yes, my lord."

They went to sleep that way.

Spur remembered the last thing he thought of. Sometimes it was harder to kill a man than other times. He couldn't understand that.

In the morning he had a big breakfast at Delmonico's, then went directly to the mill office. Lee was there. A young man sat in Karen's chair.

Lee saw Spur come in and poured him a cup of coffee.

"She's better this morning. Not normal yet. She won't talk about what happened. It might be good if you would stop by and see her later on this morning.

292

This office will crash to a stop without her around here. I told her that, and got only a slight smile from her."

"Any other problems?"

"Nothing so far. We have every man in the place on the watch for strangers, anyone doing something wrong. Our production has even picked up. If we could just nail down who is behind all of this trouble."

"I think I know," Spur said. "The trouble is I can't prove it. I can't move without proof."

"Who do you suspect?"

"Tom Monroe. He's the rotten apple. But how to prove it is another matter. The Sheriff can't do a thing either. So we wait and watch and hope he makes a wrong move soon."

"Which doesn't help me a damn bit."

"True, but you're tough." Spur finished his coffee and stood. "Going to take a little walk to Upper Town. Pay a call on a pretty girl. Any messages?"

"No. Just be cautious. I've never seen Karen so . . . so fragile. She hasn't burst into tears, but I get the idea that she could at any minute."

"By now she may be better. I'll do what I can."

Spur took his time walking from the mill around Scow Bay and over to Upper Town. He went up to the front door and knocked, and Cilla answered.

Her smile brightened. "Mr. McCoy. I'm glad you could come. I've been doing all of the talking since breakfast and I'm running out of things to say. She just sits by the window and looks out over the river and drinks coffee."

She led Spur into the parlor with three big windows that looked out at the river and Washington State across the way. Karen sat in a rocker with a magazine in her lap. She watched the far shore.

"Karen, guess who has come to visit you?" Cilla said. Then she nodded at Spur and walked away.

Karen turned and looked at Spur. He thought he saw a trace of movement in her passive face, but he wasn't sure.

"May I come in?"

She waved a hand at a chair across the room. He sat and could see her face now. It was pale, almost frozen.

"We have news about the fire. Lee said that even though the fire burned some of the timber, most of the saw logs are not ruined, and most hardly damaged at all." He went on to explain to her what Lee had said.

"Isn't that good news, Karen?"

She nodded and looked at him. "Yes, good news," she said softly. Then she looked back at the river.

Spur was encouraged by the words.

"I talked with Lee this morning. He said the whole mill office operation has clanked to a stop. Without you there to keep things going it's a royal mess."

A smile touched her mouth, then faded. "Sounds like Lee."

Spur moved his chair forward until he sat with his knees a foot from hers.

"Hey, Karen, this is Spur, remember? I'm one of the good guys. I know you had a shock yesterday." He reached for her hands, caught them and held them.

"Karen, look at me," he said sharply.

She looked up. "Yes, I know. Not all men are like Orville Ames. Most men are kind and gentle, considerate. But still. . . .''

"Still some of them aren't. True. That hasn't changed since yesterday, has it? Didn't you know that before yesterday? Karen, answer me.''

She blinked back tears, then nodded. "Yes, I knew that before."

"Karen, you're almost the same as you were yesterday. Today you're a little smarter, a little wiser. Today you have one more bad memory. That's all it is, a bad memory. Don't dwell on it. Live over it."

She looked at him quickly.

"Only a bad memory." She nodded to herself. "Yes, I like that."

"Karen, he didn't hurt you, nothing happened. He tore off your clothes, but nothing else. I got there before he could hurt you."

"Yes, yes, I know. Still . . .''

"Only a bad memory. We all have bad memories. Last night I had trouble sleeping. I had to kill Orville when he almost killed me. Have you ever killed another human being, Karen?''

"Oh, no!"

"That is one of my bad memories. One I have to live over."

Karen frowned. "I'm sorry." She seemed to relax a little. Her shoulders eased, her chin came down just a little, she leaned forward in the chair instead of sitting ramrod straight.

"I . . . I didn't think how you felt. I knew he was dead. I just . . . you know. I felt sorry for myself."

Spur laughed and she looked at him sharply.

"I'm sorry to laugh, but what do you have to be sorry about? You're young, you're beautiful, you have work where you're needed and which you're good at. You are part of a vital growing lumbering firm. You have your entire life to look forward to. You have a whole host of things to be thankful for.''

She watched him, frowned a moment, then lifted her brows. ''Yes, you're right. I'm trying to believe all of that.''

''Are you embarrassed because I helped you dress?''

''Yes, a little. I don't remember all of it. I know he took my clothes off and felt me, and then he kept yelling at me, but before he could do anything you came. Then later I bit him on the arm and ran away, and then I remember riding home. So you must have dressed me. Yes, I'm embarrassed by it.''

''Good,'' Spur said standing up. His reaction surprised her.

She stood up frowning. ''Why do you say that?''

''Because it's natural and normal for you to be a little embarrassed. Nothing to worry about. Oh, Orville did admit that he tipped the boat over on purpose. He and his wife hadn't been geting along for some time. So the sheriff can clear that up, now.''

''Then he didn't do it. . . .'' She stopped.

''He hated his wife. So he took her fishing twice a day while the salmon were running to establish a pattern, then the last day he tipped the boat over knowing she couldn't swim. You didn't have anything to do with it.''

''Oh, good.''

She looked at him and smiled. ''Goodness, my manners. Would you like some coffee or a cup of tea? I don't know why Cilla didn't offer you something. Maybe a small brandy? We have some around somewhere.''

Spur smiled. "This is the biggest coffee drinking town in the country. I've had four cups already. No coffee, thank you."

"Oh. I guess we do drink a lot of coffee." She turned. "I know, we had some little cakes, very good. And some lemonade, we got some fresh lemons. Yes. Don't move, I'll be right back."

Spur hated lemonade, and most little cakes tasted like sawdust, but he would relish them today. She had broken out of her self-imposed shell, if even just a little. It had been a good visit, if nothing else came from it.

When she hurried back, Karen had a silver tray with small cakes on it, and Cilla carried a pitcher of lemonade and glasses. Cilla smiled and nodded at him, thanking him silently.

For a moment it was quiet, then all three began to talk at once and they laughed. Spur pointed to the ladies, and Karen nodded at her sister-in-law.

A half hour later the cakes were gone and the lemonade made with lots of sugar was all gone, and Spur begged off, saying that he had to get back down to the mill.

Karen walked him to the front door and held out her hand shaking his.

"Thanks for coming to my rescue. I felt all morning like one of those logs that gets away from the raft and floats down the Columbia. I was being swept out to sea. Tell Lee that I won't be back to work tomorrow, but I will be the next day. I need to do some sewing I've been putting off, a new dress and a blouse."

Spur didn't return to the mill when he left the ladies. He went to the livery, rented a horse and saddle and took a ride. He wanted to ride out to the end of Point Adams where the Columbia at last dumps into the sea. But there was a lot of water between him and the point. He'd have to backtrack and go around another bay where a river came in.

He had heard that Fort Stevens sits on a high point protecting the bay. The fort was built in 1863 by the Union forces in case the British might side with the Confederates and send warships up the Columbia. They never did. Maybe he could see it later.

Instead, Spur rode to the last point of land in Astoria toward the downstream end, then turned and rode back slowly, watching the mighty river, wondering how he could resolve this case without simply giving up.

He searched his mind for new ways to pressure Tom Monroe without actually threatening him some way, but he could think of little. He could at least consider some kind of pressure against the man. Exactly what, Spur didn't know.

Something that would threaten to expose him and force his hand to make a grand play and hopefully a major blunder so the guilt could be assessed and placed legally.

Now with this new more interesting direction he settled down to thinking up some devilment to spring on Tom Monroe.

30

Sam Lincoln looked up as the man with a sheriff's star on his shirt rode up on a good-looking sorrel and stopped. Sam had been camped on the edge of town in a little patch of woods for two days now. He had been around town looking for work.

Sheriff Vinson spotted Sam quickly because Sam was the only Negro anywhere around Astoria. The lawman stepped down from his animal and let her graze.

"Afternoon. You must be Sam Lincoln. Hear you're looking for work."

"Yes suh, that's surely right. I'm a good worker. Yard, garden, I kin paint and clean, too."

"I'm sure you can, Sam."

The sheriff looked around. He saw a blanket roll, a pillowcase for a carpet bag, a small fire ring for cooking and a lean-to made of cut off fir boughs. On a tripod of sticks sat a small wash basin.

Sam's kinky black hair was short and clean, his shirt was clean as well.

"Sam, might be easier for you to find work in the cannery. A new one just opened and they need help. You go down to Consolidated Canning at the foot of Cass Street and tell them I sent you. Good pay, steady work. Right now is the peak of the salmon run and they need every hand they can find."

"Sheriff, I thank you, suh. Ain't ever place I get me such a good welcome. I'll be getting myself right down there."

Sheriff Vinson smiled and rode away. He'd heard some complaints about the Negro man, but as far as the law was concerned he had every right to be in town. Unless he broke the law, Sam Lincoln was welcome in Astoria.

The sheriff had been gone barely five minutes, and Sam had most of his gear picked up and packed away, when five black-hooded horsemen rode out of the brush and surrounded him.

"What you doing here, boy?" one man asked.

Sam was scared but he didn't let it show. He picked up his pillow case of belongings and held it tight. "I just talked with the sheriff, and he told me to go down to the cannery. I'm looking for a job."

"We got no jobs for your kind in this town," another voice rasped.

"Christ, we ain't got all day!" a third man snapped. "It's daylight out case you gents didn't notice."

"Don't want your kind here, black man, not at all. You best move out now and walk back up to Portland where there's a few like you."

Sam frowned, then pulled a knife from the side of his torn pants.

"No, suh. Don't aim to do that. Sheriff said I kin

stay, so I kin stay. Going to get me a job down on Cass Street.''

One hooded man slid off his horse, lit lightly and flashed a blade of his own.

"Let's see if you can use that steel, nigger!''

The hooded man was handicapped by the lack of clear vision, and when he lunged the Negro stepped back, tripped him and sliced his arm as the vigilante fell hard to the ground. He was up in a second, furious.

"You cut me!'' He charged forward again, feinted to the left, then the right, and when the Negro had committed to defend the last feint, the man moved in the first direction and drove his knife deeply into the black man's side.

Sam went down without a word. The blade slipped from Sam's hand and the hooded vigilante kicked him in the other side.

"The rope,'' the tallest of the men said. "I didn't want it to come to this, but now it's the only way.''

Sam's hands were roughly tied behind his back.

"Got no reason to do this. No reason at all. Sheriff done say I could stay.''

"Shut up, nigger. Got to learn to stay in your place.''

Two men hoisted Sam to the back of one of the horses, sat him facing backwards just behind the saddle. The rope had been thrown over a limb on a big fir tree and tied off. It was too close to the trunk but would work.

One man rode up and put the noose over Sam's head and pulled it tight, placing the knot at the exact spot alongside his right cheek.

The five vigilantes watched Sam a moment.

"Do it!" Josiah Dangerfield said. The man on the horse that also held Sam spurred his mount forward and Sam slid off the rump and dropped only a foot before the rope tightened.

The five riders stared at Sam. His neck had not broken. The rope cut across his throat shutting off his breathing.

"Take a couple of minutes," one of the men said.

"Should have had more slack."

"He wasn't as heavy as that other guy."

Sam kicked and thrashed. He was still alive! He had to get out of this. His eyes rolled as he stared at the men. Then Sam realized he couldn't breathe. He gagged and twisted and kicked, then he made gurgling noises.

Slowly Sam's eyes closed as he passed out from lack of oxygen.

A six-gun barked in the silence. The vigilantes looked up to a horseman charging toward them.

"We got to get out of here!" one of the vigilantes roared.

The man who had used the knife on Sam rode up to his body and slashed his throat from side to side. Blood spurted out in a red geyser.

"Go!" the tallest man said and they rode into the brush and woods that surrounded the growing village of Astoria on three sides.

Sam Lincoln's body swung in the late afternoon breeze. The knife had pushed the body so it moved in a small circle until at last it stopped.

Sam Lincoln was dead.

Up the unfinished street on the outskirts of town, Spur McCoy pounded forward on his mount, his Colt still in his hand. He had been two blocks away when he saw the five horsemen around the lone man and fired the shot hoping to scare them.

He raced up to the hanging man, saw his throat and spurred on past after the killers. They had taken to the woods that opened on a meadow, swinging north toward the river. Spur saw the last of three of them vanish into the growth ahead.

He kicked his mount into a gallop and charged across the meadow. He needed only one of them. Give him one and he'd get the names of the others.

The woods here made up only a narrow band before they bordered on a piece of swampy marsh that the riders wouldnot try to cross. Spur rounded it and saw two of them riding for the River Road.

His horse was faster than the others. He had picked her for speed when he selected her that afternoon. The two riders had taken off their hoods and now the two split up.

Spur was within a hundred yards of them now. He could tell one of the men was larger, heavier. His horse should be the slowest. When they parted, Spur kept on the trail of the larger man in the brown hat and dark blue jacket.

The man could ride, but he didn't have the best horse under him. He struck out into the woods, bypassed a brushy area and charged along the side of a hill. On the other side was the River Road. Above the river were the ridges of the coast range. They soon would come to the fire area where the vigilante would have almost no cover to hide in.

Slowly, Spur gained on the other rider. At last, the vigilante realized he would be overtaken soon. He pulled to a stop in a thick stand of virgin timber and darted behind a four-foot-thick fir tree.

Spur saw the man pull a revolver from his waist-band and rode to within forty feet before he dismounted and moved forward slowly, darting from cover to cover. He paused then, listening.

Nothing.

The man was not moving. He jolted to the next tree and heard the blast of a revolver, but felt no pain. He missed. The soft puff of blue smoke from the powder pinpointed where the vigilante had fired. By now he had probably moved.

Spur guessed he had gone to his right, typical of a right-handed amateur in a gunfight. Spur dashed to the next big fir and one more, then bent low and peered around it almost at ground level.

He looked past a just opening fern and spotted the shoulder of a man standing behind a tree not quite large enough to conceal him.

Spur found a chunk of a limb on the ground and threw it so it landed six feet behind the man. The vigilante whirled, coming into full view and fired as he turned.

Spur's shot crashed on top of the vigilante's useless round. Spur's hot lead smashed into the gunman's left shoulder, spinning him into the brush. Spur watched where he hit and did not see him move. He couldn't be dead.

Possum . . . he was pretending to be unconscious.

Spur moved but without making a sound. He slid his foot into the mulch with each step, he did not break a branch or let a live limb of the alder or vine maple swish behind him.

When he was ten feet from the man, he saw his right hand move slightly.

"You move your right hand again like that and

you're dead!" Spur spat at the man. "Easy. Just let go of the weapon with your right hand, spread your fingers wide, and lift your right hand. Otherwise a big chunk of lead is going to blast through your skull. You hear me, murdering bastard!"

"Yes."

"Do it, now!"

The man's hand lifted.

"Now lift your left hand."

He did.

"Use your left and push up to a sitting position."

"Can't. Shoulder's shot up."

"Use your right hand then, but don't touch the gun."

Spur had moved his sights to the man's right shoulder. He moved quicker than Spur thought he could, lifted the gun and fired. The round went wide. But Spur's already aimed weapon had a big advantage. His round smashed into the vigilante's right shoulder, slammed him to the ground and knocked the gun from his hand.

Spur ran the fifteen feet to the vigilante, kicked the gun away and confirmed his guess who the man was.

"Well, Josiah Dangerfield, district attorney and champion of justice, the top lawman in Clatsop County, is really nothing but a cowardly, ride in the night, murdering degenerate."

"I don't know what you're talking about. I was out squirrel shooting with a friend when you began to chase us."

"Sure, and you always shoot at people who try to talk to you out in the woods."

"You can't prove a thing."

"Oh, but I can. You messed up, Josiah. I am an

eyewitness to your vigilante group killing that Negro back there. The odds were that you would foul up sooner or later."

"You still can't prove a thing."

"I damn well can. First off you are going to tell me who the other men were with you. One was George Putnam. We know that Abe Quincy got burned too bad to ride, that's why there were five. Now who are the other three men?"

"Damn you, bastard!"

Spur squatted beside the district attorney and hit his bullet smashed left shoulder with the barrel of the .45.

Dangerfield screamed with pain and protest.

"Yeah, I can see how it'll go. You'll keep quiet and every two minutes I'll pound your shoulder again. That'll make it bleed like crazy. It could be a close race between how stubborn you are, and how much blood you can lose and still stay alive. Be damn close I'd guess."

"You're a lawman. You wouldn't do that."

Spur put his iron in leather and hit Dangerfield's shoulder with his fist. Blood surged. Dangerfield gasped at the raw pain, then bellowed in agony.

"Won't help a bit, Josiah. Just you and me here, and one of us is going to win. We're talking about poetic justice here. The top lawman in the county hanging people, burning them out, running them out of town, all in the name of justice. I'm waiting for a name. I figure you can bleed another twenty minutes, maybe twenty-five, but no more."

Before Dangerfield could reply Spur hit him twice in the shoulder. Josiah almost passed out.

"The names, killer. Who are they?"

"Benny Clement . . . owns the livery stables."

"Yeah, Josiah, that's a good start. Now the other two."

"I'm not in a very good legal position on this, am I?" Dangerfield asked.

"Not the best."

"Then why should I help you?"

Spur hit him twice in the left shoulder. Blood flowed more freely now working down his arm, soaking his jacket.

Dangerfield screamed with the pain. He looked at Spur with hate-filled eyes. Spur only pulled back his fist again.

"Christ . . . Fred Goudy, our barber. A decent man."

"For a cowardly, night rider killer. I'll see that he gets a decent hanging. The sixth man, who is he?"

"Don't . . . don't hit my arm again. If I tell you will you patch me up so I don't bleed to death?"

"Sure, why didn't you ask before?"

"James Ross. He's part owner of one of the new canneries. A real gentleman."

Spur snorted. He checked Dangerfield for any other weapons, found a hideout derringer in his left side coat pocket. It was wedged in where Dangerfield couldn't get to it. Spur took it to add to his collection and told Dangerfield to unbutton his shirt. Spur cut off pieces of it and ripped them up to make bandages for his two arms. He soon had the bleeding stopped.

"How many men have you killed?" Spur asked.

"Only six. All deserved to die except the Negro today. It started when a good lawyer got a killer off free as a bird. He killed his wife, and everyone knew it, yet we couldn't prove it. After the trial he stayed in

307

town and bragged about how he had killed her.

"That started it. Six of us got together and caught him and hung him, the way the law should have done."

"And then it kept going?" Spur asked.

"Not for a year. Then another case came up that we couldn't even get a true bill from the grand jury. He had raped a young girl who was so broken up about it that she killed herself. We knew he couldn't swim so we took him out and let the Columbia kill him. He screamed as long as he stayed afloat."

"You were dispensing Astoria justice."

"It was justice!"

"Burning out Fu Chu?"

"Marginal. But he had an opium den going, trapping dozens of good men on that narcotic."

"Just because it wasn't illegal didn't bother you." Spur gave up, hoisted the man to his feet and found his horse. He took the horse's reins and led it back to his own animal, then rode down to the River Road and back to Astoria.

It was dark by the time they got to the courthouse. Spur talked to the sheriff who shook his head in disgust and put Dangerfield in a cell and sent for Doctor Ulman to work on his shoulders.

"That's one asshole I don't want to die before we can hang him," Sheriff Vinson said. He looked at Spur. "What about the other three?"

"Bring you another one tonight about eight o'clock," Spur said grim faced and went out the door.

31

Spur went at once to the livery stable. The stable hand said that Mr. Clement was gone for the day. Wouldn't be back until morning. The young man was glad to tell Spur where his boss lived.

The moment Spur stepped on the porch of the Clement home he realized there was a lamp burning in a holder outside the door, as if the family expected company. He rang the bell and then stood on the wall side of the door just in case.

The door opened outward an inch or so and a strained voice came through the crack.

"Yes? What do you want?"

"I'm looking for Benny Clement. Is that you?"

"No, he isn't home. He went to Portland on the morning boat."

"Strange, his stable hand said he had just come home."

"Who do you want?"

"You, Mr. Clement. I have some questions to ask you about the death of Sam Lincoln, a black man who was hung this afternoon.''

"Don't know anything about it.''

"Strange, since you were one of the five men, one of the Astoria Vigilantes, who hung him.''

The door slammed shut and a bolt slid into place. Spur ran to the back door. It too was bolted tightly shut. The house was a two story affair, with a woodshed of one story in back. As Spur walked around the house he heard a window slide upward and he dove toward the house just as a hand gun boomed twice in the darkness.

Spur ran to the other side of the house, smashed a window with his gun butt and then ran back to the side where he had been shot at. He broke open that window, unlatched it at the bottom, threw it upward and climbed inside the house.

He heard a door slam somewhere above.

Cautiously, Spur checked out the lower level. There was no one there. Clement must have expected Spur to come. Four chairs sat at the kitchen table. Family man.

Spur looked at the stairway. It had a door and creaking steps, he was sure. He jerked the door open and let it slam against the wall. Two pistol shots slammed down the staircase and hit the wall beyond.

"Might as well come down, Clement. You've got no place to run. I've got absolute visual identification of you as one of the participants in the lynching of Sam Lincoln.''

There was no response.

"Clement, you have a choice. You can come in and face the charges of murder on Sam, or I'll hunt you down and kill you. The decision is up to you. Don't make a damn bit of difference to me. I've acted as executioner in a good many cases like these. I'm legal, you're not.''

Another shot slammed through the empty air of the staircase.

"At least you got your wife and two children out of it. I guess you aren't all asshole, after all. Just most of you. Come on in and you can take a chance you might get a sympathetic jury. Never can tell what a jury will do.''

There came no shot, but also no verbal answer.

"Clement, we both know what a .45 slug will do when it enters your forehead. There is absolutely no second chance that way. With a jury you can always hope. And it would mean another month or two of life. Isn't that worth something to you right now, Clement?''

"Yeah, worth something.'' He fired down the stairs again. "It all was going just fine, then that damned Fu Chu messed it up. He had to go and burn down Putnam's store. Putnam went wild. He kept goading us into things after that. He got us to try to burn down the laundry and then he got Quincy burned so bad, I'm surprised he lived.''

"Why jump on Sam Lincoln? What did he ever do to any of you?''

"Josiah is from Atlanta. Lost all of his accent, never can tell it. But he hates all blacks. He blames them for the war and the destruction of his family and the plantation. His family used to to work over two thousand acres down there. Had over 300 slaves. He got us going about Sam. Josiah saw him the first day he came to town.''

"Clement, a jury will take that into consideration. We don't have any eyewitnesses about the Poikela

311

hanging. You've got a chance to get off with a prison term.''

"Not me. Never have been lucky. Not a damn chance in the world. I wrote a letter to my wife while I waited for you. I was with Josiah when you chased us. I saw you take him. Right then I knew what I had to do.''

"No, Clement! There's a better way!''

Spur raced up the stairs. He was only halfway up when the hand gun at the top of the steps fired once more.

The mortal remains of Benny Clement came rolling down the steps to meet Spur, the six-gun sounding loud as it fell from the dead hand on the wooden steps.

By the time Spur found a lamp and brought it up to the steps, it was too late. The big .45 slug had gone in the right side of Clement's skull and out his forehead. The hole where the lead came out was four inches across.

Spur went back to the sheriff's office and told him what happened. They sent someone to move the body to the undertaker. That left two more for Spur. He stopped by at the nearest saloon and asked the barkeep where Fred Goudy, the barber, lived. He didn't know but somebody at the bar did. That's what's nice about a small place like Astoria.

Goudy lived two blocks over on Jefferson Street. No lights showed in the Goudy home when Spur knocked on the front door. He knocked a dozen times and at last a light came on and someone walked to the door. It opened and a woman looked out.

"Yes?'' she asked.

"Mrs. Goudy, I have to see your husband.''

"He's not home."

"I know he's here, Mrs. Goudy. Let's not make this any harder than it has to be. I am arresting him. Would you tell him if he doesn't come out, I'll have to come in."

She closed the door and the bolt slid home.

Spur waited five minutes, then he heard a voice from a half opened second story window.

"Hey, McCoy. I know you're still there. Go away."

"You're under arrest for murder, Goudy. You better come quietly."

"Not a chance. I've got my wife and three kids up here. You touch my house I'll slit their throats. I have both my sharpest straight razors with me. I'll do it!"

"You do that and then I'll have to shoot you down like a dog with rabies."

"Why you want me?"

"Vigilantes, Goudy. You're a member. You hung a man this afternoon."

"He warn't no man, he was a nigger."

"You're not much of a man yourself for running around under a black hood."

"Where are the others?"

"Dangerfield has bullets in both shoulders in the jail. Benny Clement just put a bullet through his brain. Isn't it about time you take your chances with a jury?"

"Me and the woman got to talk," Goudy said.

Spur settled down to wait. Talking it over with his wife was better than blowing his head off. She would make him see the odds of going with a jury.

A half hour later the front door opened and Goudy came out carrying a lamp in one hand, the other hand raised over his head.

"Don't shoot. I decided to let you take me to jail."

A half hour later, Spur had taken Goudy to county jail, where he shared a cell with Dangerfield and was just across from Abe Quincy. Spur went back to the street with the address of James Ross.

His wife said that James was night manager at the cannery. He always took the hardest shifts, she said.

Spur went the six blocks down to the cannery at the foot of Lafayette Street. It was the second new operation opened this year, P.X. had told him. He expected half a dozen more canneries here before long. During the peak of the salmon run the three canneries in town all worked two shifts.

The men on the night shift were advised to carry revolvers with them on their way to work so they wouldn't be shanghaied by First Mates looking to fill their quota of sailors for the big sailing ships heading for the orient.

Spur went in the door marked "office" and found only one man there. He sat in a chair facing the door and in his hand was a double-barreled shotgun. His finger touched the trigger and both barrels pointed at Spur's chest.

"I figured you'd be here before this."

"If you're going to shoot you better do it now, you'll never have a better chance," Spur said.

He saw the man's eyes waver, then he set his mouth, the chance lost.

"Ease that Peacemaker out of leather with thumb and one finger and lay it on the floor."

Spur did.

"Now use your foot and slide that revolver over here to me. Turn around and lean against the wall."

Spur did. At least he wasn't dead. The canner's hands found the hideout derringer in his vest pocket and slipped it out. He took a knife from Spur's right boot and walked back across the office.

"Sit down against the wall and lace your fingers together behind your head."

When Spur sat down he saw that the shotgun still targeted his chest.

"Twice a day we dump fish heads and guts and skins in the ocean about a mile off shore. Give me two good reasons why the midnight boat shouldn't have your carcass in the batch, all chopped up to make identification impossible."

"One reason is enough. I'm a federal lawman, a Secret Service Agent. I'm here on an assignment. The sheriff knows I came to see you. So does your wife. The reason is if you turn me into shark food tonight . . . you'll hang."

"That's a possibility. But not a very good one. I'm a lawyer and worked in criminal law for two years. You're forgetting evidence, McCoy. All anyone could have is circumstantial and situational evidence. Nothing hard, nothing factual. Who saw you come in here? Who saw you talking with me? Nobody. Your conclusion is not valid."

"Easy to say now. How many men have you killed, Ross? Not with the gang of hooded cowards. I mean how many times have you stood toe to toe with another human being and shot him in the head or sliced his belly open with your knife and watched his guts hang out as he died? How many?"

"None, so what. It's you or me."

Spur had high hopes on the thin throwing knife in his left boot. It was only four inches of blade and three of handle and not heavy. It would have to be a deadly accurate throw.

"How did you get involved with a bunch of cowards like the vigilantes?"

"Keep him talking, right? Wear him down. I've got an hour before I dump you in the grinder. How did I get in the group? I went storming into the district attorney's office one day to complain about a killer going free. One thing led to another and they invited me in."

"Do you have trouble sleeping after helping to lynch a man the way you did Sam Lincoln, the Negro?"

"Not at all. I'll sleep well tonight after a double. But I should only count one. This is boring. You better get up slowly and take a tour of the plant. That way we'll be right close to the dump vat when it's time to load it."

Spur put his hands on the floor to boost himself up, let his left hand slip past his left boot and pulled the small throwing knife with it. He slid it to his right hand as he came up straight.

Ross looked away from Spur for a second while he stood, and that's when Spur's right hand snapped back to his ear and swung forward, launching the knife on its one turn journey. The half-inch wide, double-sided blade did the turn and the sharp point stabbed through Ross's throat just as he came upright. The knife penetrated, slicing his jugular vein in half, gushing blood down his shirt.

Ross stumbled backward, dropped the shotgun, which fired one round of buckshot into the ceiling. Spur jumped around the chair and knelt beside the fallen cannery owner. Spur checked the blade. The man was bleeding to death.

The jugular does not spurt the way the carotid artery does, but a steady flow of blood spilled from the wound. There was nothing Spur could do to stop it.

Ross shook his head. "Don't bother," he said barely able to form the words. "Yeah, I was with them. We killed both men." He started to say something else, then his head dropped to the side and his involuntary muscles relaxed. A large wet urine spot appeared on his pants.

Spur retrieved the blade, wiped it on Ross's shirt and walked slowly out of the room.

The sheriff sent a wagon to the cannery to haul the body to the undertaker. Spur made out the report and the confession as given by Ross.

Sheriff Vinson sat and smoked his cigar and watched Spur.

"McCoy, you're a little slow sometimes, but you do good work once you get in action. I'd say our vigilante problem here is about cleared up—except for the trial."

"About time. But look what it cost. A good D.A. is gone, the biggest general store in town burned out, the best barber in jail, the livery stable probably will go broke with no man to run it, and a county commissioner is in jail."

"But the sickness is burned out, McCoy. We won't have to put up with any more lynchings."

"Of course you still have your opium problem with Fu Chu," Spur said.

'Not for long. The City Council has decided that Fu Chu has a public establishment, he's serving a product to people and must have a dispensing license same as the saloons. Unfortunately, we are issuing no more dispensing licenses. Fu Chu will be given notice to move, or to cease his opium den operation within fourteen days."

"Hope it'll work."

"It will. I talked to the little Chinaman. He says he was about to move to Portland anyway. Many more customers and they have a much more relaxed business climate."

Spur stood and stretched. "This one is all yours. I'll give you a written statement about the whole thing. A deposition under the jurisdiction of the court, because by the time this comes to trial I could be anywhere."

The sheriff waved and Spur headed for his hotel. It was past time for Nancy to be singing, so he didn't have to go over there. Maybe he could get a good night's sleep. He could still see that knife flying through the air, slicing into Ross as he stood.

Spur unlocked his hotel door and opened it an inch when he saw a light on. He had his Peacemaker out but knew he wouldn't need it.

"Nancy," he said and pushed the door open. She sat on the bed with a thin nightgown on and held out her arms.

"I hear you've been working overtime tonight," she said smiling.

"True," he said. "Damn true."

32

Spur woke up and watched her.

Nancy combed her long red hair where she sat in the bed beside him. Without looking at him she spoke. "About time you woke up. You snore first thing in the morning, you know that?"

"Do not."

"Do too. Who was awake and rational and wishing she could go back to sleep here, anyway? Logic wins out again."

"In Indian country, snoring is a good way to lose your hair and half your brains with it."

"This isn't Indian country, you're safe here . . . well, comparatively safe."

"Not as long as you're naked and so close. I'm in a hell of a dangerous spot. I could get raped to death right here on this bed."

"Nut."

"Egotist."

"Iconoclast."

"Sombitch."

Nancy giggled. "Now that last one I like." She stopped combing her hair, draped it over his head and then went down and kissed his lips seriously.

"Do I detect the faint rumblings of female sexual desire in that fair bosom?"

"Nothing faint about it, Buster. I figure one of us is gonna be up and gone from this backwoods burg one of these days with about an hour's notice."

"You expecting the New York stage to send you a telegram?"

"Hoping." She moved over on top of him. "Just one more time to get the day started off right."

"I'll go along with that. A small celebration for winding up the vigilante situation."

"I thought we celebrated that last night."

"Then, too."

An hour later they had breakfast in the hotel dining room, complained to each other about the food, and then Spur said he had to check in with the lumber company. "Things have evidently settled down for them, and I might just be able to get moving out of this old town . . . like you suggested."

"That was a threat at the time."

He left her in the dining room for another cup of coffee and walked up to the mill.

The first person he saw was Karen sitting behind her desk. She had a smile for him, and a cup of coffee.

"You look pretty and happy this morning, Miss Johnson," Spur said.

"Then it worked. I'm trying to be more friendly . . . so it will reflect better on the company."

"Lee in?"

Karen smiled and waved him inside.

"McCoy, you were a one man army yesterday. You always tear around that way when you get a chance? You wiped out the vigilantes in one evening."

"And afternoon. When it's ready to happen, it happens. A little bit of luck always helps out. You seem pleased about something."

"Just had a conference with the fallers. We worked out a new agreement. They get a small wage increase, and I get a guarantee of so much production per man. That way everybody wins, we're all happy."

"Have you had any more trouble?"

"Not a whisper. All the men are watching like chicken hawks, which I'm sure is helping. On the other hand, this Monroe might simply have given up trying to buy the mill at a low price. I did get another letter from Portland with a higher price. I think he's given up."

"Let's hope so. If he has, I'm about ready to get out of this town. I'm supposed to be working for the Secret Service."

"You were, you are. We're using a new system on the log chute and the rafts. We tack a color label on the butt end of every log with a number of it. We check it when it hits the river and again when it gets in a raft, and when it's sawed. Sounds complicated, but it isn't. We haven't lost a log in a week now."

"You're convincing me that I'm on borrowed time here. I should get back to Portland and a telegraph wire."

"I had a long talk with Marty yesterday. I agreed to pull out my complant against him on the spikes in the log. He said he's getting ready to go to Seattle. He has a contact up there and he thinks he can get in a good lumbering operation. I think Marty is starting to grow

321

up. We actually sat across a table at Delmonico's and talked for half an hour without getting into a big fight.''

"What about Karen?'' Spur asked.

"She's snapped back just fine. What happened with Orville was a one in a thousand fluke. Hell, she's a Johnson, she'll be fine. Kind of wish that I could get her married off, though. Having two women in the same house can get on a man's nerves sometimes.''

"Don't look at me,'' Spur said standing quickly. "I'm not a candidate.''

"I was afraid of that.''

Spur headed for the door. "Going to see P.X. and start wrapping up my business in your nice little town. If those canneries keep coming in, Astoria won't be so little the next time I come through.''

When Spur went in the saddle shop, P.X. was just munching into a cinnamon roll. He held up a tin.

"Have one, they're just baked. Second pan full this morning.''

"You've had a lot of visitors or you're going to get fat, one or the other.''

Spur ate one. It was delicious. The bread dough was sweet, the cinnamon and sugar melted together in just the right proportion and had a soft white sugar glaze over the top that set off the intense cinnamon flavor.

"I may run off with your cook,'' Spur said.

"You could probably get away with half the town for what you did yesterday. Wiped out the whole damn vigilante group in four hours. Dangerfield! Now that was a shocker to me. I had no idea. Clement I wasn't surprised at, and old Fred Goudy. The cannery guy I didn't know. How can men get so

322

twisted that they think they can take the law into their own hands?''

"Started out honorably," Spur said. "A guy who got off scott free for murder and then bragged about it. I've seen it happen before. Most of them end up the way this one did. Who does the D.A.'s work now?''

"County Commissioners will appoint somebody and then call a special election in four months.''

"Looks like my work here is wrapped up, P.X.''

"Lumber yard problem quieted down a little, or is this just a lull between storms?''

"Seems. I'll take a morning boat up the river, way I see it now. Get to Portland and the telegram office, and I'll be back in business.''

"Where to next?''

"Wherever General Halleck decides there's a fire for me to put out.''

"You work for a general? What is this Secret Service, a whole army?''

"No, the general's retired. I still love the smell of this place. What is it about leather that is so satisfying?''

"I've worked with leather for almost ten years now," P.X. said. "I wouldn't do anything else. Not now. Oh . . . I might take the job as president of the United States if they offered it to me. Nothing less.''

Spur picked up a set of saddlebags from a shelf. They were a rich brown leather, carefully crafted, with a cut out in the center throw to fit over the cantle of most saddles in use. The two inch deep bags had a small pocket on the front like a cavalry saddlebag and an overflap with straps on the end to fit buckles. The overflap was carefully worked in silver on both sides with the symbol of a thunderbird. Spur looked at workmanship. The stitching was even and tight, double stitching on stress points, and the bags were sturdy and carefully beveled.

"Made that for a man who never came to pick it up," P.X. said. "Hear he got shot down in a gunfight in eastern Oregon. Those cattle ranchers over there get on the warpath sometimes and the blood really flies."

"No price on this," Spur said.

"The man paid for it in advance. Figure his kin might come and get it, but that was most five years ago now."

"Give you ten dollars for it," McCoy said.

"Don't josh me, McCoy. There's fifteen dollars worth of silver on there."

"Sure, but you already were paid for it. Found money." Spur looked at the saddlebags again. He wasn't leaving town without them. "Twenty dollars—if you use the money to buy your wife the fanciest dress she can find in Portland."

"Deal!" P.X. said grinning and jumping up on his work table so he could shake hands with Spur. "Sandra usually doesn't go in for fancy clothes, but I'll tell her this is an order from a high official in the United States Government."

"Done," Spur said and took a twenty dollar gold piece from his pocket. "Afraid I was gonna lose that coin somewhere. I mostly stick to paper money these days."

Spur slung the saddlebags over his shoulder and tipped his low crowned black hat to P.X. He headed past a table piled a foot thick with freshly tanned cowhides.

"You stop by before you get on the river boat," P.X. said.

Spur waved that he would and walked out of the glorious smell of the leather working shop and angled back to the mill office.

Karen spotted the saddlebags the moment he came in the door and came up to look at them. She smiled at him, then touched the new leather.

"Beautiful. They took like the kind that would be used in a big parade of some kind."

"I'm not much for parades, but I will put them to good use. Glad to see you back to work."

"Yes, I decided it was time. I'll remember what happened but I won't be dwelling on it. I'm still going to smile at a man when I like him. Like I'm doing now."

"You do seem back in good form. Maybe we could even have another picnic before I leave. I've about decided that my work here in Astoria is finished."

"Oh, no! You just only arrived." Her soft blue eyes showed worry and concern. She shook the blonde hair off her shoulders and frowned. "You just can't go. We won't let you go. We need you here in Astoria."

Spur smiled. "That's nice to hear. Maybe I could stay another day. I did want to go out and try to catch a salmon. You could have taken me fishing."

"I don't like being in boats much," Karen said.

The outer door slammed and a 14-year-old boy ran inside and stopped suddenly, looking around. He clutched a white envelope in one hand and stared at Spur.

"Mister, are you Lee Johnson?"

"No, he's probably in his office."

"Where's that? They told me he was in here."

"Why do you want to see Lee?" Karen asked.

"I got this message for him. A man in a buggy stopped me and gave me this and told me to bring it right out here to the mill office and to give it to Lee Johnson. Nobody else."

"What did the man look like?" Lee asked.

The boy shrugged. "He was old, had on a suit. Old as my dad."

Spur motioned to the boy. "Lee should be right in here. Let's see."

The boy followed Spur to the office and inside.

"Young man has a message for you," Spur said to Lee who looked up from a ledger book.

"Oh?"

"Yes, sir. Are you Lee Johnson?"

"I am."

The boy stepped forward and gave him the envelope, then started to leave.

"You better stay until we see what it is," Spur said. "We might want to ask you some more questions."

Lee opened the envelope and read the top sheet of paper.

"My God!" he roared. "It's from Tom Monroe. He's kidnapped Cilla and my two babies. He's holding them hostage until I sign the enclosed bills of sale for the lumber mill and the timber land leases."

Spur grabbed the boy by the arm and hurried him out of Lee's office.

"Was anyone with the man in the carriage?"

"Yes, a woman and a couple of kids."

"Which way were they heading?"

"Oh, let's see. I was on Arch Street. He could have been heading for the River Road."

"How much did the man pay you to deliver this?"

"A dollar! A whole paper dollar!"

"All right, you can go now."

Spur went back into Lee's office. Lee sat behind his desk staring at the paper. He seemed unable to move. At last he looked up at Spur.

"McCoy, you're more used to dealing with these men than I am. What in hell can we do now?"

33

Spur took the papers Lee Johnson had just received from the kidnappers and looked at them. One was a bill of sale for the mill and lumber, the second a bill of sale for the Johnson Lumber Company leases on the timber parcels. The third was an unsigned letter to Lee.

In brief it said that if Lee did not sign the papers selling his mill and leases, Lee would never see his wife and children alive again. He was to sign the papers and bring them with him to an exchange point detailed in the letter.

Spur gave the papers back to Lee. "Don't sign them whatever you do. I'll find your family, count on it. Take these to the Sheriff and get him looking for Monroe. There's no name on these papers but they have to be from Monroe. He's the only one interested enough in the mill to do this.

"I'll be finding Cilla and the kids. You can count on that. Now go. First send someone to the livery and have the stablehand saddle up that horse I used yesterday and have the mill hand ride him up to your house. I want to start there.''

A moment later Spur ran out of the mill office toward Upper Town and the big house on the slope where the kidnapping had taken place.

Tom Monroe had planned it all carefully. He knew when Karen and Lee left for work. He knew they usually didn't come back until evening. He had found out that the only other person in the house was the cook.

He had rented the buggy three days before, and now drove up the street toward the big Johnson house with total confidence. Lee Johnson would sign the deal. He would not allow his family to be killed due to his own greed.

The first few minutes in the house were critical. He parked near the front door. No other houses looked on the front area of the Johnson house. Good.

He rapped on the door and waited.

Cilla Johnson herself opened the door. He lifted the derringer and pushed her back as he stepped inside the house.

"Not a word, not a sound, Mrs. Johnson, or I'll shoot you. Do you understand?"

She nodded but her teeth chattered. No one had ever pointed a real gun at her before! She wanted to scream, to drop on the floor and screech until Lee came.

"Take me to your cook, at once!"

They walked into the kitchen. Cilla was afraid she was going to turn and run. Run away from this danger, this problem. She had never been good about solving problems. In the kitchen the cook was finishing the breakfast dishes. She turned and smiled, then saw the gun and screamed.

Monroe pushed Cilla ahead of him, slapped the cook hard across the face and she stopped.

"No more noise. Mrs. Johnson, you find some twine or rope. We need to tie up your cook so she doesn't get in any more trouble."

Cilla's trembling fingers brought out some heavy cord from a drawer and Monroe tied the cook to a wooden kitchen chair.

"Who are you?" Cilla at last got brave enough to ask. "Why are you doing this?"

"You really don't know, do you, Mrs. Johnson? You don't have to. It doesn't matter. Now we're going to get your children."

Cilla couldn't explain it. He was about to threaten her children and some deep-seated fury made her explode. She suddenly flew at the man across the four feet that separated them. He didn't have time to lift the derringer or even throw up his hands. Her fingers clawed down his face, leaving long deep scratches. She screamed at him, kicked him. Her hands clawed again and again at him until he backed away from her.

Monroe fired a shot from the derringer into the ceiling. When Cilla paused in surprise, he slapped her hard, knocking her to the floor.

"Don't you ever scratch me again or I'll kill you!" Monroe shouted. "Now, stand up and take me to your children!"

Cilla stood slowly, rubbing her face. No one had ever hit her that hard before. Never in the face. Not even Marty. As she walked behind her, Monroe took out the fired derringer round and loaded in a new one.

They went up the staircase and to the nursery and the room beside it. In each, a child slept.

"Bring them," he said. "Take what you'll need for a few days. Do it quickly. You have ten minutes to get things together. I'll be right beside you. Now move!"

Cilla jumped, remembered the blow to the side of her face.

"A few days? I have to take all that food and milk? Will there be milk for the babies? I'm not nursing them anymore."

"No questions!" Monroe barked. "You're wasting time."

When she had a box filled with things she wanted to take, she bundled up the baby and the older one and carried them to the buggy. The man was there with the box of things. He set her beside him, put the older child beside her and the baby in her arms.

"Mrs. Johnson, we're driving part way downtown until we see someone who can deliver a message for me. If you see someone you know, pretend you don't see them. I don't want you to say a word. If you cry out or scream or attract attention to us in any way, I'll shoot your baby. Do you understand?"

Cilla's eyes widened. "Shoot my baby? You couldn't. You wouldn't!"

"Mrs. Johnson, I wouldn't like doing it, but I will. Nothing must go wrong now. You do exactly as I said or I kill all three of you. Now do you see how careful you must be?"

A half hour later they had gone down to the edges of Lower Town and found a boy to deliver the message. Then the buggy reversed itself and headed toward the Klaskanine River and its little bay and swung around past the Lewis and Clark River and on to the Pacific Ocean only five or six miles farther away.

Now they saw no one. The buggy went around the small settlement that called itself Sunset Beach and moved south along the faint track of a wagon road along the ocean.

"Where in the world are we going?" Cilla asked at last.

"To your new home for a few days. It's not as fancy as you're used to, and you'll be the cook, but at least we'll be out of the rain that's coming toward us from out of sea."

Cilla saw it, a wet-looking fog bank rolling in, but over that angry black clouds swirled and worked their way to the shore. A light rain already was spattering the calm ocean surface.

"Now can you tell me why you're doing this?" Cilla asked.

Monroe relaxed. "Yes, I think so. Can't do any harm now. I'm the man trying to buy your husband's sawmill. He doesn't want to sell it. I'm trading him his family alive and well, for his signature on a contract to sell the mill. A simple business deal."

"That's also kidnapping and extortion. My daddy is a lawyer. I've heard law talk all my life. You could go to prison for fifty years for what you did today. Oh, also assault and battery. Add another ten years to that sentence."

Monroe laughed as he turned off the coast trail into a narrow lane that led inland past a small hill and around a tiny stream that worked its way to the gray sands of the Pacific shore.

"No judge in his right mind could find me guilty."

"But daddy says that no Circuit Court judge *is ever* in his right mind. Looks like you have some problems."

"I'll have no problem at all, bitch, if there's no one who can identify me. Now what do you think about that? You're no more good to me alive than you are dead. In the process I might just strip you naked and see if that body of yours is as good humping as it looks like it could be."

"Hell, little fat man, I'm better in bed than any woman you ever even dreamed about. But I don't ever bed little fat men with bellies as big as yours."

Monroe slapped her hard and then his hand dove down the neck of her dress. She pulled herself up from where he had pushed her with the slap but did nothing to remove his hand.

"Really getting a thrill, old man? I bet you can't even get it hard anymore. Even if you did, with a fat belly that big you couldn't get it anywhere near a cunt hole."

Monroe pulled his hand away.

"You like to talk dirty, don't you? That means your little cunt is getting hot and all ready to be poked. I might just oblige you while we wait. Course I'd have to tie you to the bed posts first. Spread-eagle you."

He watched her as he pulled up to a small farm house. There were two barns, a crib, a tool shed and an outhouse that looked like it could be a four holer.

Monroe chuckled. "Hell, you like to be poked after being tied up! Heard about your kind of woman but never met one before. Damn, but you're one all right!''

"Not with you, fat ass."

He motioned her out of the buggy. She got out and carried both her babies into the house. It hadn't been lived in for a while, but it had been cleaned up recently.

"You expect us to live here?" Cilla said, her fists on her waist, her chin and her breasts thrust out.

"Damn right. Put the kids down somewhere, I got business with you." Monroe rubbed his crotch, then his fly.

"Disgusting!" Cilla said turning away.

Monroe took the baby from her, put her down on the bed in the second room. The older child he sat on the end as well. Then he went back to the living area and eyed Cilla.

"You're terrible," Cilla said.

Monroe slapped her gently on the cheek. Her eyes glistened with fire. He slapped her on her round bottom and she struggled to keep from responding. Then he caught both her breasts and squeezed until she shrilled in a scream of pain.

"Damn you!" she bellowed. "Damn you!" She stared at him. "Oh, damn. Do that again. Please do that again!"

Cilla sank to the floor and unbuttoned her blouse and threw it off. Then she lifted her chemise away and sat there on the floor her full breasts swaying.

"Please do that again," she said. Then she smiled. "Or you just go ahead and do anything you want to with me. You were right. I'm ready."

Spur McCoy ran the last hundred yards to the Johnson house. The boy with the message had come to the mill at about eleven o'clock. That meant Monroe had to be just leaving town slightly before then. Not a cold trail, but cold enough.

Spur went in the front door without knocking and called out. He heard a muffled voice from the kitchen.

Spur ran there and untied the cook who was still frightened and hysterical. He made her sip water for two minutes, then she could talk.

The cook told him everything she knew. "Yes, he was a short, fat man. He was nearly bald with fringes of brown hair. And his clothes were too large for him."

Spur told her to lay down and take a nap, then he ran out to the front door and checked for tracks. He found several in the dust of the yard. But one set overlayed the rest.

It looked like a small buggy, and one horse pulled it. He prayed for a broken shoe or no shoes or some distinguishing marks, but there were none. Four shoes, all common, the rig heading down hill.

Spur heard a horse pounding up the street and saw the mount he had used the day before. The stable boy slid off it and Spur thanked him and grabbed the reins.

Then Spur walked down the street with his horse behind him. It was easy to follow the rig until it came to Arch Street. It turned west and then was lost in a flurry of tracks made by iron wagon wheel rims and a dozen or so horses and mules.

On a hunch, Spur kept going down Arch Street four more blocks and then he ran out of town. He studied the tracks. To one side he found what could be the same small buggy moving on west. It angled toward the river on Genevieve all the way to Chenamlis, then he thought it turned west again. But he wasn't sure. He needed more than a maybe.

Spur knew it would be useless to ask anyone if they'd seen a buggy with a man and a woman and two children in it. There could have been twenty like it along here every hour.

West, why would he go west? Spur gave up on the tracks and went to see P.X. The little saddlemaker yanked a piece of stitching tight and scowled.

"I heard about it. The sheriff was by and said that Monroe's desk has been cleared out. He isn't at his boarding house. It's a damn good guess that he's the one. I heard something that didn't quite make sense two or three days ago."

He yanked another stitch string tight and glared at Spur. "Why'n hell can't I think of it? It just didn't jibe. Like a fancy New York accent, or your Boston way of talking on a black man or a Chinese. Out of character."

Spur watched the midget pushing the needle through the leather and drawing up the string tighter than was needed as he took out his frustration on the leather.

"Hot damn!" P.X. said. His dark eyes danced for a moment. "Got him! Old Doc Jackson, who used to be medical man here, now is retired and rents out a few properties he has. He stopped by to talk about a new leather belt he wants, and he remarked how he rented the old Handshoe place over on the coast. It's up from Seaside and down aways from the point.

"He said he didn't know why a body would rent that place unless he wanted to run a dairy herd. This gent didn't have an animal to his name."

"Tom Monroe?"

"Yep. Stop by at Doc's place next to the barber shop and he can draw up a map. Doc's right good at map making. He told me once. . . ."

When P.X. looked up, Spur McCoy had darted to the door and the wooden framed screen door came slamming home after he jolted past it.

P.X. watched Spur riding hard down the street toward the barbershop. "Good luck, hunter man," P.X. said softly. "Good luck."

Spur sent a teenage boy on the street running to tell Lee Johnson to come to the barbershop. Spur found Doc Jackson's place and opened the door.

Doc Jackson snoozed in the morning sun that slanted in his window. He woke up quickly, grinned and dropped his feet off the footstool.

"Well, the Federal Agent. Haven't had the pleasure. . . ."

"Yes, it's a pleasure meeting you. No time right now for small talk. There's been a kidnapping and we're hunting the man. You rented the old Handshoe place a few days back. I need a map how to find it, damn fast."

The doctor's seventy year old eyes squinted, then he nodded.

"Yep. Easy to find. Go west until you hit the coast road, follow down it past the big rock in the surf. It's the second creek leading up into little valleys to the left. The Handshoe place has a Western gate, sort of. Two poles with a cross piece and a sign that used to say HANDSHOE, but one side has fallen down."

"Thanks, that should be good enough."

Spur went outside and mounted, then looked for Lee. He rode half a block down, came back and saw

Lee riding up. Lee had a rifle in his saddle boot. He tossed Spur a Spencer repeating rifle.

"Time to go snake hunting," Spur said. "He's probably at the old Handshoe place over on the coast."

"Been there," Lee said grimly. "If he's harmed that lady or the kids, I'll torture him worse than any Apache ever thought of doing."

Spur nodded. "Let's ride. You know the territory. You lead the way, and we better hurry!"

34

Tom Monroe knelt on the living room floor of the little farm house. He had not undressed, he wasn't that much the fool. But Cilla had, willingly, quickly, and they had coupled in a rush that left them both panting and moaning and still clutching at each other.

Now he lifted her to her hands and knees, played with her drooping big breasts until she cheered, then spread her legs from behind and found her wet, used slot.

"From in back, just like a big dog," he said. He probed and she giggled and he found her wide opening and drove in until his belly and her buttocks stopped him.

"Best from the back," he said pumping hard. "Best in your tight little asshole, but we'll wait on that until tonight." He bent forward, resting on her back and caught her hanging breasts.

"Oh, yes, pussy and tits! This was a great idea. I just might not give you back. You're a goddamned sex machine, best I've ever had or heard about. Is there anything you won't do?"

Cilla grinned trying to hump rearward to meet his thrusts. "I'll do anything, long as it doesn't hurt my body. What you got in mind for next time?"

"Lord, girl, this is a number four already. You trying to wear me out the first go-round? I got to rest a little bit and take a ride to see if any of your friends know where we are."

He punched faster and faster. Cilla shrilled long and loud, and then they both climaxed at once, falling forward on her stomach and he bounced out of her. They both laughed through their panting.

One of the babies started crying.

"Damn," Cilla said. "Just when I was getting warmed up." She picked up her clothes and went into the bedroom to tend to the infant.

Tom Monroe sat on the floor for five minutes recovering. Then he picked up a rifle he had stashed in the house two days ago and went outside to put the buggy in the barn. He unhitched the horse and threw on a saddle and cinched it in place.

Monroe was not a good horseman, and he didn't plan on any fancy riding. He knew there was some chance that Johnson found out where he was headed. He had rented the place four days before from the nearly blind old doctor. He gave another name, and hoped the old Doc didn't know who he was.

But he couldn't be sure. He rode back down the lane until he could see the main coast road which was only a faint wagon trail. He saw no one coming from the north. No one at all.

Monroe rode back to the barn, tied the horse with the saddle still on, and carried the rifle back to the house. He had figured out how to defend the place. He had two rifles. One at the upstairs window that he had lifted half open. The other rifle would be beside the kitchen window that had one foot-square pane of glass broken out.

The living room had a bay window and the more he thought about it, the more he liked the idea. If he had trouble with anyone coming he would do it. Cilla was gonna be mad, but what the hell.

He went into the house and up the stairs. Cilla was caring for the brats, he decided. Tom got a chair from the partly furnished house and pushed it next to the window that looked toward the ocean. From that height he could see the waves breaking in the distance.

Monroe thought about the woman downstairs. Damn, what a woman! She couldn't get enough cock. She'd take it in any of her three holes and love it. If nobody tracked him the rest of the afternoon he was going to have one wild night. With Cilla he could do everything he had ever dreamed of before morning.

He thought about it and then realized he was nodding. He snapped open his eyes and scanned the lane and as much of the coast track as he could see. Nothing. But how long had he dozed? He had to stay awake, alert. He couldn't spoil the whole scheme now that he was so close.

One of the babies downstairs cried, and Cilla evidently got to it because it quieted down. She must be a good mother.

Motion.

For a moment it didn't register, then he saw something moving at the very top edge of his view of the coast trail. Slowly the picture there took shape and form.

Two horsemen, riding with a purpose. He ran downstairs, got Cilla and took her to the bay window.

"You're going to have to stand or sit here. Do you want me to tie you to a chair to make it look better?"

She was playing with his crotch as she talked. He rubbed her breasts through the thin dress.

"Better tie me up. I'm gonna tell them you raped me. You understand?"

He said he did, got a chair and tied her loosely in it but so she couldn't get out. He sat her almost touching the glass in the bay window. It had no curtains. They could see her as soon as they got close enough.

He ran back upstairs and levered a cartridge into the old Henry Repeating rifle. It held twelve rounds of .44 caliber rim fire cartridges. Weighed over nine pounds, but he could hit a turkey at a hundred yards with it.

By that time the two riders had turned in at the lane and sat there looking at the house. They were about two hundred yards away. With a Henry that was like shooting fish in a half full bucket.

He sighted in and put a bullet into the ground beside them. No sense killing them if he didn't have to. They could be coming with the signed papers. Not likely, though, seeing what he knew about Johnson, but possible. The other one had to be that government man, McCoy.

Damn! He hadn't figured on a whole posse. One was bad enough. Two. As soon as he fired the two men rode in opposite directions. They were circling around the house; they'd come in on the blind sides.

Getting serious. He sighted in at the rider going to

the left, tracked him, led him a bit and fired. Monroe saw the horse's head jolt to the side. The horse fell dead in a second from the big slug. He'd wanted the man.

The rider rolled off the horse and a moment later a rifle round from the other rider smashed through the top of the window where Monroe sat. He scuttered to the stairway and went down.

"Don't you hurt Lee, he's a good man," Cilla called from the front bay window.

Monroe ignored her, made sure both outside doors were bolted, then checked the windows. They were sash double hung with twist locks on the wooden bottom section. Four windows on the ground floor and all were down and locked.

Monroe looked out the side where the man was on foot. He saw him twice, but decided not to fire out the window.

Outside, Lee Johnson had hit the ground rolling when the rifle shot killed his horse. He found some cover behind a small ridge and waited. When the rifle barrel pulled in from the window he ran down a slight depression and then out across in the open toward the side of the house.

He saw movement in a first floor window and looked more closely. In the bay window someone sat in a chair. No curtains. He looked again, then worked forward until he could be sure. It was Cilla! She sat there tied to a chair. That bastard Monroe. Using Cilla as a shield!

Lee and Spur had agreed not to shoot at the house unless it was absolutely safe. Spur had fired one round into the top window. Lee wasn't sure if Spur had seen Cilla in the window.

Lee lifted up again and charged the house. He was on the side without any windows and got to an apple tree thirty feet from the side of the house without being fired at.

From there he could see the back door. The house was set a hundred feet from the start of a slant of timber that ran up the hills in back for a mile or more. A pasture for the dairy cows meandered around the bunch grass of an old swampy place and the timber and brush.

Lee and Spur had worked out a simple attack plan. Lee would harass Monroe at one side of the house and Spur would go in a window on the other side and try to nail him or force him out and away from the hostages.

Lee crawled forward until he could see the windows on the front side, but away from the bay window. Probably a bedroom. He found a rock and threw it at the window. It took three tries to hit it and the crash of the glass came loudly.

For a second Lee saw Monroe's form behind the broken pane, but he darted away at once. A few seconds later Lee heard more breaking glass, then it was quiet.

Inside the house the muffled sound of two pistol shots came, then two more. Lee guessed if Monroe came out it would be from the back door. He lifted up and ran to the blind side of the house, and worked around to the corner. He was twenty feet from the back screen door. Lee made sure he had a fresh round in the chamber of the rifle. Just like shooting deer—only this one could shoot back. He waited.

Inside the house, Spur lay behind a couch in the living room. He had come through a bedroom window and got to the couch before he saw Monroe who sent two wild revolver shots at Spur and then two more.

All had missed. Spur didn't know where the two kids and Cilla were. Then he heard a soft cry and he looked at the window and saw Cilla sitting there, tied to a chair. Now, where were the two kids?

Monroe was across the room away from Cilla. But he still didn't know where the kids were, so he couldn't shoot. Four rounds. He wondered if Monroe had reloaded. Spur found a piece of wood for the fireplace. He picked up the foot long chunk and threw it toward the door leading into what he guessed was the kitchen.

Monroe spun and fired a round at the sound.

"That's five rounds, Monroe. Your piece is dry."

"Not my rifle, asshole. And I can use it. Right now I'm pointing it at Cilla there in the window. I'm going out to the kitchen. You so much as lift your head and I'll put a slug through Cilla. You understand?"

"You win," Spur said. He heard movement, then lifted up and saw Monroe dart into the kitchen.

"Cilla, are you all right?" Spur asked.

"Yes, get him!"

"Where are the babies?"

"They're in the bedroom over there. Out of danger. He . . . he raped me, but don't tell Lee."

Spur sent two rounds through the kitchen door and at the same time ran to the wall and slid over to the opening. He looked around the door at shoe-sole height but saw no one. He swept the room, then again. Monroe stood behind a chair next to the back door.

He seemed to take a big breath, lifted a rifle he

carried and before Spur could get a clear shot past the chair, Monroe opened the screen and ran into the back yard and toward the trees.

Lee heard him coming, sighted in and then stopped. He couldn't fire. He moved his sights and sent a slug into the ground in front of him.

"Hold it Monroe or you're a dead man!" Lee called.

Monroe turned and fired his rifle at the voice, then levered in a fresh round and kept running for the woods.

Spur came to the door and fired twice, but already Monore was out of six-gun range.

Lee sent another round in front of the man, but couldn't bring himself to hit him.

Spur ran up, grabbed the rifle, but by then Monroe slipped into the brush and coast-stunted fir and out of sight.

Lee tossed Spur a box of rifle shells. "Sorry, I just couldn't shoot him."

"You should have. I talked to Cilla. She and the babies are fine, except she said Monroe raped her."

Lee stared at Spur for a second, then growled and grabbed the rifle from him. Together they ran into the woods twenty yards down from where Monroe had entered. Spur sent his reloaded revolver's six rounds of covering fire into the general area where Monroe had vanished. They made it to the woods without any problems.

Just inside the brush Spur motioned Lee to be still. They listened. They heard brush crashing to the left and both ran that way, through the heavy brush and Oregon grape and salal and red huckleberry.

Twice more they stopped and listened. They were

346

getting closer. Then the crashing stopped. They moved forward slowly, not making a sound. A high keening sound of agony knifted through the silent woods.

They had begun to climb up the side of the hill now, and the tangle of brush was alternately heavy and lighter. The sounds came from just ahead.

Cautiously they parted the brush and looked out. They were on the lip of a twenty foot dropoff. Below, on the rocks of a small creek, lay Monroe, one leg twisted under him at an unnatural angle.

"Didn't spot the drop off until he fell," Spur whispered.

A rifle round smashed through the brush beside them. The men edged back.

"You're a dead man, Monroe, give it up," Spur called. "A jury might not even hang you."

Two more shots crashed into the silence.

Lee dropped to the ground and worked his way quietly through the three feet of tangled brush until he could see over the edge. He lifted the rifle and fired.

Spur had worked up beside him. The rifle round smashed Monroe's left knee. He bleated in pain.

"Bastard! You could have killed me. Why didn't you?" He fired three times at the brush but missed flesh.

"Want you to suffer a little, you kidnapper and rapist! You threatened three lives! You don't deserve to live. Throw the rifle to the side. We might be able to save your worthless hide for a judge and jury."

Spur listened to Lee. He wasn't sure he could let the man live if he had been Lee. Monroe bellowed in pain and threw the rifle to the side.

Spur went down first, as Lee held the rifle on Monroe. Spur checked the knee and the crushed, broken leg. Lee came down.

"Gonna be a hell of a lot of work to get you out of here," Lee said. He stared at the man for a minute. "You rape my wife?"

"Hell, no! She asked me for it. She was begging for it. Being kidnapped made her hotter than hell."

Lee slugged Monroe in the face with his fist, knocking him back on the rocks of the small stream.

Monroe shook his head to clear it, then snorted through his pain. "You don't know much about your wife, do you, Johnson?"

Lee started to hit him again, then controlled himself.

Spur looked at the broken leg. "Need to splint both of them before we can move you, Monroe. Soon as I start working on that right leg, you're going to pass out."

"Get the damn sticks," Monroe said. "I won't pass out."

Spur turned to go after some downed dead branches to use as splints when he heard a cry. He looked back as Monroe pulled a hideout derringer from his pocket and fired. Lee shrilled with pain as the round hit him in the thigh. He swung down the rifle and fired, then worked the trigger guard lever three times as fast as he could and fired three more rounds into Tom Monroe's chest.

Spur jumped back and looked at Monroe. There was no pulse at his temple. Then he checked Lee.

"Looks like a .25 caliber," Spur said. "Doc will have to dig it out."

A soft Oregon rain rolled in from the ocean and began to fall.

Spur took the rifle and helped Lee stand. "We better get back and check on Cilla and the babies."

Lee stared at the dead man. "I don't understand. I just went kind of crazy. I shot him four times. I *wanted to kill him.*"

Spur put Lee's arm over his shoulder. "You did what Monroe wanted you to do. He could have shot you in the heart with that little gun. He had two rounds. What do you think he was waiting for?"

"I don't know. I'll never know." Lee scowled. "This makes me no better than those vigilantes."

Spur helped the wounded man walk down the creek to an easy place to go up the bank. "You were defending your family. You're no vigilante, Lee. You're more like a hero. Cilla will be wondering what happened to you out here."

They walked ahead through the fine rain that fell silently without any wind.

35

It was just after six that evening when Spur and Lee rode into Astoria. A sheriff's deputy saw them coming and Sheriff Vinson met them and took charge of Tom Monroe's body. They talked briefly with the sheriff, then drove to Upper Town and the Johnson family house.

Cilla hugged Spur after the children were put down and she had washed up and changed clothes quickly. Her hug was a little too familiar, Spur thought for a moment. Then she broke away and grinned.

"Don't know what the kids and me would have done without my two heroes. Glory but I'm a lucky lady." She and Lee talked a minute in the library and the big house.

"Now things are settled down," Lee said. "Monroe is out of the way. I had a letter from a mill owner up near Portland who said the big bidding war on that ties contract has evaporated. The Portland and San Francisco Railroad never got enough money to get started. He had put in a bid but it was all for nothing."

"Probably a good thing Monroe never knew that," Spur said.

Lee walked to the window and then back. "It's going to be a long time before I pick up a rifle again," he said. "Just a damn long time. No more hunting for me . . . ever. What happened out there changes a man."

"It's over and you and your family are all well, that's the important part. Tonight Doc has got to dig that slug out of you."

"You'll be heading out soon?" Cilla asked.

"Tomorrow I'll find the Justice of the Peace and swear on my statements about all of the cases the sheriff needs evidence on. Then I'll be gone up-river. I might just rent a horse and ride to give me another day to rest up a little."

The front door shut and soon Karen came in. She ran to Cilla and hugged her. Tears misted her eyes.

"Oh, glory! I'm so happy to see you! It must have been terrible. The babies are all right I heard."

She hugged Cilla again, who seemed pleased.

"Yes, everything is fine."

She hugged Lee and then Spur. "You two are my heroes. If I were the mayor I'd give you both medals!"

Spur chuckled. "How about dinner at Delmonico's instead? For the four of us. A little celebration."

"Oh, yes, wonderful!" Karen said. Cilla started to agree, then saw Lee shake his head.

"I guess we better not," Cilla said. "You two run along. I need to give the babies both baths and everything."

They rode down in Karen's buggy, trailing Spur's horse.

The dinner was good, a steak and side dishes including new potatoes and peas in a cheese sauce. Back in the darkness of the buggy, Karen pushed against Spur and kissed him.

"Mr. McCoy, if you're leaving tomorrow the way you said, this is my last chance. Now listen to me." She reached up and kissed him three times, warm, demanding, passionate kisses.

"There are three good reasons why I want you to show me how to make love. Right here, in the grass up on the hill, or in the safety of your hotel room."

"I told you, little lady—"

She stopped him with another kiss and gently put his hand on her breast.

"Please, Spur. I want the best teacher in the world, and one who I've fallen just a little bit in love with. Is that too much to ask?"

Ten minutes later he ushered Karen into his room. She had come up the back stairs with her face covered so no one would know who she was. She slipped in his door with no one noticing her.

Her face was flushed as she stood against the door watching him.

"Scared?" Spur asked.

"Yes. Not like I was when I was naked in the cabin with Orville. That was terror. Now I'm a little hesitant, curious, expectant."

She walked over and sat down on the bed and Spur pushed the bolt closed on the door.

"Ever since I was big enough to know about making love I've pushed down the idea, said no to several young boys with big ideas, and generally protected myself when men were around. It gets to be a habit. Now . . . now all of those 'no's' are in the past and I have to change my thinking and let there be one 'yes.' It's a little scary." She grinned. "But I'm not about to back out now."

Spur sat down beside her without touching her.

"Oh, Cilla seemed all worked up about something. She was alone with Monroe. Did he try to attack her or anything like that?"

"She said Monroe raped her."

Karen laughed softly. "She said that, did she? I know Cilla pretty well by now. When we're alone we have girl talk lots of times, and that Cilla does talk sexy. She loves to make love. One night she got so worked up she . . . you know . . . she used her finger and rubbed herself until she had a climax. She told me it would be impossible for any man to rape her. It might start that way, but by the time he got her blouse off she'd be so worked up and wanting it that she'd be helping him."

"Some women need more loving than other women. Now, what about Karen?"

She reached up and kissed him. Soon her tongue probed at his lips, then inside his mouth. Her hands came up and cradled his face and when she broke off the kiss she was smiling.

"Oh, that makes me feel all warm and . . . and good."

Spur kissed her again, reminding himself to go slow, let her lead if she wanted to. After several more kises she put his hands on her breasts.

"Like before," she said. He opened the buttons on the top of her dress and she helped. "Yes, yes. I want you to touch me, to feel me, rub them. They want you to.''

His hands were gentle under the chemise, and she sighed and smiled.

"I'm feeling all warm and warmer. Is that a good sign?"

He said it was and toyed with her nipples until he could feel them enlarge and stiffen. Tenderly he lifted her chemise.

"So beautiful!" he said. "Wonderful, amazing. May I kiss them?"

Her eyes widened. "Oh, glory! Would you? Oh, yes!"

He barely touched his lips to her soft white breast when she sucked in a gasp. Then his featherlike kisses rounded one breast and centered on her nipples and she moaned and threw her arms around him. Her hips jerked and her whole body vibrated with a series of quick spasms that rolled through her, bringing soft cries of pleasure from her.

"Oh, glory! Oh! Oh!" She hugged him tighter and then at last relaxed and fell against him where they still sat on the bed.

"That's the first time I ever did that!" she said softly. "Wonderful, simply wonderful."

He pulled on her skirt and she nodded and lifted the dress over her head, her long blonde hair cascading back from where it caught in the fabric and falling in delightful disarray over her shoulders and face.

She pushed her hair back and he touched her chemise. She nodded and he lifted it off. He stared. Her breasts were large, strongly nippled with areolas four inches across.

"The most beautiful part of a woman," Spur said.

He kissed both breasts quickly and then took off his shirt. She unbuttoned two of the fasteners and smiled at his bare chest with its dark hair.

She still wore drawers, the white tight-fitting garment that was waist high and extended to the knee around each leg.

"Me first," Spur said. He slipped out of his boots, then his socks and his pants. He stood there in his short underwear, then slowly lowered it until he was exposed and kicked the cloth away.

"Oh, lordy!" Karen said. She looked up at his face. "I've never seen a man all over naked before. "You're beautiful."

She looked down at his crotch and the jutting presence of his erection.

"He's so . . . so big. I don't see how . . ." She stopped and blushed. "I mean . . ."

Spur kissed her and she grinned.

"Now that is something that might frighten me."

"He's friendly," Spur said.

"Cilla keeps telling me how wonderful it is making love." Karen giggled. "Now I'll have a story to tell her."

It was another ten minutes before Spur gently eased her drawers down exposing her crotch and the blonde muff of soft hair over her heartland.

She lay beside Spur but not touching him.

"So far I don't feel much different," she said. "I'm excited and worked up . . . and feel sexy . . . and I want you to . . . to do it. But I thought it would be a lot . . . a lot . . . different."

"Making love is natural, like eating and sleeping and walking down the block. It's not some strange, dangerous bugaboo that most mothers tell daughters

355

it is. Most mothers don't want their daughters to know the marvelous feelings until they get married.''

Karen turned and caught his erection. She looked at him quickly. ''Am I hurting you?''

Spur chuckled. ''Not a bit, we both love the touch. Explore, I won't break.''

Spur's own hand caressed her upper thighs, and she began to breathe faster. She held him tightly as Spur's fingers trailed across her nether lips and she gasped.

''Oh! that was like fire. Could you touch me there again?''

He did and she smiled.

''I put a finger up inside me once and thought I was being very wicked.''

Spur did the same thing and she smiled. ''Now that doesn't feel wicked, it feels warm and so fine!''

He came out and touched her clit. She looked at him.

''That is *absolutely wild*!''

''That's what Cilla was touching that night.''

He twanged the little penile nub six times and she roared into another climax. This one twice as strong as the last one. She rolled on top of him, her hips pounding at him as the vibrations slammed through her a dozen times, jolting her, shaking her, rattling her as she moaned in total pleasure.

When it was over she reached down and kissed him.

''Now, sweet Spur. Right now I want that big thing of yours inside me. Do it before I explode!''

Spur rolled her over and lifted her knees and went down. He probed and used saliva to help the first entry. To his surprise he slid in with no restriction.

The more active the woman, the less the hymen remained, Spur remembered.

Karen squealed in wonder as he stroked deep inside of her.

Tears filled her eyes and she cried and laughed and her hips kept pumping up at him as he came down.

"Nothing ever has been so wonderful! Why have you been keeping this from me all these nights?"

"Because you're a nice girl who's going to get married and I don't want to hurt your chances."

"Spur, a silly question?"

He nodded.

"In high school, the boys used to tease me about having such big tits. They said they wanted to . . . you know. Are we doing it now?"

Spur laughed and pounded harder into her. She took all he had and pushed back at him.

"Yes, sweet Karen. Those boys knew what they wanted and I'm glad you waited for me. Yes, sweet Karen. Now we are humping. Of course, you're no longer a virgin. But don't you dare breathe a word of that to your future husband."

"I know. Men are strange about that. But how in the world are you hurting me? How can I be any different? It doesn't make any sense at all. I'll be almost exactly the same person tomorrow."

"Things will change about this in the future. Let's enjoy what we have now."

Then her wiggling hips got to him and Spur felt the gates opening and he concentrated on stroking long and hard into her marvelous body. A dozen bangs later he moaned and grunted as he shot a double load into her.

Karen climaxed again as he did and together they humped and pounded and moaned and at last fell in each other's arms drained and exhausted.

Later they sat on the side of the bed. He stroked her perfect breasts.

"Spur McCoy, I love you," Karen said.

Spur nodded. "Good, you should, if only for a few hours. I've been in love with you ever since I saw you that first day. But not forever in love, just for a little while in love."

She fell back on the bed. "Cilla is right. Making love is the most wonderful thing a woman ever does. Just laying there and . . . and humping . . . is so marvelous. Everything else just fades into the background by comparison."

She sat up. "Again! let's do it again."

Spur laughed softly. "Hey, the man needs a little time to recharge his system. We can't just cum and cum the way a woman can. We have to manufacture all that semen."

"Oh. I'm learning. But we can once more before we go home?"

He nodded. "Yes, yes. It will be a real honor and a pleasure."

About nine o'clock that evening they arrived at the big Johnson house and Cilla took one look at Karen and grinned. She stood close to Spur and rubbed his crotch so no one could see her.

"Good work!" Karen whispered to Spur and laughed softly.

Spur said goodbye to them and went back to the hotel. Nancy had left a note. She had to go to Portland to finalize her deal there. She'd be back the next day. She still had her six month contract to work out there in Astoria. Then she hoped to get a booking agent the restaurant owner knew in Chicago.

Spur settled down in his bed and decided he'd take the morning boat after all. It left about ten.

The next morning Spur talked with P.X. for half an hour. He said goodbye to Sandra, marveling again at what a composed, pleasing woman she was.

P.X. worked on a fancy leather belt.

"Pin money," he said indicating the belt. "It also buys food and pays the rent."

Spur knew the feeling.

"You coming back this way soon?" P.X. asked.

"Not unless I need to, which I hope I don't. But if I get to Portland, I'll be sure to take the boat up here to see everyone."

P.X. stopped working. "An honest opinion?"

"Fire away."

"I'm thinking of running for District Attorney. There's no law that says the D.A. must be a lawyer. If I get elected, then I'll start reading for the law. Your honest opinion."

"You'll get a lot of weird jokes about the short end of the law, and a man not big enough for a big job. Evaluation: Yes, run by all means. You're smarter than the last three D.A.'s they must have had here. Apply your common sense to the law, and you'll do fine. Then read for the law nights and Sundays.

"But be sure to keep your saddle shop open as a hedge against not being elected."

P.X. grinned. "Damned if I might not give it a try."

Sandra came through the curtain. "Thank you, Mr. McCoy. I've been trying to talk him into it ever since the current District Attorney got himself jailed.

If Percival Xavier runs, I'm betting he will win."

"So am I, Mrs. Northcliff. So am I."

Spur just barely made it to the passenger boat that ran between Portland and Astoria. On the long boat ride he would have plenty of time to work up his telegram to General Halleck. He could send it tomorrow from Portland.

For a moment the Secret Service Agent wondered where he would be going next. A recent service directive had instructed all field agents to clean up several problems within a region whenever possible rather than crisscrossing the country.

He could remember no new cases in the Far West, but he was sure that General Halleck would have a problem spot for him. That was tomorrow. Today he could play a little poker, sit and watch the river scenery go by, and remember a beautiful young lady who had just been introduced to the pleasures of making love.

Spur grinned. He wouldn't trade his job with anyone, anyplace, at anytime!

SPUR

The wildest, sexiest and most daring
Adult Western series around.
Join Spur McCoy as he fights for
truth, justice and every woman he can
lay his hands on!

_____2608-2 DOUBLE: GOLD TRAIN TRAMP/RED ROCK
                REDHEAD $3.95 US/$4.95 CAN

_____2597-3 SPUR #25: LARAMIE LOVERS
                                 $2.95 US/$3.95 CAN

_____2575-2 SPUR #24: DODGE CITY DOLL
                                 $2.95 US/$3.95 CAN

_____2519-1 SPUR #23: SAN DIEGO SIRENS
                                 $2.95 US/$3.95 CAN

_____2496-9 SPUR #22: DAKOTA DOXY
                                 $2.50 US/$3.25 CAN

_____2475-6 SPUR #21: TEXAS TART
                                 $2.50 US/$3.25 CAN

_____2453-5 SPUR #20: COLORADO CUTIE
                                 $2.50 US/$3.25 CAN

_____2409-8 SPUR #18: MISSOURI MADAM
                                 $2.50 US/$3.25 CAN

LEISURE BOOKS
ATTN: Customer Service Dept.
276 5th Avenue, New York, NY 10001

Please send me the book(s) checked above. I have enclosed $_____
Add $1.25 for shipping and handling for the first book; $ .30 for each book
thereafter. No cash, stamps, or C.O.D.s. All orders shipped within 6 weeks.
Canadian orders please add $1.00 extra postage.

Name _____

Address _____

City_____State_____Zip_____

Canadian orders must be paid in U.S. dollars payable through a New York bank-
ing facility.   ☐ Please send a free catalogue.

BUCKSKIN

The hard-riding,
hard-bitten Adult Western series
that's hotter'n a blazing pistol
and as tough as the men
who tamed the frontier.

#12: RECOIL by Roy LeBeau $2.50US/$2.95CAN
_____2355-5

#11: TRIGGER GUARD by Roy LeBeau
_____2336-9 $2.50US/$2.95CAN

#10: BOLT ACTION by Roy LeBeau
_____2315-6 $2.50US/$2.95CAN

#8:   HANGFIRE HILL by Roy LeBeau
_____2271-0 $2.50US/$2.95CAN

#5:   GUNSIGHT GAP by Roy LeBeau
_____2189-7
                                       $2.75US/$2.95CAN

HARD RIDING WESTERN ADVENTURE FROM LEISURE BOOKS

by Nelson Nye. Tens of millions of Nelson Nye titles in print! One of his most unusual and action-packed Western tales!

_____2431-4 $2.50 US/$3.25 CAN

GUNBLAZE by Lee Bishop. A returning Confederate veteran takes on an army of renegades to carve out a new life for himself in the west.

_____2410-1 $2.50 US/$3.25 CAN

SUNDANCE: TRAIL DRIVE by Peter McCurtin. He's half-Indian, half-white and all-trouble. Blazing Western action.

_____2384-9 $2.50 US/$2.95 CAN

The Exciting and Beloved Characters of

ZANE GREY

Brought to life again by his son

ROMER ZANE GREY!

Classic Western Action

_____2530-2 ZANE GREY'S BUCK DUANE:
KING OF THE RANGE $2.75 US/$3.50 CAN

_____2553-1 ZANE GREY'S ARIZONA AMES: KING
OF THE OUTLAW HORDE $2.75US/$3.50CAN

_____2488-8 ZANE GREY'S LARAMIE NELSON:
LAWLESS LAND $2.75 US/$3.75 CAN

_____2621-7 ZANE GREY'S YAQUI: SEIGE AT
FORLORN RIVER $2.75 US/$3.75 CAN